Raised by a sorceress from the depths of limbo he came into the world without a past or a name.

They called him Kyre – Sun Hound – avatar of an ancient hero; summoned as the last chance to save the dying city of Haven from the ravages of the evil witch-queen Calthar and the sea- dwellers.

But Kyre sensed that he was more than a cipher: he felt a power within him; and a past existence which lurked in his dreams and hazy memories. He had to solve the mystery of his true identity before the hour of the final confrontation.

In the sky, the Hag cast down its baleful light: the Great Conjunction was close at hand. Soon the followers of Calthar would rise from the sea and obliterate the city of Haven and its people, forever.

LOUISE·COOPER
MIRAGE

UNWIN PAPERBACKS
London   Sydney

First published in Great Britain by Unwin® Paperbacks, an
imprint of Unwin Hyman Limited, 1987.

UNWIN HYMAN LIMITED
Denmark House
37–39 Queen Elizabeth Street,
LONDON SE1 2QB
and
40 Museum Street
LONDON WC1A 1LU

Allen & Unwin Australia Pty Ltd
8 Napier Street, North Sydney, NSW 2060, Australia

Unwin Paperbacks with Port Nicholson Press
60 Cambridge Terrace, Wellington, New Zealand

British Library Cataloguing in Publication Data

Cooper, Louise
  Mirage.
I. Title
823′.914   PR6053.051

ISBN 0–04–823382–X

Set in 10 on 11 point Times by MCL Computerset, Ely
and printed in Great Britain by Cox & Wyman, Reading.

For my mother, Pat –
who told me magical stories,
and opened my eyes to wonder.
You began it all.

Chapter 1

Are you awake, in the dark and the silence?

Do you have eyes to see, and ears to hear? Do you have hands, to reach out and clutch at the emptiness?

Can you feel? Can you know hate, loneliness, love, despair?

ARE YOU ALIVE?

Yes; you are alive. You can sense blood trickling through your veins, count the muffled beats of your heart; and you know that, after what might have been centuries of waiting, sleeping without dreams, without memory or identity, you exist. And although as yet there is nothing for your awakening senses to grasp, something is approaching you. It draws nearer, like a half-recalled nightmare, and it pulls and calls, demanding that the call be heeded.

You don't want to answer. You can't name the instinct that urges you to turn and run in fear, but it's there; it's strong. Yet you have no means to resist or flee the compulsion, and the unknown beckoner is touching you, binding you, dragging you inexorably forward . . .

. . . to admit you in blinding agony into a world where you suddenly and violently exist – and in which your first acceptance of life is a long-drawn scream of pure terror.

'Wake up!'

The voice was light, crisp, demanding obedience. It spoke so close by his ear that he started; and his muscles contracted sharply with the unaccustomed movement. It took him a few moments to comprehend that the voice was female.

'Wake *up*!' The impatient edge was more prevalent. 'You breathe, you live; I know you can hear me, and you won't gain anything by pretending not to understand. Open your eyes.'

His eyelids flickered open – then shut again instantly as an intolerable brilliance seared his brain. He uttered a sound that was midway between a shout and a groan of protest, and his unseen companion sighed.

'Very well; very well. Wait ... ' A faint hissing. 'There. The brazier's extinguished, and if moonlight blinds you you're little use to man or beast and the Hag might as well consign us all to madness. Look at me.'

He took no heed: distracted by the sound of his own voice and curious at its unfamiliar timbre, his mind was elsewhere.

'*Servant, open your eyes!*'

Startled by the cold anger in her tone, he obeyed reflexively. She stood not two paces from where he lay, illuminated by a cold, dank shaft of light. A heavy mass of fair hair framed an angular face which, though still young, was harshly lined. Her eyes, watching him shrewdly and unwaveringly, were the blue-grey of a hostile sea, and she wore a black, shapeless shift, so wafer-thin that he could glimpse the outlines of her breasts beneath the fabric.

The woman stared hard at him and her eyes narrowed coldly. 'You're not quite what you should be ... but no matter. It makes no difference. Now, *listen*. I am Simorh, and the first lesson you will learn is to be obedient to me. Sit up.'

There was strength in his arms ... cautiously he raised his torso, head turning to look uncertainly about at his surroundings. He seemed to be in a chamber built from rough and heavy blocks of stone that seeped and ran with water. The chilly glow filtering from above gave little indication of the cave's proportions, but he sensed it was vast; a cheerless, empty place of shadows and echoes. A smell which he identified as brine and rotting weed hung thick in the air, and on the threshold of audibility he heard a regular, rhythmic hushing, as though some monstrous beast lay uneasily sleeping and breathing just beyond the dark walls.

He shivered, then looked down at himself. He lay on a barnacle-encrusted rock shelf, and he was naked. His body felt alien. Strong, well-proportioned, but alien. Disturbed, he looked at the woman again and tried to make his throat form words.

'Where is this place?' It was banal, but the question he really wanted to ask eluded him.

'The old temple.'

That meant nothing, and he frowned, trying to assimilate the little he knew. She was Simorh; that much she had told him. He knew her name, but –

Then the question he had sought crystallised, and with it came a sick fear.

'My name,' he said, and the fear coloured his voice as it echoed suddenly more strongly in the cave. 'What is my name?'

She smiled again, thinly and with a trace of contempt. 'You have no name. You need none, for you're nothing beyond what I've chosen to create.'

For a moment understanding eluded him. Then:

'You . . .?'

Simorh laughed harshly. 'You're slow to grasp the facts, my friend! Let me put it plainly – I have *created* you. You owe your very existence to me, and for that alone you'll learn to be grateful!'

'But I must have a name.' He looked at her cold face, and his eyes pleaded.

'Must?' Simorh echoed, unmoved. 'Why?'

'Because I exist – I *know* I exist. Please; who am I?'

'You have no identity. I've called you into existence because I need a creature like you. You have a function to perform, and that is your only value. Beyond that, you're worthless.'

The fear increased, mingling with hurt, but although

he wanted to protest he had no argument to counter her.
There were no memories in his mind, no recollection of
a past or an identity. It was as though he were new-born;
and yet he wasn't a complete stranger to the world.
Concepts such as sun, moon, earth, sea, sky, were
familiar to him; he conversed with this cold-eyed woman
in her own tongue; recognised countless points of
reference in his surroundings. He lived, and he was
whole. But he was denied the smallest clue as to who,
or what, he was.

He put a hand up to his face and felt the contours of
bone under skin and flesh. 'What colour are my eyes?'

Simorh's mouth curled. 'Don't be ridiculous! That's
of no importance.'

'It is to me! I want to know what I look like – please,
I must know myself!'

'There's nothing to know,' she said implacably.
'You're just a shade, a creation of sorcery. *My* sorcery.
And I could destroy you as easily as I created you.' Her
smile wasn't pleasant. 'So if you value the life you've
been granted, you'll do as you're told and ask no more
foolish questions. Remember that, and we'll get along
well enough.'

In a peculiarly detached way it occurred to him that
he could have risen from the shelf, taken a single step
towards her and broken her neck with his hands. The
thought was fleeting, and quelled by the same impulse
which told him not to argue further with her. If what she
said was true – and he had no way of knowing – he'd
be a fool to put her to the test; for whatever this life
might hold, it was surely preferable to oblivion? He bit
his lip uncertainly – and, surprised by the small pain,
experimentally did it again. Simorh watched him, her
expression hovering somewhere between unease and
contempt; then abruptly she turned and moved into the
embrace of the shadows.

'Here.' Her voice, at a distance, was hollow. 'Put this
about yourself. We've stayed here overlong, and even

a creation of sorcery can drown. We must be on our way.'

As she spoke she picked up a dark and shapeless object and tossed it to him. It was a cloak, long enough to cover him from shoulders to feet, and he fingered it uncertainly. 'Where are we going?'

'Back to Haven. No, don't start your questions again, damn you! Just hurry.'

He cast the cloak awkwardly round his shoulders, then, at her impatient urging, swung his feet off the rock shelf and stood up.

Water, shockingly cold, licked at his ankles. He looked down and saw it swirling sluggishly across the floor; dark, brackish and laced with an unpleasant foaming scum.

'The tide's turned.' Simorh was already moving away towards a dark gash in the rock wall which he realised was a doorway. Beyond it steps glimmered in the unhealthy light, leading away upwards. 'At high water this chamber floods to the roof; we've little time left.' She eyed him bitterly. 'I didn't risk destroying myself just to watch the sea take you before you can do your work. Stir yourself – or I'll put you under a compulsion.'

The brine smell was stronger ... not knowing what compulsion the sorceress might be capable of conjuring, and not caring to speculate, he followed her towards the aperture. The surging water splashed around their feet with a thin, furtive sound; then they were through the gap and leaving the slowly flooding cavern behind.

The stairway was narrow, the steps worn and slippery, but Simorh's surefootedness gave him confidence as they climbed towards the source of the light. The flight was quite short: they reached the top and, angling her body against the rock wall, the sorceress beckoned once for him to follow before disappearing into a cramped fissure through which the dim light was filtering. For a moment as the rock's cold blackness pressed in on him he experienced a panic-stricken sense of claustrophobia,

as though he were being swallowed and digested by a
beast made of living stone. He drew breath, forcing
himself to keep his hands by his sides and not push
frantically, futilely against the encroaching walls – and
then he stumbled out of the fissure in Simorh's wake,
and emerged into a nightscape that almost made him
bite through his tongue in shock.

He stood amid a litter of rubble and broken masonry,
surrounded by the towering, skeletal ruins of what had
once been a massive structure. Splintered pillars of
stone speared like knives into the green-black sky,
long-rotted windows gaped sightlessly, barnacles and
weed encrusted the ancient buttresses and twisted them
into fantastical shapes. And in the centre of the ruin was
a humped, featureless slab of rock, threaded with veins
of incredible colour, that might, untold centuries ago,
have been a votive altar.

A cold, sluggish wind soughed through the broken
stones, and underlying it he heard a sighing, a whisper
that ebbed and flowed in mesmeric rhythm. The sea . . .
there was salt on the air, sharp and raw in his nostrils, and
he shivered as he was assailed by a disquieting sense of
recognition.

'Hurry.' Simorh's voice echoed eerily between the
shattered walls. 'There's little time left.'

In the chilly half-light she looked insubstantial but for
the now almost brazen sheen of her hair. She beckoned,
her movements quick and peculiarly ungraceful, and he
began to stumble across the detritus after her –

And stopped, as he was abruptly caught in an ice-cold
shaft of light.

The huge, pockmarked satellite that orbited this
world had been hidden behind one of the few wall
sections still standing, but as he moved it swung into his
field of vision; a single, baleful silver-grey eye glaring
through the ragged frame of an arched window. He
stood transfixed, staring back at it as a sense of dread
filled him; then suddenly Simorh was at his side and

tugging furiously at his arm.

'Move! Move, damn you! We must *go!*'

The moon's glamour shattered; he shook his head, looked at her and saw the satellite's sickly colour reflected in her eyes. For a reason he couldn't begin to understand her look made him recoil, but he responded to her urging and they scrambled through the rubble, to emerge at last on to a narrow shingle strand, at the edge of which lapped a smooth, shifting, iron-dark sea.

Simorh stopped to catch her breath, then looked over her shoulder at the monstrous moon which, now that they were clear of the ruin, hung alone in the night sky.

'Quickly.' She spoke softly. 'The strand will be covered soon – we must reach the beach before the sea does.'

The shingle bar was a poor barrier against the encroaching tide; already, small, white-edged wavelets were licking at it and soaking the unstable mass of shale and pebbles. Simorh started along the narrow causeway, her robe snatched by the wind and blowing ethereally about her, and – yet again he seemed to have no choice – he followed. The shingle was treacherous, slippery and shifting, but the smooth stones were less painful underfoot than the rubble of the ruin. To their left the sea stretched unbroken to a hostile and distant horizon; after one glance he preferred not to look at it again. To the right, low, crumbling cliffs were half hidden by a thin mist, and the tide seeped between them and the land like a slow-moving river. The mist seemed denser ahead, hiding the unknown goal to which Simorh was leading him, although he thought he had glimpsed a rise in the desiccated cliffland, and the deceptive witchglow of a distant light. Suddenly and sharply the dread came back; the sense that he was moving towards something that he neither understood nor wanted, but was compelled to face. He tried to call out to the sorceress, who was his only point of reference in this eerie world, but the words caught in his throat. The wind soughed, the sea hushed; if he wasn't to drown, he could only follow.

Simorh stopped and turned, her face corpse-white under the baleful moon. 'Hurry!' she called. Her voice was all but lost against the vast night. He pulled the cloak more closely about himself, and hastened in her wake.

The shingle bar ended in a gentle slope to the sand of a wide, deserted bay. On the far side the cliffs became high buttresses, and the beach – that part of it still clear of the encroaching tide – stretched away into an unguessable distance. Simorh stopped, waiting for him to catch up, then raised one arm to point inland to the back of the bay.

'That way.' She set off again without waiting for a response, as though she didn't want to stay on the fine white sand any longer than need dictated. He trailed after her, tired now, and through the shifting mist saw again the fleeting, will-o'-the-wisp glimmer of lights where the sand gave way to rock once more. Then abruptly he realised that they were approaching not a bare rock face, but a crazed jumble of walls and buildings hewn out of the stone and sprawling away behind the bay towards the clifftop. The strange witchglows were nothing supernatural, merely the lights that marked the town's gate; but the realisation didn't reassure him.

'Hurry!' Simorh called again. The fog distorted her voice and muffled her figure into little more than a dark smudge. 'The Hag is setting.'

The moon had slipped down the sky and now hung threateningly over the cliffs, shrouded in mist and surrounded by a sickly corona. Its light gave the scene a cold, steely edge, and he looked away again, disturbed.

Simorh waited for him to reach her, then grasped his arm in a grip that surprised him with its strength. Her nails dug into his bicep and she hissed. 'When I give you

a command, I expect you to obey me! Don't forget that
– don't *dare* forget it!'

He stared down at her, not speaking, and she turned
away with an exasperated gesture; but not before he had
seen the fear huddling behind the anger in her eyes.
They set off again towards the town and the smooth sand
gave way to scattered rocks. But these rocks, he noticed,
were different; even-edged, as though they had been cut
by human hands. They formed, he realised suddenly,
the unmistakable outline of a broken wall.

A sick sensation made his stomach churn and he
stopped, reaching out to touch the jagged stones. They
had been hewn, though centuries ago – and wedged
between the slabs were traces of slate. He swallowed as
a fragment of memory flickered across his mind and was
instantly lost.

'The stones.' He'd spoken almost before he realised
it, and Simorh whipped round as though someone had
struck her. 'They're not . . . natural.'

He couldn't see the sorceress's face clearly enough to
read her expression, but her body tensed. 'No. They're
not natural.'

'Then what – '

She interrupted him angrily. '*Damn* you, with your
endless questions!'

A spark of rebellion took hold of him and he insisted
stubbornly, 'I want to know!'

She was silent for a few moments, then abruptly and
harshly she said, 'Very well; if you must. Nine years ago,
the tide flowed twice in one night without ebbing. It
receded, eventually, but the sand it brought did not.
You are walking on the tomb of more than half of Haven
and its inhabitants.'

The colour drained from his face and he withdrew his
hand quickly from the cold stone. Simorh's mouth
twisted in a mockery of a smile, and the mist, shifting
about her, gave the disturbing illusion of an army of
ghostly forms at her back. 'Now perhaps you understand

why I don't want to linger here.'

He nodded, not knowing what he could say. Feeling
that the sand was suddenly burning his bare feet with
every step, he hastened after her.

Haven – or what remained of Haven – was sheltered
behind a high sandstone wall in which was set a wide
arch. Two lamps burned green in the lee of small
alcoves, and as they passed through the arch he had his
first glimpse of the town that, whether or not he willed
it, was to become his home.

Haven was a straggling sprawl of low buildings,
narrow, twisted streets and small squares which seemed
to have grown rather than been carved out of the rock
on which it was founded. Pale stone houses with
shuttered windows stared blindly at him from both sides
as he followed Simorh up the winding lanes. The mist
crept around them like phantom hands, distorting
the shadows and manifesting |illusory shapes| that
flickered and vanished before they could be seen with
any clarity. There was no sound save their own soft
footsteps, and no sign of life, human or otherwise. The
quiet and the desolation were intense, and eerie.

As they climbed higher through the town, the sense
of inexplicable dread that had weighed him down since
the moment when Simorh had dragged him screaming
into this world grew stronger, although still he could find
no cause for it. Questions tumbled one upon another
through his mind, but he dared not ask them.

As they passed through the city he tried to glimpse
his reflection in the windows of the houses but every
window was tightly shuttered as though the
householders had long ago abandoned their dwellings
and left them to the mercies of wind and rain.

Or as though they feared the night . . .

He was gazing uneasily at one of the shuttered houses
when he realised that ahead of them the street ended
at a sheer wall, several times his own height. He stared

up, and was just able to make out the silhouettes of three tall towers beyond the wall before a deep wing of shadow seemed to drift across the sky and the images blurred into darkness.

'The Hag has set. This way, quickly.' Simorh turned aside to where a narrow gate had been set into the wall. She lifted the latch; the gate opened, and they passed through.

Steps led up into the mist-shrouded dark, and they began to climb. It seemed that they were in a garden, but the thin soil and the unceasing blight of salt-laden air had mocked the garden-maker's efforts; the flowers and shrubs were poor and stunted. An occasional larger bloom showed bloated and pale in the tangle, and dead or dying vegetation trailed across their path as they climbed. Then the steps ended, and they stood before a high, windowed and dimly lit structure that spread away into the dark on either side. The three towers he had glimpsed from the street were clearly visible and he realised that this place, whatever its nature, must be the seat of power in the city.

Simorh raised a hand to the arched door that faced them, and pushed. The door swung silently open, revealing a wide hallway, floored and faced with stone shot through with veins of blue, green, amber and silver. Tapestries hung on the walls; once they had glowed with reds and oranges and yellows, but their colours had faded with age and wear, and now they looked merely shabby.

The sorceress was moving towards a flight of stone stairs that spiralled up out of sight to the right of the hall. She was half way there when footfalls sounded on the steps, and moments later a man appeared.

He stopped when he saw them, and his expression changed to astonishment as he looked first at Simorh and then at the man behind her.

'Princess . . . I – we didn't expect – ' He looked at the stranger again and licked his lips uncertainly. He was a heavy-set man, blond-haired and bearded and perhaps some fifteen years older than the sorceress. And he was a warrior; his massive body ran to muscle rather than fat, and although his clothes – loose shirt and trousers, with a long woollen robe thrown over – suggested indolent and comfortable living, the short but businesslike sword at his hip belied first appearances.

'Vaoran.' Simorh stared coldly at the warrior. 'You were wrong. *All* of you were wrong. I have succeeded.'

'Yes . . . ' Vaoran's blue eyes filled with unease and he licked his lips nervously. 'It seems, lady, that you are owed an apology by those who doubted you. That I, at least, will offer, and wholeheartedly.'

Simorh nodded with tired dignity. 'Your apology is accepted. Thank you. Now, if you would be kind enough to inform Prince DiMag that I have returned and – '

The warrior's face closed instantly. 'Prince DiMag has retired to his rooms, lady. He left strict instructions that he isn't to be disturbed.'

'Don't be ridiculous, Vaoran!' Simorh's mouth narrowed into a tight line.

'With respect, princess, I'm not in a position to question or disobey the prince's order. Believe me, lady, I'm sorry.'

Simorh stiffened at Vaoran's words. Curious, her creation watched and waited for her to react. He anticipated an angry outburst, but it didn't come. Instead, her shoulders sagged as though in defeat, though when she tossed her head back there was still a semblance of pride in the gesture.

'Very well. If those are your instructions, I won't argue with you. Perhaps you'd be good enough to have our new guest taken to the Sunrise Tower – and send word to me in the morning, as soon as the prince wakes.'

Vaoran bowed. 'Of course, lady.' He glanced at the stranger again, but briefly and uncertainly. 'I'll summon a steward.'

'And a word of warning, Vaoran. He asks questions.

Don't attempt to answer them – or I, personally, will
be responsible for the consequences.'

She gave her creation a final look that suggested his
presence was more of a curse than a blessing, then
before either man could speak she walked quickly away
towards the spiral stairs.

Simorh climbed the steps swiftly, keenly aware of defeat
and trying to thrust the memory of the last few minutes
as far from her mind as she could. The knowledge that
DiMag had barred her from his presence, tonight of all
nights, was bitter wine. He had known what she was
attempting to do, the risks she would run; but still he
had avoided her.

At the top of the flight she turned and headed along
a corridor towards the furthermost of the palace's three
towers, where her private apartments were situated.

Reaching the narrow stairway that led to her tower,
she began to climb. Lamps in hanging chains had been
lit at intervals on the wall for her return. Someone, at
least, had faith in her. She climbed on, not pausing to
glance through the tower's narrow windows at the
dizzying panorama of the town and coastline beyond,
and soon reached the white door with its painted single
eye. Almost as soon as her hand touched the latch the
door was pulled open from within, and the narrow, elfin
face of a young girl peered nervously from the darkness
beyond.

'Princess!' Relief and eagerness coloured the girl's
voice, and as Simorh stepped into the unlit apartment
she dropped to one knee and kissed the hem of the
sorceress's thin robe.

Simorh smiled sadly down at her. 'Get up, Falla;
there's no need to be so formal. Is Thean in the
sanctum?'

'Yes, lady.' Falla was hastening to light a lamp, and
a warm glow shot through with soft shadows rose slowly
into life. 'We kept vigil, turn by turn, as you told us.'

She paused and looked back, her eyes huge and dusky in their frame of pale face and bobbed dark hair. 'I'm so thankful you're safe!'

She might not give thanks by the time this is over, Simorh thought, but only nodded and said, 'Thank you, Falla. Fetch Thean, and tell her the vigil can end now. I'm very tired . . . '

The girl hastened away through a curtained arch, and returned moments later with Thean at her heels. Simorh's second protegée was taller and fairer than her companion, and her normally vivid blue eyes were dulled, the pupils over-dilated, with the effects of the narcotic incense which had sustained both girls throughout their vigil.

'Princess.' Like Falla, she knelt and kissed Simorh's hem; unlike the dark girl she was bold enough to ask the question that simmered in both their minds. 'Did the work go well?'

Simorh's limbs felt iron-heavy and, partly through reaction and partly because of the night cold striking through her inadequate garment, she was shivering spasmodically. With an effort, she nodded. 'It succeeded, Thean. He is here, in the palace.'

The girls' eyes widened, and Thean said: 'Oh, lady . . . does the prince know?'

The prince doesn't know, and the prince doesn't care, Simorh thought bitterly. She had argued ferociously with DiMag over the advisability of tonight's events, and only the fact that he had no other solution to the threat that hung over Haven had enabled her finally to gain his unwilling permission for what she had to do. But DiMag had disliked having to give way to her – and he would dislike it all the more when he came face to face with her creation in the morning.

If he was willing to see her . . .

She must have shown some sign of her distress, for the girls were suddenly about her like two anxious mother cats. They ushered her through the smaller of

the two doors that led off the room, up another short
flight of steps and into her bedchamber.

'Are you sure you've no further need of us, lady?'
Falla's anxious dark eyes scanned her face.

'I'm sure, Falla. Go. You've earned your rest.'

She waited until the door closed and the padding
footsteps diminished away down the stairs, then turned
to her wide, curtained bed. The sheets smelled faintly
of salt – everything in this forsaken place smelled of salt,
though she was so inured to it that she hardly ever
noticed – and when she lay down she found she barely
had the strength to pull the blanket over herself. The
fire was burning down to embers; the kettle hissed
gently, and when she snuffed out the single light at her
bedside the crimson-edged shadows loomed and reared
over her like sentinels. She thought of what she had
achieved tonight; thought of the frightened creature she
had conjured into existence out of nothing; thought of
DiMag . . .

Simorh turned over in the bed and pushed a fist hard
against her mouth so that her ever-vigilant apprentices,
in their room above, wouldn't hear her sobbing.

Chapter 2

Simorh's creation woke screaming an hour before dawn, racked by a nightmare that faded back into shadow only as his eyes snapped open. An involuntary reflex triggered his muscles, and he flung himself from the disordered and sweat-soaked bed, staggering across the circular room until his flailing hands found a door. Fingers clawed the latch, scrabbling and wrenching and drawing blood from under his nails, but the door refused to yield.

At last he stumbled back, not knowing where he was but understanding on an animal level that he was trapped. Still part-drugged with sleep and the remnants of the nightmare, he found himself at a narrow embrasure of a window, and the shock of the cold stone sill against his skin rallied his floundering wits. Remembering, and rubbing at his eyes, he stared out at the vista beyond the walls.

The mist which had stolen up from the sea in the wake of moonset had thickened, casting a milky pall through which the thin pre-dawn light shimmered. Close by, a tower loomed out of the fog, disembodied and drifting, one window gaping like an idiot mouth near its summit; and somewhere far down he thought he could see the ghostly green witch-lights of the town.

He backed away from the window, disturbed as the fragments of memory coalesced into a more complete picture. He was a prisoner in what remained of a coastal city called Haven; that much he knew. And he had been brought here through the spell-casting of a sorceress whose name was Simorh and who appeared to be a princess of whatever dynasty ruled here. But beyond those bare facts, he knew nothing of himself or his origins, or of the world in which he had come to dwell. If the sorceress were to be believed, he had had no existence before last night; she claimed to be his creator, and he had no evidence to gainsay her.

And yet it struck a wrong chord. Nameless he might be, and without memories – but he didn't *feel* like a cipher. Locked away somewhere within him was an identity of his own that Simorh had not created and couldn't tamper with; he was sure of it, and the certainty both angered and frightened him. He *had* to discover the truth – but if the little he'd gleaned of these people so far could be trusted, he'd learn nothing from them.

There were too many ramifications, and too many of them unpleasant, for him to be able to face them now. He was desperately tired and craved sleep still; a sleep free of the evil dreams that had plagued him through the night. If nothing else, he had warmth and shelter; he lived, and, in however bizarre a way, prospered. He'd best serve his own interests, he thought, by biding his time until he could learn more of his circumstances.

He lay down on the bed again and pulled up the coarse but serviceable covering. A faint scent of brine touched his nostrils, as though the weight and warmth of his body had released something sea-born from the pallet into the room; it was a familiar smell, chilly but comforting, and he closed his eyes with a small sense of relief. Sleep came quickly, and this time there were no more dreams.

When he woke again, the false dawn had given way to full day and a dull, colourless light suffused through his room. He sat up, full consciousness returning and with it a memory of the previous awakening that made him determined not to fall prey to the same sense of disorientation and panic. He took several deep breaths, counting each one; then, calmed, climbed out of the bed.

The window was a blank white rectangle; the fog had
thickened further as morning broke, and the filtered
daylight had a flat quality that made every feature of the
circular chamber look faintly unreal and dreamlike. For
a few moments he stood on the chill flagstones, not sure
of his next move – then he saw that while he slept
someone had paid a visit to his room, for folded neatly
on a chair near the window were a linen shirt and
trousers. He picked the garments up, fingering the
coarse fabric; and an observation, unbidden, came to
him.

They should surely have provided something better . . .

The thought fled as quickly as it had come, and it left
him puzzled. He knew nothing of these people – his
captors, for want of a better term. Why, then, should
he feel disappointed and faintly insulted by the clothing
they had provided for him?

He shrugged. If this was part of the conundrum, it
could hardly be significant; the air had a cold, damp
edge to it, and he was thankful for something warm to
wear, be it peasant's garb or prince's.

The clothes fitted him surprisingly well, though the
material of the shirt in particular felt strange, making
the muscles of his back twitch with faint irritation. Also
on the chair he found a broad leather belt with a clasp
fashioned to depict a many-rayed star with a gargoyle
face, like a grotesquely stylised solar image; he fastened
it at his waist, then, without thinking, turned to look for
a mirror in which to study himself.

There was no mirror in the room. He'd forgotten
Simorh's injunction to the burly swordsman Vaoran, but
now it came sharply back to mind. *Why* was the
sorceress so anxious that he shouldn't look on his own
face? Was he so hideous? Or was she afraid that one
sight of himself might trigger memories she would prefer
him not to recall?

He put tentative fingers up to his cheeks, nose,
eyebrows. As far as he could judge there was nothing

remarkable about his features; no scars, no deformities. He pulled a strand of hair forward over his shoulder to see it: it was a startlingly vivid red, but the unusual colour stirred no traces of recognition. Beyond that small detail, though, he knew nothing of his appearance, and although in the wake of all that had happened to him it seemed a pitifully trivial matter, at this moment it was more important to him than anything else that he should find out.

He turned towards the window, wondering if the fog-dimmed glass might reflect him – but before he could peer more closely at it and see, someone knocked at the door.

He turned sharply, but the door didn't open; and after a pause the knocking sounded again. The servant, steward or whoever stood outside clearly had more regard for his privacy than the anonymous dawn visitor, and he allowed himself to relax a little.

'Enter.' His own voice was still unfamiliar to him, but the momentary *frisson* vanished as a key grated in the lock and the door finally opened.

The girl who stepped over the threshold was dressed in a simple linen shift with a woven shawl over it for warmth. Her face was small and heart-shaped, large grey eyes framed by a mass of short, unruly dark curls, and she held a covered tray carefully before her, supporting its weight on her braceleted arms. She couldn't have been above nine or ten years old.

'Good morning,' she said with an extraordinary composure for one so young. 'You must be Kyre.'

Nonplussed, and collecting his wits as best he could, he replied,

'You're mistaken, little lady. There's no one of that name here.'

She frowned, hesitated, then came forward into the room and decisively set her tray down on the table beside his bed. 'I can't be mistaken. The steward told me I'd find you in the Sunrise Tower, and this is the

Sunrise Tower.' She turned round, scrutinising him with frank interest. 'Aren't you the one who was brought from the old temple last night?'

A peculiar chill seemed to settle in his veins; hardly realising what he was about, he nodded.

'Then you *are* Kyre.' She stepped back a pace or two, studying him critically, then smiled. 'You should be proud to have such a name. Do you like it?'

'I . . . don't know.' He was struggling to find some recollection of the name, but there was nothing; not the smallest spark of familiarity. 'I've never heard it before.'

'It means "Sun-Hound" in the old tongue,' the child told him. 'Do you speak the old tongue, Kyre?'

Old tongue? He shook his head. 'No.'

'I do. Or a little, anyway. My tutor says so much of it has been lost that no one will ever speak it properly again, but I'm trying to learn. *Ky* – hound, *Re* – sun. Kyre.' She seemed to be repeating the name simply because its inflection pleased her, but the repetition did nothing to stir his memory. He merely stared back at her until, meeting his gaze, she laughed self-consciously and a bright flush came to her pale cheeks.

'My tutor also tells me I babble, like rain in the gutter, he says. I'm sorry.' She smoothed the front of her shift and then with formal gravity extended a hand. 'My name is Gamora.'

'Gamora.' Their fingers clasped briefly and he found himself wanting to smile. He wondered if this child, with her blend of ingenuousness and attempted sophistication, would answer his questions.

'Do you live here in this palace, Gamora?'

The child's expression clouded with disappointment. 'Of course I do.' Clearly she had expected him to know more about her than he did. Then she said a little primly, 'I am the *Princess* Gamora. My father is Prince DiMag of Haven, my mother is the Princess Simorh.'

'Your – ' He checked, astounded, and for a moment thought he couldn't have heard her aright. 'The sorceress – is your *mother*?'

'Yes, of course. She and my father are cousins – such a marriage is traditional. You don't know much about our ways, do you?'

He shook his head, unable to explain the effect her revelation had had on his mental image of Simorh. He simply couldn't equate the cold-eyed witch who had summoned him to this world with the mother of such a bright and sweet-natured child. And the prince, of whom Simorh had spoken so bitterly last night, was her husband ... the knowledge shed a little unhappy light on the motivations underlying the sorceress's harshness.

'When my father the prince dies, I shall rule Haven,' Gamora carried on, matter-of-factly. 'Unless I should gain a brother in the meantime.' She looked at him candidly. 'Everyone says that won't happen; so I must be ruler one day.'

He struggled out of the confusion of his own thoughts and sensed something of the dissatisfaction that lurked, only partially masked, behind the girl's words. 'Don't you want to rule?' he asked.

Gamora's eyes clouded, and she said: 'No.'

'Why not?'

'Because by then, there'll be nothing left to rule over.'

The edge of solemn maturity in her simple statement struck a cold chord in his heart; and reminded him of something Simorh had told him last night, as they crossed the sands under the bleak and terrible eye of the Moon. *Half the city swallowed and drowned in a single night, when the tide flowed twice without ebbing* ... It must have happened at almost the same time that Gamora was born.

Anxious not to alienate the child, yet desperately needing to learn, he said, 'I don't understand what you say, princess. Why should Haven not continue to prosper?'

For a moment he thought she might answer him frankly, but instead her face tightened into a sharp,

uneasy look of distrust. Her dark curls bobbed as she
shook her head emphatically. 'Eat your breakfast,
Kyre; or it'll grow cold.'

'You haven't answered my question, Gamora.'

'I – can't.' Pain flickered in her grey eyes, then the
tautness relaxed fractionally and the childish honesty
was back. 'I *daren't*. I bribed the steward to let me bring
your tray; if they even knew I was talking to you, they'd
punish me. I heard ... ' She swallowed. 'I heard them
say that you must be told nothing; not yet.' Awkwardly,
she gestured towards the covered tray on the table. 'You
should eat. Please, Kyre. *Please*.'

He immediately regretted his attempt to draw more
from her than she was willing to give. Without further
comment he uncovered the tray, and though he was in
no mood to eat he was agreeably surprised by what he
found. A plate of steamed fish, rich and garnished with
some unidentifiable herb; and beside it a cup of dark
liquid that smelled pleasantly spiced. Gamora watched
him gravely as, to please her, he drank the cup's
contents and then sampled the fish. Something about its
flavour was faintly familiar, though he couldn't place it;
he ate more than half of it before he realised that his
stomach's urgings had overcome his mind's reluctance.

He was still eating, with the child sitting attentively
beside him, when without warning the door to the
circular room opened. Gamora looked over her
shoulder – then leaped to her feet, her face suddenly
dead white but for two flaming spots of crimson on her
cheeks.

Simorh stood on the threshold. She was dressed in a
dark yellow gown, more formal than her garb of last
night, and her long hair was braided into a tight,
elaborate style. She spared a single careless glance for
Kyre, then stared at her daughter with cold anger.

'I might have known *you'd* find your way here.' The
sarcasm in her voice made Gamora's flush deepen;
every muscle in the child's body was locked rigid and

she stared blindly ahead, not meeting the sorceress's eyes.

Simorh stepped into the room and pulled the door wide open behind her. 'Out. Go to your lessons. And tell your tutor and your nurse that you are not to be allowed out of your room when the lessons are over.'

Gamora unfroze, and her eyes widened. 'Oh, Mother, please – '

'*Out!*' Simorh repeated furiously. The child fled. As she ran from the room Kyre saw the glitter of tears in her eyes, and before the sorceress could turn her attention to him, anger got the better of caution and he said harshly,

'Are children punished in Haven merely for showing curiosity?'

Simorh swung round to face him. Her lips were set in a sharp, bitter line. 'You,' she said scathingly. 'What do you know of children, or of anything else? And you won't learn the answers to your questions from her. If you don't curb your curiosity, I'll put you under a binding that'll do far worse than simply silence your tongue!'

Some of his confidence evaporated in the face of her threat. She had power, that he knew; he wasn't sure enough of himself to test it. Not yet, at least. He nodded a barely perceptible acknowledgement and she turned her back, lifting her shoulders irritably.

'Make yourself presentable,' she ordered peremptorily. 'You're to be taken before Prince DiMag, and he doesn't like to be kept waiting.'

If mention of her husband's name caused her any discomfort she hid it well. Kyre said, evenly, 'I'm as presentable as I can be with no other clothes than these.'

Simorh made an impatient sound in her throat. 'Very well. Then come with me.' She looked back at him. 'When you stand before the prince, you will listen without speaking. Don't *dare* to ask a single question or venture a single opinion. No one will want to hear it.'

With that she left the room, and he followed. It seemed that he had been housed at the summit of one of the palace towers, for immediately outside the door steps began to spiral down. Simorh skimmed down them at a speed he found hard to match, and he only caught up with her at the foot of the flight. They walked along a passage for a short way, then there were more stairs, until finally these too ended and the stairwell widened out into the tapestry-hung hall through which he had been brought on his arrival last night. Simorh didn't pause, but turned immediately and led Kyre across the hall to a set of double doors which opened to her touch. Through a maze of passages that left him helplessly confused and lost, until at last another set of doors – guarded this time – confronted them where the endless corridors branched away into shadow. Simorh strode towards the guards and was about to issue a peremptory order for the doors to be opened, when hasty footsteps to the right alerted her. She and Kyre turned, to see Vaoran approaching.

'Princess.' He halted and bowed. 'You weren't thinking of taking the creature to the court hall?'

Simorh's eyes glinted dangerously. 'Since when have my activities been of direct concern to you?'

The swordsman's face stiffened. 'I beg your pardon, madam. But Prince DiMag is conducting urgent council business.'

The sorceress sighed, as though dealing with a recalcitrant and none too intelligent child. 'Swordsmaster Vaoran, I received word an hour ago via Prince DiMag's personal steward to bring this creature to my husband in the hall.' Her voice sharpened. 'Contrary to opinion in some quarters, the prince's memory isn't deficient; so I can only conclude that you have your own unfathomable reasons for wishing to deny me that appointment.' She paused. 'I hope I'm wrong.'

Vaoran's shoulders seemed to lock rigid, and the

expression on his face told Kyre that, beneath his arrogant mask, the warrior was afraid of Simorh.

'Lady, I meant no slight; I wasn't aware of the arrangements.' With an obvious effort Vaoran forced himself to meet her venomous stare. 'But you've obviously not heard the news from the coastal patrols.'

'I'm told nothing of what goes on in this benighted place, as well you know!' Simorh retorted savagely. 'And I fail to see what relevance the reports of the coastal patrols have to my appointment with the prince!'

'Half an hour ago, madam, they brought in a prisoner.'

'A prisoner?' Simorh's fury abated visibly; the storm in her eyes was suddenly edged with an unpleasant blend of apprehension and eagerness. The swordsmaster's gaze flicked dubiously to Kyre, but she made a dismissive gesture. 'Never mind him. Tell me.'

Vaoran glanced again at the red-haird man. Simorh's dismissal had done nothing to assuage his doubts, but he didn't dissemble any further. 'They found it at the high tideline,' he said. 'It was injured; the patrol commander believes it was caught in a cross-current and dashed on the rocks by the north headland. Its own kind had abandoned it, as we'd expect of them, so the patrol brought it to the city.'

Simorh nodded. 'I see. Where is it now?'

'It was taken for interrogation. We wait only Prince DiMag's order to bring it to the hall.'

Simorh looked speculatively at the doors for a few moments, then to Kyre's discomfiture turned an indecipherable gaze on him. She said, quietly, 'Conduct us through the bodyguard's door, Vaoran. I'd like to see the creature for myself when it's brought before the prince – and it might provide a salutary lesson for our friend here.'

The warrior clearly disliked the order, but could think of no sound reason to refuse. He made a small, curt bow. 'Yes, lady.'

More corridors, more pieces of the jigsaw ... Kyre walked behind Simorh and the striding Vaoran, aware that the poor light illuminating these passages was diminishing still further, the atmosphere growing danker and closer. At last they reached a heavy curtain at the end of a dark, unadorned and tunnel-like walk, and Vaoran pulled the curtain aside to reveal a low door which opened on soundless hinges. As it swung back, Kyre recoiled instinctively. Light flooded from beyond; light, and voices susurrating like a sullen, hostile sea. And with them, the claustrophobic, uneasy smell of fear.

Simorh went through first, bending and vanishing into the comparative brilliance. He hesitated and might have baulked, disturbed by an intuitive sense that something ugly lay ahead, but Vaoran put a powerful hand on his shoulder and, preferring the unknown to the swordsmaster's touch, he shook the hand aside and followed the sorceress, to stand blinking in Haven's court hall.

The hall was vast, or seemed so. All the tall, narrow windows were shrouded by heavy curtains, while lamps burning at intervals high on the walls cast huge pyramids of shadow that reached up among stone pillars to meet at an unguessable height. Tapestries decorated these walls; like their counterparts in the outer hall they were faded ghosts of their original glory, all brillance drained from them by age and damp decay. The hall's architecture dwarfed them, and dwarfed the two dozen or so figures gathered around a raised dais near the curtained door.

'What's this?' A man's voice, angry and with a bitter edge, cut through the whispering, and Kyre looked to his left. On the dais stood a carved chair; the chair was occupied, and Kyre found himself, for the first time, face to face with the prince of Haven.

The chair was ornate and cumbersome, made of a wood so old that it was all but petrified. The high back

was carved with the same Sun-symbol that adorned
Kyre's belt buckle, and similar amulets had been cut into
the elaborate arms. Prince DiMag sat awkwardly in the
chair, one knee drawn up and both hands gripping the
arms. He was younger than Kyre had expected, lightly
built, with long, unkempt hair of the same wheat-gold
shade as Simorh's. He was dressed in crimson trousers
and a wide-sleeved, narrow-waisted coat heavily embroidered with gold thread; the garments were old, and
looked as though they had been slept in. Now the prince
turned intelligent but angry hazel eyes on Kyre, staring
at him with a mixture of curiosity and resentment.
Beyond the throne, the twelve or fifteen men who stood
in attendance also peered at the newcomer, their
expressions hostile.

'What's this?' DiMag repeated. One hand moved in
an involuntary warrior's reflex as he spoke, going to the
hilt of a cumbersome sword that hung scabbarded at his
side. The gesture, and his tone of voice, raised Kyre's
hackles and he felt a furious urge to challenge the
prince's dismissive arrogance. Simorh, however,
stepped forward, pushing him none too gently aside.

'I have named him Kyre,' she said, then added in a
sharp undertone, 'I told you I would succeed, and I did!'

DiMag frowned. 'So I see. Whatever possessed you
to bring him here, *now?*'

Simorh's mouth tightened into a hard line. 'You sent
for me, DiMag, and told me to bring him. If you then
sent a second message cancelling the first, I didn't
receive it!'

The men behind the throne shook their heads at the
princess's sharp retort, and one or two hissed through
their teeth with disapproval. DiMag stared at his wife
for a few moments and it was clear from the sudden
palpable rise in tension that no one could anticipate how
he would react. Simorh didn't back down, and abruptly
the prince flexed the fist he had clenched and smiled a
lopsided smile that had little humour in it.

'Well, well. My memory must have failed me for a moment.' He cast a raking, challenging glance that Kyre couldn't interpret about the company at large. 'Perhaps it's as well; he may find these proceedings instructive.' He raised a hand and beckoned. 'Step forward, Kyre. Let me see you more clearly.'

Kyre moved away from Simorh to face DiMag more directly. He was conscious of a multitude of eyes boring into his back, making his spine tingle, and he met the prince's stare with steady, uncowed interest.

'Sun-Hound,' DiMag said thoughtfully. His uneven smile broadened for a brief moment, then vanished. 'The princess obviously has a reason for naming you after the greatest warrior in our history. Is she justified?'

The prince's words took him aback. 'I don't know,' he said.

One of the men hovering by the throne cut in with asperity, 'Mind your tongue, creature! You'll address the prince as "my lord", not – '

'Spare me your protocol, councillor.' DiMag interrupted the man with an irritable wave of one hand. 'There'll be time enough for the niceties later – I'm more interested in finding out whether our new friend is as much of a warrior as his namesake.' For the second time he touched the hilt of his heavy sword, and his look suddenly became closed and almost possessive. 'Vaoran – give Kyre your blade.'

The burly swordsmaster stepped forward. 'My lord, is this wise? After all, you – ' he stopped as DiMag turned a ferocious glare on him, then hastily amended whatever he had been about to say. 'There are more urgent matters to attend to.'

'Your view of what is urgent clearly doesn't accord with mine,' DiMag retorted. 'Give Kyre your blade.'

Unhappily Vaoran obeyed, unclipping his scabbarded sword and holding it out hilt-first. Kyre took it with equal reluctance, unable to comprehend the look of intense dislike the warrior gave him as he handed the

sword over. His fingers closed round the hilt, and he felt
a sudden peculiar sense of familiarity. He had held such
a blade before; he understood its weight and balance,
and the tactics and skills of using it. And yet instinct told
him that his knowledge was flawed. Though the weapon
was familiar, it was also *wrong* ...

Prince DiMag rose to his feet, unsheathing his own
blade as he did so. 'We'll put your fighting abilities to
the test,' he said, his odd smile returning. 'Let's see if
you have the skill to disarm me.'

Some of his councillors began to protest, but the
prince ignored them and their voices dropped away to
disquieted mutterings. DiMag began to descend the
steps from the dais. His movements were strangely
awkward; he negotiated the steps with difficulty, and
Kyre realised that he was handicapped by a paralysis of
the left leg that gave him a terrible limp. He took a pace
back, appalled. A child could disarm the prince,
afflicted as he was; this was a travesty ...

DiMag reached the floor and stood facing Kyre, who
was a head taller. His eyes were dangerous. 'Draw your
sword, Sun-Hound,' he said.

All attention in the great hall was focused on them
now, and Kyre felt alarmingly vulnerable. What did this
hard-eyed audience expect of him? If he disarmed the
prince, as he surely must, would they use it as an excuse
to mete out some punishment to him? Or would he fare
worse by holding back and humiliating DiMag by
allowing him the pretence of winning? He felt as though
he had walked into some elaborate trap whose nature
he couldn't begin to understand.

DiMag's voice snapped him back to his immediate
predicament. 'I said, draw your sword. Show us all what
you can do!'

The prince's tone goaded him; he tugged the blade
free of its scabbard and threw the scabbard aside,
hearing it rattle coldly on the stone floor. The sword was
a good one, as he might have expected; heavy, but well

balanced and manoeuvreable, and suddenly he no
longer cared what this capricious prince or his court
might want of him. He'd not asked for a part in their
pantomime; if DiMag wished to make a fool of himself,
so be it.

He brought the blade up in a curt salute which the
prince returned – then he lunged.

DiMag didn't attempt to dodge aside. Instead, he
brought his own sword up to block Kyre's, and sparks
glittered as metal discordantly struck metal. A shock ran
through Kyre's arm to his shoulder; DiMag's reflex had
been much faster than he'd anticipated and he rocked
back on his heels, quelling his surprise.

'Good,' DiMag said, 'but half-hearted. You can do
better than that.'

His tone was careless, but his eyes were still
dangerous, the light in them verging on fanatical. Kyre
shifted his grip on the sword-hilt and advanced again,
more slowly this time, watching for any sudden move.
He had made the initial mistake of underestimating the
prince and he didn't intend to repeat it; DiMag's
limitations were obvious and one calculated strike
would put an end to this charade.

Kyre chose his moment. He feinted as though thrusting at his opponent's throat, and changed in mid-strike
to a rapid, sidestepping blow with the flat of the blade
which caught DiMag off guard. The prince swore aloud
as he realised the tactic – then with a speed that stunned
Kyre he pivoted, letting his damaged left leg take his
full weight, and his sword came slicing up under Kyre's
to intercept the blow. The sheer physical force behind
the prince's strike flung Kyre backwards; DiMag flicked
his wrist as the blades met, and Vaoran's sword was
wrenched from Kyre's hand to fly wildly, spinning,
across the hall. It crashed on the dais, scattering the
councillors behind the throne, and Kyre dropped to his
knees, clutching at his shoulder which felt as though it
had been dislocated.

DiMag stared down at his opponent. The prince's face
was grey with pain, but he forced a smile that, Kyre
thought as he returned the gaze, was far more significant
than he could imagine.

'Well, you did your best.' Laughter, albeit on the edge
of anger, lurked somewhere in DiMag's voice. 'But it
wasn't good enough.' He darted a vitriolically triumphant glance at his councillors, then turned back
towards the dais. Vaoran stepped forward as though to
assist him, but the prince waved him away.

'Thank you, swordsmaster, but as you perhaps now
realise I'm not yet a complete cripple.' Painfully,
clumsily, he made his way to the top of the steps, where
the sword Kyre had wielded lay near the throne. No one
made any further attempt to help him as he bent, with
a ferocious effort, and picked up the blade. Turning, he
held it out to Vaoran, who took it in chagrined silence;
then he sat down once more and looked at Kyre, who
by this time had risen to his feet.

'Come up here,' he said, beckoning. 'Stand beside
me. The court has had its entertainment, even if
Councillor Vaoran and his friends are disappointed by
the outcome.' He smiled thinly. 'Now I know I can
defeat you, I've no cause to fear you.'

Simorh had turned her head away, her expression
unreadable, while Vaoran's face was flushed and the
other councillors looked disconcerted. Abandoning any
attempt to understand what was afoot, Kyre mounted
the dais and stood, as DiMag indicated, beside the
throne. The prince studied his face carefully for a few
moments, then said: 'You don't understand me, do you,
Sun-Hound? You haven't begun to comprehend what
this is all about.'

Kyre didn't speak, and DiMag shrugged. 'You'll
learn, soon enough. And you might as well begin your
first lesson now.' He snapped his fingers towards a
nearby retainer. 'We've kept our unexpected guest
waiting. Tell Paravad to bring it in.'

The order was hastily relayed to the far end of the hall, where liveried guards moved to open the double doors, and one hurried away along the passage beyond. People shuffled and whispered among themselves, and the growing tension made Kyre's skin crawl. Then after perhaps a minute or two came the sound of feet in the corridor, and five men entered, escorting a figure in chains.

Leading the small party was a saturnine man in stained grey clothes. Every gaze in the hall followed him as he walked to the dais, where he stopped and bowed to DiMag before standing aside to allow his companions to approach.

Kyre stared at the being which the four guards half led and half dragged before the throne, and felt a tight, cold knot at the pit of his stomach. He had expected some kind of animal – but this creature was human. Slim, and so young that its sex was hard to determine, the prisoner had a shock of short silver-white hair and its skin, under a thin black shift that barely covered its torso, was faintly tinted a translucent blue-green. Huge dark eyes, disproportionate in a narrow and almost feline face, stared up at DiMag without emotion: either the being didn't comprehend its situation, or it was devoid of fear.

DiMag stared back at the captive, and when Kyre glanced at the prince he was shocked by the insensate hatred that glittered in the hazel eyes. Slowly DiMag ran his tongue over his lips, then he gestured to the saturnine man to approach him. As the grey-clad figure mounted the dais Kyre caught a trace of an unwholesome reek, and recoiled inwardly as he recognised the acrid and unmistakable smell of fear.

'Well, Paravad.' DiMag leaned awkwardly towards him. 'Have you persuaded it to speak?'

The saturnine man made a small, obsequious bow and shook his head. 'No, my lord. It refuses to respond. I've made use of all the customary techniques, but it is unwilling to co-operate.'

DiMag twisted a strand of his lank hair between two fingers. 'What's your prognosis?'

'To be frank, sir – and in the light of past experience – I can see nothing to be gained by pursuing my efforts any further.'

The prince nodded. 'I'm inclined to agree. Very well; filth is filth, and should be disposed of before it can corrupt everything it touches.' A savage edge, contempt mingled with loathing, had crept into his voice as he spoke. 'Was it armed when it was captured?'

'It was, sir; yes.'

'Then bring me the weapon it carried.'

The silver-haired creature continued to regard the tableau on the dais with the same hollow, indifferent stare, and Kyre's discomfort increased. Paravad's answers to DiMag's questions, however carefully phrased, left him in no doubt that the prisoner had been tortured. It exhibited no physical marks, but something in the saturnine man's look and in his smooth voice with its underlying ice told him that Paravad's methods were too subtle to embrace mere brutality, and that he derived a good deal of pleasure from his work. Kyre felt a cold sweat break out on his arms and torso.

Another guard, gorgeous in red and gold and bristling with self-importance, came striding the length of the hall to halt and bow with military precision before the dais. He carried a bizarre weapon which he held out to the prince, and, peering forward, Kyre saw that it was a long-shafted spear, the shaft polished to glasslike smoothness and shot through with opalescent tints of green and blue. The blade, glinting wickedly in the poor light, formed a long and ferocious point that branched half way along its length into a secondary, shorter blade angling away into a sweeping hook. It was a superb piece of craftsmanship, and formidably versatile; it could stab, slice, scythe, or pin and sever any flesh in its path. *And with an unpleasant, liquid feeling at the pit of his stomach, Kyre knew that, if the weapon were placed in his hands, he could handle it like a master.*

DiMag rose from his chair and took the weapon from the guard. Briefly, as the spear passed into its field of vision, a flicker of intelligent interest showed in the chained captive's eyes; then as the prince's hands closed on the haft it lapsed back into its former indifference.

Slowly, DiMag paced to the edge of the dais. The councillors were watching him intently, and the smallest sound – the rustle of a garment, an incautious intake of breath – seemed shatteringly loud against the stifling background of silence. Kyre felt as though his body were under a spell; his limbs were locked and frozen, his lungs had stopped functioning. He could only watch as, with careful precision, and clearly treasuring the moment, DiMag stepped down and approached the prisoner.

It looked up at him as he raised the blade, and for a moment its expression changed, betraying youth and vulnerability and – at last – fear. DiMag's eyes lit with an answering triumphant relish; he renewed his grip on the spear-shaft, paused – and the blade sheared in an arc that slashed the prisoner's head from its shoulders in a single blow. Kyre's stomach lurched violently as he saw blood spatter like thrown water over DiMag's hands and body. The severed head bounced and rolled, and the decapitated body swayed, arms jerking once in an obscene parody of life, before it collapsed to the floor, darker blood pumping across the marble floor.

DiMag threw the weapon aside and stared dispassionately down at the prisoner's remains. Slowly he rubbed his hands together as though washing them, spreading the crimson stains over his own skin. Then he smiled.

'Just a little fear, at the last,' he said, as though speaking to himself. 'It almost makes the trouble worthwhile.'

Kyre felt his leg muscles weakening under him. He couldn't express, couldn't even begin to assimilate, his horror and disgust at the prince's cold-blooded pleasure.

Suddenly he collapsed to his knees and, as the surprised councillors turned from the main entertainment to stare at him, he vomited violently on to the floor of the dais.

Chapter 3

Kyre was hustled back to the Sunrise Tower by two armed guards. His last glimpse of the court hall showed a party of servants moving in to clear away the remains of the corpse, and that image stayed indelibly with him long after his escort had locked the door of his room on him and gone.

He sat on the bed, staring at the floor before his feet and struggling against the sense of numbing inadequacy that had overtaken him. He had just witnessed the brutal killing of a defenceless captive; and the wanton savagery disgusted him. But he was equally disgusted with himself – he'd made no attempt to intervene, but had merely stood by, passively observing. He'd proven himself a coward, and a sick wave of shame took hold of him. Perhaps the sorceress was right after all; perhaps he *was* nothing better than a cipher, a shadow-man, and his pretensions to an independent identity were just that: pretensions.

Looking through the smeared window, he saw that the fog which hung over Haven was beginning to disperse. The dark shapes of towers and walls and roofs showed faint and ghostly through the white pall; the view was eerily depressing, and Kyre turned away with a suppressed shiver.

He loathed this place. He loathed the bleak shore with its moaning tide and shifting strand; loathed the claustrophobic city and its cold-eyed people. Whatever was amiss in Haven, whatever had driven Simorh to call him out of darkness and bring him here, he wanted no part of it.

The bed sagged with a dismal protest as he sat down once more. The room seemed to close in on him, and he put his face in his hands, not wanting to be forced to look at the bare walls. He stretched out on the bed, turning over so that his face was pressed close to the wall. Sleep would solve nothing, but it seemed a better prospect than wakefulness.

With a sigh that the room threw mockingly back, Kyre closed his eyes.

In the shadowy hall, Prince DiMag sat hunched in his chair, watching as the cleaning operation was completed. Four servants had carried away the prisoner's body and severed head in a sacking sling, and the harsh sounds of brooms swabbing the bloodstained flagstones echoed hollowly somewhere among the rafters.

Some of his councillors had left the hall; others conferred gravely at the back of the dais, and the prince noted with some irony that Vaoran was among their number. He deliberately ignored them, aware that he was the subject of their debate, and aware, too, that he could have stopped their whisperings in their tracks with a single look. But DiMag wasn't about to give them the satisfaction of seeing him behave according to their predictions. He shifted his position, drawing up his undamaged leg and resting his heel on the edge of the chair seat.

'DiMag . . . ?'

Simorh was standing a few paces away. Her posture was tautly formal, hands clasped before her; the thought came involuntarily to his mind that she looked beautiful, and it awoke old memories that, to his surprise, hurt. Then he saw the familiar unease in her eyes, and it reminded him sharply that they both no longer felt – *could* no longer feel – the same towards each other as they had once done.

When he answered her his voice was wearily sharp. 'What is it?'

Simorh blanched a little at his tone, but was

determined not to be intimidated. 'Have you a few moments to spare?'

Her voice gave away the fact that she resented having to all but plead for his attention, and DiMag noticed the strained inflection. He smiled coldly.

'I have a few moments. Especially as my councillors seem intent on conducting the court's business without reference to me.' He'd raised his voice deliberately, and was gratified to see, from the corner of his eye, Vaoran's head come up sharply. The swordsmaster glanced at the prince and then at Simorh, and his face flushed before he turned away again.

Simorh moved closer to the throne. 'I wanted to speak to you about Kyre.'

'Kyre. Ah, yes; the Sun-Hound whose stomach objects to the sight of blood.' DiMag smiled lop-sidedly. 'I admire your choice of name for the creature, Simorh; I didn't realise you had such a sense of the absurd.'

She turned abruptly away to hide her anger, and clasped her own forearms. 'He has a lot to learn.'

'Clearly.'

'He *will* learn: I'll see to that.' Her voice had a vicious edge. 'He's unmoulded, untrained – as yet he's no better than an ignorant animal.' She swung round to face him again. 'But he is what I said he would be. You can't deny that, DiMag – just as you've never been able to deny that we need him.'

DiMag didn't answer her. Instead, he levered himself clumsily upright from the chair and moved slowly towards the edge of the dais. Simorh started forward to help him before she could stop herself; he drew back, glaring at her, and her hands fell to her sides.

'We *need* him,' DiMag repeated with ferocious contempt. 'A single man – and not even a true man, but a *thing* conjured by witchcraft! You may find that enough to satisfy you, but by the Hag, I don't!' Carefully he negotiated the steps to the foot of the dais, and Simorh followed, her cheeks burning with mortification at his all too obvious aspersion.

'You know the facts as well as I do,' she hissed, aware that some of the councillors were watching them. 'You've read the scripts that Brigrandon translated – you know what Kyre is, and you know, you *must* know, why I took it upon myself to perform that conjuration!' She didn't add that she had run the risk of losing her sanity or even her life to cast the spell that had summoned Kyre to the world; self-pity would cut no ice with DiMag. 'You know what my motives were!' She had kept pace with him as he moved towards the door behind the dais, subtly trying to interpose her body in a way that would make him pause, but without success. DiMag looked at her, and his hazel eyes were cynical.

'Yes: you did it for me, or so you'd have me believe. Everyone in this damned place would have me believe that they act entirely in my best interests!' He touched his tongue to his lips, tasting salt. 'Haven needs a fighting force now as it has never needed one before. You're quick enough to champion the results of your dark arts against my disapproval – conjure me an army ten times the size of the one we have now, and I'll have good cause to thank you!'

Simorh's expression closed as she realised that nothing she could say would persuade him to unbend. 'I can't perform miracles.'

'Then you might have saved your energies, because nothing less than a miracle is going to be of any use to us!' DiMag had reached the door, and hacked aside the tapestry that hung across it before pausing to stare at Simorh. His face was white and drawn with fatigue. 'I pity that poor creature you dragged from the netherworld. We are nothing to him, he owes us nothing; yet, willing or no, he's destined to be our champion or die in the attempt. No one has taken the trouble to tell him what's required of him. He must simply do what he is told to do, without ever questioning.'

'You talk as though he were as human as you or I,'

Simorh said. 'He's not. I gave him life: he has no existence beyond what I've granted him. Questions of his desires or his feelings don't arise.'

'I wonder if he would agree with that sentiment?'

She gazed back at him, and for the first time made no attempt to hide the bitterness she felt. 'Do you think I care? Only one thing matters, DiMag; only *one* thing! And I'll sacrifice anything for that!'

He paused. Then: 'For Haven?'

His words were a challenge; he knew what she implied, and was daring her to voice it without ambiguity. Simorh's courage failed, and unshed tears glittered in her eyes as she said, 'For Haven.'

She couldn't speak to him again, but could only watch mutely as he pulled the low door open and walked through. The tapestry curtain fell into place behind him, and a small, cold draught breathed on her face. After a minute or so, when his uneven footsteps had faded along the corridor, she too went through the door and began to walk back through the maze of passages towards the main palace hall and the upper levels beyond. By the time she reached the hall, DiMag was nowhere in sight. Simorh crossed the marbled floor towards the spiral stairs that would lead her to her own tower, and had almost reached them when footsteps behind her made her turn her head.

Vaoran had emerged from the direction of the main council chamber doors and was moving – deliberately, she thought – to intercept her. Too dispirited to evade him, she slowed and allowed him to catch up.

'Princess.' The swordsmaster's voice was gentle, and he laid a hand on her arm. She flinched at the contact and saw the shrewd flicker in his eyes as he realised that he had made a tactical mistake. He withdrew his fingers.

'Princess, is anything amiss? I wondered – '

'Nothing's amiss,' she replied sharply. 'Thank you, Vaoran, but the prince and I were merely discussing a private matter.'

'I thought perhaps the prince's action was a little . . . untimely.' He nodded in the direction of the Sunrise Tower. 'The creature – the warrior – he was obviously unprepared for such vehemence.'

'There's been little opportunity to prepare him for anything he might confront in Haven, Vaoran. Time will mend that.'

'Of course, lady.' The burly man inclined his head. 'And if I can be of service in that regard, I hope you'll consider me at your disposal.'

Oh, yes; Simorh thought: *I know what that means, Swordsmaster Vaoran! But you'll have no influence over Kyre while I continue to draw breath*! She hid the sharp inner flash of fury behind an impassive mask and said coolly, 'I appreciate your concern, but I think it best that Kyre should remain under my jurisdiction.' The look in her eyes grew hard. 'You'll serve me best if you remember that.' And before he could dissemble or protest, she turned and strode away towards the stairs.

Simorh vanished, and Vaoran, after a few moments, swung abruptly on his heel and left the hall in the opposite direction. Believing himself to be unobserved, he'd made no effort to disguise the sting of his chagrin; but as his footfalls faded along one of the echoing corridors, a small figure eased out from the shadows and across the floor.

Gamora peered along the passage which Vaoran had taken, and only when she was satisfied that the swordsmaster was out of sight did she hurry on light and silent feet towards the stairs. There she paused again, flattening herself against the wall, and peeped cautiously round into the stairwell, aware that if her mother should by some mischance return she would earn more than sharp disapproval for her disobedience. She'd been sternly instructed to stay with her tutor; but she couldn't concentrate on lessons with so much afoot, and had escaped when the ageing scholar had left her

to work on her handwriting while he fortified himself
with a cup of wine.

She *had* to see Kyre again. There were so many
questions she wanted to ask him, and she couldn't
contain her impatience. Her first meeting with the
strange newcomer had kindled a sense of hopeful
eagerness that Gamora had never experienced before,
and which she couldn't understand but wanted to grasp
avidly lest it should slip away.

The stairwell was empty and silent. Gamora waited,
counting her heartbeats until she judged that her mother
would have left the main staircase where it branched to
her own tower, then hitched up her skirt and ran up the
steps towards her goal.

At first, Kyre thought that the furtive scratching sounds
at his door must be the remnants of a dream. He had
almost fallen asleep, and the small disturbance had
jolted him back to wakefulness so suddenly that he was
convinced the noise had come from within his own skull.
He sat up, rubbing a clenched fist across his face – then
stopped as he saw the door moving slightly.

A click. The sound was faint but decisive, and his
muscles tensed in response. Then the latch rattled and
lifted, and slowly the door creaked open.

'Kyre?' Gamora's eyes were huge smudges in the
blurred whiteness of her face as she stood framed in the
dim light from beyond. 'Kyre, are you awake ... ?'

'Princess – ' He got to his feet in an involuntary reflex,
and the little girl slipped into the room, shutting the door
behind her. 'What are you doing here?'

She tiptoed across the floor – pointlessly, as there was
no one in earshot – and smiled ingenuously. 'I picked
the lock. My tutor told me a story once, about a prisoner
who escaped from a dungeon, and I remembered how
it was done.' Proudly she held up a small wire con-
traption and showed it to him. 'I have to wear these in
my hair sometimes, but they have much better uses!'

Her fingers were stained with ink; she must have slipped away from her lessons, and Kyre wished that he could have been in a better condition to greet her. In his present mood, he couldn't respond to her childish enthusiasm.

Gamora, however, possessed a sensitivity beyond her tender years, and she knew instantly that all was not well with her new friend. 'Kyre, what's amiss?' she asked, her eyes wide and her voice solicitous. 'Something troubles you.' She touched her tongue to her lips in a gesture unconsciously reminiscent of DiMag. 'Did my mother take you to the court hall?'

She must have the eyes and ears of a fox ... Kyre nodded, and Gamora sighed. 'I thought she would. My father would have wanted to see you ... but there was something else, wasn't there? I heard a prisoner was brought from the shore at dawn.'

'You miss nothing, do you, little princess?'

'I can't afford to,' Gamora retorted candidly. 'Is it true? Is there a prisoner?'

He couldn't judge how much she might have guessed or how much he could tell her without distressing her. It was easy to forget how young she was. After a few moments' hesitation he said: 'There was a prisoner.'

'*Was?*' She picked up the hint that Kyre had hoped she might miss. 'Ah. Yes, I think I understand. Was it my father who killed it?'

His expression answered her question. Her small face became almost feral, and she said fiercely, '*Good!*'

'You *approve*?'

She stared at him in surprise; then comprehension dawned in her grey eyes and the surprise was replaced by a sad smile. 'You still don't understand, do you? Poor Kyre.'

Poor Kyre indeed. He turned away.

Behind him, Gamora said: 'Did you speak with my father?'

Kyre drew a deep breath. 'No. We – exchanged no

more than a few words.'

'Then he didn't tell you why we hate the sea-people so much?'

The fierceness in her last few words made him realise that her own hatred was no more than a catechism, a response she had learned from babyhood without questioning and probably without comprehending. It turned his anger to ashes – the fact that she was a child was enough both to explain and to excuse – and at the same time it provided the catalyst of clear, cold reason for which, somehow, he had been waiting.

A city rotten with the putrefaction of hatred. A ruler whose sanity was in question, and whose consort's bitterness tainted everything she touched. And a child to whom death and slaughter were a commonplace to be shrugged off with barely a second thought. Whatever Haven and its people wanted of him, whatever the role that Simorh had decided he should play, Kyre wanted no part of it. He had feared the sorceress because she claimed to hold the key to his own life or death; but what was life worth if it held no better prospect than Haven and its corruption? He'd be better dead, or consigned back to limbo, and the thought dissolved the last of his terrors. He must leave the city – where he'd go he didn't know; but he must leave.

Gamora was waiting for him to answer the question she had asked, and he dropped to a crouch so that their eyes were on a level. Reaching out, he took her small hands in his and tried to smile.

'There's much I don't understand, little princess, and perhaps I never will. But I need to leave the city.'

Her face clouded. 'Why?'

'I can't explain; not now. Can you help me, Gamora?'

Her brow creased in an unhappy frown. 'Will you come back?'

'Of course I will.' He hated lying to her, but there was no other way.

'When?' Gamora asked. 'Let it be soon, Kyre – or

let me come with you!'

'No, little one; I can't do that. But I'll come back soon.' He felt something twist inside him, and silently cursed his own serpent of a tongue. 'I promise.'

She didn't quite trust him, but she also sensed that she couldn't sway him. Gently tugging her hands from his grasp, she turned and walked slowly back to the door. 'This lock is old,' she said in a curiously flat voice. 'I'll have to lock it behind me, but when they bring you food, you can use the fork from your plate to trick it open again.' She looked back over her shoulder, her eyes haunted. 'They won't know it was me. I promise I won't tell.'

She would keep that promise, he knew, far more faithfully than he would hold to his own empty oath. He nodded. 'I understand.'

'Then, if you want to leave the palace ... there's a way that no one uses any more.' Gamora gulped back a threat of tearfulness. 'I found it by myself, and I sometimes go down into the city to explore. Here.' Squaring her small shoulders as though abruptly but reluctantly coming to a decision, she returned to his side. 'If I wet my finger and draw you a map on the floor, it'll stay long enough for you to remember it.' Licking a finger several times she drew a quick, practised series of outlines on the flagstones. When she had done Kyre stared down at it. It was simple enough.

'You must wait until dark,' Gamora told him. 'Until the palace sleeps. The fog will hide you.'

He glanced towards the window. 'The fog has lifted.'

'It will come back.' She smiled obliquely. 'It always does. I'll think of you, Kyre. I won't be able to see you in the mist, but I'll watch from my window and I'll imagine waving to me. Will you wave?'

'I will, princess.' That promise at least he could keep. 'And I won't forget what you've done.' On an impulse he leaned to kiss her forehead. 'Thank you.'

Her cheeks pinkened and she backed towards the

door, trying to hide her pleasure. 'I must go. May the Eye protect you, Kyre.' She opened the door. 'And . . . I do love my father. I know that might seem strange to you; but I do.'

The remark, unprompted and without apparent motive, was somehow disconcerting, as though the little girl had read Kyre's thoughts and was trying to defend DiMag. Before he could respond, however, Gamora had closed the door between them, and he heard the sound of the lock clicking softly back into place.

Waiting was the worst of it. He spent most of the day by the narrow window, first trying to force it open, then, when it proved rusted into place by salt and damp, simply sitting and staring out through the gale-scored glass at what little view was afforded him. Occasional sounds drifted distantly from the city, though they were muffled by the mist, which never truly relinquished its hold. Kyre kept other thoughts at bay by trying to interpret the sources of those disjointed sounds; but nothing could quite banish the constant background fear that at any moment the door at his back would open, and a summons from the sorceress would put paid to his plans.

But the summons did not come; and at last the light beyond the window began to fade as the fog closed in once more. Sounds faded into an engulfing silence, and Kyre felt as though the blood in his veins had been replaced by a burning, searing river of tension. He rose, paced; then sat down again, afraid that someone below might hear his restless movements and investigate. And at last he knew that, whether the palace slept or not, he could wait no longer.

The lock yielded to his probing with remarkable ease. The hinges creaked abominably, but the noise was short-lived and not loud enough to draw attention; cautiously Kyre eased himself through the half open door and on to the narrow landing.

Around the first spiral of the descending stairs a lamp burned low; it cast a pool of dim, sullen light, and the rancid smell of fish-oil assailed his nostrils as he passed. Beyond, the stairwell was dark; he felt his way down each uneven step, using the rough wall to guide him, and finally reached the foot of the tower. Here were more lamps, but again they were dimmed for the night, their flames nothing more than tiny pinpoints that granted the passage more shadow than light. Kyre waited, neither moving nor breathing, until the stillness and the lamps' soft, uninterrupted hissing reassured him that no one was abroad. Then he moved, a silent shadow among shadows, towards the unused staircase that would take him to the palace walls.

Thean couldn't sleep, despite the fact that she felt wearied to the marrow. The after-effects of the narcotic incense she had inhaled so deeply yesterday, and which had enabled her to keep vigil while her mistress was at the ruined temple, stubbornly refused to leave her; disjointed visions flickered at the corner of her mind whenever she tried to close her eyes and rest, and sleep seemed to mock her, an arm's length away but always out of reach.

Beyond the curtained recess her fellow apprentice Falla slept soundly on her bed; but below Thean could still hear the sounds of restless pacing that told her Simorh, too, was wakeful. She'd seen little of the princess today – there were rumours of council business which had kept her away from the tower – but had been quick to notice the strain in Simorh's eyes when she finally returned and, without exchanging more than a terse greeting with either of her neophytes, retreated to her private apartments. Since then she had paced, paced, paced; and Thean needed none of her acute psychic sensitivities to know that something was badly wrong.

The sounds below ceased suddenly: Thean rose from

her place beside the dying fire, shivering as she moved out of the narrow circle of warmth, and was about to douse the lamp when the door opened.

Simorh stood on the threshold. She wore a linen shift with a shawl thrown over it, and in the gloom her eyes were vast, dark hollows in her face.

'Thean ... you're abroad late.'

Thean curtsied. 'Yes, lady. I couldn't sleep.'

'No more can I.' Simorh paced across the room to the window embrasure, but the night and the thick fog had blanked the glass into a featureless charcoal grey. 'There's something afoot; I can feel it.' She drew a quick, sharp breath between clenched teeth, almost a hiss; and Thean said: 'Perhaps you still suffer from the conjuration, princess. It took its toll.'

'No.' The sorceress shook her head emphatically. 'It's something else, and I suspect ... ' She paused, bit her lip, then looked at the girl. 'Scry for me, Thean. Bring out your glass. I want to get to the root of this, and I won't rest until I do.'

Thean didn't know if she would be capable of calling on her talent, but she didn't argue. Crossing to a chest at one side of the room she took out a tiny sphere of green glass wrapped in a black cloth. Simorh watched while she spread the cloth on the floor and placed the sphere upon it; then as Thean crouched over the scrying-ball the sorceress moved silently to stand behind her and laid both hands lightly on her shoulders. Thean saw the sphere beginning to cloud and grow milky; from the milkiness an image began to form. What she saw, and what it meant, Thean didn't know; she was merely the medium for Simorh's own power as the sorceress drew from her uncomprehending mind the message in the crystal.

It was over very quickly. Simorh believed she knew the direction in which she should look for the source of her disquiet, and she was right. The sphere, focusing almost immediately on her thoughts and suspicions, gave her a rapid succession of clear images; and she felt her heart miss a beat painfully. *Red-haired man, grey-eyed child, empty room, tide-washed strand* . . .

Thean recoiled with a jolt as her mistress abruptly broke the psychic contact between them. When she gathered her wits, Simorh was already striding towards the outer door.

'Wait here,' the sorceress ordered savagely. 'And wake Falla. I will need you both!' And with that she was gone, the door smacking back against the wall in her wake.

Simorh wasted no time rousing servants who at this hour would be fuddle-headed and little better than useless. Instead, she ran up the stairs of the Sunrise Tower – and at the top, the open door told her all she needed to know.

For a few moments she stood on the threshold, letting her back rest against cold stone and shutting her eyes against a wave of angry despair. All she had tried to do, tried to instil, and it still came down to this wanton disobedience and foolhardiness. Or perhaps Gamora couldn't be blamed; perhaps she herself should have known that a creature of the dark might have the guile of the dark.

Turning, Simorh started back down the stairs again, and at the foot of the flight entered a side corridor that led back past her own tower and on into the depths of the palace. The nurse's room – no light showing there. But beneath the door beyond, a thin bar of comparative brightness gave away the presence of a dimmed lamp.

When she opened the door, Gamora was kneeling by the window. Her hands were cupped between her face and the glass and she was staring, moving her head in an effort to see through the shrouds of fog and darkness. Bitter fury welled in Simorh, and she threw the door shut with a crash.

The child jumped, lost her balance, and sprawled on

the floor. When she looked up, her mother was standing over her.

'Get up.' The fury Simorh had exhibited earlier was nothing in comparison to this. Shaking, Gamora obeyed, backing towards her bed as Simorh advanced on her. Suddenly the sorceress's hand shot out and she snatched a handful of her daughter's hair, pulling hard and forcing her to stop with a cry of pain.

'What have you done?' Simorh hissed. 'You disobedient, stupid child – *what have you done*?' With each syllable she shook Gamora, and, terrified, the girl began to cry. 'You unlocked the door – you let him go! *Didn't* you?' Another shake. 'Answer me!'

'Mother – '

'I said, *answer me*! And don't *dare* to tell me a lie!'

Gamora's face crumpled. 'He said – he wanted to go away. Mother, I didn't mean any harm! I only wanted to be kind to him, because ... ' She caught sight of Simorh's face and desperately swallowed what she had been about to say. Miserably, she whispered, 'He promised he wouldn't tell you ... '

'Oh, by the *Hag* – ' Simorh's rage was doused by a wave of self-disgust. How could she expect Gamora to know better? The child was impulsive and quixotic, but she wasn't truly to blame; she had thought she was doing a kindness, and couldn't be expected to understand the consequences.

She released Gamora, and said harshly, 'You foolish child; of course he didn't tell! But you should know by now that you can't hide secrets from me!'

Gamora climbed on to her bed and curled up, sobbing. 'I didn't mean any harm – '

By all that's sacred, does she think I don't know that? Simorh thought savagely. She was staring down at the child, torn between further fury and a regret that made her want to reach out and bridge the appalling gulf between them, when the door behind her opened. She whirled, and saw Gamora's nurse, her eyes heavy with sleep, standing on the threshold with a lamp in her hand.

'Oh . . . ' The woman made a hasty curtsey, clumsily. 'I beg your pardon, lady – I didn't realise; I thought I heard the little princess cry out – '

Simorh's voice shook. 'Princess Gamora has had a nightmare. You should be more vigilant!'

Gamora's sobs were subsiding, and the nurse looked dubiously from mother to daughter. 'A nightmare . . .?'

'That's what I said.' Simorh couldn't build the bridge now; the damage was done. She walked past the nurse, pausing only to say: 'Stay with her until dawn. I think she will be glad of your company.'

As she hastened away down the passage, her heart was pounding and her mind reeling with the effects of the encounter. She hadn't meant to be cruel to Gamora; her anger had been fuelled by fear, not hatred – but how could a child understand that? She didn't realise what she had done, or what Simorh must now do to put matters right. The sorceress shuddered. She didn't relish the task ahead, but it had to be faced; and she would face it.

If it wasn't already too late.

Chapter 4

Those who saw Calthar moving on the endless flights of stairs or traversing the tunnels of the citadel knew what must have brought her from her lair, though none would have dared voice their thoughts in her hearing. And if they had the misfortune to be close by when she passed, they looked only once at her face before hiding themselves in the dark, damp shadows, holding their breath, touching lips that were suddenly cold to the charms about their necks, eyes closed until she was gone.

The tortuous ways through the citadel were unlit and treacherous, but she carried no lamp. Silver hair, a shocking contrast to her darkly green-tinged skin, swung chaotically about her head and shoulders like a mad nimbus, and the robe she wore and which had been worn by a hundred predecessors flapped in crazed tatters too old and too thin to hide the lithe, powerful body beneath.

She found her quarry with unerring instinct, and flung open the low door without pausing to knock or call out. As the door slammed back and the icy wind that haunted the corridors set all the fish-oil lights dancing and guttering, the old man scrambled up from the pallet bed. One foot caught in the blanket that covered him, and he stumbled and fell, pulling the blanket with him to reveal the naked body of a girl – hardly more than a child – huddled on the pallet.

Calthar stared at the girl with shrivelling indifference, then pointed, without speaking, to the open door. The girl snatched up her garments and ran, ducking wide of the awesome interloper, and her footsteps could be heard padding rapidly, unevenly away.

The old man stood up, pulling the blanket about himself and adopting a hunched, suppliant posture, like a dog not knowing whether to fawn at its master's feet or turn tail and flee. As Calthar stalked slowly around him in a wide circle his pale eyes followed her figure with hungry eagerness: then he looked at her face and the hunger died stillborn, to be replaced by fear.

'She's gone.' Calthar's husky voice was savage, and her accusation had a deadly edge.

He drew in a sharp breath. 'Again?'

'Again, Hodek. Again. Where is Akrivir?'

The old man swallowed. 'He's sleeping. The day has been arduous, and he was – '

She hissed like a snake, silencing him instantly. For a few moments there was no sound in the chamber other than her stertorous breathing. Then she said with soft venom, 'I see. So while your worthless son sleeps and you fornicate with children, who is to watch over Talliann?'

The old man's fear flowered into panic. 'She can't have left the citadel! I – she was – '

'*She was unwatched!*' Black rage and searing contempt fired Calthar's voice with loathing, and he cowered back as though from a physical blow. 'You know where she has gone – and you know what will happen if she isn't brought safely back!' She advanced, reached out to touch his face lightly with long fingers, and he smelled the scent of corruption on her skin. 'You have neglected your duty, Hodek. You know what I'll do if you fail to make amends for that neglect!'

An ugly, incoherent sound came from the back of Hodek's throat, and her hand slowly withdrew. Her eyes glittered liked quartz. 'Fetch her back. Unless you want the Hag to reach out and touch your bones tonight, *fetch her back!*'

Whimpering, the old man scrabbled for his clothes while she watched him, the harsh staccato of her breathing making the room claustrophobic. When he scuttled from the room and shouted for men-at-arms, she followed him; she stood at his back in the vast cavern that opened to the sea, and she watched with a gaze that no one dared meet as the search party left on the sullen tide. For now, there was no more to be done. But – and she turned her head slightly to stare at the cringing Hodek wringing his hands at the sea's edge – if anything went amiss tonight, there would be payment to exact. And it would give her a cold, cruel pleasure to exact it.

Though he knew his surprise was illogical, Kyre was discomfited to encounter a thriving population in the city below the palace's high walls. He had crept down through the terraced gardens, past the stunted plants with their sickly white blooms, to the wicket-gate that finally released him into the outside world. And there, in the dim, misty streets with their glowing witch-lights, figures moved and faces peered from windows. He heard a door slam, saw a curtain twitch, glimpsed two women, wraithlike in the fog, huddled together and hurrying to be home out of the night. A small square paved with sandstone blocks was littered with the debris of market-day; somewhere a dog howled and a curt voice reprimanded it.

Kyre shivered, moving on. There was an incongruity about the scene that discomfited him; the normality of the sounds, the people, the market refuse, didn't fit with his original, indelible image of the eerily empty town. It was as though the inhabitants of Haven weren't true people at all, but ghosts from a dead past. He remembered the sands beyond the town, and what lay beneath them, and the initial shiver became a cold shudder that scoured the length of his spine.

A shutter slammed nearby; the noise carried on the thick, still air and startled him. He increased his pace, feeling the gradient of the street steepening and aware, too, that he was cold. The fog had a clammy touch against his skin and the clothes he wore hadn't been designed to counter the chill of the open night. And that realisation made him wonder, for the first time, where he was going.

Kyre had been so intent on escaping from the palace and its warped inhabitants that it hadn't once occurred to him to consider what he might do once he was free. Instinct had led him down towards the sea, but only because he had come this way once before and knew no other path. Yet the bleak shore had nothing to offer, save for the ruined, skeletal temple on the shingle strand; and no inducement could persuade him to face that terrible place again – unless his only other choice was to return to the palace.

Involuntarily he looked back over his shoulder to where the town's jumbled streets and rooftops climbed away into the fog. It hadn't occurred to him that the hunt might already be up; but there was a good chance he had been missed by now. He knew he was valuable to Haven in some way; or at least, valuable to Simorh. He didn't know how far the sorceress's powers extended, but neither did he care to put them to the test, and once she discovered him gone she'd waste no time in summoning the manpower – or something less human – to track him down.

Kyre began to run, his bare feet thudding on the hard ground, creating dull echoes. With night deepening, the last straggling lategoers had left the streets and the lower reaches of the town were utterly still. The few lights which burned in windows were going out one by one. Almost before he realised it he had reached the arch where the twin green lamps glared like unwinking eyes, and he slithered to a halt.

Still no sign of pursuit. But the silence was invaded now by a new sound that set his nerves crawling in the few moments before he recognised it. Faint, soft, imbued with a cold malignance, it was the distant, mournful rhythm of the sea. There was a power in the sound that drew Kyre against his will; he stepped through the arch, turning his face towards the huge beach that opened up before him. The white sand stretched away, gleaming before it was swallowed by the fog; he smelled brine and decay carried on a light wind, and his nostrils flared involuntarily. It was hard to discern any scale or perspective through the mist: he thought he could glimpse a deeper darkness, far off, where the tideline must be, but it was impossible to be sure. Only a dim patch of light high up and away to his left told him that the scarred satellite which the townsfolk called the Hag had risen and was glaring down through the fog at him.

The wind gusted suddenly, making the green witchlights dance, and the shadow of the arch distorted jerkily and startled him forward. A short, rocky slope, then hard stone gave way to soft, damp sand under his feet, and he turned to look back at the town through the arch's frame.

He couldn't go back. Not now; not when he'd come so far. The beach surely couldn't lead only to the ruined temple – there must be a way, however difficult, of climbing the cliffs to one side or the other and escaping inland. And whatever the hazards of freedom, it was by far the lesser of two evils.

Kyre turned his back on Haven, tasting the wet wind and trying not to shiver. Then he set off into the shifting, banking fog, across the wide emptiness of the beach.

No light burned in Simorh's tower, but this was a work which demanded darkness. The sorceress knelt on the floor of her sanctum, aware of the uneasy gazes of Thean and Falla who flanked her, and her hands shook as they gripped the two ends of the knotted length of cord she held. Her fingers felt like lead, numb with the cold that pervaded the room and unwilling to obey her, but she fought the chill, feeding on the anger that still burned in her like a banked-down fire. The rage had been directed first at Gamora and later at herself; now though, she must channel it towards another, and an image of Kyre's face formed in her mind. She latched on to it like a hungry dog, and took a deep breath, drawing all the air she could muster into her lungs as though afraid that when she tried to breathe again there might be no more. Her bones ached and she longed to be able to forget this new trial of strength, turn her back on it and sleep. But that couldn't be. She had begun this, and she must see it through; to reject her responsibility would be to admit defeat, and for that there could be no consolation.

Feel the anger, she told herself savagely. *Feed on it, take strength and solace from it. You can do this; you must do it. Feel the rage. Even if it leaves you with nothing else, feel the rage . . .*

Simorh's fists clenched tighter on the knotted cord. Then, with slow and implacable deliberation, she began to wind it and wind it in a complex pattern around her hands as her lips mouthed the silent and ferocious words of an incantation.

Kyre had believed he was moving to the South, away from the stark ruin on the strand and towards the higher cliffs which, his confused reasoning argued, might hold some better hope of sanctuary. The sound of the sea was drawing nearer, though he still couldn't tell how far he was from the water, when to his dismay he stumbled suddenly and found his feet ploughing into shingle.

The strand . . . but he'd been walking in the opposite direction; he'd have pledged his life on it! Dismayed, Kyre stopped and peered ahead, praying silently that he was wrong, that he wouldn't see the sight he dreaded.

But it was there, rising out of the fog as though floating on it like a monstrous mirage. The harsh, skeletal framework of the ancient temple, its walls jagged and broken, towering up from the shingle bar. Even as Kyre watched it seemed that the mist was thinning, drawing back from the ruin to leave it clear before him, while directly above the rotting structure the pockmarked moon hung in an otherwise empty sky.

Something that tasted sour and acid mingled with the saliva in Kyre's mouth as he stared, appalled, at the temple. He hadn't meant to come here, he had set his face in the opposite direction; and yet, tricked by the fog and the sea's echoing, he had been unwittingly drawn back to this terrible place as though bound to it by the same sorcery that had brought him to this world.

His lungs heaved as he tried to catch his breath. He wanted to defy whatever glamour it was that had afflicted him and turn back towards the cliffs on the far side of the bay's mouth; but instinct told him that the attempt would be futile. He hadn't misjudged his direction from Haven. Something had invaded his mind, twisting him away from his goal to bring him back to the place of his bizarre birth and, looking up again at the dark sky, he felt certain that the withered moon, or some arcane power linked with it, had been responsible.

His jaw clenched. He was about to turn his back on the bones of the ruin and on the satellite's dead, glaring eye, when he saw something that stopped his breath.

The mist had stolen back from the strand, exposing the giant, quiescent serpent of the shingle bar ... and out on the bar was something alive. It must have come from the sea, and now, clear of the water, it crawled over the stones, moving slowly and awkwardly as though the element in which it found itself was alien to its nature; a hunched, indistinct shape that shimmered wet and phosphorescent from the sea. Kyre stared at it, repelled and yet fascinated. And then, with painful concentration, it slowly rose until it was standing upright, and it turned to face him.

It was human. Even at this distance there could be no doubt. And one look at the frail, narrow, deathly-pale face told him that the interloper was young, and female. Ragged hair the colour of jet blew about her head, and eyes which in the darkness were huge, featureless black hollows stared at him across the distance that separated them. The chill moonlight gave a terrible flatness to her white skin so that she looked corpselike, almost two-dimensional, something from a fragmented, disturbed dream. She was clad in a long gown, and as she moved – hampered, he realised, by its waterlogged folds – the gown shimmered, as though its entire surface was covered with a myriad glittering silver pinpoints.

A painful and involuntary muscular spasm racked Kyre as he returned the alien girl's gaze. Yet what he felt was more than a physical hurt. For the first time something that he recognised as a memory was lurching to life within him, twisted beyond recognition but stronger than anything he had encountered since being dragged into this world. He *knew* her. She was – he fought for identity, for a name, but it wouldn't come; the memory, if memory it was, was distorted beyond his reach. He could only stand staring at her as though transfixed. *But he knew her*.

She turned her head suddenly, looking out to sea, and the movement broke Kyre's trance. He struggled to find his voice, wanting to call out and reassure her that he meant her no harm, but before he could utter a sound she had regarded him again, once, and was moving slowly backwards, step by uneven step, along the shingle bar.

'Wait!' He forced the word out and it sounded flat and dull against the vast night. She didn't respond, only continued to retreat from him with her odd, uneasy gait. The capricious mist was creeping back, and Kyre was suddenly afraid that she would fade into its embrace and be stolen away, leaving him bereft and alone. He had to go after her and, if she could understand him, he had to speak to her.

He took two hesitant steps forward, and the girl stopped. Though the darkness played tricks and her face was no more than a pale blur, he thought she smiled with a peculiar twisting of her lips, as though the movement were unpractised. Then she took five rapid paces back, almost scuttling, increasing the distance between them.

'Wait!' Kyre called again. 'Please – wait!'

A sound like thin and fragile laughter answered him, and the girl turned her back and ran. Her feet made barely a sound on the shingle, and the glowering moonlight set the spangles of her gown shivering and dancing like a shoal of tiny fish as she skimmed away towards the stark ruin at the end of the bar. Aware only of the fear that he would lose sight of her, Kyre set off in pursuit. The shingle was treacherously loose, sliding under his feet and threatening to throw him off balance, but even so he was faster than the fleeing girl and knew he must catch her before she reached the temple. What he would do then, what he would say, whether she would be afraid of him, he didn't know. All that mattered was to catch her.

He was no more than twelve paces behind the shimmering, hurrying apparition when a ferocious hissing sounded beneath his feet – and without any warning, five glittering silver columns erupted with the speed of striking snakes out of the shingle in front of him. Kyre yelled aloud in shock, trying to twist in mid-stride as they coiled towards him, and fell, the yell turning to a scream as one of the silver ropes cracked across his back like a whip, searing his skin. He rolled instinctively, digging hands and heels into the shingle to spring up and back – and five more of the monstrous things reared up out of the bank behind him, cutting off his retreat. They swayed menacingly above him, and cold silver sparks spat and flickered along their lengths, some spinning to the wet shingle where they hissed like furious cats. The saliva dried in Kyre's mouth as he realised that the hideous things were alive – or at least, directed by some sentient mind that could see him, that was anticipating his next move and only awaiting its chance to strike at him again.

Trapped, and sweating with fear, he turned to where he had last seen the girl from the sea. She had stopped and was staring back at him, and his first conviction that these monstrous supernatural whips had attacked him at her bidding died as he saw that she had her hands to her mouth in shock. Without thinking he reached out, trying to implore her to help him – and the silver coils twisted, cracked, slashing a fresh shower of burning sparks across his face and pitching him to his knees with a harsh cry of pain. He sprawled, and the shingle beneath him began to hiss anew, pebbles heaving and shifting as if some giant, enraged beast were thrashing under the surface. Kyre tried desperately to scramble to his feet but was thrown violently off balance again, rolling aside in a frantic but futile effort to protect himself as more sparks spat down and seared through his clothing to the unprotected skin beneath. The silver snakes reared over him, coiling and writhing as though maddened by the sight of his agony, and amid their triumphant spitting and hissing he heard another cry, a sound of distress and incoherent protest. It wrenched at his mind and, wild-eyed and crazed, he saw through the shimmering ropes the girl's figure, leaning towards him, arms held out in supplication. And behind her, something else – a blur, too indistinct to register fully on his racked brain; but he had a momentary image of dark shapes flowing from the direction of the ruin, moving towards the girl, overtaking her –

She screamed, on a high, full-throated note that contained anger and terror and protest, and at the same moment the ten silver serpent-whips curled over and came lashing down together on Kyre. The first strike was white-hot fire, and pain exploded through him with such murderous force that the shriek he tried to give voice to was a silent travesty. He had a momentary glimpse of the glittering, sparking coils rising again for a second attack – and as they bore down and struck him, a fresh wave of pain smashed his consciousness into oblivion.

Falla and Thean caught Simorh's arms as she swayed
and pitched forward. Lifting her as carefully as the
room's cramped confines allowed, they laid her back on
cushions, and Thean anxiously rubbed and patted her
ice-cold hands to restore the circulation. The sorceress's
face was deathly pale and lined from great strain, but
after a few moments she forced herself, with a
tremendous effort, to open her dull eyes.

'Fetch ... armed men,' she whispered hoarsely. 'Tell
them ... ' She coughed convulsively, and spittle ran
down her chin. 'Tell them to bring him back ... '

'Lady, are you – ' Falla began.

'*Fetch them!*' Simorh could hardly speak, but there
was venom in her tone. 'Obey me!'

'Yes, lady.' Falla scrambled to her feet and ran
towards the door. As she disappeared, Simorh struggled
into a sitting position, refusing Thean's attempts to help
her.

'I shall be all right ... leave me, Thean. Let me sleep.'
She looked at the discarded cord, and her expression
tightened with revulsion. 'Just leave me alone.'

Four heavily armed guards, venturing nervously from
Haven under Vaoran's direction, found Kyre sprawled
unconscious on the shingle strand. His clothes were
scorched in places, and there were burn marks on his
face and torso. Vaoran stared down dispassionately as
his men turned the senseless figure over. He knew the
bare details of Kyre's escape and could surmise the
methods Simorh had used to apprehend him; though
sorcery repelled him he nonetheless felt a distinct
satisfaction as he stared at the prisoner.

One of his men, whey-faced in the waning moonlight,
glanced uneasily over his shoulder towards the sea, then
indicated Kyre. 'The tide's getting closer, sir. Should we
get him back to the town?'

Preferable to leave him for the fish and crabs to eat,
Vaoran thought venomously, then pushed the thought

away. He'd do nothing to advance himself in Simorh's eyes if he abandoned her creation to the sea; this setback must be borne a while longer. But he couldn't resist taking a slow pace forward, prodding the unresistant body with his boot and then delivering a carefully judged kick to the small of Kyre's back before the others lifted him. One more bruise to suffer amid the others: a pity the creature would never know its origin ...

'All right,' he said, his voice as harsh as a seal's bark against the whispering sea. 'Move him.'

They thought Kyre unconscious, but though he was too stunned to make a movement or utter a sound, his senses were returning. Through blurred and half-closed eyes he was dimly able to make out Vaoran's figure, and he had felt the kick that connected with his spine, though he was incapable of reacting to it. As the men tramped back over the sand with his body slung carelessly between them, it occurred to him to wonder why the swordsmaster should have a grudge against him. But his mind was too stunned and cloudy to be coherent. He lapsed back into senselessness as he was borne towards Haven, and knew nothing more until the moment when he was dumped, with no ceremony and jarring force, on to the floor of the palace's entrance hall.

Kyre groaned and tried to roll over, and heard someone laugh unpleasantly. 'The Sun-Hound's had his teeth pulled, eh?' It was Vaoran's voice, and his men joined in the laughter. 'Well, he'll live. You – inform the Princess that he's here.'

Footsteps hastened away, the noise drumming in Kyre's head, and, his pride stung by the swordsmaster's sarcasm, he made a great effort and managed to lift himself on to his elbows. His skin felt as though it had been roasted and sickness churned in his stomach, but he fought down the nausea and the pain and met Vaoran's cold blue stare. The burly man smiled deprecatingly. 'Better make yourself presentable, Sun-Hound. It'd be ill-mannered of you to greet your mistress looking like a whipped cur!'

Anger surged in Kyre, but before he could muster it into any physical or verbal form he was interrupted by a sudden flurry of running feet and a woman's voice calling an ineffectual command. The dimmed lamps by the stairway arch dipped and flickered with a rush of air, and a small figure erupted from the stairwell and across the floor.

'Kyre!' Gamora's voice was shrill with distress. 'Kyre!'

Vaoran moved to intercept the child, catching her arms and swinging her towards him. 'Little princess! You shouldn't be here; where is your nurse?'

'Don't you *dare* touch me!' Gamora struggled so furiously that he was chagrined into releasing her, and as soon as she was free she darted to Kyre's side. 'What have they done to you?' she cried.

Kyre took hold of her hand before she could touch his scorched face. 'It's all right, princess. Don't distress yourself, I'm not harmed!'

'But you *are* – you're burned, your clothes, your face – Kyre, what did they *do?*'

'Gamora!' The voice, laced with exhaustion though it was, carried enough angry authority to bring the child up short. Kyre looked up and saw, in the darker maw of the stairs, Simorh, with a harassed-looking woman of middle years at her back. He had time for the sorceress's haggard features and lank, sweat-damp hair to register on his mind before Gamora had flung herself across the hall and was clutching at Simorh's skirt.

'Mother, they've *hurt* him, and he's my *friend!* Why have they done it? He wasn't running away; he promised me he'd come back!'

'Gamora ... ' This time Simorh spoke more gently, as though she hadn't the strength for a confrontation. 'Gamora, you don't understand. Go back to bed. Go with your nurse.'

'No!' the child argued. 'Not until I know why they've

hurt Kyre! I saw them from my window and they were *carrying* him, as if he was something *dead*! Mother – '

Simorh's pallor increased and she shut her eyes. Gamora was sobbing, and Kyre's sympathy for the child, coupled with the guilt he had already incurred over her innocent faith in him, made him fight back the pain he still felt and force himself, unsteadily, to his feet.

'Little princess.' His voice stopped Gamora's protests in mid-flow, and she turned, wide-eyed, to look at him.

'I'm not harmed.' He spread his arms wide, hoping that his appearance didn't give the complete lie to his words. 'See; I'm standing, I'm speaking to you. I can even smile at you.' Beyond the child he saw Simorh staring at him, her face frozen into a look of suspicious uncertainty, then his gaze flicked back to Gamora. 'I'm not hurt.'

Gamora licked her lips. 'But – why were they carrying you like that? As though you were something killed on the hunt – '

He met Simorh's eyes again, briefly. 'It was a game, little princess.'

'A ... game?'

'Yes.'

She wasn't wholly convinced, but he could see that she set great store by his word, and at last she looked up at Simorh again. 'Mother ... ?' It was the last confirmation she needed.

'Yes,' Simorh said faintly. 'A game.' The look she gave Vaoran was venomous, and she might have directed her next remark to him, but a further sound on the stairs drew the attention of everyone in the hall. Uneven footfalls ... and Prince DiMag appeared, dressed in a light woollen robe under which Kyre could see the crumpled clothes he had worn that morning in the court hall.

'So this is the cause of all the noise.' His hazel eyes raked them all in turn. 'I'd anticipated an invasion at very least – I suppose I should be gratified to find the palace unscathed!'

'Father, I thought they were hurting Kyre!' Gamora broke away from Simorh and ran to him. He stared down at her and absently stroked her dark hair. 'Did you?' Then he looked first at his wife and next at the burly swordsmaster, and the look was vitriolic. 'Why should you think that?'

Vaoran intervened smoothly before Gamora could speak. 'There has been a slight – mishap, sir; and the Princess Simorh was gracious enough to call on my services.'

'Was she, now?' DiMag said with a faint smile.

'It was a game,' Gamora insisted. 'Kyre said so!'

'Then a game it was.' The prince smiled reservedly at her. 'But the middle of the night isn't the time for games, Gamora. Not if you want to grow to be worthy of your position, and not if you want to allow the rest of us to get a night's sleep!'

The child flushed. 'I'm sorry.'

DiMag laughed with a gentleness that surprised Kyre. 'Then show how sorry you are, little one, by going with your nurse. Back to bed, now.' He touched her hair again, and she gazed at him with adoring eyes. 'Yes, Father.'

The harassed-looking woman, who had not dared to speak in the presence of her betters, took charge of Gamora with obvious relief, and the little girl was shepherded away up the stairs and out of sight, her huge grey eyes looking hungrily back.

No one moved until the two were out of earshot, then DiMag limped down the last two steps and into the hall. His movements were more awkward than they had been earlier in the day, and Vaoran started forward solicitously.

'Sir, might I assist you?'

DiMag looked at him. 'Thank you, no. I'm sure you'll find it edifying to know, Vaoran, that the damp night air does nothing to improve my disability; but I'm still capable of walking unaided.' He had by this time

reached the centre of the small group formed by
Vaoran, Simorh and Kyre – Vaoran's men had stiffened
to attention the moment he appeared and no one paid
them any heed – and slowly he pivoted on his good leg
to regard the three in turn. Then, so unexpectedly that
they all started, he snapped, 'So: who is going to tell me
the truth about tonight's ructions?'

Two vivid spots of colour flamed on Simorh's cheeks,
and Vaoran's jaw worked, though he uttered no sound.
Only Kyre's expression didn't change, and DiMag,
seeing his apparent impassiveness, gave him a sharp,
oblique look. 'Your skin and your clothes are burned,
Sun-Hound. What did you do – try to immolate yourself?'

Simorh spoke up before Kyre could answer. 'The
marks will fade quickly enough,' she said.

'Ah. I begin to understand.' DiMag looked challeng-
ingly at her. 'Why?'

'He fled the palace.' She glanced at Kyre. 'You know
why he had to be brought back.'

'*I* do; yes. But does he?'

The sorceress's expression became defensive and yet
weary, as though she resented having yet again to
propound an old and worn argument. 'That isn't
relevant, DiMag.'

The prince gazed down at the pattern of the flagged
floor beneath him, and traced a flaw in the marble with
one foot. 'I'm sure it isn't; not to you, not to me, and
certainly not to our gallant swordsmaster-councillor
here. But has anyone thought to ask the Sun-Hound
what *he* has to say?' He looked up, and Kyre was
astonished to see a measure of sympathy, albeit
detached, in his hazel eyes. 'Decisions are made in
which he has no part; events are set in train in which he
is destined to play a role without being accorded the
common courtesy of knowing what that role will be.' He
smiled bleakly. 'Were I in his place, I too might be
inclined to rebel.'

'Sir, there can be no possible comparison between –'
Vaoran began, but the prince interrupted him with
heavy irony. 'Naturally, Vaoran, there can be no
comparison between the ruler of Haven and a mere
cipher. But *I* won't deny even to a cipher the privileges
I'd grant without second thought to a dog!'

The slight emphasis wasn't lost on Vaoran, but he had
no chance to reply, for DiMag had already turned to
face his wife once more, ignoring the swordsmaster as
though he were of no consequence.

'Salve his burns, make him presentable and send him
to me.'

Her lips whitened. '*Now?*'

'Now.' DiMag repeated. 'I think the Sun-Hound and
I have a good deal to say to each other – and I doubt
he's in any better mood for sleep than I am.'

And, without waiting for a response from any quarter,
the prince turned and limped towards the stairs.

Chapter 5

The room in which Kyre found himself was in chaos. DiMag's books and papers littered every available space, and a motley collection of weapons covered the small area of wall which wasn't obscured by tapestries. A single lamp, turned low and burning with the same chilly green light that lit the town entrance, provided the room's only illumination, and a worn curtain which had once been crimson but was now dulled to the desiccated hue of an old bloodstain half covered the window.

The appearance of the room and one or two otherwise insignificant incidents had forced Kyre to reappraise his first impressions of the prince. He neither liked nor trusted Haven's ruler; there was an edge to him that raised Kyre's hackles, and he was clearly unstable, given to irrational whims; besides which, the cold-blooded way in which he had killed the prisoner in the court hall still turned Kyre's stomach when he thought of it. But the obvious affection DiMag felt for his daughter, even if he found it difficult to express, was unmistakable. And he was the first of Kyre's captors to have shown a grain of consideration for the bewildered prisoner of Simorh's sorcery.

Or did he delude himself, Kyre wondered?

'Sun-Hound.' The voice startled him, coming as it did from a deeply shadowed corner of the room, and DiMag rose from the long couch which, it appeared, served him as a bed.

Kyre turned to face him. Uncertain of his own attitude, he made a half-hearted bow which didn't quite convey respect. 'Prince DiMag.'

DiMag smiled. 'Sit down, Kyre, if you can find the space. Formal interviews are tiresome.' He moved to the window, looking out past the half-drawn curtain. 'Haven languishes in fog yet again ... sometimes it's hard to remember a time when it was otherwise.' He fingered the worn linen, then abruptly turned to face his guest. '*Ha reinn trachan, ni þrachnaea pol arcath?*'

Something stirred in an occluded corner of Kyre's mind: the words sounded alien, nonsensical, yet they triggered a flicker of recognition. But it was no more than a flicker, and he shook his head.

'I don't understand.'

'Ah; never mind.' DiMag shrugged. 'The old tongue. My tutor taught it to me when I was a boy, and my daughter's tutor attempts to instil some glimmering of it into her head now. But it's corrupted; mostly lost. I don't doubt my accent makes it all but unintelligible.' His hazel eyes were calculating. 'I wondered if it might be familiar to you.'

It was, but ... 'No,' Kyre said.

'No matter. The manuscripts which survive from the time when it was spoken are too faded to make sense anyway.' Involuntarily, and regretfully, he glanced at the heaps of papers on a table near his couch, and Kyre asked: 'You are a scholar, Prince DiMag?'

'A scholar ... ' DiMag considered this for a few moments as though the idea hadn't occurred to him before, then laughed with irony. 'I suppose I have that misfortune these days, as I can certainly no longer call myself a warrior.'

'You defeated me easily enough, in the court hall.'

'Mm. Perhaps I simply showed you up as inept; I don't know. Certainly you're no true swordsman.' Again, that shrewd, calculating look. 'Though as to what you are ... that's another question, isn't it?'

Kyre sighed. The prince was being oblique, fencing with him. Despite the salve his skin hurt and was still

sore, his body ached and he was tired; he was in no mood
to play puppet to DiMag's or anyone else's whims.

'Prince DiMag,' he said, with an edge to his voice,
'I don't know why you summoned me here. I don't
know what you want of me.' He met the prince's gaze
and felt a small satisfaction at seeing DiMag surprised
by his look. 'But I can't answer your question, and I
think you're well aware of that. The Princess Simorh
tells me that I'm a cipher, and I have no knowledge
nor any memories that enable me to disagree with her.
I don't see why you should think I can be of any use
to you.'

There was silence for a minute or so while DiMag
moved with his awkward, uneven gait back to the couch.
He sank on to it and said tiredly, 'Sit down.'

Uncertainly, and with some reluctance, Kyre moved
some papers from a chair and sat. DiMag nodded,
satisfied. 'Very well; I'll come to the point if that's what
you want. I brought you here to make a bargain with
you, Sun-Hound.'

'A bargain . . . ?'

'Yes. Does that seem so surprising?' He laughed
again. 'I assure you, I spend half my life making bargains
and coming to compromises, and by comparison with
the denizens of my court, you're a rank novice in such
negotiations! When – ' and he stopped as someone
knocked diffidently at the door.

'Come.' His change in tone made Kyre lift a surprised
eyebrow, and the servant who answered the summons
received a glare of undisguised contempt.

'Your food, my lord.' The man set a covered tray
down on the table and hastily backed towards the door.
DiMag lifted the linen cover, then snapped: 'Wait!'

The servant froze. DiMag studied the array of dishes
on the tray for a few moments, then beckoned the man
to his side and pointed at a platter of shredded fish mixed
with nuts and herbs.

'That,' he said, then indicated another dish which

looked like cooked and glazed fruits. 'And that. And
a piece of the bread.'

The servant bowed and, to Kyre's astonishment, took
a small sample from each of the plates and tasted it. The
prince stared at the wall in stony silence while the man
chewed, swallowed, and finally nodded.

'All's well, sir.'

'Good.' DiMag indicated the door with a wave of one
hand. 'I'll need nothing more tonight.'

The door closed behind the departing servant. DiMag
smiled sourly. 'There have been six attempts to poison
me in the past two years, and I don't doubt there'll be
more.'

'But who . . . '

'Who? By the Hag, d'you want to sit here until dawn
breaks listening to the list of possibilities?' The prince
gripped his own leg and heaved it clumsily on to the
couch, so that it lay straight before him. 'I have my
suspicions, but I won't play into their hands by making
accusations without proof.' His gaze raked Kyre
bitterly. 'And it's no concern of yours; no reason why
it should be. Eat.'

He *was* hungry . . . Dubiously Kyre reached out and
sampled the fish. It tasted good, and he took more,
eating with his fingers.

'Before we were interrupted,' DiMag said, 'we were
discussing a bargain.'

Their eyes met briefly, and Kyre replied, 'I still don't
see that I have anything to offer you.'

'You may not; I view it differently. And I'm prepared
to help you, Kyre. My wife has thus far refused to
answer any of your questions about yourself and why
you are here. But I am prepared to answer them –
though I'll want something from you in return.'

It was the chance for which Kyre had hoped, but he
mistrusted it. DiMag's offer seemed open-handed
enough, but the prince might be far more devious even
than he seemed.

He asked: 'What is your price?'

'That, insofar as you co-operate with anyone in this benighted city of ours, you co-operate with me. Not Simorh, not Vaoran: *me*.' He smiled thinly. 'In effect, I want your loyalty.'

It seemed straightforward; yet there had to be a motive behind DiMag's line of reasoning. The little the prince had told him confirmed his suspicions that all was far from well with Haven and its ruler; and he didn't doubt that his eccentric host had private and un-fathomable reasons for striking such an apparently reasonable bargain. Kyre had no inclination to pledge fealty to any denizen of Haven, but DiMag alone – if one discounted little Gamora – seemed prepared to treat him as a man rather than a shade, a guest rather than a hapless prisoner. And that was a gesture which Kyre was fast coming to appreciate.

He nodded. 'Very well. I agree.'

DiMag steepled his fingers before his face and studied Kyre over their lattice. 'Do you know, Sun-Hound, I find your attitude quite refreshing,' he said at last. 'You refuse to be unctuous; you refuse to make the pretence of demeaning yourself in my presence; I detect in you an honesty that's a rare commodity in Haven these days.' The lids drooped shrewdly over his hazel eyes. 'I'm not saying that I've taken a liking to you: I'm not such a fool as to do that on so short an acquaintance, and by rights I should loathe and despise you, when I consider the purpose for which you were brought here. Perhaps I will come to loathe you, I don't know; it's a risk you'll have to live with.' He leaned forward suddenly. 'And it *is* a risk. Whatever you might hear to the contrary, I still rule here. But for now, I choose to indulge my whim to treat you as a friend, of sorts.' He laughed softly. 'When you've lived in Haven a while, you'll come to understand that that's a rare concession!'

It was an extraordinary speech, and Kyre had no answer to it. Seeing that his implied threat had invoked no reaction, DiMag relaxed a little. 'We'll waste no more time,' he said, taking a piece of greyish, un-leavened bread from the tray and biting into it. 'To show my good faith, ask me a question. Anything you wish. I'll answer it, if I can.'

Kyre hadn't anticipated such a rapid change of tack, and found himself floundering. So much to ask, so many answers he craved – and he heard his own voice saying: 'What colour are my eyes?'

DiMag stared at him, nonplussed.

'Well,' he said evenly, after a pause, 'It's an easy enough question to answer, though I can't claim to comprehend why you should have asked it. How is it that you know so little about yourself?'

Kyre flushed. 'The sorceress – the Princess Simorh – gave orders that I shouldn't see my own reflection. She was adamant.'

'Was she, now? Then perhaps I begin to understand a little more than she intended.' DiMag nodded slowly, thoughtfully, and crossed to a corner of the room, where an extraordinary assortment of objects had been stacked, seemingly at random, against the wall. DiMag delved among them and dragged out a heavy, oval object. It was, Kyre realised, a warrior's shield, faced with a layer of bronze. The surface was badly tarnished, suggesting that the shield hadn't been used in many years, but the thinly-beaten metal still had enough of a sheen to reflect DiMag's face as he stared at it.

'There.' The princed wedged the shield firmly and stepped back. 'Not the ideal looking-glass, but it suffices. Satisfy your curiosity, Sun-Hound.'

Kyre slowly approached the shield. Now that he was at last to see himself he felt a stab of trepidation, and had to fight an impulse to shut his eyes. He reached the shield, stopped, stared . . .

A strong, bony face looked back at him from the shield's dull bronze surface. Wide-set eyes with a slight slant to them, broad cheekbones, generous mouth, determined jaw. Hair that fell heavy and abundant over his shoulders, and very unkempt. His face was scarred where Simorh's silver whips had attacked and burned him; but they would fade. He wasn't hideous, as he had feared. In fact there was a faint echo of DiMag in his features; of others he had seen in Haven, as if, far in the distant past, there had been a link between them.

He turned to look quickly at the prince, who was watching him with lazy interest. DiMag smiled faintly. 'The bronze distorts colour, I know. To answer your original question, your eyes are green. That's a very uncommon characteristic in Haven. I imagine the princess meant it to be otherwise, just as I imagine she would have preferred you not to have red hair. Does that strike you as significant?'

Kyre was starting to feel uneasy. 'Should it?'

'Ah; now we come to the nub of it. I wonder ... ' He shook his head. 'No. That will keep for another time. But it isn't like Simorh to make mistakes. I may dislike her power and the way she uses it, but I can't deny its efficacy – in certain areas.' With an effort he stood up, and walked to the window again. He was restless, and his mood lent tension to the atmosphere in the room. 'Do you know where she found the spell that created you? Would you *like* to know?' Kyre didn't answer – the thought made him queasy – and DiMag continued with a trace of malice: 'She found it in a manuscript which had all but rotted away, and which no one else can have studied for centuries.' He turned to face Kyre. 'That's what you are, Sun-Hound. Decayed parchment and faded ink; a jumble of words half in one language and half in another. Or that's what Simorh believes.'

'And you, Prince DiMag? What do *you* believe?'

DiMag had been walking back to the couch, but he stopped and stared hard at the other man. 'I don't know,' he said. 'I suspect there's more to you than meets the eye, but I don't yet know why I suspect it. If I thought you were privy to that information I might

decide to have it tortured out of you, if that's what it
took to get it. But you're even more ignorant than I am,
and certainly far more ignorant than Simorh.' Perhaps
then he saw a dangerous light in Kyre's eyes, for he took
an easy but nonetheless calculated pace backwards. 'A
cipher doesn't have a will or a mind of its own, and it
doesn't challenge its creator by being something that the
creator didn't bargain for. Tell me, Sun-Hound; do you
have a religious belief?'

Again the sudden and sly change of subject, as though
DiMag's favourite strategy was an oblique and obscure
attack. Kyre frowned. 'A religious belief . . . ?'

'Yes. We had gods once, or so history tells us, but we
lost them. If they ever existed at all, they probably
abandoned us when we started the long descent that has
led us to where we are today, and now we can't even
recall their names.' He saw the flicker of surprise in
Kyre's expression and added, 'Oh, yes: we thrived,
once. If you go inland from the city, you'll find nothing
but a few isolated farms and the occasional mining
village, and they're poor farms and villages at best. They
still tithe a portion of their produce and minerals to us
in exchange for our protection – for what that's worth
these days – and some still come to Haven to trade.' He
smiled cynically. 'The arrangement does no more than
maintain us all at a bare subsistence; but it wasn't always
that way. Centuries ago, Haven was a great power. Our
influence spread right across the land, and the land
prospered. We created, we traded, we had art and
music, and poetry and architecture and philosophy. Or
at least, that's what the records would have us believe;
though for all I know they might be nothing more than
the grandiose fantasies of a few drunken dreamers. The
only fact that's not in doubt is that now there's only
Haven; or what's left of it. And Haven's days are
numbered.'

'The sand . . . ' Kyre said, catching the venomous
bitterness in the prince's voice. 'The sorceress said that

the sea flowed twice in one night without ebbing, and the sand came in with the tide and buried half of the city.'

'She told you that, did she?' DiMag's eyes glittered. 'And did she also tell you *why* that disaster happened?'

'No.'

'No. She wouldn't have wanted you to know that particular truth.' DiMag resumed pacing, and Kyre watched his dogged progress with discomfited fascination. 'It happened through the agency of sorcery, Sun-Hound. Not Simorh's; but a filthy, evil, corrupted power whose wielders' sole aim is to destroy Haven and all who dwell in it.' DiMag stopped suddenly, seeming to realise that he was losing his self-control. He took a deep breath, then exhaled harshly. 'I won't deny that Simorh's skills are formidable – but beside those warped and evil demons from the sea, she's as helpless as a child!' He moved to the window. 'They draw their power from the Hag, that bloated monstrosity that floats in the sky when the sun has set and rules over the winds and the tides. Every now and then there's a conjunction – we call it the Dead Night – when the Hag rises directly over the sea and throws a spear of light across the bay to Haven's very gate. When that happens, our enemies' power reaches its height, and we can't stand against them.

'The last Dead Night conjunction was nine years ago, when the tide flowed twice without ebbing. The sea-demons came in on that tide and we tried to turn them back, but we failed. Our army rode out across the sand and met them as they came out of the sea.' He pressed his hands down on the window ledge, knuckles white, as he stared out at the fog. 'My wife stood in her tower, from where she could see the battle, and while our baby daughter slept in a cradle in the room below, she used all the power she could command to keep the city safe, keep our army safe, and it wasn't enough. What she did almost turned the blood to dust in her veins, and it was

a year before she could speak again; but it wasn't
enough. Maybe it would have been kinder if she had
died.'

'And you,' Kyre said, believing that he knew the
answer. 'You were wounded?'

'If that's what you want to call it. A spear in the leg
is one matter; a spear cursed with sorcery, and wielded
by a hand that should have been dead fifty years ago,
is another. The wound should have healed, so every
physician told me. It didn't. And no spells of Simorh's
will ever restore me to fitness.'

Creatures from the sea, enemies who drew their
power from the baleful moon: the prisoner in the court
hall ... little Gamora's savage hatred of the sea-people
...

Suddenly, his mind cast up the image of the girl on
the strand.

DiMag saw the change in his expression, the dismay
and confusion that he couldn't hide in time. The prince's
eyes narrowed.

'What is it?'

'I ... ' Kyre swallowed. 'Demons from the sea, you
said. And yet – they look human?'

'You saw the creature in the court hall with your own
eyes. They're human enough to die like any of us. Why?'

'On the strand tonight – I saw a girl.'

Suddenly DiMag's hands weren't steady. 'Where?' he
demanded.

'Not far from the ruin.'

The room was silent but for the prince's harsh
breathing. 'What did she look like?'

'Young – I think. Her hair was black, shimmering,
almost – ' he struggled for the right word but couldn't
find it. 'A white face, deathly white. Strange, vast eyes.
And – '

'*Dark*, you said? Are you sure? Not silver-haired?'
DiMag's eyes were ablaze with a feverish light.

'No.' Kyre shook his head. 'Her hair was black.'

'Then it wasn't Calthar ... '

'Calthar?'

The prince's face was venomous. 'Calthar is the source of their power. She's a vampire, a soul-eater. She's the ultimate corruption; the demon-race draws its inspiration from her as a child suckles its mother's milk. But it wasn't her you saw ... '

'She came from the sea,' Kyre said uneasily.

'Oh, yes: I don't doubt that the creature was one of Calthar's emissaries. Which can only mean she's abroad again.' DiMag shuddered. 'There's another Dead Night coming. Our astronomers have calculated it, and what you saw on the strand only serves to confirm their predictions.'

A deathly cold hand seemed to touch the pit of Kyre's stomach as a terrible suspicion entered his mind. He said, not entirely trusting his voice. 'And what has that to do with me?'

'Everything,' DiMag replied softly. 'It's the reason why Simorh summoned you into our world.' He stared at Kyre with a mixture of bitter weariness and pity. 'When Dead Night comes again, she means you to be Haven's champion.'

Kyre's throat was dust-dry, and his voice shook. 'She surely can't – '

'She can. That is your task, my friend. Haven is threatened with destruction; a conjunction is approaching, and without a miracle we can't hope to survive the attack that will surely come. Your destiny is to provide that miracle.'

Kyre's mind floundered, and his only clear thought was to ask himself whether DiMag, or Simorh, or both, were insane. The idea that he, a single man, should be expected to stand against an army of enemies was sheer, deluded madness. He owed no loyalty to Haven, he had no past to call on: to the best of his own poor knowledge he wasn't even a warrior!

DiMag was still watching him, and said suddenly, 'I

know what you're thinking, and maybe it *is* a kind of
madness. But there's a great deal you don't understand.'

'Then tell me,' Kyre said tightly.

'No.' The prince shook his head. 'I'm no true scholar,
despite my pretensions; you're demanding your answers
of the wrong man.' He moved stiffly towards his couch.
'You should seek out Gamora's tutor, old Brigrandon,
and put your questions to him.' Abruptly, he turned
towards his couch. 'I think, Sun-Hound, that for the
time being we have no more to say to each other. I've
been honest with you, as I promised, but for now I can
tell you no more.' Pausing, he looked back at Kyre.
'Remember the pledge you made to me in return, and
you won't find my word wanting. I'll grant you complete
freedom within the palace, and you need answer only
to me. But *always* remember your pledge!'

He sank down on the couch, and reached out to pull
at a bell-rope which hung by the wall. Kyre couldn't
speak, couldn't find words to say that made any sense;
and, seeing that he wasn't about to argue, DiMag added,
'My own guard will show you the way back to the Sunrise
Tower.' He smiled wryly. 'Good night, Kyre. Sleep well
– if you can.'

Calthar was waiting when they brought the girl back to
her room. She stood bathed in the eerie blue glow which
suffused through the womblike cavern, watching as the
escort party stopped on the threshold. The men would
come no further than the narrow embrasure; the
sanctum was barred to them by the twin prohibitions of
tradition and their own fear, and Calthar treated them
to a glance of withering contempt when she saw how
uneasily they shrank back from the girl, afraid to touch
her. Then they withdrew, and the girl entered the cavern
alone.

After an initial struggle she had suffered her recapture meekly, and as she faced Calthar her huge, dark
eyes were empty of emotion. A tranquil and dreamy

smile softened the line of her thin lips, and Calthar felt
a familiar mixture of rage, resentment, jealousy and
disgust boiling within her like a brew in a cauldron. The
girl was in one of her lucid phases – otherwise, she could
never have had the self-possession to escape in the first
place – and was quite capable of speaking if she chose
to. But she wouldn't choose; and no power could force
words out of Talliann unless Talliann willed it.

She paced slowly towards the girl, moving among the
stalactites that hung like giant, ossified claws from the
cavern ceiling. Her steps were slow and deliberate, and
on the cave walls with their cold sheen of abalone a
hundred reflections of her lithe form and fluttering,
ancient robe performed a distorted dance. Talliann
didn't react in any way, and Calthar felt her patience
ebbing towards a dangerous level. The girl needed a
sharp and bitter lesson to bring her to heel and make
her understand and knuckle under the responsibility
that lay on her shoulders: but, though the knowledge
ate at her like a cancer, Calthar knew that hers could
never be the hand to administer that lesson. As Priestess
of the Hag and heir to the Mothers who had reigned
before her, she was feared by the sea-dwellers above all
others: save one. And it rankled cruelly that Talliann,
this child, this fey simpleton whose sanity had been in
doubt from the first day of her existence, should
command more respect from her people than Calthar
could ever do; a respect made all the stronger by the love
and reverence which went hand in hand with it. For that
reason alone, Calthar couldn't touch Talliann. She
didn't dare.

The priestess stopped pacing, and stared at her
charge's impassive back. Still Talliann didn't move, and
Calthar expelled a long, hissing breath that expressed
a bare fraction of the frustration she felt.

'Why?' she demanded hoarsely. 'Why did you go?'

Talliann raised her head, but that was all. Swift as a
snake, Calthar moved across the floor until she was

facing the girl. Her face was distorted with anger, but
when she looked into Talliann's black eyes something
she saw there made her hesitate. The depth of the girl's
hollow look was daunting; her gaze seemed to drink in
her surroundings, draining the strength from everything
she saw. A cold worm of discomfort moved in Calthar
and she looked away.

'Child, you try me!' The sorceress's voice was harsh.
'Time and again you are told what you must do; time
and again you try to thwart me. Will you never learn?'

The girl's vast, dark eyes fastened on her face and
Calthar repressed a shudder. 'You are precious to us,'
she added, forcing the words past her tongue and teeth.
'More precious than anything, as well you know. We
can't risk your safety, Talliann. And if you continue to
defy the rules we have made for your own good, then
that freedom you have enjoyed must be denied you. Is
that what you want?'

Uncertainty flickered in the girl's gaze for a moment,
swiftly followed by dread, before her face became an
impassive mask once more.

'I thought not.' Calthar smiled thinly. 'Then if you
wish to avoid such a stricture, answer my question.'

Small, sharp teeth showed over the girl's lower lip.
When she spoke, it was as though words were an
unfamiliar medium to her.

'Ask ... '

Better, Calthar thought. Aloud, she demanded:
'What did you find on the shore?'

Talliann's deathly pale brow creased in a frown that,
for a moment, made her face ugly. 'I saw ... '

Calthar waited.

'I saw ... ' And suddenly the frown was gone, and
the girl's face was radiant. She turned towards the
priestess and said, as though struck by a revelation. 'He
has come back!'

It made no sense, and the all too familiar anger of
frustration clutched Calthar. 'Who?' she demanded, her

voice rising to a furious pitch. 'What are you talking about?'

Talliann began to laugh. The sound was like bright water lapping over stones, and it grated on Calthar's ears until she thought she would scream with the pressure of it – and then it stopped as suddenly as it had begun, and Talliann repeated, in the voice of a child, 'He has come back.'

There was death in Calthar's eyes as she stared at the girl. She didn't understand this new tack, and doubted if Talliann comprehended it either. But the wretched child had encountered someone on the shores of that hated city: someone who seemed to have obsessed her. She had unfathomable but immovable reasons for not wanting to reveal the truth, and Calthar drew only one conclusion from her stubbornness – that the mysterious interloper had some direct connection with Haven.

She spoke, but this time with a terrible gentleness. 'My child, my sweeting, you are tired. You must sleep. Sleep until night comes round once more.' Moving forward, she took Talliann's arm. 'Sleep, Talliann. Rest. Leave all to me.'

Talliann moved meekly under her guiding hand, allowing herself to be steered towards the back of the cavern. A short flight of uneven steps led up to a place where the hanging stalactites formed a forest of twisted, encrusted pillars. Among these lay a single, huge shell, its gaping interior lined with the tangled, black and green fronds of sea-bed weed. This was Talliann's resting-place, the womb from which, years ago at the Hag's great conjunction, Calthar's sorcery had summoned her: as they approached the shell, Talliann stopped.

'I will see him again.' Her tone was flat with utter certainty, and then she tilted her head to one side and gave Calthar an old, sly look. 'I *will* see him. For if I don't ... perhaps there will be no great conjunction. Perhaps it will not come. Perhaps I will see that it does not.'

Calthar's breath hissed between her teeth, but her voice didn't give away the fury that Talliann's words had rekindled. 'You'll see him, precious one. You will.' *Who?* she thought. *Who?*

'Soon . . . ' Talliann's voice took on a sleepy, sing-song quality, and Calthar felt relief. The girl's strength was waning fast, her stamina failing as it always did when her emotions were roused; for now, there'd be no confrontation.

'Soon,' she echoed. If Talliann comprehended the venom in her voice she showed no sign of it, and Calthar watched as she stepped into the shell and sank down on the bed of weed. Talliann's eyes closed, and the priestess expelled a sharp breath. The girl's sleep would be long and deep; time enough to see what might be seen, and do what might be done. Something was afoot, and it must echo the omens which her Mothers had spoken in her ear since the Hag's last fullness. Their message had grown stronger each night: perhaps now she had the first clue to what they had been trying to tell her.

Within less than a minute, Talliann slept. Calthar watched her for a short while, satisfied by the gentle, even rhythm of her breathing, then she left the chamber and traversed the dimly-lit passageways that ran like a maze through the rock. She met no one on her journey, and at last reached the vast, echoing emptiness of the cavern which led out to the open sea. Here she stood for a while on a rock spur, staring down at the black water that slapped with a sluggish yet inexorable rhythm against the stone beneath her feet.

Time and inevitability . . . the sea ate eternally at the rock, wearing it away with inhuman patience, content to let aeons pass in the knowledge that it would eventually triumph. Calthar felt no such contentment. Her soul was warped with thoughts of chaos and destruction and she scorned the sea's stoicism. Damn time, and damn patience. The Hag's night was at hand.

She drew breath, and with sinuous grace slipped into the sea. The water's buoyancy lifted her and she drew its strength into her bones, becoming one with the swell, moving smoothly out on the undertow as a wave drew back towards the cave mouth and the vast, empty night beyond. Her robe flowed around her like decaying weed, tangling about limbs that shone beneath the water with a silver-green phosphorescence. She drew breath again, feeling brine flow through her mouth and nostrils and into her lungs as she dived deep, deeper into blackness, water replacing air as the medium of life, breathing and drinking, eyes wide and filled with an aching, lusting hate as Calthar, sorceress, priestess, Mother born of Mothers, swam with the ease and grace of a sea-serpent towards the open water.

Chapter 6

The verbal knife which DiMag had inserted into what was left of his composure was no match for the sheer exhaustion that overtook Kyre when he reached his room in the Sunrise Tower. He slept too deeply for dreams to plague him, and when he woke the fog had cleared and a weak sun hung above the horizon, throwing a spear of light through his window.

Recollections of the bizarre interview with Haven's prince came back as Kyre opened his eyes, and his first reaction was a surge of furious anger. At last he had discovered what Haven wanted of him, and the revelation was a goad that fired and fuelled the rage in him. A champion – or, more accurately, a pawn, a fool to stand up in the face of a deadly enemy and fight a battle which he had no hope of winning. How they expected him to fight, what they expected him to do, he couldn't begin to imagine: the entire concept seemed utterly mad. But it was the purpose for which Simorh had called him to this world.

And as for Dimag . . . his view of him was now utterly ambiguous. Though he still couldn't say that he liked the prince, he had learned enough last night to understand and sympathise with his ingrained bitterness. Yet despite his openness, and his avowed belief that Kyre had an identity which owed nothing to sorcery, DiMag had made it clear that he was as ready as Simorh to use him without scruple. His escape attempt had proved, painfully and beyond doubt, that Simorh could control him, and if he proved unwilling to co-operate with her plans, he had no illusions that DiMag would prevent her from using her powers to force him into compliance. Man he might be, with a soul and mind of his own: but to DiMag and Simorh he was no better than a slave chained to their will.

Or was he? The fury was under control now, banked down like a smouldering fire, and Kyre knew that he had two choices. He could allow his confusion, his fear of Simorh's sorcery, to gain the upper hand, in which case he was a coward and deserved nothing better than the metaphorical collar and chain with which the people of Haven meant to hold him. Or he could stand up to them, resist their efforts to intimidate him and show them that he would neither cower nor submit.

DiMag had perhaps sensed the rebellion simmering within Kyre when he offered his bargain last night. Kyre was still prepared to stand by their agreement, but whether DiMag would keep *his* word was another matter. The prince was mercurial at best, and Kyre didn't care to place too much trust in his pledge. But DiMag had promised him freedom within the palace bounds, and that at least was something he could put to the test. At the same time, he might serve his own purposes further by seeking out Gamora's tutor and putting to him some of the questions which DiMag had been unable or unwilling to answer.

He climbed out of bed, crossed the room and tried the door. It was unlocked, and he smiled faintly. Well and good; but how far would his new freedom extend? Everthing depended on DiMag's preparedness to abide by his word. Testing that preparedness would prove an interesting experiment.

He opened the door wide and looked out. There was no one to be seen, nothing but the dimly-lit and empty staircase. Kyre listened for a moment to be sure, then, hearing no sound, left his room and began to descend the long, winding stairway into the heart of the palace.

No one attempted to impede Kyre as he made his way through the palace's corridors. He encountered a steward, who stonily ignored him, two female servants who whispered behind their hands, and a pale-haired, uneasy-eyed page who pressed close to the wall and slid by, avoiding the tall man's gaze. Reaching the deserted main hall he paused for a few moments to look again at the tapestries which hung on the walls. What little remained of their faded richness was washed out by the cool daylight filtering from outside; surrounded by cold stone and with no lamplight to soften their edges they looked ghostly and wan. The main doors stood ajar and a shaft of sunlight cut a narrow swathe across the floor, bringing with it a scent of fresh, salty air that lured him. He crossed the marbled floor, pulled one of the great doors wider open, and stepped outside.

The morning was chilly, and though the chill struck sharply through his clothes and made him shiver, its freshness helped to dispel the sense of cloying uncleanness that had been growing during his imprisonment. He stood on a terrace that ran the length of the palace wall and curved away round the side of the building, edged by a low and intricately carved balustrade. Overhead the sky was a pale, washed blue, patchworked with clouds that scudded before a strong wind, and below him the palace garden sprawled, sere foliage and struggling, bloated flowers given a touch of life by the sunlight. In the distance Kyre could hear the hushing moan of the sea, and instinct – he had nothing else to go on – told him that this was, for Haven, a perfect autumn day.

He stood still for a few minutes, breathing in the mingled scents of brine and damp soil and warm stone; then as the sun's strength began to counter the bite of the wind he turned and walked slowly along the terrace towards the palace's seaward side.

The perimeter wall was too high to allow him any sight of the town, but the lack of any noise from beyond the wall was something he found a little disturbing. With the fog gone and the day fine there must be bustle and activity in the streets of Haven; but no sound of it reached the palace. The quiet was profound, and eerie.

But the quiet wasn't to last. Kyre had almost reached the corner of the palace where the terrace swept round in a graceful, flying arc, when a door rattled somewhere nearby and light footsteps scurried on stone. A shadow skittered across his path, and Gamora appeared round the curve of the terrace, running.

'Kyre!' She just managed to stop before cannoning into him. She was pink-cheeked and breathless, her dark curls bobbing, unbrushed, around her face, and the sight of her lifted Kyre's spirits.

'Princess!' He caught her under the arms and lifted her off her feet; something he wouldn't have had the temerity to do before last night. 'What's the great rush?'

'I saw you from the window,' Gamora told him, tripping over her words in her eagerness. 'And I told my tutor you must come with us, that I *insisted* – Kyre, are you all right?'

The chaotic mixture of subjects made him want to laugh but he squashed the impulse, not wanting to offend her dignity. Last night she had flown to his defence, his one friend in a sea of hostility; he owed her a debt.

'I'm fine and well, Gamora.'

Her eyes narrowed suspiciously. 'You suffered no hurt? You *promise*?'

'None. May the Eye close on me if I tell a lie!' And instantly he was nonplussed by the phrase he had used. *Where had it come from? He'd never heard it before; and yet it had come easily and naturally to his tongue, a careless oath* . . .

It seemed, however, to satisfy Gamora, for she smiled. 'Good! Then you won't be too tired to accompany us.'

This time he did laugh, at her doggedness. 'I'll

accompany you gladly, princess – if I know where it is
you're going!'

'We are going, I suspect, wherever the little princess's
whims lead us!'

The new voice, with its underlying hint of weary
humour, startled them both, and Kyre looked up. The
man who had followed Gamora's flying progress at a
more leisurely pace was probably as tall as Kyre himself,
though the stoop he affected took the edge from the
impression. He was getting on in years, lean, and
dressed in a motley of subdued colours that indicated
either lack of taste or complete indifference to his own
appearance. In youth his hair had clearly been peppery-
fair, but now it had turned grey and was swept back from
his face in two unruly wings. Broken veins under the
coarse skin to either side of his nose suggested that
drinking was something more than a pastime. But his
smile, as his grey eyes met Kyre's, was frank and
friendly, if a trifle sardonic.

'The Sun-Hound, if I may presume to make an
educated guess?' he said. 'Good morning. I'm most
intrigued to make your acquaintance.'

'Tutor Brigrandon?'

'Ah.' Brigrandon's look became self-deprecating.
'For my sins, yes. And there was I, hoping to keep you
guessing for a while. Clearly I'm not the only one whom
the little princess takes into her confidence!'

'Prince DiMag spoke of you last night.'

'Did he?' Kyre realised suddenly that, despite the
manner he affected, Brigrandon could easily match
DiMag for shrewdness.

Gamora danced on the spot, catching her tutor's
sleeve and tugging it. 'Master Brigrandon, you
promised! And if we don't hurry, the tide will turn!'

Brigrandon looked down at the little girl and said
severely, 'When you reach my time of life, Gamora,
you'll understand that *hurry* is not a polite word!'

She was unimpressed. 'But you promised! And you

said that Kyre could come with us!'

'Very well; very well.' The tutor sighed and looked at Kyre again. 'I throw myself on your mercy, Sun-Hound. The little princess insists that you accompany us on our recreational walk, and if you don't agree to her demands I'll never hear the end of it. My future is in your hands.'

The request suited Kyre's purpose admirably, as it would give him the opportunity to question the tutor without making his motive or his eagerness obvious. Besides, he was beginning to like Brigrandon. He smiled again.

'My conscience wouldn't let me live with the consequences of a refusal,' he said. 'I'm at your disposal.'

There *was* activity in the town, but it had the same muted, faded and secretive quality that seemed to typify everything about Haven. Kyre was surprised when Brigrandon led him and Gamora to the same wicket-gate through which he had entered the palace on his arrival, and disconcerted to find three more solemn-faced children, two girls and a boy, waiting there to join their party. The girls curtsied to Gamora and the boy bowed, but no one made any attempt to introduce Kyre, and he had to suffer the discomfort of their mute and poorly disguised curiosity as the gate was opened and they left the palace grounds.

It seemed odd for the heir to the throne of Haven to be walking through the streets without any form of ceremony or security. Kyre might have expected crowds to line the way for a glimpse of their princess, but to the people they passed Gamora might as well have been any fisherman's child. One or two women making their way towards the market square paused and smiled with sad fondness at the little girl, and Brigrandon nodded to a few of the folk they passed, but aside of such small courtesies they were ignored. Even the presence of the red-haired stranger – and Kyre reasoned that rumours, at least, of Simorh's sorcerous creation must have reached the streets by now – did little to rouse the townspeople's interest.

And so they walked down through the town until they came to the city wall. Kyre hadn't expected Brigrandon to lead them this way, but he said nothing, only quelled a small shiver of memory as the small party went under the arch and out on to the vast sands of the bay.

The tide had withdrawn to a brilliant line on the horizon, reflecting the sky in a hard, sapphire blue. Its restless murmuring was a deep and constant vibration which Kyre sensed in his bones rather than heard; breakers gave a glittering white edge to the sapphire and added to the feeling of distant menace which he couldn't dislodge. To either side the coastline stretched away, the cliffs deceptively colourful in sunlight: he made himself look at the tall, impassive rock faces to the right of the bay, not wanting to gaze in the opposite direction where the gauntly malignant silhouette of the ruined temple marred the scene.

The four children, freed from the constraints of the palace and the town, broke away immediately from Brigrandon's supervision and ran across the white sand towards a cluster of fallen rocks that held sheltered, secret pools. Their exuberance made Kyre think of young animals newly released from cages, but as he and the tutor followed at a more leisurely pace he couldn't banish the thought of what lay beneath the sands. The disturbance must have shown in his face, for Brigrandon, having studied him obliquely for a minute or two as they walked, suddenly said:

'Princess Gamora was less than a year old when it happened, Kyre. The others weren't even born. No reasonable man can expect them, at their age, to respect something that played no direct part in their lives.' Brigrandon's long, flat-knuckled fingers fidgeted at his side, tapping a deep pocket in his faded coat as though he debated whether or not to delve into it. In the pocket something bulged, and at last the tutor sighed.

'One shouldn't mourn forever. It's unhealthy, and life continues with complete indifference to our sorrows. But now and again it's hard to put the old memories away.'

Kyre looked down at the sand beneath his feet. For a moment he felt as though, with only a small effort, he could have seen through it to the carnage preserved in gruesome tableau beneath, and the thought struck him to the core. 'You lost someone in that tragedy?' he heard himself ask softly.

Brigrandon's eyes were bright and hard as he stared at the children, who by now were indistinguishable figures in the distance. 'Both my sons fought with our army on that night, and my daughter's husband with them,' he said, putting a detachment into his tone that didn't deceive Kyre for an instant. 'My duties kept me at the palace, but my wife went to my daughter's house to keep vigil with her. The house was only one of many engulfed by the sand, and the young men were only three of hundreds killed in the battle.' He shrugged, blinked, then thrust his restless hand into his pocket and drew out a small leather flask, reinforced with silver filigree. The cork came free with a faint sucking sound, and Brigrandon held the flask up towards the sea in a mocking and faintly defiant gesture. 'Here's to them all. May the Eye always watch for their enemies.' He drank deeply, then held the flask out to Kyre without a further word.

He didn't want the drink; he felt queasy and his stomach rebelled at the thought. But to refuse would be to insult the memories that tormented the old tutor. He took the flask. 'The Eye preserve them all,' he said, and drank.

Brigrandon put the flask away again and they walked on in silence for a while. Gamora and the other children had reached the rocks and were climbing among them, oblivious to the sombre mood of the two men. At last Brigrandon spoke.

'So you, too, curse or bless by the Eye.' He glanced
at Kyre. 'I'm surprised you've developed the habit so
quickly. Or was it simply a courtesy?'

Kyre stopped walking, aware that they had both been
waiting for this moment when the first barriers would
be breached.

'I don't know,' he said. 'All I can say is that it's not
the first time I've called on it – despite the fact that I
don't even know what it is I'm calling on.'

'Ah.' Brigrandon turned to stare at the distant sea.
'Now the picture begins to make some sense.' He
paused, then with the manner of one who had considered a number of options and come to a decision,
added, 'Let's walk a while. The children won't miss my
attention, and I'd like to talk to you. I imagine we might
have quite a lot to say to each other.' He nodded towards
the shingle bar. 'The old temple seems as good a place
as any to make our goal.'

Before he could stop himself Kyre said, 'I'd prefer –'
then bit his tongue.

'You'd prefer to avoid the place?' Brigrandon
regarded him shrewdly. 'Yes; a lot of people feel that
way. But in your case, I think it might be wiser to fight
those feelings.' Without expanding on that cryptic
statement he set off towards the shingle bank, and Kyre
had little choice but to follow. As they walked, he forced
himself at last to look up at the grim skeleton of the
temple. Under the bright sun it looked less baleful than
when the cold moonlight had etched it, but nonetheless
he couldn't stop his mind's eye from superimposing the
memory of night and darkness and the horrors they had
brought over the comparatively peaceful scene.

That, and the image of a white-faced, hollow-eyed girl
in a bizarrely spangled gown . . .

Brigrandon's voice broke into his uneasy thoughts.
'Do you know anything of the temple's origins?'

'No. Nothing.'

Shingle crunched under their feet as the sand gave

way to the bar. Now that he'd faced the ruin, Kyre found he couldn't stop staring at it. 'If you want the full story, you'd have to learn the old language of Haven,' Brigrandon said. 'And that's an impossibility now; it's so many centuries since it was spoken that our knowledge of it is unreliable at best. We keep the remaining fragments alive out of some misplaced sense of tradition, but for any practical purposes it's little short of useless. If you saw the numbers of rotting manuscripts preserved for posterity, which now we can't even translate with any accuracy – ' he broke off and smiled. 'I'm sorry; I'm in danger of being diverted on to my favourite topic. We scholars are uncomfortably aware of the shortcomings in our historical knowledge, and it rankles. To return to the point: the temple fell into disuse far back in our history, but – as far as we know – its original name was the Shrine of the Eye.'

Kyre looked sidelong at the older man. Unprompted, Brigrandon was moving into the territory he wanted to explore. 'A shrine?' he said. 'I thought that shrines were the homes of gods. And according to Prince DiMag, Haven has no gods.'

'That's true enough; or at least we've lost the gods we might once have had. But we still have the sun that shines in the sky, and though we see little enough of it, it still rises each day and grants us continuing life. In Haven, the sun is known as the Eye of Day; hence the naming of the temple.'

'Sun worship?' Kyre forced himself to look at the ruin again.

'I don't believe our ancestors ever personified the sun as a god,' Brigrandon said. 'Their view of the powers that influence this world was a little more parochial. But certainly the Eye has always been revered. And in times gone by it had a human champion, whose sworn duty was to defend all that the sun's image stood for. One might well think of him as the Hound of the Sun.'

His tone was so mildly careless that it took Kyre a few

moments to realise the significance of what he had said. When it struck him, he stopped walking, feeling a cold, ghostly hand clutch at his vitals.

He said, quietly yet dangerously: 'What?'

'Ah.' Brigrandon, too, halted, and rubbed at his chin. He seemed a little disconcerted. 'So they *haven't* told you about the original Kyre? The one after whom you were named, and in whose image you were made?'

Kyre was stunned by the question. He managed to maintain a calm expression, but his eyes burned hotly. 'They have not.'

'Ah,' Brigrandon said again. 'That is rather as I suspected.' He reached towards the pocket where his flask was concealed, then changed his mind and let his hand fall to his side. 'I'm well aware of the Princess Simorh's injunction that you should be kept in ignorance; and I'm aware, too, of the interest that Prince DiMag is taking in you, although' and he smiled wryly, 'the prince's reasoning is sometimes a little cryptic. But I imagine DiMag anticipated that you'd eventually find your way to me with your questions.'

Despite the angry uncertainty that Brigrandon's revelation had reawoken in him, Kyre smiled thinly. 'He did.'

'Then he'll expect me to answer those questions. The prince knows me well enough to realise that, whatever my shortcomings, I won't be a party to deception or evasion. So he wants you to know the facts; that much we can deduce, though I wouldn't care to take a wager on his reasons.' He sighed and shook his head. 'It's as likely as not that his sole motive is to spite Simorh. A sad state of affairs ... But, however convoluted the reasons, the circumstances have at least placed you in DiMag's favour. That's more of an advantage than you might think.'

He echoed the prince's comment of the previous night, and again there was an implication that Kyre didn't comprehend. 'Why should I not think it an advantage?' he asked.

'Oh, there are some who might not view it in that
light. Think on it: a crippled ruler who has become a
virtual recluse, no prospect of a son to succeed him, a
decimated army which he can no longer lead ... '
Brigrandon paused. 'In such circumstances there's no
shortage of ambitious men who might be tempted to
view Prince DiMag as a lost cause.'

I want your loyalty, DiMag had said last night. Kyre
was beginning to understand.

He turned and looked back across the bay to the
straggling sprawl of Haven against the cliff face. In
sunlight the old city was quite beautiful, the stone
mellow and specked with tiny, glittering diamonds of
brilliance where the light caught particles of quartz
embedded in the rock. The three towers of the palace
rode high and proud over the scene, their windows
glittering. Yes; a beautiful city. Beautiful, and riddled
with intrigue, corruption, decay ...

Brigrandon said quietly: 'I'm willing to answer your
questions, Kyre; or at least I'm willing to try. But I don't
know whether you'll like what you hear.'

Kyre smiled bleakly. 'I want to know the truth,
Master Brigrandon.'

Shrill voices impinged on them from somewhere in the
distance, and the old scholar looked towards the sea.
'This isn't the time or the place for further talk,' he said.
'Here come the children – we must return to the city, and
I've lessons to give them this afternoon. We'll meet again
later, my friend. Come to my rooms this evening, eat with
me, drink with me. Then we'll see what can be done.'

They turned their backs on the ruined temple and
walked back to the sand, intercepting Gamora and the
other children as they came racing from the direction
of a rocky outcrop. Gamora's skirt was wet and she
carried her soaked shoes in one hand; in the other she
held a shell she had found and which she was anxious
to display to Kyre.

'Look, Kyre!' The little girl's face radiated delight as she held her treasure out to him. 'Look how thin the sea has worn it – and the colours are so beautiful!'

The shell was as large as Gamora's hand, and almost translucent. Its inner surface was lined with mother-of-pearl and, catching the light, it shone like a coruscating rainbow. Kyre smiled. 'It's lovely, princess.'

'I shall keep it in my room, and look at it every day,' Gamora declared.

The other children hung back while she chattered happily, though Kyre was aware of their curious eyes surreptitiously watching him. At last the small party started back towards the city gateway. They had almost reached the sandstone arch when a group of some half-dozen men, armed and wearing crimson sashes over the shoulders of their heavy leather jerkins, came marching in quick formation out of the city. Their leader saluted Gamora, who was too engrossed with her shell to notice, then the patrol tramped away across the sand towards the tideline.

Kyre hung back from the arch, watching the men. 'Do they patrol the beach every day?' he asked.

'Each time the tide turns,' Brigrandon told him.

It was yet another ritual, another hollow tradition. Though sometimes, Kyre thought, the patrols found more than just the sea's flotsam. He recalled the sea-creature which had died at DiMag's hand in the great hall of the palace, and suppressed a shudder.

'Cold?' Brigrandon asked.

'No.' Kyre shook his head. 'Just – thinking.'

With the children trailing behind them, they walked under the arch into the claustrophobic city.

Hodek's palpable fear of her was a goad to Calthar's temper, fuelling the loathing she felt for the man and for the gaggle of spineless sycophants he gathered around himself to bolster his flagging confidence. She had deliberately summoned them to her outer chamber

rather than to one of the main halls of the citadel as
precedent dictated; she wanted them to feel the power
that cocooned this place, and she wanted them cowed
by it. She would show them that, whatever the grandiose
titles with which Hodek and his minions dignified
themselves, the Mothers ruled here, and she alone
spoke with their voice.

She sat cross-legged on a dais that had been carved
from a single giant slab of obsidian. This chamber was
small and cramped, unfurnished save for the dais and
a few fish-oil lamps set on high ledges and placed so that
their light cast grotesque and unnerving shadows.
Calthar knew the value of outward impressions, and
took satisfaction from the unease in the faces of the
council as they shuffled into the chamber and arranged
themselves as best they could in its confines. She waited
until they had settled, then said, without preamble,

'You have all had my message, and I assume you
understand both its urgency and its significance.' They
heard the rage underlying her tone, and exchanged
glances. 'I have summoned you in order to inform you
of how I intend to deal with the matter.'

Hodek cleared his throat, the sound hollow and dead.
'Before we move to that, Calthar, I – ah, we all – feel
that certain aspects might need further clarification.'

At Hodek's side, a young man whose hair was a
bizarre pattern of silver streaked with black, and who
bore an ugly birthmark on his right cheek, nodded. His
blue eyes watched the sorceress levelly as he said, 'It's
my opinion that we should speak to Talliann, and hear
for ourselves what she has to say – '

Calthar stared maleficently at him, and the young
man instantly subsided. Akrivir, son of Hodek and
second only to his father as an object of Calthar's
contempt. It was rare to find them speaking on the same
side, for Akrivir loathed his sire, and, though he'd never
been able to uncover the full truth, held him responsible
for his long-dead mother's untimely end. His hatred for

his father was matched only by his hatred for Calthar; though where he despised the one, he feared the other. He was no threat to the sorceress: indeed, she found in him a further source of amusement, and had deliberately elevated him at an early age to her council so that she might enjoy the bitter quarrels which invariably developed between him and Hodek, and added to the old man's chagrin.

As Akrivir withered beneath her savage stare, Calthar knew full well what had prompted his desire to speak to Talliann. He adored the girl, and to Calthar the idea was more pitiable than his sire's undying obsession with herself. Akrivir had hopeless dreams of becoming Talliann's lover or even consort, just as Hodek wanted Calthar and had once dreamed that he could tame her. The boy, in Calthar's view, was as big a fool as his father: Talliann was not for him, and he could no more hope to court the fey girl than to possess the Hag herself.

'Clarification.' Calthar repeated Hodek's word with soft venom, her tone making it into an obscenity. 'Speaking to Talliann.' She let the words hang in the stale air until their very last resonance had died away, and her eyes were huge and deadly, reflecting splinters of light from the veins of pyrites and quartz that shot through the rock walls. Her tongue flickered out over her lower lip, then with a violence that made every man in the chamber start with shock she barked out, 'You are *fools!*'

She rose, uncoiling, and the lamps flickered, giving off streamers of oily smoke as her sudden movement disturbed the still air. Calthar stepped down from the dais and faced the councillors, who shrank back at her approach. She was a head taller than any of them, and stared down at their pale faces with undisguised scorn.

'My message needs no clarification,' she said savagely. 'I haven't called you here to listen to inept bleatings about the finer details of what has happened

– nor,' she added with a searing look at Akrivir, 'to listen
to the blandishments of a lovesick sea-worm!' Ignoring
the suppressed fury that showed in his eyes at the taunt
she whirled, her ragged robe dancing about her body.
'The simple facts are these: our enemies have a new
champion whom they intend to use against us on the
night of the Great Conjunction. Talliann – who was
allowed to leave the citadel through the laxness of those
who should have known better – encountered this
precious new pet of theirs, and she has taken it into her
head to want him brought here to the citadel.'

Calthar began to pace. 'Talliann, as we know, has
always been given to unpredictable whims and fancies,
and in the past her thoughts have been easy enough to
steer in more profitable directions. This time, however,
she is immovable. I have cajoled her; I have reasoned
with her; I have threatened her.' She glanced towards
the back of the chamber, where a low, heavy door,
bolted, marred the rock, and from the corner of her eye
saw Hodek blanch. 'But my efforts have availed nothing. Talliann is adamant – and if her desire is not
granted, she will refuse to play the part required of her
during the Great Conjunction, when we launch the final
assault on our enemies.'

Someone swore softly, others set up a troubled
muttering. Calthar turned to face them again. 'I see you
appreciate the nature of our problem. Without Talliann,
the opportunity afforded us by the Great Conjunction
is worthless. Yet if we don't accede to her in this, we
will have nothing from her.'

Akrivir spoke up sharply. 'It won't be an easy
conundrum to solve. We can hardly send warriors into
their stronghold simply to – '

Calthar silenced him with a look. With soft venom,
she retorted, 'When your advice is required, you will be
informed of the fact. Until then, hold your prattling
tongue!

'The solution to our conundrum is something that I

and I alone can contrive. I need no help from the council
– all I need is, by tradition, to inform you of what I
intend to do, and to have your sanction. I assume that
sanction won't be withheld.'

It was a threat rather than a question. Akrivir, who
alone might have voiced another objection, thought
better of the idea, and Hodek nodded eagerly.

'Tell us, Calthar. Whatever you want, we'll do your
bidding!'

Calthar's sanctum was dark. She needed no illumination; she knew every inch of her domain, and knew that
no uninvited foot would ever dare trammel her privacy.
Crouching now on a narrow ledge that overlooked a
small and bottomless pool, she was utterly still, as she
had been for hours past, waiting and watching with the
awesome patience of a hungry predator. And at last her
vigil was rewarded.

Such a pitifully simple device in her hands, yet it was
more than enough. The land-dwellers' command of
sorcery was beneath her contempt; they'd know nothing
of the alien presence in their midst until matters had
moved far beyond their influence. And the mind of a
child, so innocent and malleable, was a dark delight to
manipulate.

Inwardly, Calthar felt a desire to laugh. But no sound
escaped her throat except for the steady, rhythmic
breathing which had continued hour after long hour.
She gazed into the pool, seeing beyond its featureless
black surface to something that moved in another place
and another dimension. Now and then her lips formed
an invocation to the Mothers whose guiding inspiration
lived within and around her, but the invocation was
silent and she made not the smallest sound. She
watched. And she smiled.

Chapter 7

Thean was on an errand, and, lacking her moral support, Falla hadn't the courage to stand up to the first of the two visitors who called on Simorh that morning.

Swordsmaster Vaoran had heard the news that the Princess was unwell and unable to leave her tower, and it offered him the opportunity for which he'd been waiting and hoping to speak to her alone. Falla's insistence that her mistress was not strong enough to receive callers met with polite but icy disinterest, and it took the burly warrior less than a minute to browbeat her into leading him to her private room.

Simorh had attempted to rise at her usual hour, and had collapsed. The power she had wielded against Kyre last night, following so closely on the heels of the ritual with which she had conjured him into the world, had drained and exhausted her and the damage would take some time to heal. At last, with the help of Falla and Thean, she had left her bed, but she was too enervated to do anything other than lie on a couch by the window. At the sound of Vaoran's heavy tread she looked up, and the swordsmaster was shocked by her appearance. Her fair hair was lank and lifeless, hanging in brittle tendrils around a face made haggard by strain and exhaustion. Her skin had become parchment-yellow and deep shadows smudged her eye-sockets, while her hands, folded on the embroidered wool blanket which the girls had wrapped about her for warmth, kept shaking in unpredictable, palsied fits. Youth and vitality had deserted her, and she looked desperately sick. Yet

her sickness didn't prevent a spark of anger from
flickering in her eyes when she saw her visitor.

Anxious to forestall that anger before she could give
vent to it, Vaoran approached the couch and made a
knee to her. It was an archaic gesture, long fallen into
disuse, yet it had the desired effect, as Simorh couldn't
ignore such a compliment without giving unjustifiable
offence.

'Swordsmaster.' With an effort she pulled herself
more upright on the couch. Falla ran forward to help,
but Simorh waved the girl away. She was beginning to
understand how DiMag must feel ...

'Princess, I came as soon as I heard the news of your
illness,' Vaoran said solicitously as he rose to his feet
once more.

Simorh looked up at him. *Shrewd eyes, as blue as the
sky, calculating ... yet there was something else in them
which he couldn't quite mask and she couldn't quite
recognise.* She returned a wintry smile.

'Thank you for your concern, Vaoran, but I assure
you it's misplaced. I'm not ill; I'm merely exhausted. I'll
be fully recovered in a day or so.'

He smiled. 'So I heard, lady, but I confess I couldn't
banish my doubts. I wouldn't have dreamed of intruding
on you, but my anxiety was such that I had to set my
mind at rest.'

'As you see, I'm in no danger.'

'Indeed, and I'm very thankful. I feel a keen
responsibility for what happened.'

'You?' She looked at him, surprised. 'Why should you
be in any way to blame?'

He made a small, self-deprecating gesture. 'As both
councillor and military commander, the fact that the
creature – the Sun-Hound – ' he uttered the name as
though it were distasteful to him, 'was allowed to escape
from the palace *must* be my responsibility. You had
personally given orders that he should be confined and
watched, and those orders were not complied with. If

I find the man who allowed – '

Simorh interrupted him with a sigh. 'Neither you nor your soldiers nor any palace servant was at fault, Vaoran. The culprit was my daughter.'

'Princess Gamora?' The swordsmaster was taken aback.

'Gamora is quixotic and impressionable,' Simorh said tiredly. 'And easily dazzled by anything unfamiliar or mysterious. No doubt she found it exciting to champion a new friend.'

Vaoran frowned and moved towards the window. After a few moments' silence he said: 'I see. I'd wondered . . . ' he hesitated, then shook his head. There was a long pause, during which the sound of Falla moving about at the far side of the room set Vaoran's nerves on edge. Then Simorh said sharply,

'*What* had you wondered, Vaoran?'

He turned to face her again, his movements ponderous and deliberate. 'It's of no moment, madam; not now.' His blue eyes focused on hers. 'I'd simply wondered if Prince DiMag had countermanded your order and hadn't informed me of the fact.'

In the ensuing stillness he could hear her breathing. The sound was sharp, quick, unhealthy; fury underlay it, though she hadn't the physical strength to give it form.

'Haven asks a great deal of you, Princess Simorh. You have made great sacrifices for this city, and I wouldn't want to see such sacrifices come to nothing.'

Simorh stared down at her hands, willing them to stop shaking and twitching. Her fingers gripped the blanket, though the grip was weak. 'And what,' she asked evenly, 'has this to do with Kyre's escape?'

Vaoran hesitated, then: 'I am simply concerned lest the control you have of him should be undermined. The Sun-Hound is your creation and your slave; but there could be factions within the palace which might wish it otherwise. I . . . ' He hesitated, then smiled at her, a little sadly. 'I simply wish you to know that, if I can be of help to you in resisting such factions, I'm at your service.'

There was silence for some time. Simorh was aware that Vaoran watched her carefully, alert for any reaction. He was a hard man to read: she thought she had the measure of him, but she could never be certain, and his apparent solicitousness made her doubly wary. At last, her voice utterly neutral, she said:

'Thank you, Vaoran. I appreciate your kindness – and your honesty.'

'Believe me, lady, I have only the best interests of Haven at heart.'

'I know. And I shall think on what you've said.' She looked up again and gave him a smile that he hadn't expected. 'Thank you.'

It was a signal to leave, and Vaoran had the wisdom to acknowledge it. He had achieved what he wanted; the seeds were sown and as yet he could expect no more. Time and changing circumstances would dictate what occurred from now on. He only hoped that he had succeeded in winning at least a small measure of Simorh's trust and appreciation.

Simorh watched the curtain fall behind the swordsmaster, then listened to the sound of his heavy footfalls as Falla led him down the stairs to the anteroom. She thought she heard a murmur of voices from below, though they were too faint to be recognisable: then more footsteps sounded on the stairs and her eyes widened as the curtain was pushed aside again and DiMag stood facing her.

'DiMag – ' She started up, as he came into the room. His eyes were intent on her; and he took a chair a short distance from the couch.

'Well.' He continued to look at her, and she couldn't interpret the look. 'I'm sorry to find you in such straits.'

'I'll be fit enough in a few days.' She smiled uncertainly, wondering whether she had imagined the

flicker of sympathy and concern in his eyes and hoping
that she hadn't.

'You shouldn't have done what you did. It wasn't
necessary – Kyre could have been brought back by other
means, without the need for you to endanger yourself.'
He paused. 'Do you still mean to go ahead, even after
the risks you've already run?'

'Yes.'

'Knowing that what you plan might kill you?'

'Does that matter?' she fired back. 'It seems to me
that I must take that chance, or sit and wait passively
for Haven to be destroyed! Death might lie at the end
of either road; but my way at least leaves no room for
shame.'

DiMag drew breath in a sharp, angry hiss. 'You failed
nine years ago.' The pitch of his voice dropped. 'We
both failed.'

'Yes. But I succeeded this time. I brought Kyre to us.'

'Did you?'

'I don't know what you mean.'

'You summoned a creature to this world, I'll not deny
that. But what manner of creature? For I'll tell you this
– he's no cipher, and you didn't create him.'

Simorh stared at him, but didn't speak.

'One.' DiMag counted on the fingers of one hand as
he spoke. 'He doesn't look as he was meant to. Oh, don't
think I'm not familiar with the ritual you used; I may not
be a sorcerer, but I can read those rotting manuscripts and
I'm acquainted with the old tongue! What was it: "his hair
and eyes shall be like to the earth that gives us life, brown
as the bark and the sweet nut that grows on the tree". And
here is your Sun-Hound, red-haired and green-eyed; not
what you bargained for at all. Two: he has a will of his own
– again, not what was intended. Three: the fighting skills,
which should be the pivot of his motivation, seem to be
non-existent; or at least, if he *can* fight, it's with no
weapon familiar to us. Oh yes, Simorh; you summoned
him. But *what is he?*'

Inwardly, Simorh was fighting down the small voice that told her – as it had tried to tell her since the night of the ritual – that DiMag was right. She couldn't allow that thought to gain a hold on her, for if she did, her hopes would crumble to nothing. She *must* believe in herself.

'Whatever Kyre is,' she said, 'it doesn't matter. I'll use him, DiMag, as I always meant to. And don't think you'll stop me. You won't.'

The prince rose and turned away, and she couldn't see his face. 'Very well. We understand each other, and I'll waste no more of your time or mine.' He swung round and his hazel eyes were hot with suppressed anger. 'You'd best build up your strength for your creature, Simorh. I've no doubt that you'll need it!'

For a moment they stared at each other, and the barriers between them were a suffocating, palpable presence. Then DiMag bowed formally and curtly, and, without a further word exchanged, turned on his heel and limped from the room. As the outer door closed – quietly, and not with the slam she expected – Simorh realised that she was biting her tongue so hard that she could taste blood. She leaned back, closing her eyes and forcing her jaw to relax, and wished that she had it in her to cry.

Descending the tower stairs was a slow and difficult process, but DiMag welcomed the distraction of the effort, for it took the worst edge from the turmoil in his mind.

He had gone to Simorh's rooms with the intention of trying to bridge the chasm between them, at least enough to make her understand his own doubts and fears. Meeting Vaoran on the threshold of her chambers had surprised him considerably and the glint of triumph in the burly man's eyes had set his hackles up.

In times past DiMag had never doubted his wife's

loyalty, but now so much had changed that even that foundation had cracked. The love they had once shared was gone, wiped out in a single night by the events that had left him a cripple and almost destroyed her mind; for nine years they had been espoused in nothing but name while the gulf between them grew ever wider. And what use was a maimed man, a warrior who could no longer fight, a prince who could no longer properly rule, to a woman like Simorh? DiMag had faced that question long ago, and had made the decision to turn away from his consort rather than live with the hypocrisy of maintaining a false image. He had nothing to offer her; she wanted nothing from him. And so perhaps it was natural that she should have begun to look elsewhere.

But Vaoran, of all men? It made his own position begin to look very precarious. Vaoran was shrewd, intelligent and ambitious, and being at the beck and call of a crippled master wasn't to his liking. And Simorh ... whatever her loyalties in the past, she, too, looked to the future. If Vaoran could convince her that her consort no longer served Haven's interests, her old allegiances might well be changed.

DiMag reached the foot of the stairs, where a wide corridor led away towards his private rooms, and paused to regain his breath, angered by the lameness that had made the descent so arduous. If only he could be *sure*. Half-founded suspicion was worse than certainty, for it let the imagination run riot. He needed to delve, to discover whether there was truth in the doubts that had been sown in his mind – yet who could he trust to help him? That, perhaps, was the greatest irony of all.

Slowly he moved along the corridor towards his chambers. As he approached, the guards who stood on permanent duty moved forward to open the door for their master. DiMag didn't acknowledge their presence, but walked past them into his sanctuary and, with a brief exertion of angry energy, slammed the door at his back.

Swordsmaster Vaoran rarely entertained guests in his modest apartment on the fringe of the palace's barracks. His habits tended to be ascetic; he drank only in moderation and, as far as any of his men could tell, was uninterested in the women who would have made themselves readily available to a man of such high standing. But on returning to his rooms after his visit to Simorh, he found, as he had anticipated, a visitor awaiting him.

The caller rose as Vaoran entered. He was a plump man of advancing middle years, dressed in the red tunic and gold sash of a royal councillor, and he nodded with grave courtesy as the swordsmaster closed the door.

'Good morning, Councillor Vaoran. I fear I was a little early for our appointment: I trust you'll forgive my invasion of your privacy?'

'Not at all, Councillor Grai. I'm later than I'd planned: my apologies.' He indicated for Grai to sit down again and crossed to a carved cupboard that dominated the sparsely furnished room. 'Some refreshment?'

'Ah – thank you. Wine would be welcome.' The plump man's gaze followed Vaoran as he poured drinks for them both, and he accepted the cup that was put into his hands.

'Thank you. Did you succeed in seeing the Princess Simorh?'

'I did, yes.' Vaoran took a chair opposite his guest. 'Though I'll admit the interview fell short of my expectations.' He smiled, a private smile. 'Or at least, my hopes.'

Grai pursed his lips. 'Her attitude, then, hasn't changed?'

'Not to any degree.'

'I see.' Grai sighed. 'It makes me sad to see her so inflexible. I would have thought that by now she might be coming round to the view that there can be little hope for the prince's future. Lame as he is, embittered as he is – Haven needs a much stronger man.'

Vaoran fingered his cup. 'You know I agree with you,
Grai. But without the princess's support, our position
is still too tenuous for us to risk making our views more
public. They're shared by a good proportion of the
people – but the people also share our sympathy for the
princess's predicament, and any move that could be
construed as a threat to her would be a grave mistake.'

'That's true, so far as it goes. But the princess has no
political standing, not by comparison to – '

Vaoran interrupted him, an edge to his voice.
'Political standing doesn't enter into it; she has power
of another sort, as we both know. But even that's not
relevant, Grai. It's vital – vital to *me* – that the Princess
Simorh should come to see the situation from our point
of view, and that she should not be coerced in any way.'

'Ah.' Understanding showed in Grai's eyes: he had
forgotten Vaoran's personal considerations. 'Of course.
But if she persists in her loyalty to the prince, who is,
after all, her husband – '

'In name only.' Vaoran smiled again, a little bleakly.
'And that can't be an easy burden for her to bear. She
knows that under DiMag's rule Haven has little to hope
for, and she has the future of little Gamora to consider.'
He looked up, met Grai's eyes with a hot, hungry gaze.
'Simorh is loyal to the man she married, but she is more
loyal still to Haven and her child. A time will come when
she must decide between them. And when it does come,
I shall be on hand to help her in any way that I can.'

There was a long pause, then Grai nodded. 'Time,'
he said reflectively. 'More time.'

'Yes. Just a little more. For Haven's sake.'

'If anyone had told me I'd be taking on a new pupil at
my time of life, I'd have called him a liar or a fool or
both.' Brigrandon smiled drily and raised his mug in
Kyre's general direction. 'Bad luck to your enemies!'

Kyre returned the smile with an element of reserve

and took a mouthful of ale. They were sitting in the clutter of the old scholar's private study, the table between them strewn with the remains of a substantial meal, and beyond the tall, narrow window darkness had finally fallen, bringing back the creeping fog.

Brigrandon had been drinking steadily for two hours or more – ever since Kyre's arrival, in fact – but though his speech was a little slurred and his movements beginning to lack co-ordination, the brain behind the physical mask was still active enough. As both set their mugs down again, Brigrandon slapped the heap of parchments that lay beside his empty plate.

'Well, my friend, there you are. The entire history of Haven, myth, legend and fact, painstakingly sifted and translated and written into comprehensible form by my humble self!' He paused, then patted the pile more gently and let his hand rest on it. 'The pinnacle of my life's achievement; a pretty story for the edification of little children.' Ironic bitterness crept into his voice, showed in his faded eyes for a moment as he looked up; then the dry smile was back. 'Don't worry; I don't expect you to read it. It's simply my credential; proof to you that I can answer your questions.'

Kyre returned the smile. 'I don't need proof, Master Brigrandon. And I'm grateful to you.'

'*Ach!*' Brigrandon waved a hand dismissively, almost swatting the near-empty flagon that stood perilously close to his elbow. But despite his studied carelessness, Kyre could see the old man was touched. 'You haven't had your answers yet,' Brigrandon added. 'Wait and see if you still feel like thanking me by morning.' A long pause, then: 'Well, my good friend who thirsts after knowledge – I'm at your disposal. Where would you like to begin?'

On the brink, at last, of the revelation he craved Kyre felt a sudden reluctance, and found himself dissembling. 'Are you sure I don't inconvenience you, Brigrandon? The hour's late.'

The scholar shook his head. 'These days I tend to spend my nights drinking rather than sleeping, so I might as well talk while I drink.' He reached for the flask and poured himself a generous measure of ale, spilling a fair quantity over the table. 'Yes; I know what you're thinking, and you're right: drunkenness and I are old acquaintances. But it doesn't impair my mind, more's the pity; so it needn't give you an excuse to put off the moment. If you back away from the questions now you'll only crave the answers another time, and that kind of torment isn't pleasant to endure. So.' He took a long swallow from his cup. 'Ask.'

Kyre was tempted to follow Brigrandon's example. More drink would bolster his courage, and he needed courage to counteract the formless fear that lurked inside him. But he also needed a clear head, and that was the most vital thing of all. So he resisted the temptation, only fingering the stem of his own cup as he forced himself to formulate the one question that was at the nub of everything.

He said: 'Prince DiMag tells me that Haven needs a champion, and he and the Princess Simorh intend that I should fulfil that role.' As he spoke, the old anger was rekindled and it helped him to elucidate. 'You tell me that there was another Kyre, another Sun-Hound, long ago, and that I've been made in his image and given his name. I can only conjecture that I'm meant to do what he might have done, were he alive now.'

Brigrandon pursed his lips. 'A few inaccuracies, but that is, in essence, true.'

'Then I want to know this. Who was the first Kyre? What did he do? And why does Haven want me to emulate him?'

There was silence for some while. The fish-oil lamp that illuminated the room sputtered fitfully to itself, and in the far distance Kyre thought, or perhaps only fancied, that he could hear the uneasy moan of the sea. Then at length Brigrandon spoke.

'Three questions, and I think they require only one answer.' He leaned forward and refilled his cup again, this time with greater deliberation. 'I'll have to admit that our records are incomplete. The old language hasn't been spoken for so many generations that it's all but lost, and the fragmented version we *have* retained is probably inaccurate. But, in essence, Kyre – the *original* Kyre – ruled Haven many centuries ago. He was a warrior as well as a prince, and under his rule the city's army was a powerful force – a very far cry from the pitiful remnants you see today. The sea-demons must have feared Kyre and his soldiers; and – '

'The sea-dwellers?' Kyre interrupted him abruptly. 'You're saying that even then they were at war with Haven?'

Brigrandon smiled sadly. 'My friend, that is the oldest of conflicts. We have only shards of knowledge from that time, but everything points to an enmity as ancient as the Hag herself. And it was the sea-dwellers who, finally, were Kyre's undoing. Have you heard of what is known as Dead Night?'

'Yes. Prince DiMag spoke of it.'

'Well, such a conjunction took place during Kyre's reign, and the sea-demons planned to use the power it gave them in a single massive assault against Haven. There was a sorceress who lived among them then; we don't know her name, but she was a vampire, a devourer of souls – '

Vampire and soul-eater ... Kyre recalled DiMag's description of the sorceress Calthar, who he said ruled in the sea-dwellers' realm now. Surely, they couldn't be one and the same?

'She drew her power from the Hag, and she used that power to bring about Kyre's downfall during the Dead Night battle,' Brigrandon went on. 'They met face to face out on the strand, and though he was the finest warrior Haven has ever known, he couldn't prevail against the demon-inspired sorcery she used. She slew him.'

Brigrandon paused for more ale, drinking slowly and then wiping his mouth with the back of his hand. 'It's said that when Kyre died, at the very moment when the soul-eater's spear struck him down, the world stopped in its track and a great and terrible cry of protest echoed up from the very bowels of the earth.' He smiled with dry self-deprecation. 'Of course, that's an embellishment – I don't doubt there were ancient historians as guilty of poetic licence as I confess I've been at times. But no matter: whatever protest the world might have made, the Sun-Hound died.'

Kyre's mouth was dry and there was a bitter taste on his tongue: he drank more ale. 'And?' he prompted.

'And . . . ?' Brigrandon repeated.

'There must be more.'

'Oh yes; there's more. The Sun-Hound had a consort. Her name is lost, and we know nothing of her, save for one fact.' The old scholar fingered his cup. 'She was a witch, a sorceress. Not of the order of the monstrous creature who trapped and slew Kyre; but she had power. She didn't fight at Kyre's side, but she stood in the very same tower that the Princess Simorh occupies now, and tried to use her magic to save him. When she realised she had failed, she killed herself rather than live on without him. But before she died, she wove a spell, a talisman to protect Haven from the demons from the sea. And the spell formed part of her dying prophecy.' He looked up and his eyes met Kyre's uneasily.

Kyre said: 'Tell me, Brigrandon. What was her prophecy?'

The old man shrugged. 'Do I need to tell you? She decreed that, should Haven ever be threatened with final annihilation by its enemies, one could be summoned to the world who was made in the image of her lost lord. And she left behind a rite by which that one – that cipher – could be imbued with the spirit of the first Sun-Hound, so that he might face the vampire-witch from the sea and defeat her.'

For a long while there was silence. Brigrandon was staring into his cup, his face tight and uneasy. Kyre stared blankly ahead; in his mind's eye was a picture of DiMag in his gloomy sanctuary, then, superimposing that, the image of Simorh's taut and bitter face.

He said at last: 'They want me to fulfil the prophecy and be a second Sun-Hound. They want me to face that same creature, that – that soul-eater – who killed the original Kyre – '

'Not the same creature,' Brigrandon said. 'She's long gone from this world. But her descendants live on.'

'The same creature, or another – what's the difference? They want to pit me against her, in the hope that *I* can succeed where the greatest warrior in your history *failed*!' He drew in a violent breath. 'They are *insane*!'

The scholar looked away, lifted his cup and drained it. 'You wanted the facts from me, my friend. Now you have them. I warned you that you might not like what you heard.'

Kyre took a cold grip on his rising fury. He had no justification for venting his anger on Brigrandon: the old man had done no more than answer the questions put to him. 'This prophecy,' he said. 'It's in one of these manuscripts of yours?'

'As far as we can translate it, yes. It exists. Don't doubt that.'

Another long silence, while Kyre's eyes lost their focus again. At last he spoke. 'Go to bed, Brigrandon. I owe you a debt, but I can't repay it. I need time to be alone, to think.' He frowned, seeming to drag himself back from another, unimaginable plane of thought and existence. 'I'd like to stay here, if you'll allow it: at least until the sun rises.'

'Of course.' Brigrandon rose, lurched, and a sheaf of papers fell to the floor with a heavy thump. The lamp in the centre of the table rocked alarmingly, throwing grotesque shadows across the wall, and the scholar

began to move slowly towards a curtained recess,
steadying himself by clutching at the furniture. He was
drunk, and Kyre envied him.

Brigrandon reached the curtain and hacked it aside
at the second attempt, revealing a narrow, unadorned
bed in the recess beyond. He hesitated, swaying a little
on his feet, then shook his head sadly. 'Stay as long as
you will, if my snores don't disturb you. And if you need
a sympathetic ear when tomorrow comes, I shall be
here.' His fingers tightened on the curtain fabric and he
stepped into the recess. 'I have one last thing to say to
you, and it's something you may heed or ignore as you
choose. The first Kyre was prince and ruler of Haven,
and he was beloved of a sorceress. He was also free from
those disabilities that cripple the man who rules Haven
now. Bear that in mind, my friend, in all your dealings
with Prince DiMag. Good night.'

Kyre waited until the small sounds of Brigrandon
readying himself for sleep had ceased, then reached out
to the lamp and turned the wick up so that shadows
shrank back from the table. The smell of fish-oil
pervaded the room but he barely noticed: a peculiar and
terrible sense of peace was settling on him. He knew:
at last, he *knew*. And there was something awakening
in him, a new courage and a new certainty that he would
not accept the fate that Haven had planned for him.
Whatever its perpetrators might name him, he was not
Kyre. And that was a lesson they would soon begin to
learn . . .

The tide had risen to the full, drawn back to the ebb,
and now was rolling in again, following the slow,
muffling march of the fog. It crept over the shingle bar,
over the bay's smooth sand and the streets and houses
petrified beneath, and as it quietly, rhythmically ate the
land away, the Hag rose and rolled with it, first a grey,
bloated spectre on the horizon, then a shining eye that
gazed down on the sea and shot the wavetops with silver.

Cross-currents and undertows moved among the stark black rocks and beat in the mindless rhythm of centuries against the crumbling cliff faces; out at the end of the submerged shingle bar the ruined temple rose from the swell, impassive, an old skeleton etched against green-grey dark.

Haven slept, while two green witchlights under a sandstone arch burned defiantly against the night. One lamp glowed in a window of the palace, casting its dim radiance over the struggling white blooms in their wasteland of a garden. A prince tore unknowingly at the woven blanket which covered him, lost in the grip of an all too familiar nightmare. In her tower Simorh also dreamed, and tried to interpet her dreams even as she slept. And the Princess Gamora, smiling with the illicit pleasure of knowing that her nurse slumbered soundly in the next room and would never, ever guess that her young charge lay wakeful, played in the dark with the shell she'd found on the beach, watching its shimmering surface catch and reflect the refractions of moonlight that shone through the fog, through the chink at her curtained window. It seemed to speak to her, whispering stories of strange and beautiful places, conjuring vivid pictures in her mind, and she longed to answer the shell's call and see the dream-worlds it promised her, to slip away and tell no one of her secret, not even Kyre. It would be such an adventure.

And Calthar, a motionless and infinitely patient predator in the pitch-black of her sanctum, gazed into the fathomless dark pool that told more than was natural, and smiled as her lips formed silent, secret words. While not far away in the labyrinth which Calthar ruled, Talliann turned in an unnatural sleep, unconsciously fighting the strictures that shrouded her mind, and whispered a name that her waking mind didn't know. A name from long ago, another age, another history. Something that had been dead when the history she knew began.

Chapter 8

Dawn came, the sun showing as a dim, pale ghost amid the fog that shrouded the city and muffled all sound and all movement. Kyre had fallen asleep at Brigrandon's table, and only stirred when the first diffused rays touched his face. In the recess the old scholar slept on: and as the strengthening daylight slowly dwarfed and dimmed the lamp at his side Kyre rose, stiffly and with an effort. A glance towards the curtain that separated Brigrandon's bedchamber, a moment's hesitation, then he strode to the door. His quarrel wasn't with Brigrandon. He was determined to face those who were responsible for his situation: and when he did, his fury would know no bounds.

The early morning air was bitingly cold, with a clammy, bone-penetrating dampness permeating it, and by the time he had entered the main wing of the palace via the terraced walk – the only route he as yet knew – the damp was clinging to his face and arms, and mingling with the chill sweat of his anger. The hall was cold and desolate, with no lights burning and no servants in sight; he hesitated only a moment before striding towards the stairs. At this hour DiMag was likely to be in his chambers, and that was well and good. He wanted the prince alone, without the encumbrance of his court.

As he climbed the stairs, taking them two at a time, Kyre's hands were beginning to shake. He clenched and unclenched his fists in an effort to stop the spasms, but they continued to assail him, spreading through his arms until he felt like a coiled spring ready to explode from confinement at the smallest provocation.

The landing: still no one in sight. But as he turned the corner he saw the one obstacle he had forgotten – the constant guard set at DiMag's door. Two men, anonymous in their uniforms, staring fixedly at the opposite wall, unmoving.

Kyre slowed. The sentries paid him no attention. Then, at some unknown signal, one of them turned about and opened the door beside him. Kyre heard a murmur of voices; DiMag's, quick and sharp, another which he knew but couldn't place; and then the bulky figure of Swordsmaster Vaoran emerged, ducking his head to clear the low lintel. The door slammed at his back and he turned towards the stairs – then stopped.

'You – ' He didn't dignify Kyre with a name, and contempt underlay the irritation in his voice. 'What are you doing here?'

Kyre's fists clenched again, involuntarily this time, as the anger latched quickly on to his dislike of the warrior. 'My business is no concern of yours.'

Vaoran's eyes narrowed, and as the other man made to brush past him he reached out and gripped Kyre's arm. 'You're not planning on seeing the prince, are you, my friend?'

His words were an open challenge. Kyre froze, and stared at him, glad to find that he was the taller by a few inches. Skilled swordsman Vaoran might be, but suddenly such considerations were irrelevant. Beyond them, he saw, the guards were surreptitiously but avidly watching.

'And if I am?' he retorted softly.

Vaoran smiled. 'Prince DiMag has no time for you, creature. He isn't interested in you. I'll give you one warning, for the sake of your own continuing good health – '

He got no further before Kyre's fury erupted. He could no longer control it; his clenched right fist came

up and slammed with all the force he could put behind
it into Vaoran's face, whilst at the same moment he
swung his left arm and followed with a bone-cracking
blow that knocked him off his feet. The swordsmaster
hit the floor like a boulder; even as he rolled over, and
the two sentries started forward to help him or restrain
his attacker or both, Kyre swung round. The guards
couldn't co-ordinate themselves in time to prevent him
from thrusting between them, and before they could
stop him he had flung open the door to DiMag's
rooms.

The prince froze, startled, as Kyre burst in. He had
been in the act of putting on the crimson coat he wore
during court business, and looked faintly ridiculous with
one arm half in a sleeve. When he saw the look in his
unexpected visitor's eyes, the muscles of his face tensed
visibly.

'I want to talk to you,' Kyre said savagely, '*Now*.'

'My lord – ' One of the sentries appeared at Kyre's
back, sword drawn. 'We couldn't stop him, he was – '

'*Get out!*' DiMag interrupted the man with such
ferocity that he jumped back, and Kyre helped him on
his way by pushing the door shut, hard, at his back.

DiMag let his coat drop to the floor and limped slowly
across to the bed. He fingered the tasselled rope that
hung beside it and said levelly, 'If I should pull this, my
servants would be instantly summoned. Though
whether they'd reach me before you had committed
murder is a matter for conjecture.' He turned to face
Kyre again. 'What do you want?'

Striking Vaoran had blunted the edge of Kyre's anger,
but enough remained to fuel the fires inside him. He
took a step forward, noted with some satisfaction how
DiMag matched him with a pace back, and said, 'Last
night I talked with Brigrandon. He told me the legend
of the first Kyre.'

'Ah,' said DiMag.

'And I learned the nature of the legacy which he and

his consort left to this benighted city.'

'Ah.' DiMag had the good grace to look away.

'Haven wants a hero,' Kyre said viciously. 'That's what you told me, isn't it? A hero, to save its corrupt and decaying bones from final ruin!' He clenched his teeth, trying to get his breathing under control, then swung round. 'You are a *liar!*'

He couldn't, in the grip of his anger, find the detachment to read the expression in DiMag's hazel eyes, but an observer might have seen the flicker of regret and sympathy that touched them briefly. Then the prince said evenly: 'I didn't lie to you, Kyre. Perhaps I distorted the facts a little, or put my own interpretation on them. But I didn't lie.'

'You're a master of rhetoric, my lord prince!' Kyre cried. 'You knew the truth. You knew what the word *hero* meant in your terms! Not a fighter, not a saviour – just a human sacrifice to be cloaked in the trappings of a myth and sent to face impossible odds, to satisfy the doubtful premise of a prophecy which no one understands, and which probably doesn't even exist!'

Silence fell sharply in the wake of his accusation, and the two stared at each other until, abruptly, DiMag broke the deadlock by glancing aside.

'You're growing eloquent. Somehow, I hadn't expected that of you. No – ' He raised a hand as Kyre seemed about to erupt again. 'Don't take offence. I'm simply saying that it adds more weight to my conviction that there's more to you than any of us knows.' A brittle smile. 'Though you might accuse me of putting my own interpretation on that, as well as on everything else.'

'Damn your interpretations!' Kyre retorted. 'I've heard enough of your dissembling – I want the truth from you, and I won't be satisfied until I have it!'

'No. I don't suppose you will. Very well – I should at this moment be in the hall, but it seems court business must wait a while.' He moved towards his couch. 'Sit down, Sun-Hound, and stop being so stiff. Now: the truth.'

'All of it.'

'As you wish.' DiMag lowered himself carefully on to the couch. Kyre made no move to sit but paced to the window; after a few moments DiMag steepled his fingers and stared at them. 'You have, it seems, correctly anticipated the Princess Simorh's plans for you. And I won't deny that they're my plans too, though not from choice; but I'll come to that later. Yes, there is a prophecy, and yes, it is fragmented and we can't be sure that our interpretation of it is accurate. We lost any true understanding of our old language at about the time we lost our gods, whoever or whatever they were. But the prophecy exists, my friend. You are living proof of that, for the spell that summoned you to our world is an integral part of it. And the prophecy says that, when Haven is faced with final ruin, our enemies' sway can be broken only if one created in the Sun-Hound's image faces and defeats the sorceress from the sea.'

'But I'm *not* the Sun-Hound!'

'Created in his image,' DiMag repeated with emphasis. 'Maybe my wife failed in fine physical detail, but in all other respects she fulfilled what was required. No; you're not the true Kyre. But you will *become* Kyre, and you'll face Calthar. It's the only hope Haven has.' He stared at the wall. 'And I bitterly, bitterly regret that it has to be so.'

The angry words that Kyre had been about to utter died on his tongue. He hadn't expected such an admission from DiMag, yet the prince's tone and his expression told him beyond doubt that he meant what he had said. And it set all his preconceptions suddenly adrift.

'Why?' he said.

The prince looked at him. 'Why do I regret it?'

'Yes. It makes no sense.'

'Oh, but it does,' DiMag insisted. 'I don't revel in the

idea of human sacrifice. I faced Calthar once: it was her hand that gave me the wound that won't heal, and the fact that I'm still alive and not consigned to whatever her torment she inflicts on her victims is her joke on me. I wouldn't willingly wish such a fate on any living creature: I'm not that much of a monster, whatever you might believe.' His face hardened. 'But neither am I such a fool as to plead high principles when we are threatened by a power which we can't combat by honourable means. If we must fight sorcery with sorcery, I'm not· about to spurn a valuable weapon – especially when it's the only weapon we have left.'

He got up and walked slowly to join Kyre at the window. 'I didn't think Brigrandon would tell you so much, so early or in such a way. I'd hoped to introduce you to the idea a little more – shall we say – gently. And I don't mind confessing I'd ·nursed fond hopes that, given time, you would come to sympathise with our plight and could be persuaded to take on the Sun-Hound's mantle of your own free will. That was a mistake.' He smiled bleakly, then turned to look directly at Kyre, his gaze steady and very frank. 'I realise now that, had there ever been a chance of such an unlikely hope being fulfilled, we destroyed it by keeping the full truth from you.'

Kyre stared back at him. 'There could never have *been* such a chance. Haven means nothing to me; I have no loyalties here. How could you possibly think I would comply willingly?'

'Oh, I know; I couldn't reasonably expect it of any mortal man. A cipher, maybe; but not a mortal man. But you're not entirely devoid of pity or affection. You might have been persuaded to agree for the sake of the child who must one day rule in my place.'

'Gamora . . . ?'

'Yes.' DiMag gazed out into the mist. 'She's touched you; even I can see that. And I'm not surprised; there's something in my daughter that the rest of us have lost.

Innocence, gentleness, goodness, call it what you will; I haven't the right words. But I know you've grown fond of her, and I'd begun to hope that – '

'No.' Kyre interrupted harshly. 'You'll not appeal to me that way; not by using Gamora. You've told me what you want of me, but I'm not willing to make such a sacrifice. Not for Gamora, not for you, not for *anyone!* You have no right to demand it of me!'

'*Right?*' DiMag tensed, his eyes angry. 'I have *every* right – and indeed a *duty* – to use any means at my disposal in the fight to save my city and the people who dwell in it! Dead Night is almost on us, and we can't stand against it as we are! What makes you think I owe you any more than you owe me?'

Kyre's jaw clenched. 'I won't do it, DiMag. And if you think I will, may you be damned for it!'

'Your will doesn't enter into it!' DiMag snapped. 'If we have to force you, we'll force you. And you've already experienced what Simorh can do. I doubt if you'll stand for long against the torment she can inflict on you, to secure your co-operation.' He turned, limped across the room like a caged animal. 'Do you think I *want* to do this? If you were the cipher that Simorh meant to conjure with her sorcery, the question wouldn't arise. The fact that you're not complicates matters, but in the end it can make no difference!' He stopped, turned to face Kyre, his face strained. 'If there was another way, I'd take it. My conscience doesn't rest easy with the thought of sending a man who has done me no wrong to almost certain death. But if there's a chance – *any* chance – that you might be my sole means of defeating a deadly enemy and giving my daughter a future, then I'll gladly live with my conscience!'

Kyre said, his voice shaking: 'I could kill you, Prince DiMag. That, too, would solve your dilemma.'

'You could try,' DiMag sneered. 'But I doubt if you'd succeed; even lame as I am, I'm a far better swordsman than you'll ever be. And besides, it would do you no good. Destroy me, and you'd still have Simorh to contend with. Can you cut down her silver whips with a blade?'

Kyre sucked in his breath, remembering the experience and not wishing to relive it.

'Kill me, and you'll not have a friend in this world,' DiMag added. 'Leave Haven, and Simorh will bring you back. Jump from the Sunrise Tower or drown yourself in the sea, and death is the best you can hope for.' He looked up. 'This way, at least you have a chance. So why not take it?'

Kyre felt fury rising in him again, and it was made all the stronger by the knowledge that DiMag was right. Abruptly he turned away, and his voice was harsh as he said, 'We have nothing more to say to each other.'

'Apparently not. But think on what I've said, Kyre. It might bear further contemplation.'

There was silence for a few moments, acute and claustrophobic. Then Kyre strode to the door, and as DiMag stared moodily out over the fogbound city he left the room without a further word.

'Kyre! Kyre, wait for me!'

He stopped at the sound of the eager young voice, and felt every muscle in his body tense as the renewed anger threatened to get control of him. Gamora's feet pattered in the corridor and then she was beside him, catching hold of his hand and smiling happily up at him. She had come from the direction of the Sunrise Tower, and he surmised that she had been searching for him.

'Kyre, come and see what I found in the garden this morning! There is a flower that – '

Kyre interrupted her. 'Shouldn't you be at your lessons?'

She was taken aback by his tone, but it only dimmed her enthusiasm for a moment. 'Master Brigrandon was drunk last night and he's still sleeping it off, so he can't teach me! Oh, Kyre, you *must* come – '

'Must?' The word was like salt in a raw wound and he turned such a look on the little girl that she took a step back, her grey eyes wide with hurt. DiMag had tried to use this child to blackmail him emotionally, and at this moment Kyre could almost have hated Gamora. It was only with a great effort that he reminded himself that she couldn't be held to blame, and couldn't be expected to understand his hostility. He forced his face muscles to relax, and shook his head as though to clear it.

'I'm sorry, princess; I'm a little ... distracted.'

'Then let me cheer you! We could walk on the beach, or I could show you some of the old passages through the palace that are never used now!'

She was pitifully eager to please him, and he couldn't bear the thought of her company. However fond he might have become of her, it wasn't enough to change his mind. DiMag's ploy wouldn't work. He owed Gamora nothing.

'I'm sorry,' he said again, more sharply. 'I'm busy, Gamora – I have things to do.'

'Can't they wait?' Gamora pleaded.

Kyre felt as though he were trapped between fire and ice, and he wanted only to escape from the pressure she was putting on him. His eyes hardened, and he disentangled his fingers from hers with an abrupt movement. 'No. They can't wait.'

Tears filled Gamora's eyes, but she made no further attempt to appease him, only watched with uncomprehending misery as he walked away from her towards the stairs.

Kyre only stopped when he reached the terrace that ran along the palace's seaward side. The fog had if anything grown even thicker, so that it was barely possible to see three paces ahead; but the silence in which it cloaked the world, and the emptiness of the terrace, offered desperately needed solitude.

He sat on the balustrade, staring into the fog's blank wall and trying to ignore the rank, vegetable smell of the decaying garden below him. He hadn't meant to hurt Gamora, but her innocent face and bright chatter were more than he could bear now; he needed to be utterly alone, while the rage in him burned itself out.

He'd gone to challenge DiMag, had found his worst fears confirmed, and at the last had had nothing with which to fight back. The prince was right: no matter which way Kyre turned, all roads led to the same inevitable end. If he believed for a moment that he could call on reason and justice to sway DiMag, he was as wrong as it was possible to be; and he had no power to prevent Haven's rulers from using him in any way they chose.

What was it DiMag had said? *If there was another way, I'd take it.* Surely, Kyre argued with himself, *surely* this ancient, obscure and barely understood prophecy wasn't Haven's only hope? So much of the city's history had been lost, or twisted in translation from a dead language: Brigrandon, whose knowledge couldn't be faulted whatever his weaknesses, had freely admitted as much. And if the prophecy was wrong, or misunderstood, then somewhere in the mouldering records there must be another answer. Haven's rulers wanted him to fight an enemy he had no chance of defeating, and on that futile thread hung all their hopes. So great was their desperation that they were willing to sacrifice him in a cause that could avail them nothing. But Kyre was determined that he shouldn't be forced to die for Haven without fighting that destiny to his last breath. And he believed – perhaps foolishly, but it was all he had to cling to – that if an alternative could be found, DiMag would be true to his word.

But how and where to search? He raised his head, drawing the clammy air deep into his lungs, and faced the realisation that he didn't know where in all of Haven to begin. And yet a thought was invading the darker recesses of his mind; something that had no logic yet which refused to let him alone. Instinct; intuition. He had no reason to trust it, but it had sown the seeds of a conviction that the answer lay not in the walls of Haven, but in the conundrum of his own lost identity.

It didn't make any sense. Kyre shook his head and rose from the balustrade. His hair and clothes were damp from the cloying fog, and he was cold; but the cold went deeper than mere physical chill. He didn't know how or when Simorh meant to perform whatever mouldering ceremony it was which would theoretically place the Sun-Hound's mantle on his shoulders; but he believed that she would delay no longer than she had to, and then nothing he did or said could save him. He might have less time than he realised.

He needed to think. Gamora wouldn't be likely to seek him out again today – when he could, he promised himself, he'd make amends to her for his unkindness – and so the Sunrise Tower seemed as good a sanctuary as any other, and more palatable than this eerily forsaken place. What his efforts could avail him, Kyre didn't know. But he must at least try.

He turned, and walked slowly back into the palace.

DiMag was tired. These days he didn't seem to have the stamina he had once possessed, and the earlier clash with Kyre had taken more of a toll than he'd anticipated, so when it became clear that the court business would drag on well into the evening he felt depression settling on him like an unpleasantly heavy cloak. He hadn't eaten all day and his stomach felt hollow, yet the idea of food made him queasy. All he wanted was to sleep without dreaming.

Earlier in the day, a vigilant servant had discovered the presence of a virulently poisonous herb known colloquially as Forktongue in the palace kitchens. It was obvious that the deadly leaves had been intended for DiMag's own table, and, once alerted, the court had

gone through the ritual of setting an investigation in
train. For the sake of protocol the prince's advisers had
felt obliged to formally express their shock that anyone
in the palace could have planned such a crime, and be
seen to pursue the conspirators diligently. They had
failed to trace the culprit, but DiMag had no illusions:
he knew that his councillors would have been better
pleased had the matter never come to public notice. Had
the herb been discovered and removed without fuss or
recrimination, the entire incident could have been set
aside and conveniently ignored. And there were some
who might have preferred that the discovery had never
been made at all.

He pulled himself upright in his chair. The councillors
were debating the nature of repairs needed to a ceiling
in the palace's west wing, and DiMag forced himself to
crush a black desire to stand up, damn them all for
bleating sheep if they had nothing better to occupy their
minds, and walk out. His head hurt, his leg ached more
fiercely than it had done for some time – but if he was
to continue to rule Haven unchallenged, he must be *seen*
to rule Haven, however trivial the business at hand.

Two of the councillors were beginning to argue. Their
rising voices shook the prince out of his stupor, and he
was about to call them to order when a new disturbance,
beyond the door at his back, made him pause. Women
shouting, or sobbing; he couldn't tell which ... His
advisers also heard it, and fell silent, frowning in
surprise.

'My lord – ?' one began.

DiMag made a quick negative gesture, then signalled
to one of the guards at his back. 'See what's afoot.'

The man moved to obey, but before he could reach
the curtained door it burst open and Simorh flew into
the room.

'What is it?' Alarm coloured DiMag's voice as he
looked at his wife. She was in her night clothes,
barefoot, and her face was white, haggard and blotched

with tears. 'What are you doing here? You should be abed – '

In a great, sobbing breath, Simorh cried, 'DiMag, Gamora has gone!'

'Gone . . . ?' He didn't comprehend; his mind was too fuddled with tiredness to think clearly. 'What do you mean?'

'She's not in the palace! She's run away, and I – I can't touch her! I scried, I used all the power I could muster, and she wasn't there, I couldn't touch her mind. She's *gone*, DiMag – there's no trace of her anywhere in Haven!'

Chapter 9

'She thought Gamora was with me.' Simorh darted a look of bitter venom at the nurse, who stood wringing her hands in mute anguish. 'It was only when it began to grow late that she thought to *look*, to *see* – '

DiMag's grip tightened on her shoulders as her voice rose towards a hysterical pitch, and she subsided against him, though she was still shivering violently. Even through his own fear and distress a part of his mind was disturbed by the strangeness of the familiar yet all but forgotten sensation of holding her. His wife, known but long estranged, yet instinctively turning to him in a time of great need ... it stirred a complex tangle of emotions which he couldn't begin to interpret.

He said, thrusting the thoughts away and praying inwardly that he sounded more certain than he felt, 'We'll find her. She can't have been gone long, or got far.'

'But *why* did she go?' Simorh cried. 'She had no *reason!*'

DiMag knew what she was thinking, and he shared her unspoken terror. There were people in the palace whose interests might be well served by Gamora's disappearance. As a hostage she would provide the one certain means of ensuring his own acquiescence to whatever her captors wanted of him. Abdication, his life in exchange for hers – there was nothing he wouldn't agree to for his daughter's sake, and the fact was well known.

But he dared not dwell on such a possibility, or allow

Simorh to dwell on it either. The search had already begun, directed by Vaoran, who, whatever DiMag's differences with him, could be relied on in a crisis. If Gamora was still in the palace she would soon be found; if not ...

He'd already heard the bare bones of the story, such as they were. Gamora's nurse had missed her shortly after darkness fell; finding that Brigrandon hadn't seen the little girl all day, she sent a servant to see if Gamora had visited Kyre, and when this too produced no sign of the child the nurse assumed that Gamora must be with her mother. She didn't like to disturb the princess – who frightened her more than she cared to admit – and so it was only when Gamora's bedtime had long passed that she began to worry. She had plucked up enough courage to approach Simorh at last, and it was then that the truth began to dawn.

Simorh couldn't begin to explain the sense of dread that crept through her when she realised that Gamora was nowhere to be found. There was no logic in the feeling; chances were that the child had gone off on some secret errand of her own devising and would return soon enough to face a scolding. Yet the sensation persisted, and when Gamora's favourite haunts were searched without result, Simorh knew with an unassailable instinct that something was desperately wrong.

Thean and Falla had pleaded with her not to overtax herself, but she wouldn't hear them. Using her scrying glass, she had fought back her weakness in a frantic attempt to touch her daughter's mind, and had found nothing. She knew her own skills well enough to reach two possible conclusions. Either Gamora had gone somewhere far beyond Haven, where her mother's magic couldn't reach, or she was dead. And so, hurling the glass aside in a frenzy of grief and terror, the sorceress had fled from her tower and run to the court hall where DiMag and the council were in session.

DiMag told himself over and over again that Simorh must be wrong when she claimed that Gamora wasn't in the palace or even in the city. She was ill, her abilities at a low ebb; it must be that she was simply too weak to touch the child. Over and again he tried to convince her, too, though he couldn't tell if he had succeeded. And in the meantime, they could do nothing but wait.

He looked up suddenly as the doors at the far end of the hall banged open, and saw Kyre coming towards him. A sharp spear of suspicion flared in DiMag as he recalled the acrimony with which they had parted; but as the other man approached and the prince saw his expression better, the suspicion abated.

Kyre stopped in front of the dais, looking quickly from DiMag to Simorh and back to DiMag. 'She isn't found?'

'No. But she can't have gone far.'

'What can I do?'

'As much as any man can do.' DiMag smiled with no humour. 'Though of course, you have no obligation.'

Kyre coloured. 'In this, I have.' He was thinking of the unhappy encounter with Gamora that morning, of the misery on the little girl's face as he walked away from her. Could she have been so upset by his treatment that she had run away? It was unlikely in the extreme, but it couldn't be ruled out. Gamora was impulsive, her emotions easily moved: if the hurt had gone deep, who could predict how she might react?

He said: 'Where are you searching?'

'At the moment, in the palace.' DiMag frowned. 'Though if you have any thought, any clue that might lead elsewhere, for the sake of all that's holy don't hold it back!'

Simorh's head came up sharply. 'Why should he know anything?' she demanded venomously. 'What does *he* have to do with it?'

'Hush.' DiMag touched her hair, trying, though awkwardly, to soothe her. 'Gamora looks on Kyre as her friend. She might have said something to him that will help us.' And as she bowed her head again he looked over her shoulder at Kyre. 'Did she? Did Gamora say anything to you?'

Kyre shook his head helplessly. There was nothing – except, ridiculously, the image of Gamora on the beach, holding up a shell she had found and turning it so that the sunlight glinted on its rainbow surface.

'No,' he said. 'Nothing.'

Simorh looked up again. In her thin, strained face her eyes were dark and featureless hollows that reminded Kyre shockingly of the deathly pale girl on the strand. 'Find her,' she said, and her voice was as empty as her eyes. 'I don't care what you have to do; what *any* of us has to do. Just *find* her!'

Gamora's talent for avoiding people she didn't want to see was as finely developed as her talent for finding those she did; and, still smarting from the sting of Kyre's inexplicable rebuff, she had made her way back to the gardens that morning by a tortuous route that avoided the gazes of all but a few unimportant servants. There she hid herself among a tangle of limp and fading bushes, careless of the damp underfoot and of the leaves' unpleasantly slimy caress, and while the short day wore on she idled her time away, scooping the thin soil aimlessly into little heaps, shredding foliage with her fingers, sometimes singing tuneless dirges to herself in an effort to pass the hours without thinking about her own disappointments. But that was impossible. Her father was busy, her mother ill – they wouldn't tell her what the illness was, but Gamora knew well enough – and her tutor would give her no lessons today. Her nurse did nothing but fuss and scold, and now her friend, her only real friend, had been unkind to her and she didn't know why. Several times the sense of injustice brought tears to Gamora's eyes, but she bit them back stoically, reminding herself aloud that she was a princess and future ruler of Haven, and future rulers didn't cry.

She cradled her shell, which she'd taken to carrying everywhere with her. When she was older, it would be different. When she was older, people wouldn't simply smile and ruffle her hair when she gave an order; they would obey, the way they obeyed her father. She didn't want to rule, but if she must then she would make the most of it. And when she was older, she would marry Kyre. *Then* he wouldn't speak sharply or turn away from her, because if he was unhappy she would know how to cheer him.

She looked up, and realised that the light was fading. The fog hadn't lifted all day, and now as the invisible sun dipped towards the sea it seemed to be closing in, like the dark, formless cloak that sometimes haunted her in bad dreams, rising up from the floor around her bed to slowly engulf and suffocate her. Gamora shivered. She could hear moisture seeping in the ground beneath her and it sounded like the fog breathing, *in-out, in-out,* a waiting, predatory animal. She scrambled to her feet, shuddering as the tendrils of the undergrowth seemed to snatch at her ankles, and ran for the comparative safety of the overgrown path. She kept running until the terrace wall loomed out of the darkening mist ahead, and only stopped for breath when she reached the safety of the steps.

Gamora didn't want to go back into the palace. The gathering dark unnerved her, but at this moment it seemed a better prospect than the scolding she was sure to receive from her nurse if she returned to her room. She felt alone, unloved, unwanted. Very well then; she'd go away. And if her disappearance gave them all a fright, so much the better; it might shake them into paying more attention to her in the future.

She turned the shell over and over, marvelling at the way the rising moonlight reflected every colour imaginable in the mother-of-pearl. Then she held it to her ear, to see if she could hear the sea. But instead of the sea the shell seemed to be whispering her own name.

Gamora ... Gamora ...

Gamora smiled, hesitantly at first then with growing eagerness as she realised her imagination wasn't playing tricks on her.

Gamora ... Come and see, Gamora. Come and see.

Images crowded into the little girl's mind, of night and the sea and the world transformed by the pale shimmer of moonlight into something magical and wonderful. Such places! Such beautiful, unknown lands ...

Come and see, Gamora. Come to me, and I will show you wonders beyond imagining. Come to me, and all these wonders will be yours ...

The shell seemed to take fire with an inner light of its own; sparkling like pearl and diamond and emerald and sapphire all at once.

Come and see. It isn't so very far. Come and see ...

She wanted to see with her own eyes, instead of merely in her imagination, the beautiful things that the shell-voice had promised her. And they were out there, in the night, only waiting for her to come.

She left the grounds by a back way, rarely used, that took her around the palace's outer wall and down into Haven. The fog muffled her footsteps and distorted shapes and shadows in the empty streets; it created an eerie illusion of being deep under water, and more than once Gamora started, heart pounding painfully, at imagined horrors looming out of the dark. Under other circumstances she might have turned tail and bolted for home, but the shell in her hands gave her confidence, and in her mind she seemed still to hear it whispering encouragement to her.

She reached the archway at last, and stopped between the alcoves with their dimly glowing lamps. Ahead lay the bay, vast and empty, no longer the familiar playground of bright days but something unknown and fraught with danger. Yet even as Gamora's courage faltered, the shell seemed to speak to her again, whispering her name, calling her, urging her to be brave enough to leave the town's dull lights behind and move on into the dark. She stepped through the arch, felt the hardness of paving under her feet change to the yielding, shifting texture of sand. Grains trickled into her shoes; she kicked them off, and started barefoot across the huge expanse of the beach.

Fog enfolded her in soft shrouds. Somewhere high above, she knew, the Hag sailed the sky and gazed down at her, but the old moon's scarred face was lost in the dense whiteness. Even the sea was no more than a distant, muted susurrating without form or direction; but though she could see no more than a few inches before her, Gamora padded swiftly and unerringly across the sand. Now that the shell had assuaged her fears she felt exhilarated; the challenge of being alone in the night thrilled her, and she believed fervently that the promised *something* to which the shell was leading her would be worth any risk and any peril.

The sound of the sea grew louder, closer. A capricious gust of wind pounced from the west and ruffled the fog, momentarily pushing its veils aside so that Gamora had a brief glimpse of sullen, dark waves, crowned with yellowish scum, a bare twenty yards away. The tide was very low and must be about to turn: she ignored the sudden *frisson* of unease that assailed her, and hurried on.

Moments later, the sand turned to shingle beneath her bare feet. Gamora stopped, realising that she must have reached the long bar that stretched out into the bay's north-easterly arm and knowing that there was nothing now between her and the ancient, ruined temple.

Surely, the shell didn't mean for her to go *there*? She couldn't – fear of the place was inbred in her, as in all the people of Haven, and even her insatiable curiosity had never been enough to overcome it. But as she hesitated, not knowing whether to wait, turn aside or flee back to the town, a voice, lilting and gentle and so sweet that it made her ache inside, called out to her.

'*Gamora* ... '

It wasn't the shell this time. The voice was different
– and it had come from a way off, somewhere out on
the shingle bar. The little girl bit her lip ...

'*Gamora* ... '

She wanted, so desperately wanted, to answer. The
sweetness of the voice hinted at love and kindness and
beauty, assuaging her loneliness and reaching to the
depths of her soul. Yet she dared not answer. The
shingle strand was too grim a barrier.

'*Gamora... come to me, Gamora. Don't be afraid...*'

The breeze rose again, from the north this time,
shredding the mist so that it rolled aside – and Gamora
saw an unearthly figure waiting for her on the bar.

Vast eyes, as black as the night-shrouded sea, gazed
at the child from a deathly white face about which the
wind flung tatters of raven hair. Dressed in a dark,
sleeveless robe, the woman looked so fragile that her
bones might have been spun from strands of glass, her
flesh insubstantial as sea-foam. A faint, silver nimbus
surrounded her, tiny motes sparkling and dancing, as
though she had come down from the moon and brought
a trapped piece of its light with her; and love, longing
and an inexplicable pity welled up in Gamora as,
transfixed, she returned the unwavering gaze.

The woman inclined her head with a slow and almost
childlike movement, as though to regard Gamora from
another angle. Then she smiled – Gamora saw only a
darkness where her mouth must be – and, raising one
long, frail arm, beckoned with a fluid motion.

Gamora felt her feet starting forward involuntarily.
For an instant she tried to fight the impulse, but the
momentary doubt was eclipsed by a renewed surge of
emotion. This was what the voice in the shell wanted;
this strange, fey creature, whoever she might be, was
the one who would lead her to promised wonders. And
she trusted the voice. It was her friend.

As the little girl broke into a run, the woman laughed, bright, shimmering laughter that the fog couldn't quell and that made Gamora want to laugh with her. Then she turned, her robe rippling suddenly with dark hints of blue and green amid the black, and skipped away along the shingle bar. Dropping her precious shell – somehow it no longer seemed important to her – Gamora picked up her skirt and broke into a stumbling run, her voice cutting through the murky night like the cry of a small, lost bird.

'Wait! Oh, wait for me!'

The figure ahead of her stopped, jerkily like a marionette, and spun back to face Gamora. Her laughter pealed out again and she held out both her arms, feet dancing restlessly in the shingle, unable to stay still.

'I'm coming!' Gamora cried. 'Wait for me!'

Their progress along the shingle bank was a bizarre game of catch-if-you-can. Just as Gamora thought she would reach the strange woman and touch her she skipped away again, dancing across the slippery stones, so light that the little girl believed she might at any moment take to the air and fly away into the fog.

She couldn't tell how long the weird game went on; time was meaningless, and only her elusive quarry mattered. But suddenly there were walls looming out of the fog; huge, crumbling ramparts gashed by the decayed eyes of what had once been windows; shattered columns towering among them, great, fallen stones impeding the way. Gamora stumbled to a halt, catching her breath on an involuntary, indrawn gasp of shock as she realised that the shingle bar had ended and she stood among the ruins of the shunned temple.

Not fifteen paces away the strange, shimmering woman had also stopped, and waited between two monstrous piles of broken masonry, gazing back at Gamora. This time, Gamora knew, her elusive friend would not run away; there was nowhere left to run.

'*Gamora*.' The woman smiled, and the dark hollows of her eyes were suddenly lit with an inner fire that drew an answering smile in the child. Gamora didn't hesitate, but ran across the uneven ground, arms held out in greeting. Their hands linked, and the little girl felt fingers that were slender, frail, yet strong and warm curl round her own. A sensation that she had rarely felt in her short life flooded through her; the knowledge that she was wanted and welcomed, that she, and no one else, mattered.

The woman laughed again. Now that they were at close quarters, Gamora was surprised to see how young the stranger was. There was something other-worldly in her look: her face was small, sharp and narrow, her lips thin if gracefully curved, her eyes, like her hair, utterly black. Without the sea-shell's enchantment to cloud her mind Gamora would have feared her, but the spell had too great a hold on her, and she felt nothing but the adoring eagerness that had led her to this moment.

'Pretty. So pretty.' The woman's voice was mellifluous and dreamy, and Gamora's captivation deepened. Hesitantly, not sure if she dared speak lest she broke some unwritten rule, the little girl said: '*You* are pretty. What's your name? Tell me, please!'

'I am Talliann.' The dancing silver motes in the nimbus around her spun faster, shimmering.

Gamora's fingers tightened on the thin hands she held. 'Will you be my friend, Talliann? I want so much to talk to you, and the shell said there were things you'd show me.'

Talliann inclined her head as though considering the child's plea, and her eyes took on a faraway look. 'There are so many things I can show you,' she said at last, still dreamily. 'So many . . . and so much I want to know of the place where you come from.'

'I can tell you! Gamora cried eagerly. 'We *can* be friends – please say we can!'

'Yes.' Talliann raised her head slowly. She seemed

to be gazing at something high on the ruined wall, though when Gamora followed her direction there was nothing to be seen but the ancient stones and the grotesque silhouettes of carved figures, gargoyles mutilated by age and the elements. Perhaps, she thought, Talliann was trying to see through the fog to the moon – and then the breath caught violently and painfully in her throat as one of the broken gargoyles moved.

Fear broke through the enchantment, and Gamora made an ugly, inarticulate sound, stumbling back, eyes wide and staring in horrified disbelief. She tried to let go of Talliann's hands, but Talliann's grip abruptly tightened and she couldn't free herself. High overhead, distorted by the fog, an indistinct shape was detaching itself from the crumbling wall, moving unevenly yet with an appalling, reptilian grace, like something fast and lithe awakening after a long sleep. And as it moved, climbing down towards a window embrasure, Talliann watched its progress with empty eyes.

'*No!*' Gamora found her voice at last, and pulled with all her strength to free herself from Talliann's grasp. 'No, let me go! Stop it, Talliann, *please!*'

The grip on her fingers tightened still further, belying Talliann's gossamer-frail appearance, and despite the panic exploding within her Gamora couldn't help but look again at the wall and the thing that moved on it. It had reached the embrasure now and crouched there, a nightmare making ready to pounce. A cascade of tangled hair flowed over its hunched shoulders, and though its features weren't discernible, the glitter of its eyes was visible under the wild mane of hair. Then a voice, husky, triumphantly malignant, floated down through the fog to where Talliann and Gamora stood rigid.

'*Good, Talliann. Very, very good.*'

Gamora screamed and twisted violently in an effort to free herself, but Talliann's grip slid to her wrists. She jerked once, hard, and Gamora was pulled off balance, staggering across the rough ground and colliding with her. With her arms securely pinned, the child could do nothing but watch in frozen trepidation as the creature on the wall – human, animal, demon, she didn't know and was too terrified to guess – contorted its limbs to a seemingly impossible angle and, like a monstrous spider, began to descend, climbing lithely among the smashed stonework. As it neared the ground deep shadow swallowed it, but still Gamora could hear its movements above the harsh sound of her own gasping breath. Then it was down – she heard the slither of feet on shingle, and a rustling sound – and something detached itself from the shadow-pool at the wall's base. It crawled, flowed, across the broken ground, then its shape changed and it rose upright, solidifying and resolving into human shape. Its crown of tangled hair shivered like an animal's mane, and around the long, powerful limbs the tattered shreds of ancient garments fluttered and coiled. Gamora tried to shrink back as it advanced, but Talliann blocked her path; the child felt hot tears sting her cheeks as terror and an awful sense of betrayal fought for precedence in her reeling mind. The figure drew closer, then a hand, the fingers bony and tipped with long, ragged nails, shot out and took hold of her jaw in a pincer grip. Gamora shut her eyes tightly, but couldn't open her mouth to scream or plead or be sick, though she wanted to do all three at once. A powerful smell of brine assaulted her nostrils, mingled with the reek of decaying seaweed, and she uttered a small, helpless, wordless sound.

'Look at me, Gamora.' Close to, the husky voice had an undercurrent of terrible cruelty. 'Open your eyes, and look at me.'

Gamora tried to fight the compulsion to obey, but it was impossible; her eyelids were forcing themselves apart against her will. The fog and the walls of the ruin swam before her, then her vision focused and she looked into Calthar's face.

The green eyes, chillingly, unhumanly and calculat-
ingly malevolent, sapped the last shreds of Gamora's
will. The child's limbs stiffened and she could only stand
rigid and helpless as the sorceress tilted her head at a
painful angle to see her the better, her fingers making
small, stroking motions across Gamora's chin in an
obscene parody of affection. Then she smiled, and in the
darkness the effect was savage.

'Good . . . ' she said again. 'We have what we came
for.' She glanced at Talliann, the old resentful malice
stirring behind her eyes. 'Release her, Talliann. Your
part is done.'

Talliann's grasp relaxed a little but she didn't let go.
When she spoke she was incoherent, as though Calthar's
presence had disturbed her composure and clouded her
thoughts. 'I don't want . . . ' she said. 'I don't want . . .
you to harm my friend.'

'Why should I harm her?' Contempt gave a rasping
edge to Calthar's voice. 'She's valuable to me – and you
know full well why; just as you know that this whole
affair is at your behest!' She gave Gamora a venomous
little shake, 'Don't try to argue with me now. Let go of
the child!'

Slowly the defiance faded from Talliann's eyes,
leaving her face expressionless, and her hands fell away
limply to her sides. She stepped aside with a shuffling,
crablike motion, and Calthar turned her head to stare
up into the fog. The tide had turned and the first sliding
incursion was inching its way across the shingle bank;
somewhere below her feet the sorceress could hear
water moving into the temple's underground chambers.
Dawn was still far off, but the Hag would set soon; she
sensed the old moon's light waning, and with it her own
power. The return journey should be delayed no longer.

She turned once more to Gamora. The child still stood
frozen, all movement arrested. Only her eyes held any
animation, and the stark terror in them irritated Calthar
intensely. Still gripping Gamora's chin, she raised her

left hand and drew a symbol in the air before the little
girl's face. Gamora's eyes closed instantly, and as she
slumped, Calthar caught her and swept her up in her
arms. Then she looked at Talliann.

'Go,' she commanded.

Talliann frowned faintly. Her lips parted and she half
raised one arm before letting it drop again. 'I . . . don't
want . . . '

Calthar's mouth hardened into a vicious line. 'Go,'
she said again, softly, in a tone Talliann knew well.

All intelligence left the fey girl's eyes. She bowed her
head, black hair whipping across her face as a capricious
gust of wind caught it. Then she turned and began to
move with her odd, shambling gait to where the sea
waited.

Chapter 10

They gathered at first light in the walled courtyard behind the palace; some two hundred hard-eyed soldiers together with courtiers, councillors and as many palace servants as could be spared from essential duties. A soft, dreary rain had just begun to fall, darkening stonework, soaking clothing and dripping from hair and cloak-hems.

DiMag waited until the entire company was assembled, then emerged on to the palace steps to address them. The prince looked haggard and ill; from his vantage-point just inside the doorway Kyre saw him falter twice as he stepped outside, and feared for his ability to get through the necessary formalities. But nothing would induce DiMag to stop now, however exhausted he might be. A night's intensive and organised searching had proved that Gamora was not in the palace precincts, and DiMag sensed in his bones that, whatever had befallen her, time was of the essence if she was to be found.

The assembly fell silent as he appeared. His gaze swept over the sea of upturned, uneasy faces for a few moments, then he cleared his throat.

'My friends of Haven.' The prince's voice mirrored his bleak weariness. 'As you all know by now, my daughter, the Princess Gamora, is missing. She disappeared last night and despite extensive searches we can find no trace of her. We have established beyond doubt that she is not in the palace, and therefore the search must be intensified and extended to the city and all surrounding areas.' He hesitated. 'I don't need to tell you that her wellbeing is of paramount importance to me and to my wife. Nothing else matters beside her safe return, and I ask you, *urge* you, to stint nothing in the search for her. She must be found, whatever the cost.' Another pause, and DiMag seemed to be struggling to get himself under control. 'If she is found – *when* she is found, and brought safely back – then whoever finds her will earn the highest measure of reward that I can bestow.

'I can say no more to you at this stage. You have all been assigned to search-parties; your leaders should now report to Swordsmaster Vaoran, who has designated areas of the city and its surrounds for each party to comb. And if any one of you can provide a clue to my daughter's possible whereabouts – any recollection, any hearsay, *anything* at all – then I urge you to bring the information to me in the court hall immediately.

'That is all. Search diligently and thoroughly – and thank you.'

DiMag turned and walked back into the palace. At his back a murmur of voices was rising, and the search-party leaders were already pushing their way through the crowd and climbing the steps to find Vaoran. The prince moved away into an antechamber, accompanied by several of his more senior advisers, and Kyre hesitated, unsure of what he should do. Across the room, on the far side of the window, men were congregating around the burly figure of the swordsmaster, and for a moment, as Vaoran glanced up, Kyre caught his eye. The look he received mingled open hostility with contempt and an unpleasant edge of triumph: Kyre felt his hackles rise, and looked quickly away. But he could still sense the cold blue eyes staring at him, and after a few moments he turned his back with a deliberate movement and walked quickly away into the side chamber.

DiMag saw Kyre enter the room, and left the knot of anxiously conferring councillors to intercept him. Kyre took in the appalling strain on the prince's face and made a quick, formal bow. 'How can I be of use?'

With the shadow of their last encounter still hanging over them, DiMag hadn't expected him to maintain such an open-handed response. For a moment his mask slipped and a flurry of emotions showed on his face; then he had himself under control again.

'I want you to go with Vaoran.' He gripped Kyre's upper arm and steered him out of the councillors' earshot. 'I know it's not an assignment you'll relish, but I have good reason.' He looked up shrewdly at the taller man. 'Take his orders, Kyre, and do what he tells you. But if the orders he gives seem to detract in any way from the urgency of finding Gamora, I want you to report to me immediately. Do I make myself clear?'

'You're not suggesting that Vaoran – '

'No, I'm not. I don't believe for a moment that Vaoran would harm my daughter. But no more do I believe that he'd be above using her, if he could, to secure my co-operation in his own schemes.' DiMag paused, and studied Kyre's face suspiciously. 'I'm gambling on my instincts by being this frank with you, Sun-Hound, and despite our differences I think those instincts are sound. But if you fail me, or if you betray my trust, you'll suffer for it.'

Kyre's eyes narrowed. 'I won't see Princess Gamora hurt. Or used – against anyone.'

The prince nodded. 'That's what I thought, and it's why I'm taking the risk of relying on you. Go, now. Report to Vaoran and tell him I've assigned you to his search party.'

Kyre turned to leave, then stopped and looked back. 'How is the Princess Simorh?'

DiMag shrugged. 'Much as anyone might expect. She suffered a bad relapse, but she's well tended in her tower.' His eyes were suddenly haunted, belying the estrangement between himself and his wife. 'As things are, we can't hope for anything better.'

Kyre could make no reply to that. He headed towards the door, and the prince turned back to his councillors.

Horse-riding was a new experience for Kyre, yet one which seemed elusively familiar. As Vaoran's party filed out of the courtyard gate and into the twisting city streets, he sat easily on his mount's high, narrow back, controlling it with relaxed and practised movements of his fingers on the reins. The swordsmaster made no secret of the fact that he resented Kyre's presence in his party, and, bar an initial curt order to mount up and move out, pointedly ignored him.

They rode through Haven, not towards the sandstone arch but up, along streets that grew narrower and steeper until finally they emerged from the city on to the clifftop. The open emptiness of the high ground was a shock after the close and claustrophobic atmosphere that permeated Haven; grey, sere moorland stretched away into the wet haze, broken only by the occasional patch of windburned gorse and untrammelled by any path. In the distance Kyre glimpsed what appeared to be a cluster of low buildings, and beyond them an indefinite spread of crop-bearing fields; but the drizzle made it impossible to discern any real detail. The prospect did not look appealing.

At Vaoran's order the riders turned right along a hard-packed track that followed the cliff's ragged edge; the swordsmaster waited until the party was strung out along the path before jerking his horse to a halt and looking back.

'We'll ride beyond the bay, until the track ends. I want the first five in line to watch inland, the rest to look down to the beach. Use your eyes as you've never used them before; and if any man sees anything untoward – *anything!* – report it to me immediately!'

His voice carried harshly on the still, damp air and

the edge of emotion was unmistakable. Despite his dislike of the man, Kyre couldn't fault Vaoran's zeal. He spurred his horse as the party moved on again, and kept his gaze fixed firmly on the huge crescent of the bay below. The tide was half out and ebbing, and the shingle bar lay like a shining snake in the shallows, gleaming under the dull sky, the ruined temple reduced, from this height, to the dimensions of a child's toy. Grief constricted Kyre's throat as he thought of Gamora and what might have befallen her. In all of Haven she was the one innocent undeserving of any harm, and the memory of how he had rejected and dismissed her so cavalierly at their last encounter added guilty remorse to the sorrow. If Haven had had gods, he thought, he would have prayed fervently to them at this moment that she might be found safe and unhurt.

It took two hours to traverse the winding path along the clifftop, and when the track at last petered out into dead patches of shale and thin grass, no clue had been found to Gamora's whereabouts. The weather was worsening; the cloud-cover had thickened and crept lower, seeming to meet the land in places, and the early drizzle had developed into steady rain that drove stingingly in from the sea and soaked the men and their mounts through. The tide was by this time at its lowest, and Vaoran pointed towards a steep but negotiable gully that cut a scar in the cliff and led down to the sand.

'We'll make our way down to the bay, spread out and comb the beach while the tide's at the ebb,' he shouted back.

He turned his horse towards the decline and one by one the men followed. Kyre, at the tail end of the file, experienced a brief but nauseating moment of vertigo as his mount began to slither down the gulley and the cliff fell away to either side; with an effort he collected his wits and concentrated on the saddle pommel as the riders made their cautious way towards the beach.

Reaching the sand, they spread out in a wide arc that

stretched from the cliff face out to the tideline. Kyre
positioned himself in the lee of the cliff – it offered no
shelter from the driving rain, but he felt happier with
the greatest possible distance between himself and the
restless sea – and slowly the line of riders began to move
forward, eyes focused on the ground around them, alert
for any clue. Kyre hung back a little behind the main
formation, anxious to take in every detail of the rocks
and pools that littered the foot of the cliff, and morbidly
aware that at any moment he might glimpse a tangle of
dark hair or a small, white limb protruding from the
weed and boulders. Ahead of the party, perhaps a
quarter of a mile away though obscured by the mist and
rain, the ancient temple stood between them and
Haven, and he couldn't banish a purely intuitive yet
powerful gut feeling that Gamora's disappearance was
somehow connected with the ruin. Though he couldn't
see it, it drew him, its presence a constant and disconcerting goad.

Someone shouted suddenly, the sound peculiarly flat
in the heavy atmosphere, and a horseman broke from
the line to canter towards Vaoran. Kyre reined in,
watching though he could hear nothing of the con-
versation between the two men. He saw Vaoran shake
his head and clap the rider's shoulder as though in
commiseration, then the swordsmaster raised his arm
and signalled everyone to move on.

The temple drew nearer, its jagged pillars looming
out of the grey day as though they hung in mid-air with
no foundation to support them. Kyre's horse shied
nervously at the apparition and he had difficulty calming
its stamping and side-stepping. At last he reined it to a
halt, meaning to settle the animal before riding on; and
as he leaned forward to stroke the horse's neck in an
attempt to reassure it he glimpsed a flicker of movement
by the cliff face.

Involuntarily, Kyre jerked so hard on the reins that
his horse snorted sharply and almost sat on its haunches.

The cliff here was pocked with caves, some no more than narrow slits in the rock wall, others gaping like dark, idiot mouths; and it was in the shadows of one of the wider caves that he had seen the movement.

'Who's there?' Kyre moved his horse a cautious pace or two nearer the cliff, peering forward and mentally cursing the water that dripped from his hair into his eyes. 'Come out – show yourself!'

A slithering sound answered him, as though someone or something was climbing carefully across the piles of rank seaweed that littered the place. Then he saw a pair of eyes, shining luminously in the gloom, and the outline of a pale arm that rose and, jerkily, beckoned.

He looked quickly over his shoulder. The rest of the search-party were still making their slow way onward and no one seemed to have noticed the fact that he was now some way behind them. Kyre thought of Vaoran's order, then recalled DiMag's last words to him, and stilled the shout that had been on the tip of his tongue. He neither needed nor wanted anyone to back him up, least of all Vaoran . . .

His horse grew nervous as he edged it towards the cave, fighting the bit and kicking up flurries of sand until he was forced to dismount and lead it. The hand still beckoned, though he could no longer see the shimmer of the eyes; whoever lurked in the cave had drawn back into the darkness as he approached. He called out softly, 'I'll come no further. Who are you, and what do you want?'

Again there was a slithering sound: then a figure emerged slowly from the cave's black interior into the twilight just beyond the entrance. Small, thin, skin pale with an odd blue-green tinge that he'd seen before, and white hair that whipped around its shoulder as a wet gust of wind caught it. It was dressed only in a loincloth and its body was so scrawny as to be all but sexless. In one hand it held a spearlike weapon, identical to the one with which Prince DiMag had killed his prisoner; its grip on the spear seemed negligently careless but Kyre wasn't inclined to take any chances. He held up one hand, palm outwards, in what he hoped would be interpreted as a pacific gesture.

'Can you speak?' he asked. 'Do you understand me?'

The sea-dweller smiled, showing small but ferally sharp teeth. Then it said, in a voice that was bizarrely modulated and sounded as though water rather than air flowed through its lungs, 'Sun-Hound?'

Kyre's throat constricted. *How could it know*? He swallowed and replied with an effort, 'Yes. I'm the one called Kyre.'

It nodded. 'You're searching for the little princess.'

'Gamora ... do you know where she is?' His pulse was starting to pound.

The creature laughed, and revealed its free hand, which hitherto it had kept hidden behind its back. Something glinted like a captive rainbow in its grasp; then it brought its arm up in a sharp motion and threw the object directly at Kyre.

He stumbled back, and caught the thing by reflex rather than judgement as it arced towards him. It was a shell, the inner surface brilliantly pearlescent and reflecting every colour of the spectrum. Gamora's precious shell, which she had found on the beach while they walked with Brigrandon ...

The pounding in his blood swelled to a suffocating pitch and he looked up, wild-eyed.

'*Where is she?*'

'With us. Safe. I can take you.'

Kyre felt sick with horror. Gamora was in the hands of her people's deadliest enemies. He tried to get a grip on the combination of fury and panic that threatened to overwhelm him. If Gamora was a prisoner, why was this creature so eager to take him to where she was held? Gamora was a far more valuable hostage than he could ever be; her captors could surely want nothing from him?

The creature impinged on his chaotic thoughts. 'I can take you,' it said again. 'But you only. No other.'

'Why?' Kyre demanded hoarsely. 'Why me?'

It shrugged. 'I didn't question the order.' Another feral smile. 'If you want her to live, you must come.'

It was an ultimatum that he couldn't argue with, and he dared not doubt for a moment that, if he didn't comply, Gamora would be harmed. He wanted to ask a hundred different questions, but there was no time. The decision must be made, now.

'Well?' The sea-dweller cocked its head in a faintly mocking challenge.

He cast another look back towards the sea. The horsemen were well ahead now, his absence still unnoticed. He thought of Gamora . . .

'Very well,' he said tersely.

The creature's smile became a wide grin. 'Come, then,' it told him. 'This way – quickly.'

It emerged from the cave mouth and started away at a run in the opposite direction to Vaoran's receding party. Taken aback, Kyre loosed his horse's reins and set off in pursuit. The sea-dweller moved with a peculiar, loping gait that looked ungainly but nonetheless covered ground fast; keeping up with it on the wet, soft sand was hard work. They were still in the lee of the cliff, and at first Kyre didn't hear the hoofbeats approaching from behind, as the rush of his pulse pounding in his ears masked all other sound. Only when a voice bellowed at his back did he realise with a sudden shock that his absence had been discovered.

'*You!* What in the name of the Eye d'you think you're doing?'

The sea-creature stopped in a tangle of limbs, hissing with alarm. It cast a rapid glance back, then snatched Kyre's arm, pulled hard and snarled, '*Run!*'

Jerked almost off his feet as his companion dragged him away from the cliff and in a direct line towards the sea, Kyre had no chance to think what he was doing and time only for the briefest glimpse of the horsemen bearing down on them. Someone must have looked back and seen him with the sea-dweller; now the soldiers were pounding head-on towards them, Vaoran in the lead and yelling at them to stop. He looked desperately at the sea, and knew they couldn't reach it before they were run down.

'Run!' the creature screamed again, furious or frightened, Kyre couldn't tell which. He tried to force his legs to move faster, but his calf-muscles ached savagely and he could make no better speed.

The leading horses changed direction, stringing out in a curve that would cut the fugitives off before they reached the tideline. The animals were far faster than any runner, and suddenly the dark blur of Vaoran's horse swept between them and the sea. Kyre and the creature instinctively swerved, only to reel back as another horse veered in from the left. The two animals converged, forcing them into a narrow bottleneck, and as other mounted men came to reinforce their leader, Kyre and his companion stumbled to a halt, hemmed in and trapped.

Vaoran stared down at Kyre, and though the swordsmaster's heavy figure was little better than a silhouette against the sky Kyre could sense the undisguised loathing radiating from him.

'So what have we here?' Vaoran said with soft malignance. 'A turncoat and a traitor, a sandworm who consorts and plots with sandworms ... '

The sea-dweller bared its teeth and snarled. Vaoran's horse shied violently, alarmed by the aggressive movement and not liking the smell of brine from the creature; Vaoran jerked the reins viciously to discipline it, and his blue eyes focused on the white-haired being. His chest heaved as though with some livid emotion he was determined to contain, then he gestured to one of his men.

'Kill that,' he said with flat disinterest. 'We'll give the

prince's pet a more protracted lesson; but kill that now and leave its entrails for the gulls.'

Kyre wanted to shout a protest, remembering Gamora, but the sea-creature was faster than he was. Before anyone else could move, it brought its spear up in a bizarre movement from the wrist, and the weapon cut a whirling, lethal arc through the rain, slashing across the unprotected chest of Vaoran's horse. The animal shrieked and reared, tipping the swordsmaster out of the saddle; other horses milled in panic, their riders frantically trying to keep them from trampling their fallen leader, and in the confusion the sea-creature thrust the bloody spear, shaft-first, into Kyre's hands.

'Follow me!' it hissed, its huge eyes glittering with a fanatical light. 'Or the child will be dead before nightfall!' And it was gone, darting like quicksilver through the melee and running towards the sea.

Kyre cursed, a voluble oath that he hadn't realised he knew, and tried to shoulder his way through the stamping animals in the creature's wake. Vaoran, hoarse with shock and rage, shouted, '*Stop him!*' and a horse slewed into his path, the rider snatching his sword from its scabbard and lunging towards him. Kyre felt fear and fury and desperation well up like a tidal wave; and with them came an instinct that surged out of his lost memory. The spear in his hands suddenly seemed to be alive; he flicked his wrists, holding the shaft double-handed, and the ferocious blade sheared like a striking steel cobra to meet the sword as it came down. The metals clashed with a searing, discordant note that set Kyre's teeth jarring, and sparks hissed in the rain. The swordsman swore, trying to untangle his blade: Kyre held it trapped on the divided point of the spear until the moment was perfect – then with another swift, expert twist he brought the spearblade back and, in the same movement, hamstrung his assailant where he sat.

The man's screams were an ugly counterpoint to the

renewed whinnying of the horses as the smell of blood panicked them afresh, and even Vaoran's roaring frustration couldn't cut through the din. Still gripping the spear, Kyre shoulder-charged the wounded man's horse; the animal jumped aside, stiff-legged with terror, and he was through the knot of men and free. He started to run, following the faint footprints of the sea-creature; inspired by desperation he gave no thought of what might lie ahead of him, and halted only when his feet splashed into the shallows of the turning tide.

Behind him there was shouting: he looked back and saw someone stumbling across the sand towards him. Vaoran ...

'Come back!' The swordsmaster was mad-eyed, his rage beyond control, and at the sight of him the shock of what he'd done struck Kyre like a physical blow. He had wielded the sea-dweller's spear as though born to it – he'd hamstrung a man, perhaps killed him – he'd had to do it, for Gamora's sake: *but where had that deadly skill come from* ?

He looked frantically over his shoulder at the sea. Vaoran meant to kill him, and he couldn't trust himself to defeat such an expert warrior. He didn't want to die – and he couldn't fail Gamora!

He backed away into the sea until the water was swirling round his thighs. There'd be no chance for explanations; the swordsmaster wouldn't listen, and perhaps in his place Kyre might have felt the same. The sea was his only chance.

He took another step backwards and felt the beach begin to shelve steeply under his feet. He didn't even know if he could swim, but it was too late to consider that now; he must learn, or drown.

Vaoran was closer; he couldn't afford any more time. Taking a deep breath, Kyre shouted, 'They've got Gamora! I *have* to go, or they'll kill her! Tell DiMag – they've got Gamora!!'

Whether Vaoran either heard or understood, he

didn't know; he turned and, with a silent mental plea to any benevolent power that might be listening, flung himself into the path of a breaking wave.

Green water smashed over his head and bore him down; it was stunningly cold and he almost gasped in a lungful of the sea before his head broke surface and he found himself beyond the wave and carried on a strong cross-current. Instinct took over and he kicked out, feeling his legs and the sea's buoyancy propel him clear of the current and into deeper water. Salt stung his eyes, nose and mouth before he learned to breathe between the swells of the breakers. He thrashed his arms, trying to match their stroke to the thrust of his body – and suddenly co-ordination came; it was easy, and he was swimming strongly.

As though he'd been born to it . . .

He forced the chilling thought away, knowing he must concentrate on pure physical survival. He'd swim until he was clear of the bay, then come ashore at a place where Vaoran's men couldn't reach him: it was impossible to think beyond that point until he was safe –

Kyre yelled aloud and swallowed sea-water as something gripped his ankle. He lost his stroke and twisted, flailing; then whatever held him pulled violently and he went under in a swirl of bubbles and foam. Down – he kicked but couldn't free himself – and then through the murky, turbulent darkness he saw luminescent eyes and a hand that grasped his foot, while another hand beckoned with a slow, smooth motion. Beckoned him down . . . He turned his head frantically from side to side, trying to tell the sea-creature that he must breathe air, not water, but it only showed its teeth in its feral smile and beckoned again, nodding so that its pale hair flowed like waterborne weed.

It must know he couldn't survive more than a minute or two under water – it meant to drown him! Kyre kicked again, with all his strength. He'd lost most of the air in his lungs with the shock of being pulled down; there was a mad drumming in his ears and his head and chest felt as though they were about to burst apart. He had seconds, at most, before muscular reflex would force him to open his mouth in a fruitless and desperate compulsion to breathe.

The creature nodded, more emphatically, as though reading his thoughts and urging him to begin the terrible process of drowning. The gloomy undersea world seemed to be turning crimson; the sea was like blood, his captor an appalling scarlet apparition, and the drums in his ears were beating harder, deeper, louder – and suddenly he could bear it no longer. A spasm racked his throat and diaphragm, his mouth opened and he gasped for air.

A fountain of bubbles gushed by his face and blinded him, and he felt the stinging, searing attack of salt. He shut his eyes, limbs flailing helplessly ... and the drumming in his head faded, the pressure in his chest receding as his lungs expanded in relief. Expanded ... contracted ... expanded again ... *he was breathing!* Shocked and bewildered, Kyre opened his eyes to see the sea-dweller, one hand still gripping his foot, grinning at him in the murk. It nodded and made an open-palmed gesture as if to say: *you see?* Kyre stared back at it, aware that they were both drifting on the heavy undertow – he could see neither the sea bed, nor any glimmer of light from the surface – but suddenly not caring. He was breathing, as easily as he breathed on land, but what flowed through his lungs was *water* ...

Realising that he at last comprehended what had happened to him, the sea-creature released its hold. It turned, moving with lazy grace, and backfinned with its hands to keep its position against the current. Then it pointed ahead, into swirling darkness.

Stunned, wondering, Kyre turned his body about until he was angled forward half way between the vertical and the horizontal. The caress of the sea, buoying him and giving strength and flexibility to his limbs, was relaxing and invigorating. He felt as though his stamina could be endless here in this gentle, watery world.

Tentatively he nodded to the creature ahead of him to show that he was ready. Then, as it moved slowly away, he flexed his muscles and propelled himself forward, following it into the deeps.

Chapter 11

DiMag said evenly, without looking up from the notes he was making, 'I see.'

Vaoran stared down at him. Two spots of colour were flaming on the swordsmaster's cheeks, and he couldn't keep the anger he felt out of his voice as he asked sharply, 'My lord, what do you intend to do about it?'

'*Do?*' The prince turned round in his chair so fast that Vaoran took an involuntary pace back. They were alone in DiMag's private apartments. DiMag's eyes were venomous with dislike and disappointment, and his mouth set in a tight, ugly line. 'What, my good swordsmaster, would you *suggest* that I do?'

'The creature is a traitor! He has betrayed Haven! My lord, I've believed all along that he shouldn't be trusted; though I don't wish to sound sanctimonious, I – '

'Then don't!' DiMag snapped viciously. He got up, the chair scraping noisily back. 'According to your own report, the last you saw of Kyre was when he plunged into the sea to escape your wrath. Which, as I doubt if he can swim, probably means that he is dead. In which case, you've had all the satisfaction you're going to get – unless you want me to have the sea fished until his corpse is found, so that you can take pleasure in dismembering it?'

Vaoran didn't answer, but DiMag could hear suppressed fury in his stertorous breathing. The prince smiled sourly. His swordsmaster and councillor might well harbour deep-rooted resentments, but he wouldn't dare act on them. Not yet, at any rate. Then the smile faded.

'Vaoran, you have done me a great disservice,' he said, turning his back and walking away towards the window. 'Thanks to your prejudice and stupidity, the sorcerous work which my wife' he stressed the word, subtly but noticeably, 'performed at great risk to herself has been destroyed and brought to nothing.'

Vaoran's face purpled. 'The creature betrayed you, Prince DiMag!'

'Did he?' DiMag looked back at him, eyes narrowed. 'How can you be so certain?'

'By the Hag, he murdered one of my men! One of my best soldiers – he bled to death on the sand before my eyes!'

'Maybe Kyre killed him to save his own life? Maybe you didn't give him the chance to explain himself?'

Vaoran stared at him. 'What in corruption was there to explain? The creature was *consorting* with those demons, in league with them! I'm not about to start doubting the evidence of my own eyes!'

'No, of course not. And so you were ready to kill him without a further word being said.'

Vaoran sucked in a harsh breath. 'Yes. I was. Because my faith lies in Haven, not in the unproven mouthings of a creature dragged into the world out of hell!'

DiMag turned slowly to face him, and wished fervently that he had a sword in his hand. He said, softly, 'Get out of my sight.'

Vaoran held his gaze for a few moments. Then, with a disgusted exclamation, he turned and left the room, slamming the door behind him.

Grai was waiting where the corridor turned at the junction with the main stairs, out of sight and earshot of the sentries at DiMag's door. He stepped out of the shadows as Vaoran approached and, judging the swordsmaster's mood, prudently said nothing while they descended the flight together. Only when they reached the entrance hall did Grai at last speak.

'Well? Did it go as you anticipated?'

'Worse.' Vaoran glanced sidelong at the plump councillor. 'My evidence wasn't enough for him; he began *defending* that monstrosity as though it were his blood brother!'

'Um.' Grai sucked at a strand of his beard, a habit which irritated Vaoran, and his eyes focused on the middle distance for a few moments as he contemplated. 'Well,' he said at length. 'Then it seems our prince is as unreasonable as ever.'

'Indeed. In fact I might go so far as to suggest that he's on the verge of losing his reason. Not a happy omen for the future of our city.'

Grai nodded sagely. 'Certainly it isn't. Though whether the time is yet right to suggest such a thing more publicly . . . ?' He let the question hang unfinished, and Vaoran hunched his shoulders.

'Not yet, Councillor Grai. We need, I think, just a little more time.' He smiled grimly. 'If the condemned man is given a long enough rope, then he'll sometimes save the hangman a tiresome task.'

The councillor uttered a short, wheezing laugh. 'Succinctly put. I take your meaning, and I agree with you. We've learned patience; we can endure it a little while longer. Now, I shall leave you to refresh and victual yourself after your arduous morning.' He patted Vaoran's arm in an absent-minded gesture and started to move away, then stopped and looked back. 'Oh; one small matter. The last words the creature shouted to you, about Princess Gamora. Did you mention that to the prince?'

'No. I thought it might be more – tactful – not to reveal it as yet.'

'Tactful.' Grai smiled. 'Tactful. Yes. What the prince doesn't know can't trouble him. Wise of you, Vaoran.' He smiled, and walked away.

'*DiMag!!*'

Simorh's scream brought Thean and Falla running from the room below. They found the sorceress collapsed on the floor among a tangle of blankets, hands flailing and sweat gleaming on her skin as she struggled out of the grip of a dream.

'Lady! Lady, it's all right, you're safe in your tower!' Thean, who was the stronger of the two girls, pinioned Simorh's arms and fought to calm her while Falla unravelled the blankets that cocooned the sorceress. Simorh moaned and burst into tears, and between them her apprentices lifted her back on to the couch from which she'd fallen.

'Falla, fetch the physician!' Thean said urgently.

'No!' Simorh's body jerked and she swatted weakly at the ministering hands. 'Not the physician – send for the prince, send for DiMag. I must speak to him!'

'Madam, you're in no condition – '

'*Ohhh!*' Bitter exasperation was in Simorh's groan and she wiped at her face with the sleeve of her robe. 'Don't argue with me! I *must* see DiMag.' She gripped Thean's wrist, her nails digging so painfully into the flesh that the girl winced. '*Do as I say!*'

The girls exchanged an uneasy glance, then Falla straightened and ran towards the door.

DiMag was still seething from his interview with Vaoran when a servant brought Falla's message from Simorh. For a moment it was on the tip of the prince's tongue to dismiss the man with a curse, but an odd instinct forestalled him. His senses were unnaturally and painfully acute today, and something in the tone of the message alerted him. He found Falla waiting nervously in the corridor, and smiled to reassure her.

'Well, Falla. What's amiss with your mistress?'

The dark girl shook her head. 'I don't know, my lord. She woke from a bad dream and she was very distressed – she begged to see you.'

'Very well. Lead the way.'

They made as good speed as DiMag was able, and within minutes were climbing the stairs to Simorh's tower.

'DiMag!' As they entered her bedchamber the sorceress tried to rise, pushing the anxious Thean aside. The prince read the urgency and strain in her face, and glanced at the two girls. 'Leave us.'

He waited until the door closed behind them, then knelt beside the couch. 'What is it? Have you had a vision?'

Under other circumstances Simorh might have been gratified by his eager concern, but she was too distraught to notice. She caught hold of his wrist and the words spilled chaotically from her tongue. 'I saw Gamora. In a dream – DiMag, I saw her!'

DiMag felt his chest constrict. He knew his wife well enough to set great store by the dream-images that sometimes came to her, and to trust her interpretation of them. His fingers clamped over hers and he demanded urgently, 'Where? Is she alive?'

Simorh nodded. 'She's alive, and unharmed, but ... the place where she is; it's ... ' She shook her head helplessly. 'I don't *know*, DiMag; I can't see it clearly. It's as though she were in another world, another dimension.' Tears sprang to her eyes. 'I don't know that place, and I can't touch it.'

Dread settled like a monstrous weight in DiMag's gut. 'Simorh, what you saw – ' he could hardly bring himself to utter the suggestion, but forced the words out. 'It wasn't a place of death ... ?'

'No!' She was vehement. 'She is alive; I *know* she is. Besides – Kyre was with her.'

'Kyre?' His face lost its colour and her eyes widened.

'Yes, Kyre. Why is that significant?'

DiMag released her hand and stood up. He couldn't bring himself to meet her frantic gaze as he said, 'Vaoran came to me half an hour ago, with news – '

'Of Gamora?' Simorh's voice was shrill.

'No. Listen to me. Kyre was with Vaoran's search party; I sent him. He encountered a – ' he hesitated, swallowed, 'one of the sea-creatures, and Vaoran tells me that he and the creature were attempting to slip away when they were apprehended.'

Her face was suddenly very still. 'What happened?'

DiMag shrugged. 'Much depends on what you choose to believe. According to Vaoran, there was a fight, one of the soldiers was killed, the creature escaped to the sea – and Kyre went with it. He was last seen in deep water, swimming.'

Simorh didn't speak for some while. From stillness her expression had taken on a pinched, tight look, her eyes haunted and introverted. At last, she said: 'Do you believe that report, DiMag?'

The prince sighed. 'I don't know what to believe. All I do know is that Kyre hasn't returned.' He looked up. 'And yet you saw him – '

'With Gamora. Yes.'

He bit his lip. 'Does that mean they *are* dead?'

'No.' Less vehemence this time, but her conviction was unshaken. 'They both live; I know it, and I feel – *sense* – that they're together. But wherever they are, DiMag, we can't reach them, and the search parties won't find them.'

DiMag sucked in a long breath. 'I don't know what to do, what to think. If you're right, then – ' he shook his head violently. 'There are so many possibilities. *Why* did Kyre go? How did he find Gamora?'

'I'll find out,' Simorh said savagely.

He looked at her. 'You're not strong enough.'

'I don't care. I don't care what I have to do. I'll find out what's happened.' Her eyes were feverishly bright. 'There's no other choice.'

DiMag paced the room slowly. Tiredness made his limp more pronounced than usual, and Simorh had to look away, disturbed by the awkwardness of his gait. 'Is our Sun-Hound a traitor?' he said at length, speaking more to himself than to the sorceress. 'Vaoran believes it. I don't.' He turned, faced her again. 'You brought him here; you should know the truth.'

She cast her eyes down. 'When I get him back in the palace, I'll find out,' she said viciously.

'If you get him back.'

'*When.*'

'As you please.'

Simorh gripped her upper arms. 'It *has* to be "*when*"; don't you understand that? Kyre is our only link with Gamora!' She stared at DiMag's taut, bitter face for a few moments, then abruptly turned over on the couch, away from him. 'Go away, DiMag. Send out our search parties and leave me alone; I can't talk to you.' Her shoulders heaved and she drew in a gulping breath. 'I know what you're thinking. Kyre has brought this on us, and I brought Kyre to Haven. Very well: it's all my fault, and I confess it. But I'll change that. If I die trying, believe me, I'll *change* it!'

She was crying, and DiMag couldn't touch her, couldn't even approach her. The division between them was too wide. He turned away and limped towards the door, only pausing when his hand was on the latch.

'I don't believe Kyre took Gamora from us. There's far more to this than we understand, and I'm not such a fool as to take Vaoran's glib tales at face value.' He looked down at his own feet and added softly, 'You don't know me very well, do you, Simorh?'

Simorh jammed a clenched fist into her mouth in an effort to stem the shuddering, silent sobs that racked her and seemed to jar from the top of her spine through to her heels. She didn't hear the gentle sound of the door closing as DiMag left the room.

Time had become an alien and meaningless concept. They might have been travelling for an hour or a day or a year, moving ever onward through the dim, swirling world of the deeps, a world of greens and blues and

greys, ever changing, ever revealing some new wonder
as they swam on. Here was a formation of crystalline
rock, shaped into fantastical sculptures; a castle from
a childhood dream. Here was a vast bank of weed
moving above their heads with slow, inexorable grace
as though directed by some alien intelligence. Here
were shoals of fish with brilliant eyes, which darted aside
like a shower of glass slivers at their approach, passing
by a fingersbreadth away yet always eluding capture.

Kyre felt as though a new and unplumbed range of
senses which he hadn't known could exist had been
suddenly and stunningly awakened. The freedom he felt
at moving with such ease and speed through the water
was like a heady drug; there was a new dimension of
power in him and he wanted to laugh and scream and
weep all at once with the sheer exuberance of it. The
fight on the beach was forgotten, Gamora was
forgotten, Haven was forgotten; he knew only this deep
and beautiful new world and he wanted to experience
it with every part of his being.

But the sea-creature that guided him knew the
urgency of its mission, and though it was content to
indulge his eager exploration, it nonetheless continued
to lead him towards their goal. To Kyre, the creature
was a flickering will-o'-the-wisp that he followed
without pausing to consider the wisdom of what he did;
he was too caught up in the miracle that had overtaken
him to think beyond the moment. But at last something
new impinged on his mind. The smooth tide on which
they swam was changing: cross-currents buffeted them,
stirring up sand from the sea-bed and churning the water
into murk. And then above his head there were traces
of shimmering, shivering light, and a distant booming
sound that seemed to echo in his bones.

His companion jack-knifed gracefully to cut across his
path as, suddenly confused and unsure of himself, he
twisted about in the water. It took hold of his wrist and
gestured towards the surface before turning upwards

and kicking out strongly. Kyre's limbs moved reflexively to match the creature: there was an exhilarating sense of speed, of energy – and then their heads broke out into salt-laden air.

The sea-dweller snorted a stream of water from its nostrils, then took several shallow, rapid breaths, drawing oxygen into its lungs. Kyre, unprepared for the transition, found himself choking and spluttering in a medium that was suddenly alien to him; only when the creature gripped his jaw in one hand and punched the palm of the other against his chest did he cough water from his lungs and feel his throat begin to work again. The change was agony, a stinging clash of wet salt and cold air, and he continued to cough convulsively, offering no resistance as his guide towed him towards what his streaming eyes could only dimly make out to be a high ledge. A wave helped them on their way; Kyre's body scraped painfully against rock, and then hands were taking hold of him, dragging him from the water, pulling upward. He fought them, not wanting to leave the sea, but his efforts were feeble and, like a stranded fish, he was dumped on the harsh, barnacle-crusted surface of the ledge.

Three men were waiting for them on the ledge. Two were getting on in years; the third was a good deal younger, a bizarrely distinctive figure with his silver-streaked black hair and the ugly birthmark on his face. He watched Kyre with intent interest as the guide climbed lightly up the side of the ledge and stood before the reception party.

'I have done as I was instructed,' it said, and bowed quickly to the assembled company. 'This is the one she wanted.'

Hodek stared down at Kyre, who was only now beginning to try, painfully and not yet with any success, to sit upright. He ignored the waiting guide, and it was Akrivir who finally answered.

'You've done well,' he said, a little bleakly. 'You'll

be rewarded.' He nodded a dismissal, and the guide headed towards a dark recess in the cavern wall. As he passed, Akrivir intercepted him; they exchanged a few words in low tones, then the guide disappeared.

Hodek's companion stroked his own chin thought-fully. 'It seems a pity that we have to maintain this charade. My vote would be to kill this creature now.'

Akrivir smiled cynically, and Hodek scowled at his colleague. 'Take a blade if it pleases you, and run the creature through,' he countered sourly. 'You'll be the one who answers to Calthar, not me!'

The other man shrugged and turned away, and Kyre, whose fuddled mind had been alerted by the exchange, managed at last to raise his head.

'Who are you?' His voice was roughened by the salt and cracked on the last word. He rubbed at his eyes, trying to clear them – and as he focused on the group before him, he remembered at last why he had been brought here.

Hodek glowered down at him. 'You are the one they call the Sun-Hound?'

Tension began to replace the weakness in Kyre's limbs. 'Gamora . . . ' he said, then the strength returned to his voice. 'Where is Gamora?'

Hodek sighed with theatrically exaggerated patience. 'I asked you a civil enough question. Be so good as to reply in the same manner!'

Kyre felt himself starting to shiver. *A cave, above sea level – the stronghold of Haven's enemies . . .*

'Yes,' he heard himself say. 'I am the one called Kyre . . . ' He shook his head, trying to clear the last vestiges of confusion and shock, then repeated, 'Where is Gamora?'

'The child is well,' Hodek told him.

'I want to see her!'

Hodek cleared his throat with genteel deliberation. 'I think,' he said, 'that we might do well to establish one or two minor details before we progress any further. The

child, as I said, is well – for the time being. While you
co-operate with us, and do as we ask rather than wasting
our time with tiresome questions, she will remain well.
If, however, you decide to be contentious, her health
may take an unexpected turn for the worse. Now.' He
smiled unctuously. 'Shall we begin again?'

Kyre forced himself to nod.

'Good.' Hodek clasped his hands together and Kyre
heard the knuckles crack loudly. 'Akrivir will escort you
to your destination. Ask no questions, say nothing;
simply follow.' He stepped aside and nodded to Akrivir,
who, without speaking, jerked his thumb towards the
mouth of a black tunnel at the back of the cavern.

Suspicious, but not willing to argue in the face of the
implied threat to Gamora, Kyre went with him. As they
reached the tunnel he looked back and saw Hodek
watching him. His demeanour was far from reassuring,
and Kyre turned his head quickly away.

As Akrivir and his charge vanished from sight, Hodek
let out a long, hissing breath. Like his fellow councillor,
he'd wanted no part of this ridiculous charade, but
Calthar had insisted on it, down to the finest detail and,
as usual, without deigning to make her reasons known.
The familiar mixture of desire, fear and loathing
churned in his blood as he thought of the priestess, and
it awoke his old fantasy that one day he would defeat
Calthar at her own game. A delusion perhaps, but a fond
one: nothing would have given Hodek greater pleasure
than to reverse their established roles and see her
crawling at his feet.

His colleague was still staring at the tunnel mouth,
and his voice broke in on Hodek's pleasant reverie.

'I still don't begin to comprehend why Talliann should
want such a creature brought here,' he said. 'What could
she possibly want with him?'

'How should I know what moves Talliann?' Hodek
retorted. 'The girl's even madder than Calthar.' He
smiled, not pleasantly. 'Perhaps she's at last beginning

to awaken to the joys of the flesh?' And he cackled. 'Let her have her diversions while they last.' 'Once she's done what's required of her, there'll be no more need of troublesome children or recalcitrant Sun-Hounds, and Calthar will know exactly how to deal with them both.' He patted his companion's arm. 'You'll see, my friend. You'll see.'

Chapter 12

Kyre was hopelessly disorientated. His escort had led him for what seemed like mile upon mile through the unlit tunnel; he could see nothing, and only the sound of Akrivir's footsteps a few paces ahead kept him on course. In the pitch darkness the sounds echoed disconcertingly, and he had lost all sense of perspective, so that it seemed the blackness before his straining eyes was a solid wall that he must at any moment run hard into. But the impact he feared didn't come; and at last a glimmer of light showed ahead.

They emerged from the darkness so suddenly that his pulse missed a sharp and painful beat. One moment there was nothing but the featureless tunnel, with only a faint, nacreous patch of illumination drawing indistinctly closer; then with no warning the passage turned at an acute angle, and opened on to a shocking vista.

Kyre swore aloud and flailed wildly for support as vertigo hit him like a solid wall. Akrivir caught hold of him, steadying him and smiling grimly at his shock, and he could only stare and stare at the impossible scene.

They stood on a ledge that jutted out from the soaring wall of a titanic cavern. Before them and to either side sheer rock fell away into an echoing chasm, swallowed by a blackness so intense that Kyre had the terrible feeling he could have reached out and down and taken physical hold of the dark. Across the abyss's sickening gulf the opposite wall of the cavern rose towering towards an invisible roof, and to Kyre's stunned eyes it seemed that the far cliff before him was alive with a

scene out of an unimaginable hell. Staircases scarred it,
like great swathes cut from the rock by a huge and
petulant hand, while distorted, spindled towers and mad
buttresses reared out of the wall at grotesque angles,
each one pricked by windows that shimmered and
flickered with deathly pale light. And it seemed – though
his battered and straining senses could never be sure –
that tiny figures moved against the monstrous backdrop,
dimly phosphorescent as they were caught by the lights
like moths in a flame, throwing the whole scene into
crazed and terrifying perspective. And somewhere, so
far below that he didn't dare think on it, he heard the
confined and angry moan of the sea.

Akrivir took his arm, pointing with his free hand, and
spoke for the first time. 'That way,' he said curtly.

Reluctantly Kyre looked in the direction he indicated.
To the right of the ledge a flight of narrow stairs swept
down in a sharp curve, hugging the cave wall. They
ended – or seemed to – just before utter blackness
devoured them; and Kyre's stomach lurched as he saw,
meeting the stairs, the slender span of a rock bridge that
arched away across the chasm. From here it looked as
fragile and insubstantial as a single thread from a
spider's web, and all his senses recoiled at the thought
of what his escort expected of him. But Akrivir wasn't
about to take any argument, and shock had drained
Kyre of the strength to resist. Like a man dreaming he
stepped on to the first stair, the second, beginning the
dizzying descent towards the bridge. Akrivir went
before him: he forced himself to concentrate on the odd
piebald of his hair immediately ahead to keep thoughts
of what might lie below the stairs' sharp outer edge at
bay, and, mesmerised and numb, arrived at last at the
point where the slender bridge speared away into
emptiness.

He was hardly aware of the crossing. What hidden
mental reserves he called on to enable him to walk out
over the abyss he didn't know; but somehow his feet

moved, one before the other, and by slow and halting degrees he saw the far cliff with its insane architecture draw nearer, nearer; until, sick with fright and tension, he stumbled from the bridge's quivering span and into the heartland of the sea-dwellers' citadel. His legs threatened to give way beneath him in sheer reaction, and Akrivir watched him patiently. When he was finally able to straighten up, he thought he detected a glimmer of amused sympathy in the other man's blue eyes.

'The crossing takes a little getting used to,' Akrivir said.

'Yes ... ' Kyre fought back an impulse to laugh, aware that it might turn into hysteria, and, encouraged by the fact that his escort was at least willing to speak, ventured a question. 'Where are you taking me?'

Akrivir shook his head, smiling faintly again. 'Don't ask me: I won't give you any answers.' He hesitated, then added more quietly: 'Not yet, at any rate. Come on.'

Taking Kyre's arm again, he drew him away from the edge of the bridge and into a tunnel which could have been twin to the one by which they had reached the cave. But this black corridor was short: within less than a minute they had entered a wide passage lit by chain-hung lamps, with side lanes leading off at intervals. And in this maze there were sounds of voices, footsteps, people – *people*? Kyre asked himself dazedly – talking, laughing, shouting, the sounds of voices echoing like a faint, random chorus from all directions. Akrivir led Kyre through caverns that might have been a deliberate parody of the market-places of Haven, roads and squares, streets and alleys – this whole cliff was a single, vast warren, a city within rock within the sea; a living microcosm of a world. And as they threaded their way deeper into the citadel the distant voices became more substantial, and Kyre began to see more and more of the sea-folk who inhabited this crazed place. They emerged from their dwellings or paused at their work to watch the two men pass, and the impressions they left on his spinning mind were as varied as he might have found among any gathering in Haven. Here was a man, sly-eyed and suspicious; here an ancient, toothless couple who pointed at him and mumbled to each other and shook their heads; here a naked child, silver-haired and so beautiful that it might have been the very personification of innocence, snatched away by its mother before it could stray too close to the interloper. And he *was* an interloper, Kyre realised. This was a world apart from Haven; a world populated by beings to whom he was a freak and an oddity. His skin was the wrong colour, his hair was the wrong colour, his face and limbs were misshapen, his eyes and mouth in the wrong proportion . . . if humanity was judged by the norm, then in this citadel he was unhuman.

And yet he could breathe water as they did; and he could wield the double-bladed spear as their warriors learned to do . . .

Bewildered though he was, the sights and sounds and salt smells of the citadel fascinated him as surely as though he were under a spell, so that when Akrivir halted with no warning he collided with him.

Akrivir, who had lapsed once more into taciturn silence, pointed to a side tunnel that led away from the main thoroughfare. Kyre's eyes were drawn to the tunnel, and it was a few moments before his vision adjusted to the brilliance that lit its carved and curving walls. The whole passage must have been carved through a vein of pure quartz: it shone and sparkled with a rainbow of colours brought to brilliant life by the myriad lamps depending from the ceiling, and in the vivid light he could see carvings – beautiful carvings, of fish and shells and strange forms he couldn't name – decorating the entrance. They turned into the tunnel, and as they traversed it Kyre could only stare in admiration at the sheer beauty of the place. Whoever had cut this passage from the living rock had been a master of his craft.

The passage was short, and ended at a door which, incredibly, seemed to be made from a single gigantic shell, fluted bands of coral and green creating a perfect symmetry. It swung easily, gracefully back at a touch, and Kyre stepped through into a lofty-ceilinged hall.

For one bizarre moment he thought he must be back in the raftered court hall of Prince DiMag's palace. The chamber was huge, lined with tall, arched windows and dominated by a raised dais on which was a great, carved chair. Between the windows hung tapestries woven in shades of blue, green and grey, shot through in places by threads of vivid crimson that drew the eye. Below the dais stood a long table and several chairs, all empty. Kyre stared, trying to assimilate the shock of such a familiar scene. And then he realised that the windows weren't true windows at all, but shapes cut from pure white quartz, opaque, giving on to nothing. And the tapestries weren't woven from flax or linen or wool, but from the sea's harvest; weed and coral strands and the skins of unnameable, water-dwelling things. The table and chairs were made from pieces of shell, exquisitely crafted and dovetailed in organic curves. And the great chair was not wood, but a single piece of jade hewn from the ocean bed.

Akrivir indicated the table. As they drew nearer Kyre could see that a place had been set before one of the chairs as though anticipating a solitary diner in the bizarre hall; around it were dishes brimming with what must have been food but looked, to Kyre, alien and strange. They reached the table and Akrivir drew out the chair. 'You might as well sit,' he said. 'And eat. You'll be waiting a while.'

Still dazed, Kyre obeyed; he picked up an ornately carved silver knife but made no attempt to do anything other than finger it abstractedly. Seeing that he wasn't about to serve himself Akrivir sighed, and, at random, heaped delicacies from the dishes on to the plate before him. Kyre paid no heed; he was too stunned by the bizarre anomalies of the treatment he was receiving at the hands of those who, in theory, were his mortal enemies. All he could do was stare around the fantastic hall, his eyes drinking in the shimmer of quartz, the cool glow of marble, the elusive glitter of small fountains – *fountains*? Yes: they weren't an illusion; he could see them along the walls, cascading down into small pools near the floor and reminding him that this was a world where water reigned unchallenged.

He was forced out of his fascinated trance by Akrivir's voice. 'Eat,' he said again. 'Nothing's poisoned.' To prove the point he picked up a handful of food and carelessly devoured it. Kyre came back to earth and, not knowing or caring what he chose or whether it might poison him or not, stabbed at something which looked like a small, spined fruit, and tasted it. The fruit gave as he bit, and an exquisitely fragile and elusive flavour filled his mouth, tingling on his tongue. He looked up, startled, and Akrivir suppressed a laugh before pouring a pale gold liquid from a ewer into the cup at his right elbow. 'Try that,' he said. 'You'll find they go well together.'

Again, a delicacy to the drink; whether it was strong or innocuous he didn't know, but the taste left him longing for more.

It was only when he heard footsteps that he realised his escort had turned away from the table and was leaving. Akrivir made no farewells, said not a word, but merely headed for the door; and Kyre rose quickly, thinking to call out to him. But before he could speak Akrivir stopped, looked back and shook his head, forestalling anything Kyre might have said. For a moment only there was something akin to sympathy in his eyes: then they hardened again and he strode away, leaving Kyre alone in the hall.

For some moments he stayed motionless, half on his feet in an awkward, ungainly posture, simply staring at the shell door while awareness of his solitude slowly dawned on him. It was a discomfiting sensation to be left alone in such vast and impassive surroundings, and slowly he subsided back on to the chair. His hosts – if that was an appropriate term for them – wanted him to remain here, and they wanted him to eat. Very well: he would play along with their wishes. It seemed he had little to lose; however royally he might be treated he was effectively a prisoner, a hostage for Gamora. He would wait, and let them reveal in their own good time what they wanted of him.

Kyre looked down at the food on his plate. Trying, with poor success, to quell the sick pounding of his heart he began, cautiously but deliberately, like a man who knows the meal before him might be his last, to eat.

Gamora gazed up wide-eyed at the woman beside her and said, her voice awed, 'I didn't think he'd come . . .'

Calthar met her stare and was amused by the admiring innocence she saw in the little girl's face. Aloud, she said, 'You must learn to trust me, child, and understand that what I say, I mean.'

Gamora blinked and peered again through the quartz window that overlooked the hall and its solitary occupant. The window was a device of Calthar's, showing an opaque face to the hall yet allowing any watcher to view the great chamber, albeit distortedly, from the far side, and the fact that something so simple was heralded as a work of genius by the citadel's council irritated the sorceress almost to distraction. Gamora pressed the palms of her hands against the quartz as though willing it to melt and allow her through. She seemed to be thinking hard: then suddenly she turned to Calthar again. '*Why* did he come?'

'For you, sweeting.' And that was no less than the truth. At first Calthar had doubted that Haven's new pet could be moved to fulfil Talliann's desire through the lure of this child. Though she'd given no hint of it to Hodek and his acolytes, she had had severe misgivings about the viability of her scheme to bring the creature to the citadel, and the ease with which it had been accomplished had surprised her.

But then, she'd reckoned without the qualities of Gamora herself . . .

Calthar had no maternal instincts, and scorned the idea. But in this child who stood at her side, this little princess of Haven and designated future leader of her sworn enemies, Calthar had seen something of the qualities that motivated other, less pragmatic souls, so often to their own downfall. Gamora's initial defiance, when she had woken to find herself in the citadel, had roused grudging respect in the sorceress; the child had more courage than Hodek and all his crew together. She hadn't cried, she hadn't screamed, she hadn't grovelled; she had simply demanded, with an imperious indignation that belied her years, to be released. Calthar had been very amused by her determination. And later, when she realised that she was a hostage and there would be no release, she had accepted the fact of her imprisonment with mature dignity. A child worthy of her station, Calthar thought. A pity that she had been born to the scum of Haven; in other circumstances she would have been ideal material for the sorceress's own schemes.

But there was nothing to be gained by wishing. Gamora had other uses; and second only to her value as a lure for Kyre was her ability to add to Calthar's knowledge of affairs in Haven, and now the pattern was beginning to make some sense.

Calthar was amused by the Haven rulers' fond delusion that they could turn the tide of events by invoking such a worthless prophecy. She knew enough about the true Sun-Hound's story to scorn the idea that any cipher created in his image could hope to live up to such a legend, and considered that, if her enemies were prepared to put faith in such a vain hope, they were greater fools even than she'd thought them. In truth, their new champion was more valuable to the citadel than he could ever hope to be to his creators – and now, with Gamora's innocent revelations to guide her, her plans were beginning to resolve exactly as she had wanted.

Gamora's voice broke in on her thoughts. 'My mother couldn't command Kyre,' the little girl said sombrely. 'She wanted to, but – ' and she broke off as she realised that Calthar was listening intently. Calthar saw doubt in the child's eyes and said gently,

'But what, little one?'

'Nothing.' Gamora hunched her shoulders and turned away, and Calthar felt an odd sense of satisfaction.

She let her hand come to rest lightly on Gamora's shoulder. 'No one controls your Sun-Hound, my sweeting. He came because of you.' She dropped to a crouch so that their faces were on a level. 'Haven't I told you how much he cares for you? Don't you believe me now?'

'I . . . ' Gamora bit her lip. 'I *think* so . . . '

'Look.' The priestess rose, drawing Gamora with her as she moved closer to the quartz window. 'He eats: he drinks. I promised you he would be treated as an honoured guest, and so it is.' She smiled thinly. 'Don't people keep the promises they make to you in Haven?'

Gamora's face closed and she hung her head mutely, unwilling to answer. Well enough; her silence was confirmation in itself, and helped to weaken any hostility she might have left.

Calthar gestured towards the window, drawing Gamora's hungry gaze. 'Well now. Don't you want to go and greet your Sun-Hound?'

Gamora looked up at her dubiously, and Calthar gave a soft laugh. 'I told you that I keep my promises. Come; we'll go together. You shall greet him first, and then I'll join you and meet him for myself. You've told me so much about him that I'm very eager to make his acquaintance.' She held out her hand and, after an uncertain pause, Gamora slipped her fingers into the sorceress's palm. Calthar smiled, and led her towards the door.

'*Kyre!*'

The familiar voice was so unexpected that Kyre started violently where he sat, knocking his cup over and spilling a small flood of wine across the table. Staring to the far end of the hall he saw a small, dark-haired figure racing towards him, arms outstretched, and in astonishment he rose and hastened to meet her.

'Kyre!' Gamora's headlong rush ended in a chaotic collision, and as he lifted her into the air she flung her arms round his neck, kissing him soundly on both cheeks. 'Oh, Kyre, you *came* for me! You're really *here!*'

'Princess!' He hugged her tightly, far more moved than he could have anticipated by her welcome. Then, remembering their circumstances, he set her down, held her at arm's length and looked carefully at her. 'Are you well, Gamora? Have you been hurt in any way?'

'No, Kyre, of course I'm not hurt!' She was laughing at his absurdity. 'This place is beautiful, *wonderful* – and the lady has been so kind to me!'

'Lady?' There was something in her look, something he couldn't quite pinpoint, and it made him uneasy. 'What lady?'

'She gave me this.' Gamora put a hand to her hair, where a circlet of exquisitely fashioned pieces of mother-of-pearl sat atop the chaos of dark curls. 'And this – ' She pointed to a similar necklace around her throat. 'And a bracelet and a ring too, and a new dress ... ' She stepped away from him and pirouetted, childishly coquettish. 'She says I'm a princess, and a princess should have a crown, and jewels, and beautiful clothes ... Kyre, do you think I look pretty?'

'Of course you do ... ' He fought back the doubts, knowing that she needed his reassurance. 'You're every inch a princess, Gamora. But – '

The child interrupted him, words spilling eagerly from

her lips. 'And she *said* you'd come here, if I wanted you to. She promised – and you did; so she was right!'

She, again and again . . . Kyre said: 'Who is *she*, little one? Who is this lady?'

At last Gamora stopped skipping and twirling. 'Her name is Calthar,' she said. 'She rules here, and everyone's afraid of her. I was afraid of her at first, but I don't think I am any more; or not very, anyway. She's so kind, Kyre, and she's shown me so many lovely things.' The flow of words paused, and the child gazed wide-eyed around the hall. 'I haven't been in here before. It's *lovely*.'

That look in her eyes again . . . there was something underlying the bubbling high spirits, and Kyre's growing misgivings grew. Before she could continue, he caught her under the arms and lifted her on to the empty chair next to his own, searching her face for the elusive clue. She smiled happily at him, and he forced himself to smile back.

'Gamora, you must forgive me – I've only been here a little while, and I don't really understand all you've told me. Princess, how did you come here? And *why*? All Haven is searching for you!'

Gamora's gaze slid away from his and she made a *moue* with her lips. 'I ran away,' she said flatly. One hand hovered over the dishes on the table; she selected a morsel and ate it. 'This is nice.'

Kyre persisted. 'Why did you run away?'

She shrugged, still not looking at him. 'Nobody took any notice of me. Father was busy, Mother was ill. Master Brigrandon was drunk again. And you didn't have any time for me.' At last she met his eyes, though obliquely, and her gaze was reproachful. 'And the shell told me that I could see some wonderful things, so I went.' Another shrug. 'Why shouldn't I?'

Though he had no memories of childhood, Kyre began to understand what had moved the little girl; the loneliness and desolation she must have felt. And he was largely to blame for it. Gently, he asked, 'But how did you get here, Gamora? Who brought you?'

Gamora paused with her hand, clutching another morsel of food, midway to her mouth. 'The other lady,' she said, and now she sounded dubious. 'The one with the black hair.' Then she looked up and met his gaze candidly. 'She's very strange, Kyre. I went out to the strand by the old temple, and I saw her there. She ran away and I tried to catch up with her, but when I did, she ... she was strange. She's very beautiful, but I think she must be ill. Calthar told me she's sometimes ill, and I mustn't mind her. But I think she brought me, though I can't really remember much about it.'

The picture Gamora painted was bizarre and disjointed; but one image caught in Kyre's mind. *The lady with the black hair* – he recalled the unearthly-looking girl he had seen on the shingle bar; the black-haired one who had run from him. And Calthar ... A vampire, DiMag had called her ...

'Gamora.' He took hold of the little girl's hands, knowing that he had to cut through her innocent enthusiasm, even if it meant shattering her happiness. 'Gamora, don't you understand where you are? These people are Haven's enemies!'

Her face clouded with uncertainty. 'That's what everyone's always *said*. But – '

'It's the truth! Your father and mother are half out of their minds with fear for your safety – how d'you think they'd feel if they knew you were in their enemies' stronghold?'

'Oh, Kyre ... ' Gamora's eyes were suddenly tragic. 'You don't *understand*. Calthar says – '

He interrupted sternly. 'Calthar says. Why should you trust Calthar?'

'Because she's *kind* to me! She made promises, and she *kept* them. You've got to meet her, Kyre, then you'll see!'

And suddenly he knew what was wrong. Gamora's

voice, her inflections, her gestures, were all as he knew them. But beneath the sparkle in her eyes was a blankness, an emptiness, as though all she had ever known or believed or experienced had been leached from her mind.

Gamora was bewitched ...

'I've told Calthar all about you,' the child went on eagerly. 'She's waiting to meet you – ' she screwed her head round at an impossible angle, looking towards the far end of the hall, then cried delightedly, 'Here she is!'

Kyre looked up, and saw that a tall figure had silently entered the hall and was moving towards them. By some means which he couldn't guess at, Calthar had judged her moment perfectly. The precision of her entrance made something deep within him turn as cold as ice.

Gamora turned back to him, her face lit with triumph. 'Now you'll see, Kyre – *now* you'll see!'

Kyre rose as Calthar approached. The movement was unconscious; an involuntary combining of courtesy with the realisation that he didn't want to be at a disadvantage when face to face with her. Impressions assailed him: her height – she was as tall as he was; the faintly phosphorescent sheen of her skin; the nimbus of shimmering silver hair; her easy but reptilian grace; the gaunt yet voluptuous body beneath the tatters of the ancient robe. And her eyes. They were molten fire in a face that was, by a crazed paradox, repulsively beautiful; they drew Kyre as surely as if she'd put him under a spell with one flick of her fingers. Then the hypnotic moment broke as Calthar stopped two paces from Kyre and extended her hand.

'Sun-Hound. Welcome to our citadel.'

Her voice was a throaty contralto, and unexpectedly warm. Kyre joined his fingers with hers – and as they made contact, he felt something in her touch that sent a shivering cascade of sharp needles through all the nerves in his spine. She had real power, there could be no doubt of it; the way she regarded him made him feel that her eyes saw far deeper than the planes and contours of his face.

Gamora had scrambled down from her chair, and now skipped to the sorceress's side. 'Isn't he handsome, Calthar? Isn't he just the way I told you?' She looked quickly from one to the other, then added with satisfied finality, 'I'm going to marry him when I grow up.'

Over the little girl's head Calthar caught Kyre's eye, and there was amusement in her wry smile. 'I'm sure he'll make you a worthy consort, sweeting,' she said, and her use of the affectionate term chilled Kyre's blood.

Calthar pulled out a chair and sat down with sinuous grace. She continued to study Kyre for a few moments more, then said: 'Gamora has told me a great deal about you, Sun-Hound. It seems that you have at least one loyal and true friend in Haven.'

Kyre glanced sidelong at the child, wondering just how much she had told this woman. 'I know,' he said.

'And in fact,' Calthar continued, 'it was for her sake and her sake alone that you were willing to come to the citadel. Am I right?'

'Yes.' He had nothing to gain from hiding the truth.

She smiled. 'Then by showing your loyalty to the little princess, you've unwittingly done me a great service, Kyre.' Turning, she reached out to stroke Gamora's hair. 'Sweeting, I want to talk to your Sun-Hound, and it's talk that would bore you. In your room there's a present waiting for you; a new plaything. Why don't you go along and see what it is, and I'll bring Kyre back to you later.'

Conflicting desires made Gamora hesitate. She wanted to stay, but ... 'A present?' she asked uncertainly. 'For me?'

'Waiting for you in your room. Go and see.'

'Yes ... ' Curiosity overcame all other considerations. 'Yes, I will.' Gamora smiled shyly at Kyre, then left the table and ran towards the door. Half way across the hall she remembered her dignity and slowed to a careful walk, pausing once to look back over her shoulder and wave. Just for a moment he saw again that utter blankness in her look: then the shell door closed behind her and he was alone with Calthar.

And far away, in Haven, a sixth sense brought to his mind the sound of Simorh screaming . . .

Chapter 13

Calthar smiled, stretching out her long legs as she reclined in the chair next to Kyre. 'As I said a few moments ago, you've done me a great service, Sun-Hound.'

Kyre watched her, fascinated by her easy grace yet too wary to unbend. 'My service was to Gamora,' he replied shortly.

She shrugged a concession. 'From your point of view, yes; I won't argue with that. But there's someone else here to whom your presence is equally important. And what matters to her, matters to me.' She began to pace again. 'To all intents and purposes, Kyre, I alone rule in the citadel. But everything I do, everything I decree, every move I make, is for the sole sake of Talliann.'

Black hair and a deadly white face; the shingle strand and the cold stare of the Hag; a girl he knew, and yet did not recognise ... The image passed fleetingly through his mind and the shock of it must have shown on his face, for Calthar laughed softly.

'Yes: it was Talliann you saw on the bar near the ruined temple.'

She saw immediately that the gamble she had taken was paying off. She knew the power Talliann possessed, however innocently or erratically it might be wielded; her one doubt had been as to whether the girl's influence could snare Haven's champion as easily as it had snared her own people. Now, the doubt was assuaged.

She coiled about into a new posture on the chair, enjoying his inability to stop staring at her. 'Talliann wants to see you again, Kyre, and my first desire is to please her. That's why you come to us as a guest – '

'Guest?' The blatant contradiction snapped Kyre out of his trance, and the spell of Calthar's fascination broke as he interrupted her angrily. 'I hardly think so! Your emissary made it clear that Gamora's safety depends on my compliance – and that message was uncivilly stressed by another of your minions when I was hauled out of the sea. Is that your idea of how a benevolent host should behave?'

'What other device would have persuaded you here of your own free will? Kyre, the little princess is in no danger: she never has been. I used her to lure you here, but believe me, that is the full extent of my crime!'

She was lying. The emptiness behind Gamora's bright eyes had told him the real truth. And yet, despite what he knew, Kyre's interest was aroused beyond his ability to stem it. Betraying nothing of his inner turmoil in his voice, he asked, 'Why should I be important to Talliann?'

Calthar made a display of hesitating before she replied: 'Because I believe you may be able to help her.'

'*Help* her . . . ? Lady,' he said carefully, 'I came here from Haven, the city of your enemies. I'm no friend to you, nor to your Talliann. I owe you nothing; I have nothing that you can possibly want. Why should I be able – even if I were willing – to help either of you?'

It was the reaction Calthar had expected: she hid her amusement and leaned towards him. He didn't back away – that pleased her – but when she laid a long-nailed hand on his arm she felt the skin beneath her fingers flinch involuntarily.

'Are we your enemies?' she asked, quite gently. 'Since your arrival here you've met with no violence, no unkindness, no threat: nothing that suggests hatred.' She saw reluctant confirmation in his face, and continued, 'You may be *from* Haven, Kyre, but you're not *of* Haven; that much I know from Gamora. You owe loyalty only to those who have proved themselves your friends. And by bringing you to our citadel, I'm backing my belief that you're wise enough to acknowledge that.'

He couldn't deny that her argument was valid. He'd heard only Haven's side of the conflict between the two cities; he knew nothing of the rights and wrongs surrounding the grievances that had begun the unending war. Haven had done him few favours so far: and then there was Talliann. He savoured the name. It was familiar, strangely familiar. *Talliann* . . .

Calthar saw the seeds of uncertainty in his mind and felt the inner pleasure of vindication. She said, softly and with a hint of apparent reluctance: 'I'm also gambling on my instict that you were – shall we say, not entirely unaffected by your first meeting with Talliann, and that her wellbeing might be of some interest to you.'

Her eyes, in the hall's peculiar light, seemed to have caught fire, and Kyre felt something contract and constrict within him. Calthar had struck to the heart of his greatest weakness. That first encounter, brief though it had been, haunted him: he could still recall every detail of the shock of recognition, of realising that he *knew* her. Somehow, Talliann held a key to his lost identity – and now he had the chance to see her again. Despite his fears for Gamora, despite the danger they might both be in, he couldn't turn his back on that chance.

His pulse had quickened and there was a suffocating sensation in his throat. He said: 'You say I might help her. But why should she need my help?'

Calthar sighed, and looked down at her own bare feet. 'Because, Kyre, Talliann is afflicted.'

'Afflicted . . . ?'

'It's not a word I like using, but I can think of nothing better,' Calthar continued. 'She is . . . childlike. Given to moods and whims that no one else can fathom; moved to joy or grief or fury by random emotions that even I can't begin to divine.' She pursed her mouth painfully.

'At times she's lucid enough, but more often than not her mind is like a whirlpool that she can't control. For her own safety she has to be constantly attended and watched lest she unwittingly do some mischief to herself. She has no worldliness, and not the smallest sense of personal danger.'

'Are you saying she's mad?'

The sorceress shook her head emphatically. 'No. Flawed, perhaps; but not mad.' She looked up again and met his eyes with apparent candour. 'Talliann is like a daughter to me. Her wellbeing and her happiness matter more to all of us than any other consideration.' *And that*, she thought with private amusement, *is no less than the truth*! 'I admit to you, Kyre, that I don't understand her reasons for wanting you here. But you have had a very profound effect on her; when she speaks of you she speaks more coherently than at any other time; and that gives me hope.' Her voice took on an angry edge as she added, 'Do you really think I would allow Haven's prized champion free run of my citadel without a vital reason?'

That challenge forced a new twist on Kyre's perspectives. He couldn't trust her, *dared* not trust her; yet what she said had a seductive kind of logic. And the fascination, the chilling lure that Talliann held for him, weakened his resolve still further.

His face, as he struggled to reconcile conflicting thoughts, was an open book to Calthar. She moved closer to him, until they were mere inches apart.

'I won't try to influence you against your will, Kyre,' she said softly. 'You can leave the citadel now and go back to Haven, if that's what you want: no one here will prevent you. But what have you to lose by one meeting with Talliann?'

She knew she was taking a risk; if he was contrary enough to call her bluff, then her plans would need rapid alteration. But her judgement was almost always sure, and it proved so again. Kyre had no grounds for arguing with her. And he *wanted* to see the girl.

'Very well. If it'll please Talliann, I'll agree to it.' He managed a faint, wry smile. 'As you say, what have I to lose?'

To Kyre's inexpressible relief, the way to Talliann's sanctum didn't involve a second crossing of the dizzying bridge over the abyss. It was a short and simple route, the only anomaly being the utter absence of any other soul to see them go by. No curious faces gazing from doorways, no passers-by pausing to point and whisper to each other, no ingenuously gaping children drawn quickly out of his reach by anxious parents. Word of a stranger's presence in the citadel must be widely abroad by now, but no one came near them.

They climbed stairs, Calthar moving with such easy agility that he was hard pressed to keep up with her, and finally the stairs ended before yet another shell door. As it swung open, Kyre felt as though his stomach had inverted itself within him. The sickness of doubt, of fear – but most of all, of a ravening anticipation. Cool, blue light poured out from beyond the door, and shapes moved within it like phantoms, coming towards them. He saw the shimmer of wide green eyes, the outlines of young bodies, filmy shifts, pale, flowing hair: then the four girls who guarded Talliann's sanctum moved aside like a tide ebbing, bowing before Calthar. Kyre couldn't be sure whether or not he had imagined the flicker of stark terror in their eyes before they lowered their gazes and fled.

The cavern beyond the door was like something from a bizarre dream. Around the curving walls, abalone reflected an incredible montage of images, distorting colour and perspective. Stalactites speared down from the roof and were multiplied a hundredfold by the mirrored surfaces. Disorientated, Kyre let Calthar take hold of his hand and lead him deeper into the incredible maze: then, at the back of the cavern, something moved independently of the reflections.

She stood half way up a short flight of uneven steps where the floor rose steeply at the back of the cavern. Black hair, hollow eyes, a faint sound like a child's first, shivering breath –

She saw them, and came down the steps so fast that she almost lost her footing and fell. Her body was young and lithe, and modest in a grey shift that fell to her ankles. For the first time Kyre was able to look long and clearly at her, and he felt something within him constrict as the shock of recognition renewed itself. The small, fragile face, the unclipped black hair falling like ragged silk about her shoulders, the wide, deep eyes, dark as her hair was ... She wasn't truly beautiful – Simorh unencumbered by bitterness and illness would have been far lovelier – yet she was more familiar to Kyre than anyone or anything he had encountered since he had been brought to this world.

But Talliann ignored him. Instead, she stopped five paces from Calthar, her slight frame shaking with anger.

'*Where have you been*?' Talliann's voice was shrill and she wrung her hands together as though violently washing them. 'You *told* me, you *promised* me; you –' and she stopped as, with a silent gesture, Calthar indicated the man at her side.

Talliann swung round, and focused on Kyre for the first time. Her eyes were like twin lunar eclipses, vast black pupils surrounded by a glittering silver corona. For a terrible moment Kyre felt as though they were sucking out his soul: then the girl's lips parted to reveal sharp, even teeth as her breath caught in her throat.

'You've come back ... ' She whispered the words as though they were some dreadful, secret talisman, and as she continued to stare at him she began to shiver feverishly. Then she put a hand to her mouth, biting at her knuckles; and Kyre was shocked to see bright blood trickle down her wrist –

'Talliann!' Calthar spoke sharply, as if reprimanding

a disobedient child, then when Talliann paid no heed the sorceress swore volubly. One long-nailed hand snaked out and pulled Talliann's arm forcibly away from her mouth. 'Stop that!' She glanced quickly at Kyre, and her voice changed. 'See your guest, sweeting. He came, as you wanted him to.'

Talliann's mouth puckered. She looked uneasily from Calthar to Kyre, back to Calthar again, and whispered: 'Thank you . . . '

There was an uncomfortable silence. Then Calthar said: 'Well?'

Talliann looked at her blankly.

'You wanted to see him, child. He's here.' Impatience tinged Calthar's voice. 'Don't you have anything else to say?'

Talliann's eyes took their fill of Kyre again, until he had to look away from her hollow stare. She wiped her bloodied hand thoughtlessly on her shift. 'No,' she said flatly.

Calthar sighed as the girl turned her head away. 'I feared something like this might happen,' she said softly. 'Best leave her.'

'*No –* ' The protest was involuntary, and had little to do with the sorceress's admonition. In a single moment Talliann had taken Kyre's soul and then rejected him, and the sense of loss was almost beyond bearing.

'Yes, Kyre.' Calthar drew him back, towards the door. 'You can do nothing for her at this moment. Leave her, and in a while she'll recover.' She glanced at the girl, who hadn't moved a muscle but stood rigid, the picture of mute stubbornness. 'She knew of your arrival, but the shock of seeing you . . . ' she shrugged, leaving the sentence unfinished.

He could only acquiesce. Calthar led him towards the door, and as they reached it he hesitated, looking back. Talliann had turned her head, and was staring over her shoulder at him. Her blank expression had vanished, replaced by a fearful and painfully intelligent urgency, and she mouthed something that Calthar couldn't see. Kyre frowned, not comprehending, and might have spoken; but she shook her head frantically, a plea for secrecy and silence, and hastily turned away.

Calthar hadn't noticed the swift exchange. As she stood back to usher Kyre through the door, she glanced briefly over her shoulder. Talliann was standing with her back to them, head bowed, immobile. Calthar smiled faintly, and left the chamber.

As always when Calthar stalked the citadel's corridors, no one impeded her progress. Young and old alike studiously avoided crossing her path, withdrawing into doorways or side streets, moving back to the edges of the wider public areas as she passed by. Voices were lowered to whispers at her approach and faces were averted: no one wanted to catch her eye for fear of also attracting her volatile and unpredictable temper.

But for once they needn't have worried, for Calthar was lost in thought. She had seen Kyre escorted from Talliann's chambers to the unused stateroom that she had ordered prepared for him; the room had housed a retired but still respected military adviser until old age had recently sent him to his final rest, and the former dwelling of a high-ranker was ideal for an apparently honoured guest.

Calthar intended to maintain that particular charade for the time being, despite the grumblings of Hodek and some of the other senior councillors. Haven's new pet had aroused her curiosity, for Gamora's picture of him had been far from accurate. Whatever else he might be, Kyre was not a sorcerously-created shell. Had he been so, Calthar would have recognised the signs immediately; but this man had a will, a personality, a self-motivation that no cipher could ever possess. That led her to draw two possible conclusions: that the information Gamora had given her was wrong – which she wasn't inclined to believe – or that Kyre wasn't what his professed creators had expected.

So, then, if this new Sun-Hound wasn't a cipher of the original, what was he? A number of possibilities had occurred to Calthar, but none of them satisfied her. She wanted – *needed* – to learn more. And she suspected that Talliann might hold the clue.

Calthar hadn't been deceived by the girl's behaviour at the fiasco of a meeting; but Talliann's motive in behaving as she had done was another matter. Her fascination with Haven's pet bordered on obsession – Calthar had never known her to react in such a way to anything before, and the possible implications intrigued her. Since the moment of her arrival in the citadel Talliann had been flawed, and even the power of the Mothers hadn't been able to unravel the mystery of her strangeness. Hers was the one soul in the citadel that Calthar couldn't read easily, and yet within Talliann resided a power on which the sorceress had come to depend. As a medium, the girl was unsurpassed; but though Calthar could influence her – by terror if by no other means – and channel power through her to her own ends, she needed Talliann's co-operation if such sorcery was to achieve its full potential. Usually her co-operation was simple enough to secure, but occasionally something in Talliann rebelled, and she would make some demand, something irrational, incomprehensible, which must be fulfilled before she would be compliant again. That particular trait lay at the root of Calthar's contradictory feelings towards the girl: on the one hand Talliann was a prize, a jewel, to be cherished and protected; on the other, the sorceress violently resented her, envying the fundamental hold that she exercised, however unwittingly, over all around her. Without Talliann to impede her, Calthar could fulfil her own ambitions to rule unchallenged. Yet those same ambitions relied on Talliann's innate powers. There were other means, other methods, but they were more perilous; and to destroy Talliann, as in dark moments

Calthar yearned to do, would be to destroy one of the roots of her own strength.

But now Haven's new champion had come into the picture and had touched something deep within Talliann: so much so that the girl's wellbeing and sanity seemed to depend on his presence in the citadel. That was what intrigued Calthar most of all. There was no logic, even by Talliann's bizarre standards, in her sudden preoccupation, and the sorceress could only surmise that she had sensed something within Kyre that had so far eluded her own judgement. Trying to wring that information from Talliann would be a fruitless exercise, as what she didn't know she couldn't tell: she'd do better, Calthar thought, to make Kyre her target. His wouldn't be an easy mind to manipulate, but in Talliann and Gamora she had in her possession two invaluable weapons. With care, and a modicum of manipulation at the right moment, she might create for herself an advantage that would ensure her enemies' final downfall. And she had waited a long, long time for that.

Talliann had been waiting, tense with impatience, when Akrivir cautiously opened the door of her sanctum. He had hardly been able to believe the nature of the message that had reached him via one of her servant girls, suspecting that either Calthar or his father might be playing some joke at his expense. But Calthar didn't indulge in petty games, and even Hodek was unlikely to trouble himself with such a small spite. No: Akrivir believed that the summons must be genuine – and one look at Talliann's pale face as he entered the cavern had confirmed it.

But when he heard what it was she wanted of him, the stirrings of faint hope which had moved within him died. Her plea was simple. And he didn't want to do it.

She stood before him now, close enough for him to have reached out and taken hold of her hands, though he made no attempt to do so. He was staring at the floor, not wanting her to see what was in his eyes, and he felt as though invisible fingers had taken hold of the muscles in his chest and were squeezing them. To do what Talliann asked of him would be to admit finally to what he had always subconsciously known: that she was not, and could never be, for him.

She was waiting for an answer, and bleakly Akrivir realised that he couldn't refuse her. Whatever the outcome, whatever blow it might deal to his own dreams, he cared enough for Talliann to help her in any way he could.

She said, her voice desparate, 'I *have* to see him, Akrivir. I *must* speak with him alone, without Calthar knowing.' She turned away. 'You're the only one I can trust.' A pause. 'I'm sorry.'

So she understood. He hadn't realised it, and the knowledge was both a comfort and a bitter irony. He couldn't let her down: she was prepared to put her trust in him, knowing the risk she ran, and if he could do no more, he could at least justify her faith in him.

He stepped forward and, knowing that she'd forgive his presumption, laid his hands lightly on her shoulders. 'I'll bring him, Talliann,' he said gently. 'And I'll make sure that no one knows of it.'

She swung round to face him again, her dark eyes wide with gratitude – and, he thought, with sympathy. 'I don't know what to say. Thank you, Akrivir.' Her hands came to rest on his arms. 'You're a true friend.'

He smiled wryly. 'I hope I always will be.'

The quarters that had been assigned to him were, Kyre was forced to admit, rooms fit for an honoured guest. No comfort had been spared; he had a huge bed liberally draped with woven covers, a table and chair made of what looked like coral and inlaid with abalone, floor coverings that were warm to his bare feet, tapestries on the walls, even a small fount of sweet water playing into a pearl-lined pool, though how the sea-dwellers could obtain fresh water in this vast undersea fortress he couldn't imagine. He wanted for nothing ... save the answers to some very disturbing questions.

The last look Talliann had given him, and her failed attempt to convey a message, flickered, knifelike in his brain. On the strand, when he had first set eyes on her, a thread of his uncharted memory had been twisted violently to the surface, and this second confrontation had painfully and unnervingly confirmed it. Now he knew that Talliann in her turn had recognised him, but she had been anxious not to reveal that fact to Calthar. That didn't fit with the image of Talliann's protector, friend and mentor that Calthar claimed for herself; but it *did* fit, all too well, with Kyre's instinctive mistrust of the sorceress and her motives.

He wanted to see Talliann again – it was more than a desire; it was an aching need inside him. But he was also aware of the value of caution: and one barrier was the presence of Gamora.

Kyre glanced sidelong at the little girl, who sat beside him happily devouring the remains of a tray of food. It seemed that she had only to ask for something and it was done: her wish to see Kyre's quarters and then share the meal prepared for him had been granted instantly, and when she had expressed dissatisfaction with his clothes, which, though dried out, were stained and stiffened with sea-water, new garments had been brought for him immediately, made from a cool, thin silver-blue fabric, and Gamora had triumphantly placed one of the narrow twisted-shell circlets favoured by many of the male sea-folk on his head, declaring that now he looked as fine as she did. It was an exaggeration: for Calthar had spared nothing in fulfilling her promise to make Gamora every inch a princess. She wore a sea-green and silver gown in the elaborate style of citadel noblewomen, and a filigree of silver threads had been twisted cunningly through her hair so that her bobbing curls glittered when she moved. Even her own father and mother in Haven would never have dreamed of granting her such luxuries; they would have been no more than an unfulfilled dream in the child's mind.

But Kyre knew Gamora well enough to realise that the lure of such trappings, however desirable they might be, could never undo the conditioning that had taught her to hate the sea-dwellers with as much passion as anyone else in Haven. Her own father, whom she loved, had been crippled by them; though she was a baby in her cradle at the time, she had been brought up with the story of the Dead Night battle that had buried half of the city, and its inhabitants with it, beneath the sand of the bay. Kyre himself had been shocked by the eager light in her eyes when she heard of DiMag's slaying of the captured sea-warrior. No: it would take far more than a green and silver gown and the shimmer of abalone to make Gamora forget her own heritage.

Yet now, in Gamora's eyes, Calthar could do no wrong: and that gave Kyre a chilling insight into the strength of the bewitchment the sorceress had cast over the little girl.

He could imagine how easy a target a child like Gamora must have been for Calthar's spellbinding. For a while, as he talked with the sorceress in the great hall, he too had come close to succumbing to the allure of this strangely beautiful place and its fey-looking inhabitants, and he could understand the effect it must have had on the mind of a lonely, imaginative child. Haven by comparison was an ironically-named travesty, at least on the surface; he had seen nothing of beauty within those crumbling walls, or in the minds of its people. Simorh, vicious and embittered; DiMag with his warped and unpredictable moods; Vaoran, ambitious, untrustworthy; even old Brigrandon, who preferred the relief of a drunken stupor to the demands of cold reality . . . the contrast with what he had seen in the sea-citadel was acute –

And invidious. A man dying of thirst in a desert might

sell his soul for the chance to find an oasis. But all too often, the oasis proved to be nothing more than a mirage.

'Don't you think so, Kyre? Don't you?'

Gamora's voice at his elbow broke the web of his concentration. He looked down to find that she had finished the last of the food and was watching him eagerly.

His train of thought fled. 'I'm sorry, princess. What did you say?'

She pouted. 'People *never* listen to me. Except for Calthar: she does. I *said*, don't you think the great hall here is so much nicer than at home?'

He forced himself to smile at her. 'It's very beautiful, yes.'

'All those fountains, and the windows that aren't really windows at all but quartz. And the tapestries aren't faded the way all of ours are.' She swallowed a last morsel that she'd been chewing and rolled her eyes appreciatively at the taste. 'When I grow up, I'll have fountains like those.'

Kyre couldn't bring himself to meet her gaze and see again the emptiness behind the look in her eyes. This hiatus had to be broken – but he was no sorcerer; he could do nothing against Calthar's skills. There must be another way . . .

He was about to make some inconsequential reply to Gamora's last remark when a sound alerted him, and he turned quickly to see the door swinging open. Expecting a servant, he froze when, instead, he saw Akrivir on the threshold.

'Sun-Hound.' Akrivir nodded to him, and forced a quick smile for Gamora, who was watching him with interest. His eyes, as he looked at the little girl, were wary.

'Come in.' Kyre rose, wondering what could have brought the young warrior to his room. 'Join us.'

'Thank you, but I – haven't the time.' Akrivir darted another look towards Gamora, and suddenly Kyre realised what he was trying, silently, to convey. He took a step forward. 'You wanted to speak to me?'

'Yes. I won't detain you for more than a few moments.'

Gamora had already begun to lose interest in the exchange, and Kyre walked to the door. Akrivir caught his arm, drawing him outside, and pulled the door to behind them so that they were hidden from the child's view. He glanced swiftly in both directions, then said without preamble: 'I bring a message from Talliann. She wants to see you, and it's vital that Calthar shouldn't know of it.'

Kyre's pulse quickened. 'When?'

'As soon as possible.' Akrivir hesitated, and Kyre saw an odd mixture of resentment and fellow-feeling in his blue eyes. 'I'll take you to her myself: but there's a problem.' He nodded back towards the room. 'The child.'

'She isn't – ' Kyre began, but Akrivir cut him short, gripping his sleeve.

'You know as well as I do what Calthar's done to her!' Undisguised hatred flared in his voice momentarily before he got himself under control again. 'She can't be trusted. The Hag alone knows it isn't her fault, but if she knows anything she may betray you.' He bit his lower lip. 'I'll do anything to help Talliann, but I don't want to die doing it!'

Kyre realised abruptly what lay behind Akrivir's blend of friendship and hostility towards him, and suddenly he felt shamed. Akrivir must be a true friend indeed if he was prepared to sacrifice his own hopes for Talliann's sake – and it meant that he was the one inhabitant of this citadel whom Kyre could trust without reservation.

He eased the door open a crack and looked into the room. Gamora's small head was drooping over the table; as he watched, she yawned widely, seemingly hardly aware of what she did, and slumped further forward.

'She's falling asleep,' he said quietly, then looked at the other man again. 'If I put her to bed, she won't wake for some hours. I can come with you now.'

Akrivir didn't meet his gaze for a few moments, and when he did his eyes were intense. 'Very well. But on one condition.'

'Name it.'

'I want your promise that you'll do nothing that could harm or endanger Talliann in any way.' He paused. 'For I tell you now, Sun-Hound; if you hurt her, I'll kill you.' He smiled, jerkily and without humour. 'That's my promise.'

Kyre said: 'I'd never harm Talliann, Akrivir. And I think you know it, or you wouldn't be here now.'

Akrivir continued to stare at him for a while. Then he nodded, acknowledging the tacit understanding between them.

'I should hate you, Kyre,' he said. 'But if you can help Talliann, there'll be no enmity between us.' And with that he turned away. 'I'll wait for you at the end of the passage.'

Kyre returned to his room feeling tense with excitement. Gamora was by now asleep; the sound sleep of a happily exhausted child; and she didn't stir as he lifted her from her chair and carried her to his own bed. Laying her down, he covered her with a blanket and stood for a moment gazing down at her with sad affection. Then – he couldn't name the emotion that moved him, but had to make the gesture, however small – he bent down and kissed her forehead.

'Sleep well, little princess.' His voice was a whisper. 'I'll open your eyes, and restore all that's been lost to you. I swear it.'

Akrivir led Kyre on a complex and clearly little-used route to Talliann's sanctum, and in the distance he could hear the murmuring sounds of the citadel's great warren about its business. Since his arrival here he had lost all sense of time; without the strictures of night and day to contain it, it seemed that the sea-dwellers' stronghold never rested, and it could have been noon or deep night in the world outside for all the difference it made.

At first they hastened along in silence. Akrivir was constantly alert for any sign of movement ahead or behind, and Kyre felt it prudent to say nothing. But there was one unanswered question which wouldn't let him alone, and at last he had to ask it.

'Akrivir – why are you doing this?'

The young man looked back over his shoulder, surprised, and slowed his pace. 'For Talliann,' he said shortly. 'Because she wants it – and because I think you may be able to help her where I've failed.'

Kyre stopped, suddenly suspicious: he'd heard almost those exact words before. 'That's what Calthar told me,' he said. 'And she – '

Akrivir interrupted him with a laugh, a short, sharp bark that conveyed cynical disgust. 'Oh yes: I'm sure she did!' He stepped closer to Kyre, gripping his upper arm. 'If you take anything that Calthar says at face value, then you're running your head into a noose!'

Pure loathing burned in his eyes, and Kyre said, 'Do you hate her so much?'

'*Hate* her?' Akrivir echoed. He hunched his shoulders, staring at Kyre and apparently weighing the risks of revealing what he wanted to say. 'If I could kill her, Kyre, if I could eradicate her filthy corruption from this citadel, I wouldn't hesitate for one instant!' He turned, started to walk on but more slowly. 'She isn't the only cancer that I want to cut from our city; but she's the most malignant.' Furious emotion made his voice shake. 'I wouldn't care about what she's done to me; I can live with that if I must. But Talliann ... '

'What about Talliann?'

'Don't be a fool!' Akrivir said ferociously. 'You've seen it for yourself! Talliann's a prisoner – Calthar keeps her that way because it suits her machinations, and any tales she spins you about Talliann being like a daughter to her are lies. Calthar *uses* her, just as she's using your little princess, and trying to use you. She's far more dangerous than you know, Sun-Hound. And there's not a living soul in this citadel who dares speak against her.'

Slowly, the pieces of the jigsaw were beginning to fit together ... More quietly, Kyre asked, 'And what of you, Akrivir? What has she done to you?'

He made a dismissive gesture. 'It's an old tale now, and it doesn't bear repeating. Besides, it's no longer relevant: it's Talliann who matters.' Abruptly he stopped walking and turned to Kyre again. His blue eyes were blazing, and Kyre saw fear, hope and bitter, impotent anger in his look.

Akrivir said: 'Get her away from the citadel, Kyre. Get her away from Calthar's influence, before she's destroyed by it. It's her only hope. It's the only hope for us all!' And he swung round and strode on.

Kyre hastened after him, but the words that came to his tongue died unspoken. He realised that to make such a plea had cost Akrivir dearly: but the young warrior's outburst had confirmed his own suspicions beyond all doubt. Talliann, Gamora, himself – all victims of Calthar's scheming.

But why? he asked himself. *What did the sorceress mean to gain from them*?

They were climbing a flight of stairs, and he realised that Talliann's door lay directly ahead of them. He *had* to know more –

'Akrivir.' He caught his companion's arm, halting him, and spoke in an urgent whisper. 'What does Calthar plan to do?'

Akrivir looked back. 'Ask Talliann about the Great Conjunction,' he said flatly. 'And if you can, believe me when I tell you that I'd kill Calthar to stop it if I could.' He took the last few steps two at a time, and laid his hand on the shell door. 'Go to her, Kyre. Talk to her. Help her.' Their eyes met briefly, then Akrivir looked away. 'I'll be waiting.'

Cool, blue light washed over Kyre as he stepped through Talliann's door. The mirrorlike walls of the cavern played tricks on his eyes; as he moved, strange reflections skipped among the stalactites and he tensed, anticipating a challenge. None came . . . and then he realised that one of the reflections wasn't a reflection at all.

She moved quickly towards him, eyes widening with eager recognition – then stopped, like a frightened animal surprised far from the safety of its nest. Her voice was fearful.

'Akrivir brought you?'

'Yes.' Kyre gazed at her as unfamiliar emotions moved within him.

She nodded. 'Did anyone see you? Are you sure you weren't followed?'

'As sure as I can be.' He closed the door behind him, feeling his pulse quicken anew.

For a moment Talliann seemed to be struggling to find words, then abruptly she said: 'He was the only one I could trust, and I was so afraid of Calthar finding out . . . Kyre, I have to talk to you.'

He took her hands, wanting to reassure her: she was wary of him, and acutely aware of the risk she was taking in trusting him. He wished he could find a way to tell her that he shared her fears.

'We may have very little time,' she said. 'Calthar never sleeps: she may come here at any time.' She glanced again towards the door. 'Often I can sense when she's near, but not always.'

'There's so much I want to ask you,' Kyre told her. 'Since I saw you on the strand by the ruined temple, I've – '

'I know. I felt it, too.' Her hungry gaze searched his face. 'I know you, Kyre. I don't know who you are, but I *know* you. And my dreams – '

'Dreams?' Something clutched at his nerve-ends.

She nodded. 'I've had those dreams for as long as I can remember. They're like . . . ' she hesitated, 'like an omen, a portent. Something I must tell you, and something I must do.' She looked at him again, her gaze painfully candid. 'I forget so much, Kyre, and my mind is often confused – but I always remember those dreams. *Always*.'

Her fingers clenched in his grasp. He said nothing, sensing that there was more she wanted to impart and that she needed to take her own time. But his stomach was churning with excitement.

'I've often slipped away from the citadel, and gone to the bay where the ruin is,' she said at last, the words coming more hurriedly now. 'I've seen the town lights glowing through the fog, and I've wanted so much to go there, but I couldn't. *Dared* not. Yet I knew that was where I'd find you, Kyre. And I so much needed to tell you . . . ' she shook her head, bereft of further explanation, and he prompted gently,

'Tell me what?'

'What the dreams have warned me I must tell you. About Calthar. About what she means to do, what she *will* do, unless'. . . ' She stopped again, drew a painful, gasping breath, then calmed herself with an effort.

'You must leave here, Kyre,' she said urgently. 'You must return to Haven, and warn them, and help them.' She bit her lip. 'In five nights from now, the Great Conjunction will occur. Do you know what that means?'

She echoed what Akrivir had said, what he had told Kyre to ask her: and he remembered the Dead Night of which DiMag had spoken with such bitter loathing. 'It's the night when the moon throws a path of light direct to Haven's portal. There'll be a battle – '

'No,' Talliann said quickly. 'Not *a* battle. *The* battle: the final confrontation. That's what Calthar means it to be. She says Haven is so weakened, so racked with internal conflict, that it can't hope to stand against the

.

power of the Hag.' Her teeth clenched, as though the
next words were painful to her. 'Calthar will send that
power against Haven on the night of the Conjunction.
And I shall be the medium through which she wields it.'

'*You*?' Kyre was stunned.

'Yes.' Talliann's gaze was hollow. 'Don't you understand? Calthar has told you that I'm – afflicted, she
calls it. But this thing, this force, that sometimes
possesses me – it isn't madness. It's the Hag. And it's
Calthar's doing. I'm her puppet; I've been her puppet
since I came to the citadel. She binds me by the power
of the Hag, and she uses me to bring that power to
manifestation. I'm the key to her strength.'

Kyre stared at her as Akrivir's cryptic words suddenly
and shockingly made sense. A prisoner, an unwilling
victim of Calthar's machinations – now he understood
Akrivir's bitterness, and the young warrior's urgent plea
for him to get Talliann out of the citadel. He put his arms
around the girl, wanting to comfort her and soothe the
distress that her words had aroused. She pressed herself
closely against him, her body rigid with tension, fighting
against tears.

'I don't want it to happen,' she said desperately. Her
voice was muffled by emotion, and he felt her fists
clench against his chest. 'I want to stop it, but I can't;
my will isn't strong enough. But you ... ' She
shuddered, then looked up at him. 'You can stand
against Calthar. That's what the dreams have been
telling me. You must go back to Haven, and you must
help them!'

Again he remembered what Akrivir had said, and in
that moment he knew that no power in the world would
persuade him to flee the citadel without her. He started
to speak, but before he could express what was in his
mind Talliann said:

'There's one more thing I must do. The dreams told
me of it, and I've been waiting all this time until you
came to me ... ' Freeing herself from his grasp, she

stepped back and fumbled with something at her throat; he glimpsed an elusive shimmer of silver under her groping fingers, then heard the small, thin sound of tiny metal links snapping. The girl expelled a long breath, as though she had been relieved of an onerous burden, and held out to him the pendant that she had taken from around her neck.

'Take it,' she said, and there was a tremor in her voice. 'It's yours by right – the dreams told me so.'

He stared down at the necklace in her palm. Threaded on the broken silver chain was a piece of ice blue quartz shaped like a droplet of water. A glimmer of recognition flicked through his mind, startling him: he looked closer, and saw, embedded in the crystal structure, the unmistakable image of a shimmering, open eye. The Eye of Day, by which the people of Haven swore ... the symbol of the Sun-Hound!

He looked at Talliann, his eyes wide and his voice unsteady with disquiet. 'How did you come by this?'

'Calthar gave it to me. When I first came to the citadel.'

The disquiet blossomed into a terrible foreboding. 'When you first came ... ?' Kyre's throat was suddenly very dry. 'But I thought you were born in this place.'

She laughed, the sound shocking him with its mixture of bitterness and irony. 'No. Didn't Calthar tell you that much? I wasn't *born*, Kyre. I was *summoned*. *She* summoned me. I know nothing of myself before the moment when I opened my eyes to find myself lying in a great shell, with *her* looking down at me.' She clenched her teeth and shivered. 'I don't know how long I've been here, or where I was before, or even who I really am ... if I have an identity at all. I know nothing ... save for my dreams. Kyre, does that mean I'm mad?'

She could have been telling him his own story ... and something moved deep within him, lost memory stirring again. 'No,' Kyre said emphatically. 'You're not mad, Talliann.' *Far, far from it ... yet the recollection wouldn't come; he couldn't unlock the door –*

She fingered the pendant again. 'I've always worn this, for as long as I can remember. Yet whatever Calthar says, I know it isn't truly mine. It's yours, Kyre. *Yours*. And you must take it. That's what my dreams have been trying to tell me.'

She was shivering with confusion and distress, and as her grip became unsure the pendant began to slide through the lattice of their fingers. Reflexively Kyre caught at the chain, supporting the quartz in his palm –

The shock of the contact made him shout aloud and drop the pendant. It fell to the floor, and they both stared at it. Then Talliann put a clenched fist to her mouth and whispered: '*Please* . . . '

He didn't want to pick it up. For an instant, as the quartz touched him, he'd had a revelation that had struck him like lightning from an empty sky. Now it was gone, spinning away back into the locked rooms of his mind. But though he'd lost it, the memory of its presence still reverberated in his head: he knew that if he should touch the quartz again, the revelation would return.

And that thought terrified him.

Then a voice inside him said: *Coward! This is what you've been looking for, yearning for, since the moment when you woke in the ruined temple and knew you weren't Simorh's cipher! You have the chance you've craved to learn the truth at last – are you going to baulk now?*

Talliann was watching him. Her eyes glittered unnaturally brightly, and he felt the depth of her longing, her hope. He couldn't betray her trust.

Kyre stooped, his hand hovering over the pendant. For a moment, terror overcame him like sick, toppling vertigo: he fought it back, knowing that he had to do this, that there was no other way for him.

His hand closed over the quartz.

And in his head, the world exploded.

Chapter 14

Talliann!

Her name was a litany in Kyre's mind, and it brought with it the centuries-old pain of love and loss, of agony, of longing. Long days under the sun of Haven; cool nights when the heady perfume of the palace gardens drifted up like strong wine to their open window. Haven had been whole then, her streets and squares sprawling cheerfully out over the bay, her markets thronged, her harbour alive with industry as the fishing fleet which was her living, beating heart scudded in on the friendly tide. By day she was a peaceful golden refuge basking under the sun's eye: by night she was veiled and mysterious, glittering with a myriad tiny pinpoints of light while the old moon gazed quietly down from her dark throne . . .

The past jarred suddenly with the present. The old moon . . . the *benevolent* moon, not a maleficent object of loathing and fear, but a friend, a guide, a light in darkness. They had ruled, he and Talliann, under the beneficence of sun and moon together – until the greed and treachery of an enemy within the gates had shattered their idyll.

He remembered a name then, and with it a memory that awoke bitter hatred. *Malhareq* . . . There had been fear, pain, and at last the long, black road through agony to death. Then centuries of nothingness, before an ancient ritual, in the hands of a desperate sorceress who meant only to conjure a creature in his image, had called him back from the void.

He *was* Kyre. No cipher, no surrogate: he was the

Sun-Hound who had ruled Haven so long ago. The quartz pendant which he now clutched tightly in his hands had been his own talisman and a thing of great power; lost on the night his betrayer took his life on the sands of the bay, it had waited through the centuries for him to reclaim it, waited for the moment when the key locked within its crystal facets would at last turn the lock of his memory and release him from limbo.

Haven had forgotten so much! The realisation went through him like a sword-blade and he wanted to weep for his city, and for all that its inhabitants had lost. He knew, now, what he had known in those far-off days: that there should be no conflict between the worshippers of the sun and the worshippers of the moon; that they had been one, that the circle had been complete. Land and sea in equal measure had formed their domain; until the avarice of one woman, one sorceress, had betrayed them all.

Slowly, Kyre raised his head and looked up. He couldn't remember falling, but he was on his knees on the floor of Talliann's sanctum. She stood like a statue before him, her black eyes huge with awe, uncertainty and fear, and he felt as if his heart were shattering as he realised that, though she knew him in her dreams, though she sensed and clung to the link between them, she recalled nothing.

Talliann, my beloved, don't you remember how we were betrayed? Don't you remember Malhareq, whose soul ached for power, the priestess who called down the moon and turned her benevolence to evil? Remember her face, Talliann. Don't you see her in the woman who uses the Hag's power against you now, the woman who has ensnared Gamora, the woman who means to destroy those who were once our people? Don't you see that long-dead sorceress come back to life in Calthar?

'Talliann ... ' He spoke her name aloud, rising unsteadily to his feet. As he approached her, the look in her eyes changed and hope began to replace the confusion. In her damaged subconscious mind she knew that he had undergone a revelation; she saw the change in him – but she couldn't share it. Remembrance of her own true self, of their past life together, was still beyond her.

Calthar must have used the pendant, the Sun-Hound's talisman, to conjure Talliann here to the citadel. How the talisman had fallen into her hands Kyre couldn't begin to guess, but he believed that the sorceress must be unaware of its origins. Her motive in summoning Talliann to the world had been a mirror image of that which had driven Simorh to summon him; and, like Simorh, Calthar didn't yet know the true identity of her creation. If she were to discover it – as she surely must before long – Talliann would be in mortal danger.

He believed, too, that he now knew the nature of the driving force behind Calthar's desire to destroy Haven. So much had been lost with the dying of the old language that Haven's history as DiMag and his scholars interpreted it had become grossly distorted. They had made a legend of his life and the manner of his dying, and the legend was false. They spoke of an age-old war, of the vampire-priestess from the sea who had lured the Sun-Hound to his death. But when he had lived and ruled in Haven, there had been no war. There had been no sea-citadel. And the enemy who brought about his downfall had been within his own gates.

He remembered Malhareq's face as though she were standing before him: he had seen the echo of her warped soul in the eyes of the sorceress who now ruled over the citadel. And if Calthar should triumph, and Haven fell, she would betray the people from the sea as surely as her long-dead paradigm had once betrayed Kyre.

He had to return to Haven. His mind was moving like a riptide, propelled by the shock of his reawakened memory. There was still so much confusion, so much he had to unravel: but his first and most urgent need was to get Talliann and Gamora away from the citadel and Calthar's malignant influence. DiMag and Simorh must be told the truth, and warned of the imminence of Dead Night. And Talliann . . .

He looked at her again, and the emptiness in her eyes nearly shattered his heart. She must be healed, her memory unlocked as his had been – and he had only one hope. Once, Talliann had worn a talisman that was twin to his own. The two stones had been symbols of Haven's pride and prosperity. Singularly or in conjunction they had great power; as this quartz he now held in his hand had restored his lost self, so its twin would surely restore Talliann.

If it could be found . . .

'Talliann.' He took hold of her hands, saw her surprise at his sudden urgency. 'This pendant – it was given to you by Calthar?'

'Yes.'

'Has she another? Think, Talliann, please– is there another stone like this one?'

Her brow creased in unhappy confusion, and she shook her head. 'No, I – I've never seen such a thing.' The silver chain was tangled in their linked fingers; she stroked the quartz uncertainly. 'She sets great store by this stone: she told me that I must wear it always. But she has no other.'

Kyre shut his eyes in relief. *Then the talisman's twin was somewhere in Haven* . . .

He remembered Akrivir's warning and opened his eyes again. 'Talliann,' he said, 'do you trust me?'

'Trust . . . ' She searched his face: her look clouded, but only for a moment before she replied, 'Yes. I trust you, Kyre.'

'Then leave the citadel with me. There's no time to lose – we must go back to Haven, you, me and Gamora. I can't explain it to you now; there isn't time.' *And you wouldn't understand, my love; not yet* . . . 'But in Haven you can be free of Calthar's influence. And we can stop what she means to do. I *know* we can!'

Talliann's eyes filled with terror. 'No,' she said. 'I can't flee; I daren't try! If she finds us together and realises what we're doing, she'll – she'll – ' A shudder shook her body and Kyre asked urgently,

'She'll what? What is it?'

She shook her head violently and made an inarticulate, ugly sound. 'She'll take us to the Mothers.'

'The Mothers?' Something unpleasant lurched in the pit of Kyre's stomach. The name signified nothing to him, and yet it triggered a warning.

'Don't ask me what that means,' Talliann pleaded. 'I can't explain . . . there are things in her inner sanctum that shouldn't exist; things she can summon out of . . .' She shuddered again. 'I can't talk about it. Kyre, I'm frightened!'

'Talliann, she won't know we've gone until it's too late. Akrivir will help us, and once you're safe in Haven she'll have no hold over you!' He squeezed her hands more tightly. 'You said that you trust me – trust me in this!'

The quartz that lay between their palms seemed to pulse suddenly hot under his skin. Talliann gave a little cry of surprise, as though she had felt it too – and when she looked at him again, there was a glimmer of dawning understanding in her face.

She said, slowly, as if awed by the realisation of her own feelings, 'I *want* to come with you. I'm afraid, but I *want* to . . . '

'Then come. There's nothing to fear!'

She couldn't entirely shake off her doubt, but his urgency and her desire were giving her confidence. 'Yes.' She looked up at him with shaky determination. 'I'll come.'

He wanted to kiss her; but the gesture would have been incongruous. She wouldn't yet have understood his reasons, and he couldn't afford the time to try to explain. The urgency of their predicament was too pressing.

He said, 'Akrivir is waiting outside. I think we can trust him to help us.'

She nodded. 'He ... loves me.' A sad little smile twisted her mouth. 'More, I think, than he has ever dared to show. He's been a true friend to me, and he won't fail me now.' She touched his arm lightly. 'Call him, Kyre.'

Akrivir had maintained a discreet distance between himself and the door, but at Kyre's soft call he came quickly into the sanctum. As the two men looked at each other, Akrivir's eyes narrowed: he sensed the change in Kyre even if he couldn't guess at its nature; and mingling with the wariness in his look was a new understanding – and a new respect.

Briefly, Kyre told him what they meant to do.

'Yes.' Akrivir looked at Talliann for a few moments, his eyes pained. 'It's for the best. She'll be safe with you; safe from Calthar.' He frowned, as though touched by something he'd have preferred not to recall, then his expression cleared and he added briskly, 'The sea-cave is your only means of escape, but there are many ways to reach it. This place is riddled with old, forgotten passages. I'll guide you as far as the bridge, and Talliann knows the way from there.'

'We must take Gamora with us,' Kyre said.

Akrivir frowned. 'She won't go willingly; not while she's still under Calthar's bewitchment.'

'I know. But she'll still be sleeping – if we can get her away from the citadel before she wakes, she won't fight us.' Then an alarming thought occurred to him – how to transport Gamora through the sea? He'd learned that he could breathe water as easily as air, and now he understood why; but the little princess was another matter.

'Talliann,' he said urgently, 'how was Gamora brought to the citadel?'

'In a shell.' She realised what he was thinking. 'There are several – like great clams, in which someone can lie

and be drawn through the sea without water getting in.'
She hesitated. 'Calthar has often used them, to – to bring
victims from the land . . . '

Akrivir's expression said clearly that he understood
her meaning, and Kyre pushed away thoughts of the
fates those victims might have suffered. 'Can we take
her back to Haven in the same way?' he asked.

Talliann nodded emphatically. 'I know how to seal the
shells. And I know where they are kept.'

'Then we must waste no more time.' He looked at
Akrivir. 'Is it safe to leave now?'

'I'll check.'

'Akrivir – ' The young man looked back, and Kyre
added, 'What of you? If Calthar discovers that you've
aided us, she'll kill you.'

Akrivir smiled humourlessly. 'She won't find out. I've
learned ways of averting any suspicions Calthar might
harbour about me.' Hot determination showed in his
eyes. 'Just concern yourself with taking good care of
Talliann.' And he turned towards the door.

Abducting Gamora was unnervingly easy. Akrivir led
Kyre and Talliann back through a maze of dark tunnels,
and waited in the shadows while they slipped through
the shell door to fetch the little girl.

The cavern was dimly lit; on the wide bed Gamora
slept soundly. She didn't stir when Kyre wrapped her
in a light blanket; and when he lifted her into his arms
she simply sighed and put one thumb in her mouth
before sinking back into her dreams.

Talliann peered at the sleeping child. '*If she wakes…*'
she began in a whisper.

'*Pray she doesn't.*' He tried to smile reassurance at
her, but knew it was unconvincing: the real danger still
lay ahead of them.

Outside, Akrivir pointed at an unlit side tunnel. He was
clearly nervous, but tried not to convey it. 'This is the
safest way. Take care how you step; the floor isn't even.'

They moved as quickly as the darkness and Kyre's burden allowed. Akrivir's knowledge of the tortuous warren was sure; he led them through so many twists and turns that Kyre was soon utterly disorientated, but at last, after an unguessable time, a patch of light glimmered hazily before them.

'The bridge is directly ahead,' Akrivir whispered. 'I won't come any further; I'll serve you better by diverting anyone who might come this way in the next few minutes.' He looked at them, and even in the gloom Kyre could see the strain in his face. 'This is the most dangerous part of your journey. If anyone should see you as you cross, they could alert Calthar.' He touched Talliann's shoulder gently, tentatively. 'Take care.'

Talliann laid one hand over his. 'I'll never forget what you've done, Akrivir. Good fortune go with you!'

The young warrior turned away so that neither of them could see his expression. Gruffly, he addressed Kyre.

'I don't pretend to know what will come of this, Sun-Hound, but if we've thwarted Calthar's plans I, for one, will rejoice.' He looked up, blinking rapidly. 'Five nights from now, we'll know the truth of it. When that time comes I may have to face you as an enemy – believe me when I say I hope it doesn't come to that.'

Kyre acknowledged his words with a grave nod. 'I, too,' he said. 'Goodbye, Akrivir. Thanks are inadequate, but you have them.'

Akrivir's smile was fleeting. He squeezed Talliann's fingers once, quickly, and was gone.

Talliann waited until his footfalls had faded into silence, then said softly, 'Well . . . now we must face the worst of it.'

Kyre drew a deep breath in an effort to control the sick feeling conjured by the knowledge of what lay ahead. They approached the tunnel mouth and Talliann moved slowly, cautiously out on to the ledge beyond. He saw her poised against the dim phosphorescence

filtering through the titanic chasm, then she looked over
her shoulder, put a finger to her lips and beckoned for
him to hurry.

He stepped out on to a ledge that was no more than
a narrow buttress hanging over emptiness. All around
him the vast dimensions of the cave reared into the dark,
and far, far down in the abysmal depths below the sea
boomed its muted, threatening song. There before him
was the bridge, arching from the cliff wall and soaring
out into the gloom. In stark contrast to the mad jumble
of towers and minarets and stairways that clung to the
face above him, the cavern's far wall seemed all but
blank; only one solitary light, glowing like a lost firefly,
marked the point where the bridge finally joined with
the distant cliff.

Talliann glanced up fearfully at the insane vista
toppling out of the gloom at their backs, scanning for
signs of anyone moving on the network of staircases, but
Kyre couldn't bring himself to risk looking at that
vertiginous horror. At last, as satisfied as she could be
that all was clear, Talliann beckoned once more to him
and stepped out on to the bridge.

He knew the span was wider than it looked. He knew
he had crossed it once without mishap, and could do so
again even with Gamora in his arms. But no logic or
reason could banish the black terror that closed in on
him as he set foot on the spearing arch of rock. The
hollow immensity of the surrounding dark clutched at
his bowels, attacked his sense of perspective until he
sensed himself only as a crawling speck in an infinity of
indifferent nothingness, a tiny spider teetering across a
single, frail gossamer strand. He struggled to drag his
awareness out of the abyss's grip and focus on the figure
of Talliann moving steadily and surely through the
gloom ahead; but it was hard, so hard. The bridge
beneath his feet seemed to quiver fractionally, sending
horrifying messages through every nerve to his brain:
if he spoke, if he so much as dared to breathe, he knew

that the echoes of the sound would fall away and away, on and on until they were swallowed in the vast distance, and that would take a very long time ...

Kyre was beginning to lose hold of his desperate conviction that the nightmare of the crossing would ever end when he saw that the light that marked the limit of the bridge, and which had seemed so minute and so far away when he began, was only a few paces ahead of him. He heard the slap of Talliann's bare feet as she gained the safety of the ledge, then he was following her, casting off the yawning emptiness, and the bridge was behind him.

They exchanged a look that expressed their relief at the end of the ordeal far better than any words could have done, then Talliann peered cautiously at the bundled figure in Kyre's arms.

'She still sleeps,' he murmured, and privately thanked fate for it. If Gamora had woken whilst they were on the bridge, she might easily have panicked and sent them all to their deaths.

Talliann nodded, and they moved on. Two flights of narrow stairs slanted up the cliff wall from the ledge; but instead of climbing upwards as Kyre anticipated, Talliann instead took the lesser flight that led down into the deeper dark. Some twelve steps – which, though nothing in comparison to the bridge crossing, were nerve-racking enough – and then a side tunnel opened in the cave wall. They hurried through blackness: then more light appeared ahead, and at last they emerged into the sea-cave.

Cool air wafted against their faces; Kyre drew breath and tasted salt on his tongue. The cavern was deserted, and lit only by a soft phosphorescence from the water that lapped just a few handspans below the rock shelf. Kyre could hardly believe the good luck that had followed them thus far: superstitiously he thrust the thought away, forcing himself not to look back over his shoulder, and set Gamora gently down as Talliann hurried to a recess at the far side of the cave.

'Here ... ' She tugged at something invisible in the shadows, breathless. 'The shells ... '

He went to help her. In the alcove lay what looked like two giant clams; but the double shells had long since lost their original occupants and were worn smooth, their surfaces shining softly in the reflected light. Kyre himself could have huddled within the capacious space they offered; for Gamora, they would make as comfortable a refuge as he could hope to find.

Between them they dragged one of the shells out on to the rock shelf, and Talliann ran her hands along the ridge where the two facets met. There was a faint sound, as of air escaping, and the shell's two halves sprang apart.

'Quickly,' Talliann said. In the strange light her face was devoid of all colour. 'Fetch the little princess!'

Kyre turned to where he had left Gamora – and his heart lurched. Gamora was sitting up, her eyes wide and astonished, tousled curls falling over her face. Her gaze flicked around the cave, taking in her surroundings, and she said in a small voice, 'Kyre ... ? Kyre, where are we? What are you doing?'

Talliann made a small, frightened sound in her throat and covered her mouth with one hand. Kyre hastened to Gamora's side, crouching beside her and taking her small fingers in his.

'Don't worry, princess.' He hoped he'd succeeded in keeping the trepidation he felt out of his voice. 'There's nothing amiss; you're quite safe.'

'Safe ... ?' She repeated the word mistrustfully. 'But – '

He had to tell her the truth: if he lied, she'd know it instantly. Glancing quickly at Talliann, he said, 'Gamora, we're going back to Haven.'

For a moment the little girl simply stared at him. Then her brows knitted together and her mouth turned down in an ugly line.

'No!' she said.

'Gamora – '

'*No!*' A peculiar light sparked to life in Gamora's eyes. 'I don't want to!'

'Princess, listen to me, *please!*' Without realising what he was doing he took her by the shoulders and shook her. 'It isn't safe to stay here! If Calthar – '

'Calthar's kind to me!' Gamora shouted defiantly. 'She's my *friend*, I *like* her! I won't go home! *This* is my home now!'

He couldn't argue with her. There was no time; and Calthar's bewitchment stood as an impassable barrier to any attempt at reason. Frantically he looked back over his shoulder at Talliann.

'Prepare the shell,' he exhorted her; and to Gamora: 'Princess, we're leaving. And you're coming with us!'

As he spoke, he snatched her up from the rock floor. A terrible, adult look came into her eyes, a look of shrewdness, guile – and Kyre had no time to wonder why she didn't struggle before Gamora opened her mouth and screamed like a thing possessed.

'*Calthar*! *CALTHAR*!!'

'Gamora!!' Kyre's yell expressed shock and fury in equal measure; he swung the child off her feet, spinning round and starting towards where Talliann crouched by the open shell. Gamora was still screaming, he couldn't silence her – and then Talliann's eyes started with horror as she focused on a point behind his back.

They erupted from one of the entrance tunnels, a running phalanx of armed men, their spear-points glittering cruelly in the reflected light from the sea. He couldn't count them; there might have been ten, twelve, fifteen – but they moved with trained precision, fanning out to circle the three frozen figures on the ledge and leaving only a narrow, impossible escape corridor between them and the water.

From the corner of his eye Kyre saw Talliann's lips form words, as though praying for salvation; though no sound escaped her. The circle of warriors closed in; fine-honed blades bristled inches from his body . . . then one man, clearly their leader, stepped out from the group of spearmen and stood, feet braced, his own spear held at an arrogantly negligent angle. He smiled.

'Put the child down.'

Slowly, heart pounding, Kyre set Gamora back on her feet. The little girl darted out of his reach then looked back at him, triumphantly defiant.

'Good.' The warrior took another pace forward, gratified when Kyre backed away from the menacing point of his spear. 'We'll see, shall we, what the land-cur is made of?' He feinted with the blade; its tip skimmed past Kyre's collarbone and missed cutting him by a hairsbreadth.

'*No!*' Talliann shouted furiously.

The man licked his lips. '*Yes*, lady,' he said. His tone hung midway between reverence and patronage as he attempted to shore up his authority in her eyes. 'You have been the unhappy victim of a conspiracy, and until your eyes can be opened to the truth, I must command your obedience. I ask you to stand aside!'

'How *dare* you!' Talliann fired back. Her voice rose shrilly, echoing against the sea's boom in the cave. Her black eyes glittered and she shrieked, 'Leave Kyre alone! *Leave* him, do you hear? *Obey me!*'

Terror spiked her voice, and Kyre realised that her desperate effort to command the sea-warrior wouldn't work. She was losing control of herself, too inexperienced to demand obedience: but she gave him the chance he needed.

The warrior leader turned his head towards Talliann. His eyes focused on her – and Kyre sprang at him.

His tormentor yelled with surprise as two hands locked on his spear haft. Instinctively he pivoted, trying to jerk the weapon free, and Kyre twisted his body and kicked out. His heel slammed against ribs, and the warrior's shout choked off into a rattling hiss of pain.

He went down, taking four of his soldiers with him in a flailing tangle of limbs, and Kyre shouted to Talliann,

'Get Gamora away! Don't wait – get her away!'

He had no time to see if she obeyed him, for the sea-warriors surged at him and he was suddenly in the midst of a chaos of clashing blades. He heard Gamora scream and it sounded like a scream of protest, he saw his opponent getting to his feet, face distorted with rage: and then he was fighting for his life.

He should have known that the odds were too great, the outcome of the fight a foregone conclusion. Someone in the warriors' ranks had thought fast, and any seaward escape was blocked before he could hope to use it. He was surrounded, and though by the time it was over two sea-warriors were dead and another three wounded, he couldn't hope to prevail against so many. He'd sustained more cuts than he could count, though none enough to disable him, but at last a spear-point whirling at his face made him duck, he lost his footing and, trying to defend himself from the stabbing blade, went down. Something connected with sickening force against his temple, stunning him; he sprawled face down on the rock, his own spear pinned under his body, and two warriors pinioned his arms and knelt on his spine and legs before he could try to rise.

He heard someone sobbing wildly, though the sound seemed to come from a very great distance and was confused with the surging noise of the sea. He felt as if the sea was inside his skull, roaring in his ears: one cheek was pressed painfully against the cold, damp rock floor and his blurred vision only extended as far as ankle height. All he could see was a pair of feet, and the wicked glint of a spearhead as it hovered inches from his face. A toe prodded painfully into Kyre's kidney. He forced himself not to react, and watched the spear intently. It tensed, poised – Kyre hoped against all hope that he could judge the moment of the impending strike and roll clear – and then a new voice, appallingly familiar, cut through the babble and commanded immediate quiet.

'*Cease that!*'

The spear-tip grated against the rock as the warrior stumbled back, and a wave of cold nausea went through Kyre as he heard Gamora's childish voice cry out 'Calthar!' in tearful relief.

He sensed the tight circle of warriors around him falling back; in the ensuing silence the sound of Calthar's feet padding across the rock, and the rustle of her robe, was nerve-racking. As she stood over him his nostrils caught a breath of something unclean.

'Get up, Sun-Hound,' she said. He held his breath, didn't move. She sighed. 'I know you're conscious, and you hear me. *Rise.*'

He raised his head, painfully. Calthar stood two paces away gazing down at him, and Gamora hovered at her side. The little girl was also staring at Kyre, but her eyes were empty and her smile meaningless. A short way away Talliann stood beside the open shell. She was gazing down at the rock beneath her feet and though he couldn't see her expression Kyre could sense the aura of rigidly fearful defeat that emanated from her.

Calthar said nothing for a few moments, but her gaze bored through Kyre as though her eyes could strip away skin and flesh and bone and see through to his innermost thoughts. Then she raised one hand and snapped her fingers at the warriors gathered at her back.

'Leave.'

Her tone demanded instant obedience: they started to shuffle away. Kyre watched them go, and the sickness returned to his stomach. Calthar saw the burgeoning light of fear in his eyes, and smiled. Then she held out a hand. 'Talliann. Child, come here.'

'N-no . . . ' Talliann shook her head: her body jerked as though an invisible hand had violently shaken her, and her fists clenched at her sides.

'Don't argue with me, Talliann.' Calthar's voice was

soft, cajoling, lethal. 'Come here.'

Impelled by a force she was incapable of controlling Talliann shuffled across the rock floor, reminding Kyre of the ungainly, shambling creature he had seen on the shingle bar; the creature she became under the Hag's influence. But her face didn't reflect her compliance. Every muscle was tightened almost beyond endurance, and tears of bitter impotence shone on her cheeks. She stopped some six paces from Calthar, then sank to her knees as if unable to bear the weight of her own body any longer.

Calthar nodded, satisfied, and looked again at Kyre. While he watched Talliann he had been aware of the spear still lying beneath him, and one hand had moved, tentatively, to close over the haft . . .

'No, Sun-Hound,' Calthar said.

His hand stopped moving. She was smiling at him again, and there was murder in her smile. Then she raised one hand and made a careless gesture, as though brushing away a small, buzzing insect. Kyre found himself sprawling aside, his elbow smacking painfully against the rock as he lost his balance: before he could haul himself up again Calthar reached out with one foot and carelessly kicked the spear out of his reach. Then she took a single pace towards him.

Talliann made a thin sound, half way between a gasp and a sob, and the sorceress's hot stare fastened on her. She looked back, not flinching, but her expression was bleak with despair.

'Wh-what are you . . . going to . . . do?'

'Child.' Again that terrible gentleness, that appalling parody of affection. 'You have disappointed me. You have both disappointed me. And now you must pay my price. You know that price, Talliann.'

'*No!*'

'Yes.' She looked at Kyre again, and abruptly the last remnants of the mask she had worn slipped from her, revealing the true nature of the soul behind Calthar's

face. Kyre stared back, transfixed, and in that moment
he re-lived his first encounter, so many centuries ago,
with the embodiment of evil who had led him to
destruction.

Calthar said: *'Sun-Hound, you will meet my
Mothers!'* And in that moment Kyre understood what
was to come, and the horror of it nearly split his mind.

It was as though a vast, rotting throat had opened and
breathed the stench of the grave into the sea-cavern.
Kyre heard Talliann's high-pitched whimper of fright,
saw her clap a hand over her mouth as though to stop
herself from vomiting. He couldn't help her; he couldn't
move as the appalling fetor swept over him, assaulting
his nostrils and his lungs. Bile erupted in his mouth and
he choked it back, his eyes widening as he stared, unable
to rip his gaze away, at Calthar – or rather, at the thing
that Calthar was becoming.

Part of his mind tried to hold on to reason, tried to
tell him that the light in the cave wasn't being eaten by
a darkness so black that it defied sanity. But the rock
walls were fading, the sea's roar dimming away, and
Calthar, sorceress, priestess, Mother born of Mothers,
was metamorphosising. A cold, deathly, nacreous light
flowed from within her, the awful phosphorescence of
something long dead. Her wild corona of hair grew rank,
a crown of mouldering seaweed; the tatters of her robe
were a spider's-web scum clothing her shimmering
body; the flesh of her face melted until her skull was a
gaunt and sunken sculpture of skin stretched taut over
the jagged contours of naked bone. She smiled and she
was lipless, teeth locked in a hideous rictus. She threw
back her head, and her indrawn breath was a death-
rattle.

And Kyre understood the true nature of the Mothers.
They had ruled the sea-citadel since Malhareq, their
first matrix, had fled Haven with her followers after his
death. They were its founders, its motivators, its

controllers, each Mother born and shaped and trained
to follow her predecessor and take the reins of power.
And though no sorcery could keep the eventual death
of their bodies at bay, they clung to this world with a
terrible tenacity, unwilling to relinquish their hold on
the forces that kept alive that first principle of hatred
for the land-dwellers, who had been their kin until the
betrayal that had sent the Sun-Hound to his death. They
could not rule Haven as Malhareq had planned to do;
so instead they sought to destroy what they could not
have.

Though centuries passed and each Mother's body
died, still their minds, their wills, their power, lived on
and returned to the citadel through their rotting corpses:
and Calthar was every one of them, and every one of
them was Calthar. She made her lair among their bones;
she drew her strength from the dust of their mortal
remains; she took her inspiration from their corruption.
And each and every one inhabited her body and her
soul. As her mask fell away she became her own
immediate predecessor; a corpse, worm-eaten, its hair
crumbling, its flesh shrivelling towards disintegration;
then that disguise slipped too, and Calthar was a living
skeleton whose only adornments were tatters of
shrivelled and blackened skin. And further back, and
further back, through brown and brittle bone, through
crumbling marrow, through an apparition in which
motes of rotting dust made mockery of the human form
... until eyes that Kyre knew too well – the eyes of
Malhareq, first Mother of all, who had hated him and
coveted what he was and what he had – glared like twin
suns from the empty memory of a skull.

Then, shearing like a blade through the mesmerising
horror of what Kyre was witnessing, came the shrill
sound of a child's scream.

Gamora! The name was a talisman, snatching him
back from the monstrous corridors of memory into the
reality of the cave. Kyre's mind jerked into focus, and

the scene before him resolved into a ghastly tableau that slammed into his brain. Talliann on her knees, arms flung across her face to protect herself from the horror that Calthar had become. The sorceress, changed beyond recognition as the primeval force of the Mothers surged through her and stripped away the trappings of life: bone and skin and mould and decay flickering about her in a gruesome aura, her arms outflung as she welcomed and relished the monstrous intrusion of the dead –

And Gamora.

The bewitchment was broken. In her fury, Calthar had forgotten her precarious hold on the child, and the spell that had held Gamora in her thrall had shattered. The little girl was hunched on the rock floor, arms clapped over her head, shrieking in panic as the full horror of what Calthar had become smashed into her mind. And her screams, the pity and fury they awoke, broke the thrall in Kyre's own brain. *This monstrosity had bested him once – she'd not best him again!*

He flung himself across the ledge, hands groping blindly for the spear that Calthar had kicked aside, and as his fingers closed round the shaft he felt a surge of energy, of the old power he had once commanded. He brought the spear up, feet finding purchase as his muscles propelled him upright, and, not allowing himself a moment for thought, he lunged at the hideous, shimmering thing before him.

The spear plunged in just below the apparition's heart, and a high, wailing screech threatened to split his eardrums. The searing eyes erupted, changing into a decayed skull that opened the hinge of its jaw and hissed a foul wind of putrefaction into his face: he twisted the blade, his screams blending with Gamora's, and the skull grew skin, yelling insensately. Then flesh appeared, tendrils of hair writhing and snatching at him, and suddenly the monstrosity was Calthar and nothing but Calthar, and the nacreous glow was devoured by the natural light of the cavern, and at his back the sea was booming while the sorceress doubled over, bright blood flowing from the gash the spear had opened between her ribs. Hatred blazed amid the shock in her eyes and she staggered as though drunk, then fell to her knees, hands scrabbling on the rock, a choking, rattling sound emerging from her throat as she coughed more blood –

'*Run!*' Kyre's own voice roared in his ears and he was dimly aware of Talliann's shocked face swimming before him. He started towards her, stumbled over something that lay in his path, and Gamora's huddled form registered in his stunned brain. He swept her up and bundled her unceremoniously into the open cavity of the shell. Talliann rushed forward, and the shell's two halves slammed together. Almost before Kyre knew what was happening the shell was sliding towards the edge of the rock ledge. It hit the water with a resounding splash, and Talliann was poised to follow it, arms outspread, momentarily frozen like a statue on the edge of the sea –

The creature behind him snarled. It was a desperate, defeated sound, but there was still a horrible, malevolent strength in it. Kyre cast a glance back over his shoulder and saw her crouched on the shelf, hunching over her wound which flowered scarlet. Only her eyes were alive, and they burned, burned –

He heard the break in the sea's rhythm as Talliann dived. With a tremendous effort he tore his mesmerised gaze away from the sorceress, and his muscles propelled him in a powerful arc as he launched himself into the welcoming ocean.

Chapter 15

A breaking wave carried Kyre in to shore and drew back to leave him sprawled on the shingle bar, his spear clutched in one hand. A violent fit of coughing racked him as his lungs struggled to cope with the change from breathing water to breathing air, but at last he raised his head and looked around him.

'*Talliann!*' His voice was hoarse, and the cry brought on another bout of coughing. Painfully he tried to struggle to his feet. '*Talliann!*'

There was movement further along the shingle bar. Kyre forced himself to stand on legs that felt too weak to support him properly; then saw her. She was on all fours further along the bank, water streaming from her black hair as she wrestled with the great closed shell, which had beached close to her, trying to drag it clear of the sea's pull. He stumbled across the loose shingle to lend his strength to hers, and between them they hauled the shell out of the undertow, securing it above the waterline. They straightened to catch their breath, and Talliann went into Kyre's arms and clung to him, feeling small and desperately vulnerable in his embrace. It was some while before they released their hold on each other, and when at last they moved apart neither of them could speak.

Talliann dropped to her knees again, and slid her fingers between the shell's two halves. It sprang open, revealing Gamora's huddled figure inside.

'Princess.' Kyre spoke gently, reaching out to ruffle the little girl's dark curls. 'We're home, princess.'

She didn't stir. Her eyes were shut and she seemed
to be asleep. He shook her shoulder, but still there was
no response.

'Gamora?' She should have come out of her faint by
now . . . Kyre gathered her into his arms, lifting her from
the shell's confines. She was a limp, dead weight in his
arms, her head dropping back at a disconcerting angle,
and he looked uneasily at Talliann.

'I can't rouse her . . . '

Talliann crouched at his side. She reached out as
though to touch Gamora – then withdrew her hand
quickly and uttered a sharp, fearful cry.

Kyre's stomach turned over within him. 'What is it?'

'*Calthar!*' There was stark horror in Talliann's voice,
and she looked up involuntarily towards the sky.
Nothing was visible through the night fog, save for the
dim, jagged silhouette of the ruined temple at their
backs; but Kyre could feel the presence of the bloated
moon beyond the fog's grey shrouds.

Tallian whispered: 'She's under an enchantment,
Kyre. Can't you see?' Her eyes were huge with fear.
'Calthar isn't dead. She's regained her strength, and
she's cast a bewitchment. She couldn't reach you or me;
but the little girl . . . '

A desperate desire for her to be wrong made Kyre
protest. 'Calthar couldn't have recovered, not in this
time!'

'She could. You've seen for yourself the sources from
which she draws her strength.' Talliann shuddered.
'Kyre, we daren't stay here. We must get Gamora to
Haven, quickly, before she strikes again!'

As she spoke, Kyre felt an awful premonition seize
hold of him. Involuntarily he looked seaward, and his
blood ran cold. Adding its own terrible confirmation to
Talliann's urgency, the fog was ripping apart, slowly,
softly, like a fine fabric tearing, letting through a shaft
of cold light that spilled down from the sky and turned
the entire scene into a savage etching of black and silver.

Talliann was a spectre drained of all colour, and Gamora's small body looked like a corpse in his arms under the Hag's deadly glare.

'Hurry!' Talliann pleaded, her voice near to breaking. Kyre needed no further urging: he gathered Gamora more closely and securely to his chest, Talliann snatched up the spear he had discarded, and they set off across the unstable shingle towards the dim grey miasma of the bay's crescent. Reaching the sand they quickened their pace, and Kyre was thankful at last to see the witchlights of Haven's portal ahead, glowing through the fog like remote, feral eyes. He couldn't judge the hour but guessed that it must be deep night; there'd be no one abroad in the town now, and little chance of their being challenged before they reached the palace.

They arrived at the arch and Talliann faltered, terrified of what lay behind them yet baulking at the thought of what might await her within the hostile walls of the town. Despite his burden Kyre managed to reach out and touch her arm reassuringly: she drew a deep, grateful breath and then nodded, indicating that she was ready to continue. As they entered the portal, Kyre resisted an urge to look over his shoulder lest he should see the Hag's pockmarked face staring balefully down at them: then they had passed by the twin green lamps, and Haven enfolded them.

Fog lay in pale, still pools in the winding streets, deadening even the small sounds of their bare feet on the stone paving. Shuttered houses stared with blank, empty eyes; not even a scavenging animal slunk through the shadows. Kyre could feel Talliann's fear of the town as a palpable aura, but he himself was looking at it with newly awakened senses. So familiar, yet so decayed; its old glories and beauty long gone ... as they padded through a twisting maze of alleys, avoiding the squares and public places, old memories came back more and more strongly until he could almost have superimposed a ghost-image of Haven as he had once known it over

Haven as it was now. The sensation was disquieting, disturbing; as it assailed him the quartz pendant burned hot against his skin, as though some sentient force within it shared and echoed all that he felt.

And then at last the high perimeter wall of the palace showed ahead, the wicket-gate a darker blur in the pale sandstone. In the wall's shadow Kyre gently set Gamora down – but as his hand came to rest on the wicket-gate's latch Talliann said softly:

'Kyre . . . I'm afraid to go in there.'

In the darkness her face was a white oval, her eyes black hollows. He took her hands. 'It's all right. I'm with you – nothing can hurt you, Talliann. *Nothing*.'

'But they – ' She stopped, swallowed. 'Will they accept me? I've come from the citadel; that means to them, I'm . . . evil. And if Calthar – '

'Calthar can't touch you.' He squeezed her fingers hard, and the urgent determination he felt lent an edge to his voice. 'And no one here will harm you. You're safe here; we're both safe. Trust me, Talliann.'

She lowered her head, her expression hidden from him. Then with a quick, impulsive gesture she lifted his hands to her face and kissed them. 'Yes,' she said. 'Yes: I trust you.' She met his gaze again and added, her voice stronger, 'You know I do.'

She watched as Kyre lifted the latch of the wicket gate and slowly, cautiously, eased it open an inch or two. Nothing moved in the dark beyond, and no voice challenged him. He pushed the gate wider . . . still no sound and no movement. Kyre gathered up Gamora's inert body again, and, with Talliann close behind him, slipped through the portal into the dank, silent grounds.

He heard Talliann's soft gasp as she stared at the strange vista of the gardens. Mist drifted in thin, milky coils among the rank shrubbery, giving the low-lying bushes a bizarre semblance of independent life; the bloated white flowers that haunted the garden were beginning to rot now, releasing the sweet-sick odour of

decay into the damp air. The girl stayed close, touching
his arm as though needing the reassurance of physical
contact and shrinking back from the dead blooms as they
made their way along overgrown paths towards the
terrace.

Only the ornate stone balustrade was visible above
the pooling fog; the terrace seemed to float on it like
a ghostly ship on a curdled sea. But there was a light
shining dimly from a window near the top of the steps,
and Kyre realised that it came from Brigrandon's
rooms. The old scholar was still awake: he above all
others would be able and ready to help them reach
DiMag.

He turned to Talliann, and indicated the soft blur of
light.

'Those are the quarters of Brigrandon, Gamora's
tutor,' he whispered. 'He's a good and trustworthy
friend – we'll find sanctuary with him.'

Her answering look told him that she still couldn't
assuage her fears, but she said nothing, only nodded and
followed him up the terrace steps. As they stood before
Brigrandon's door she started to shiver, then when Kyre
rapped a quick, furtive staccato on the wood she shrank
back into the shadows. For a few moments it seemed
the knock hadn't been heard, and Kyre was about to rap
again when the door abruptly jerked on its hinges and
opened a crack, spilling a finger of warm yellow light
out on to the terrace. The figure in the doorway was a
silhouette, but Kyre recognised the set of the scholar's
shoulders, and the unruly wings of his hair.

'Master Brigrandon.' His voice was a whisper.

'Who's that?' The door opened a fraction wider, but
Brigrandon was cautious. Kyre wetted dry lips.

'It's Kyre, Brigrandon.'

There was a pause, then, slowly, the door opened
wider. They stared at each other for what seemed a very
long time: then Brigrandon said softly,

'Well, now. I'd always believed that sobriety was a

certain cure for hallucination. It seems I was wrong.'

The dry, familiar tone – and the old man's calm resignation – gave Kyre a sense of acute and desperately needed relief. 'I'm no phantom, Master Brigrandon,' he said. 'And I urgently need your help.'

Brigrandon stepped back, pulling the door fully open. 'Come in, quickly,' he said. 'Where by all that's sacred have you – ' and his voice choked off, his eyes starting in their sockets as the lamplight from the room beyond him spilled across the huddled figure in Kyre's arms.

'May the Eye preserve us!' The incredulous oath came on a harshly indrawn breath. 'You're brought her back!' He looked as though he were about to cry.

'Brigrandon, I have to see DiMag and Simorh!' Kyre stepped over the threshold, shouldering the old man aside, for Brigrandon seemed transfixed by the sight of the child. 'Gamora is bewitched – she's in a trance, and I can't rouse her. And there's more, far more.' He looked over his shoulder and called softly: 'Talliann ...'

She emerged from the darkness and stood under the lintel, every muscle tensed like a wild animal poised to flee at the smallest sign of danger. Brigrandon stared at her, not comprehending, and Kyre added quickly, 'There's no time for full explanations, Brigrandon. We've come from the sea-dwellers' citadel, and we've news – it's desperately urgent!'

'Bewitched ... ' Brigrandon repeated in a bemused tone: and then abruptly he shook his head as though to clear it. 'Kyre, forgive me. Your appearance was such a shock, I – I hadn't dreamed anything like this might happen. It caught me unawares.' He straightened his back, and the old, shrewd intelligence was back in his eyes as he crossed the room to a couch by a banked but still warmly glowing fire. 'Set the little princess down here. And your friend ... ' He looked up at Talliann, who hadn't moved. 'Come in, child; come in and get warm. You're soaked, both of you.' He watched as Kyre laid Gamora down on the couch, then gave him a searching look. 'Bewitched, you say?'

Kyre thanked providence for Brigrandon's pragmatism: no histrionics, no rebuttals; even his questions were brief and to the point. 'It's the work of a sorceress called Calthar,' he said.

'*What?*' Brigrandon's eyes narrowed.

'You know of her?'

'Enough. And if this is her doing, then I can only pray that the Princess Simorh has the power to counter it.' He glanced again at Gamora's motionless form. 'We must get word to her immediately. And the Prince – have you tried to get into the palace?'

Kyre felt Talliann press close against him. She'd come further into the room at Brigrandon's bidding, but she was still nervous. 'No,' he said.

Brigrandon's mouth tightened to a hard, thin line. 'That's just as well. As things are now, I'd give little for your chances of reaching him unscathed. Orders have been issued to kill you on sight.'

Kyre was appalled. He had anticipated hostility from DiMag, but nothing so extreme. 'But surely the prince doesn't – ' he started to say.

'They're not Prince DiMag's orders,' Brigrandon interrupted grimly. 'They're Swordsmaster Vaoran's. And he has enough men willing to obey his authority over their prince's, and put a blade in your back before you have a chance to tell your story.'

So matters had moved on ... DiMag had hinted at the precariousness of his position on more than one occasion, but Kyre hadn't imagined it could come to this so quickly. It made his own mission all the more urgent.

Brigrandon said, compounding his unease, 'There are few enough servants who can be trusted in these days, my friend, let alone soldiers. I'm not even sure that I can rely on my own men any more.' He hesitated, considering, then added, 'I'll take you to the prince myself.' He met Kyre's eyes, and his look was painfully candid. 'It's the only safe way.'

Talliann was beginning to shiver violently as the
warmth of the room clashed with the deep cold in her
bones. She was unsteady on her feet, her eyes heavy,
and Kyre said, 'Talliann is exhausted, Brigrandon. She
needs to rest.'

'Then she shall stay here.' There was sympathy in the
old man's expression as he looked at the girl. 'It might
be for the best anyway. But we must take the little
princess with us. If you carry her, that will force
Vaoran's followers to think before they make any
attempt on your life.' He sighed. 'It doesn't please me
to have to say such a thing, but it's the bald truth.'

Kyre didn't argue. He knew Brigrandon well enough
to realise that the old scholar was given neither to
fabrication nor exaggeration. If anything, he would
have understated the situation.

He nodded. 'I'll do whatever you think best.'

'Then we must go.' Again Brigrandon looked at
Talliann, and his smile was kindly. 'Dry yourself, my
child, and warm yourself. You'll find blankets in that
alcove there: take as many as you need. We'll lock the
door behind us, so you'll be quite safe until we return.'

She turned uncertainly to Kyre, and he stroked her
wet hair back from her face. 'Brigrandon's right. You
can trust him.' He kissed her forehead lightly, felt her
relax a little. 'Sleep, Talliann. There's nothing more to
fear.'

They left two minutes later, Brigrandon leading the way
with a lantern, while Kyre, carrying Gamora in his arms,
followed. Again Kyre felt the bizarre clash of past and
present as they entered the palace's outer hall: the faded
tapestries, the dulled marble, the chill air of neglect all
clashed with his newly awakened memories of past
prosperity and glory. The hall was virtually unlit; only
Brigrandon's lamp kept the depths of shadow at bay as
they moved towards the arch and the stairs beyond. No

footstep broke the quiet, no voice challenged them as they climbed, and within minutes they had reached the corridor that led to DiMag's rooms.

'The prince will probably be awake,' Brigrandon said in a low voice as they paced silently along the passage. 'He hardly sleeps these days; since the little princess disappeared, he . . . ' And abruptly he stopped speaking as they both heard the sound of footsteps ahead of them.

There were five men in the party that came round a corner of the passage, and Vaoran led them. Kyre had time to recognise the faces of two senior councillors and a high-ranking army officer before the burly swordsmaster's eyes focused on him. Vaoran stared for a moment in sheer disbelief: then his shocked voice hissed,

'*You!*'

'No, swordsmaster!' Brigrandon stepped in front of Kyre as Vaoran pulled his blade out of its scabbard. 'Kyre is here to see the prince!'

Vaoran looked contemptuously at the old man. 'Get out of my way, scholar,' he said softly. 'You know the order I've given regarding this creature.' Behind him, quietly, the army officer also drew his own sword. Brigrandon, however, wasn't to be intimidated.

'I take my orders from Prince DiMag,' he replied crisply. 'And Kyre and I have business with him – urgent business. I'll thank you, Vaoran, not to impede us!'

He started to move forward, then stopped as he found himself face to face with the tip of Vaoran's sword.

'Stand aside,' Vaoran said.

'Vaoran, don't be such a fool! Don't you understand?' Brigrandon flung out one arm and pointed to the bundle in Kyre's arms. 'Kyre has brought the Princess Gamora back to us!'

There was a stunned silence. Then, so quickly that the old man had no time to react, Vaoran struck Brigrandon with the flat of his sword, knocking him out of his path. Brigrandon reeled back, striking his head against a lamp-bracket on the wall. He lost his balance and fell, and Kyre and Vaoran were left facing each other.

Vaoran glared for a moment at Kyre, the challenge of disbelief in his eyes. Then he stepped forward and snatched back a corner of the blanket that covered Kyre's burden.

One of the men at his back swore softly as he saw Gamora's still, pale face, and the muscles in Kyre's jaw tightened convulsively. Had it not been for the precious burden in his arms, he would gladly have killed Vaoran. He had encountered men like this before; ambitious men, who sought to take power from their rightful ruler and invest it in their own hands. He had been their victim once, when Malhareq had aroused their greed; now, it seemed, it was DiMag's turn. And looking into Vaoran's eyes, he saw the confident satisfaction of a man who had almost achieved his goal.

Vaoran's face suffused with angry colour, and he brought up the point of his sword so that it hovered inches from Kyre's face.

'Set the child down,' he said, enunciating each word with careful, deadly precision.

'I'm taking her to DiMag.'

Vaoran stepped closer, the sword-point now no more than a fingersbreadth from Kyre's mouth. 'I'll count to five, creature, and then – '

'Vaoran, stop this!' Brigrandon, though still groggy from the blow to his head, stumbled forward. Seeing what was afoot, the army officer moved to intercept him; they grappled, anger lending strength to Brigrandon's struggles, and Vaoran shouted, 'Get that old fool out of the way! Quiet him, if you have to run him through!'

'*Swordsmaster Vaoran!*' The new voice cut savagely through the clamour. Startled and chagrined, the officer sprang away from Brigrandon, and Vaoran froze. The other councillors shuffled aside, making way for DiMag, who had emerged from his rooms at the sounds of the disturbance.

The prince had lost weight, his fair hair was ragged and unkempt, his face grey and pallid. Only his hazel eyes burned with feverish energy. He was fully dressed – if he slept at all, he slept in his clothes – and one hand gripped the hilt of his heavy, unsheathed sword. He ignored Brigrandon and the councillors, and gazed with undisguised hatred at Vaoran.

'Put down your blade.'

'My lord, this cur – ' Vaoran began explosively.

'I said, put it down.' DiMag's face was stony. 'Or I'll cut off the hand that holds it.'

His tone left no one in any doubt that he both could and would carry out the threat unless his order was obeyed. Vaoran hesitated a bare moment, eyes reflecting his fury at being humiliated before his companions. Then, slowly, he lowered the sword until its tip touched the floor.

Now DiMag stared at Kyre. His eyes registered doubt, suspicion and above all a terrible weariness. He opened his mouth to speak, but before he could say a word Brigrandon stepped forward and touched his sword-arm lightly.

'My lord prince,' the old scholar's voice was gentle. 'Kyre has brought the Princess Gamora back to us.'

'Gamora . . . ?' Every trace of colour vanished from DiMag's skin, as for the first time he focused on the wrapped figure in Kyre's arms. He put the back of his hand to his mouth, and for an instant Kyre saw terror in his look – terror that he might wake at any moment to find he had been dreaming. He said: 'It's true, Prince DiMag.'

'My lord – ' Vaoran started to bluster angrily, and the prince rounded on him.

'*Silence!*' He limped forward, and peered into the folds of the blanket. He stared at his daughter's face for a very long time, then closed his eyes and swayed. Brigrandon hastened to steady him as he seemed in danger of falling, and after a moment DiMag pulled himself together. He patted the old scholar's arm in a gesture of thanks, then said, 'Brigrandon, find a servant. Send for the Princess Simorh and tell her to come at once to my chambers.'

'I'll go myself, sir – '

'No. No; save your legs, my friend. Send a servant. I'll want you in my rooms . . . and Gamora's nurse; she must be roused – '

'My lord,' Brigrandon said, 'there's something more you should know.' He glanced helplessly at Kyre, and Kyre decided that there was nothing to gain from hedging.

He said quietly, 'Prince DiMag, Gamora has been bewitched. We can't rouse her.'

'Bewitched?' DiMag frowned, then his eyes hardened with a glimmer of understanding. 'Yes,' he said. 'Yes . . . I suppose I should have anticipated something of that nature. It was what Simorh dreamed.'

'And who has bewitched her?' Vaoran demanded. His confidence was returning, and his expression was dangerous. Kyre was about to make a furious retort when DiMag held up a hand, forestalling him.

'Swordsmaster Vaoran,' the prince said icily, 'I have heard enough from you for one night. I want none of your accusations, your spites, your vendettas.' His eyes met the taller man's, and Vaoran blanched. 'Get back to your quarters.'

'Prince DiMag, this is an outrage! This creature comes crawling back to Haven after betraying us all, and you – '

'*He has brought back my daughter!*' DiMag snarled. 'And that's more than you and your entire army could do!'

Vaoran recovered himself, and sneered. 'Oh, yes; he has brought the little princess back! But at what price?'

For a moment DiMag glared at him. Then he said, with incredible venom, 'I told you go. I expect to be obeyed.'

'My lord, I demand – '

'You're in no position to demand anything!' The prince's hand tightened on his sword hilt and Vaoran, disconcerted, backed an involuntary step.

'Go, all of you,' DiMag said more softly. 'My daughter has been returned to me, and for the moment that is all I care about. You may convene the council in the morning, and they'll have a full report from my own lips then. Until that time, I will kill any man who dares to disturb me.' He raked the small group one last time with a withering stare, then looked at Kyre.

'Bring her to my chambers,' he said quietly.

As he followed the prince along the corridor, Kyre could almost physically feel the heat of Vaoran's hatred. DiMag still clung to enough authority to best the swordsmaster in a direct confrontation, but the situation was obviously deteriorating fast. Vaoran had influential friends among both the council and the army; it might only be a matter of days before he felt sure enough of himself to make his bid to oust the prince from rulership. And DiMag knew it – Kyre had seen the unease in his eyes, the awareness that his future was balanced on a knife edge. When the council convened in the morning, and heard the full story of what had happened in the sea-citadel, it would divide them even further.

The guards at DiMag's door saluted and stepped aside to allow them through. They entered the familiar room – doubly so now to Kyre, for he recalled that it had once been his own – and Gamora was laid gently on the prince's couch. DiMag sat beside her, taking her hand and chafing gently at it as he gazed at her. Kyre stood by, not wanting to disturb him, and neither spoke until Brigrandon returned from his errand. Then, as the door closed behind the old man, DiMag looked up.

'I don't know what to say to you, Sun-Hound,' he said quietly. 'You've brought my daughter back, and that's a service I can never repay. But this ... ' he indicated the child's immobile form. 'I don't know what to do. I don't know what to think.'

'She's alive, Prince DiMag,' Brigrandon broke in. 'That at least we can all be thankful for. And if the Princess Simorh can – '

'*If*,' DiMag stressed harshly, then looked at Kyre again. 'Who did this, Kyre? Who was responsible?'

'It was the sea-sorceress: Calthar,' Kyre said.

DiMag's expression became a dead mask, as though all reaction, all emotion, had been instantaneously shut off. 'Calthar.' He repeated the name, but Kyre could tell that to do so cost him dearly. 'So she still rules?'

Kyre nodded.

'And she has enchanted my daughter ... ' He rose, limped across the room to a small table on which stood a flask and several cups. As he poured wine for himself his hand was unsteady.

'She should have been dead these fifty years,' he continued, and now his voice was dangerous. 'Her worm-eaten corpse should have rotted away while my grandfather was still young, not lived on to – to – ' He shook his head, unable to express what he felt.

'I know,' Kyre said, and something in his voice made the prince pause. Their eyes met, and DiMag saw a haunted echo of the horror that the other man had witnessed in the citadel.

'Prince DiMag, there's more behind Calthar's evil than even you realise,' Kyre went on. 'What she has done to Gamora is only the beginning. What she plans to do – *will* do, if we're unable to prevent it – is far worse.'

DiMag studied his face for a moment. Then: 'Tell me,' he said. 'The sooner I – ' And he broke off as the door flew open.

Simorh stood on the threshold. She was clad only in a night shift, and her eyes were wide and frightened. Her wild stare focused on each man in turn, then she said in a small, confused voice, 'DiMag ... ?'

The prince pointed wordlessly to the couch. Simorh turned, saw Gamora: and burst into tears.

Kyre and Brigrandon looked away in discomfort as the sorceress dropped to her knees at her daughter's side, head bowed over the child's body, racked with sobs which were all the more pitiful for being silent and desperately controlled. This was a side to Simorh that Kyre had never thought to see, and he was moved by her distress. He exchanged a glance with Brigrandon, but neither spoke; and DiMag simply stood gazing towards the window, seeming to see into a private world. Then Simorh looked up. Her face was blotched with tears and her voice shook as she cried,

'*Who did this to my child?*'

She didn't need to be told of the enchantment; like Talliann she could sense it. Kyre would have answered her, but DiMag forestalled him and said, with quiet bluntness,

'Calthar.'

'*What?*' Her eyes narrowed, and she got unsteadily to her feet.

'Kyre brought Gamora back,' DiMag said. 'And he says he has news that – '

'Damn his news!' Simorh's voice was razor-edged. 'That whore's spawn has enchanted my daughter – I'm not about to waste time listening to tales!' She swung round. 'I want Gamora taken to my tower, *now!* If anything can be done, I'll – '

'Lady, wait,' Kyre said sharply.

She stopped and stared at him, astounded and infuriated by his temerity. 'How *dare* you – '

'I dare because I must!' Kyre cut across her fury. 'Calthar has done far worse than bewitch Gamora. If you don't listen to me now, all your efforts to rouse her will be worth nothing – for in five nights' time she plans to destroy every soul in Haven!'

Simorh stared at him, and DiMag said softly, '*Dead Night* . . . ?'

'Dead Night. They call it the Great Conjunction. And it will take place five nights from now.'

'Fourteen,' Simorh said sharply. They both turned to look at her. 'Not five nights. Fourteen. Our astronomers have calculated it.' But her voice didn't carry conviction.

'Your astronomers are wrong,' Kyre told her. 'The sea-dwellers know to the moment when the conjunction will occur, and this time Calthar means to annihilate Haven.'

'How can you know that?' DiMag demanded.

'Because I was in the sea-dwellers' citadel, with Gamora.'

Simorh was about to retort angrily, but DiMag's hand on her arm stayed her. 'You followed her there?' he said.

'Yes.'

Simorh turned angrily to her husband. 'DiMag, you surely don't believe him? If it's true – if he *has* been among the sea-demons – then how did he reach their stronghold? And how was he able to get Gamora away?' Her angry gaze raked Kyre. 'He claims to have rescued her, but for all we know he could be in league with our enemies! How do we know that his story isn't part of a trap?'

For a moment there was a painful silence. Then Kyre said:

'Princess Simorh, I don't expect you to trust the man you summoned out of limbo. But would you be ready to take the word of the one after whom you named me? Would you trust the true Sun-Hound?'

Brigrandon was the first of them all to grasp the implication. The old man sat suddenly down on a chair, and DiMag looked at him in surprise. 'Brigrandon? What is it?'

The scholar was staring at Kyre, and after a moment he replied, 'I think, my lord, that something has happened which none of us had bargained for. Am I right, Kyre?'

'Yes. You're right, my friend.' And Kyre held out his

arm to display the quartz pendant tied about his wrist on its silver chain. 'How it came to be in the citadel I don't know. But when Talliann placed it in my hand, it turned the key in my mind – and I remembered what I truly am.'

DiMag said querulously, 'Talliann?' but Brigrandon ignored him. He was staring at the pendant with an almost childlike awe and, looking quickly into Kyre's face for permission, reached out to touch it with a reverent fingertip.

'This is the one,' he whispered at last. 'Just as our oldest records describe it. The amulet of the true Sun-Hound ... '

'*What?*' Simorh's eyes widened and she came forward. Shock registered on her face and she said in a low voice, 'No ... it isn't possible!'

DiMag came to stand beside her. His arm slipped round her shoulders as he too looked at the pendant, though Kyre doubted if he was even aware of the gesture. Then he looked up, and understanding began to dawn in his eyes.

Kyre smiled wryly at him. 'Prince DiMag, at one of our earliest encounters you asked a question of me that I couldn't answer. You said: *Ha reinn trachan, ni brachnaea pol arcath?*' He saw the prince's face pale at his flawless accent, and repeated the question in DiMag's own language. '"Can a prince return, if his land is lost?" I can answer you now, by saying, *Kena halst reinn crechen ha brachnaea voed creich*.'

DiMag whispered a translation. '"Only with the death of the last prince can a land truly die" ... ' His voice was barely recognisable, and Kyre smiled.

'Even in my time the old tongue was used only by sorcerers and scribes,' he said. 'It's little wonder that it's all but vanished now.'

'DiMag!' Simorh turned to him in sudden panic. 'DiMag, this can't be true! I know what I did, I know what manner of creature I brought to this world! What you're thinking, what you're saying – *it isn't possible!* '

'Madam,' Brigrandon put in gently, 'you believed that you had created a man in Kyre's image, but you were wrong.' She looked wildly at him, and though she fought to refute it, realisation was in her eyes. Brigrandon smiled at her with infinite pity and infinite respect. 'Your powers reached further than any of us ever dreamed, princess. You have called our Sun-Hound back from the dead!'

Servants had carried Calthar back to her chambers, but they didn't dare enter her inner sanctum. And so, inch by maddened inch, she had crawled through the door that held such terror for others, and into the heavy darkness beyond. Blood trailed across the floor in her wake; her face was twisted with pain but also with a black, ravening fury. One would pass: the other would endure.

She should have known what he was! Clutching her ribcage with one shuddering hand, feeling her own life-force spilling between her splayed fingers, Calthar knew hatred of an order she had never before experienced. No ordinary mortal could spill her blood: many had tried during her long life, but the power of the Mothers made her impervious to any weapon wielded by her enemies. Yet this creature, this false champion of Haven, had succeeded where all others had failed, and that could mean only one thing – he was no false champion. Centuries after Malhareq, first and greatest Mother of all, had sent him to his death, the Sun-Hound had returned.

And she had let him slip through her fingers, taking Talliann with him . . .

There were steps in the gloom, leading down. Calthar clamped her teeth together and dragged herself over the rim of the pit. Half way down she was forced to pause to allow the air that eluded her to return to her lungs. Her breath rattled in her throat and ribcage and she tasted blood in her mouth: she spat, coughed, spat again and crawled onward. And at last her groping hands felt something soft that yielded beneath her fingers, and she knew she had reached sanctuary.

She lay panting like an exhausted animal, spittle and blood mingling on her chin as she marshalled her thoughts. There must be a reckoning. Sun-Hound or no, Kyre would pay for what he had stolen; and the price would be Haven's destruction. The Mothers were angry and demanded recompense; she, as their avatar, would be the instrument of their revenge.

Calthar wanted Talliann back: but if need be, she could and would do without her. Though she had created the girl for a purpose, Talliann's flaw had always made her at best an uncertain channel for the power Calthar drew on. The price was worth paying – but if her recapture proved impossible there was another vehicle for her power, a darker vehicle; one that had lain dormant and waiting throughout the years of her rule. It could be summoned only once, and could not be banished again save by destruction; but Calthar no longer cared for the risks. The Mothers' hour had come. From the grave, from rotting dust, they would rise again in triumph: and Haven and all who dwelt within its walls would die.

Calthar's breath hissed in her throat, an insane blend of pain and pleasure and anticipation. She huddled further down among the debris that carpeted the floor of the pit, closed her eyes, and her mind reached out. *Heal me*, she said silently. *Heal me, and I shall bring about a vengeance to fulfil our deepest dreams!*

Later, she couldn't have said how long she lay in that place before the first tingling of returning strength began to course through her veins. When the sensation came, she smiled, and her limbs moved, sluggishly at first but then with greater confidence, through the bones and the dust among which she sprawled. She felt the wound Kyre had inflicted healing, fading to nothing more than a ragged white scar. She felt the blood she had lost regenerating within her, flowing fresh and alive in her arteries. And she felt the strength, the life-force, seeping from the mortal remains of her predecessors in the pit, the crumbling, powdering corpses from which she drew both knowledge and an awesome rejuvenating power. She breathed deeply and drew the force into her, letting it spread through her to make her whole again. And when she was whole, she closed her eyes and spread her limbs wide, listening to the vengeful thoughts of the Mothers among whom she lay; until the inchoate sounds and words in her head coalesced into a single clear prospect, and she knew what she would do.

Calthar rose to her feet. Dust and cobwebs clung to her hair and to the tatters of her robe. For a few moments she stood motionless, revelling in the sensations of union with and regeneration by her long-dead predecessors. Then she moved towards the steps that would lead her out of the pit, and her wide mouth twisted in a terrible, purposeful smile.

Chapter 16

Simorh watched the departure of the servants who had brought Gamora to her tower, then said: 'There must be no disturbance. Nothing.'

'I've posted guards to stand watch at the outer door, and also at the foot of the stairs.' DiMag smiled painfully. 'There are still a few I can trust.'

She nodded. 'Very well. Then we'll begin.'

Kyre felt Talliann's fingers entwining nervously with his, but his thoughts were too chaotic to allow him to do more than squeeze her hand in an attempt at reassurance. Since the shock of his revelation, much had happened – and much had changed. He had feared that DiMag and Simorh would find it impossible to accept the truth, but he had underestimated them both: they believed, and the pendant had added more than enough fuel to the fires of their belief. They had listened in silence while he told his full story: his encounter with the sea-dwellers' messenger and the ensuing fight on the beach; Calthar's serpentine scheming; his secret meeting with Talliann and the revelations the pendant had brought; and finally, the horror of confronting the Mothers and their escape from the citadel. And he had told them the truth about the sea-people and their war with Haven: that the history to which they had adhered for so long was flawed. The old tongue, corrupted by centuries of change and neglect, had led them into the false belief that the conflict was unending and unresolvable; an eternal battle between two separate races who could never hope to find accord. Kyre knew better:

for when he had lived and ruled in Haven, the two races had been one. And he believed that, were it not for the legacy which that first power-hungry sorceress had handed down through the Mothers to Calthar, they could be one again.

The truth, Kyre had told them gently, was in their manuscripts. But even in his time the old language had fallen into decay; since then the decline had progressed so far that truth had become occluded and the legends distorted by generations of misunderstanding. He couldn't expect DiMag and Simorh to abandon the teachings of generations past and accept what he told them without question. But he could offer them one thing which was, perhaps, more valuable than anything else – the presence of the first Kyre, the real Sun-Hound with his knowledge and his memories of their lost past, among them once again.

He wished he had had the chance to speak with DiMag alone, for he knew that, now his identity had been revealed, the prince feared him. DiMag's attitude was an uneasy blend of deference and defiance, and Kyre wanted to reassure him that he had no wish to rule in Haven as he had once done. The city was DiMag's by right; Kyre was no usurper. He had returned, but his place was at DiMag's side, not on his throne. Yet DiMag, beset by opposition, painfully aware of his own instability, had doubts. So far he had quashed them, but nonetheless Kyre wanted to give him the reassurance he craved.

And then there was Talliann . . .

Brigrandon had brought her to the prince's chambers at Kyre's request, and DiMag's first encounter with the girl who, for nearly ten years, had been the embodiment of all that was evil and corrupt had been hard. Talliann had no knowledge of her true self – but, unexpectedly, it had been Simorh who had had the insight to see past the myth to the underlying reality. And it was Simorh who had told Kyre of the second amulet – Talliann's amulet – which, so legend had it, had been lost when the Sun-Hound's consort committed suicide after her lover's death. The story she related had hurt Kyre like a sword-thrust; yet it gave him a glimmer of hope. Talliann had died in Haven, and the clue to her talisman's whereabouts lay somewhere in their most ancient manuscripts. With both its twin and its rightful wearer gone, they believed, beyond recall, no one had ever troubled to search for it. But now Brigrandon, who in his capacity as royal tutor was also curator of Haven's historical records, was about to begin that search. Kyre could only hope and pray that the scholar would succeed in time.

Talliann herself had so far had little to say. She was still dazed with weariness, and most of what was revealed had been beyond her ability to comprehend. Kyre had hoped that with their return to Haven some of her forgotten past might come back to mind, but he had been disappointed: nothing seemed familiar to her. She was still very wary: she sensed DiMag's hostility and feared him because of it, and even with Brigrandon, who had shown her nothing but kindness, she was cautious. But to Kyre's great surprise, the one person whom Talliann seemed prepared to trust was Simorh, and, perhaps a little unwillingly on both sides, a rapport was developing between them. The sorceress's sixth sense had forced her to overcome her prejudices: she saw and recognised the nature of the power latent in Talliann, and knew that if she was prepared to acknowledge the true Sun-Hound she had no choice but to acknowledge his consort.

A sudden darkening of the room broke his chain of thought and he looked up, blinking, to see that Simorh had extinguished the lamps. The only light now came from a small brazier placed near the head of the pallet where Gamora lay, and by its uneasy glow everything in the deeply shadowed sanctum looked grotesque and distorted.

Simorh had changed her shift for the same thin black robe she had worn on the night she conjured Kyre to the ruined temple. Her hair, loosed, shone faintly in the dimness, and her eyes were bright pinpoints as she silently gestured to them all to take their allotted places.

They took up their stations: Simorh before the brazier at Gamora's head, DiMag by the child's feet, Kyre and Talliann on opposite sides of the pallet. The only sound in the room was the slow, regular hush of Simorh's breathing as she focused her concentration on the spell and began to slip into a trance. Then, slowly, she closed her eyes and held out both arms, fists clenched. The brazier's light reflected fierily on her skin, and her hands opened with a fluid gesture to allow twin streams of a dark powder to fall onto the coals.

The brazier hissed, and vivid flames of blue and green leapt up, engulfing Simorh's hands. She didn't flinch, though by the suddenly vivid light Kyre saw her jaw clench with momentary pain. Then, with the flames still writhing about her fingers, she began to chant.

It was a corruption of the old tongue, and the few words he could recognise set cold claws into Kyre's spine. Simorh's voice was pitched to the lowest register her throat could produce, her tone guttural, the words twining and twisting on her tongue. The chant grew more rhythmic, more insistent; shadows danced about the room, forming brief and strange images that made Kyre shudder, and the air seemed to thicken and grow clammy with a claustrophobic sense of anticipation, as though something that lurked and waited beyond the borders of the senses was slowly closing in. The power that emanated from Simorh's quivering form was building, building; still she chanted, calling on every reserve within her –

And Gamora's eyes snapped open.

The strangled cry that broke from DiMag's throat was stifled instantly as the brazier went out, plunging them into darkness. For a moment that seemed to last an eternity the silence crawled with near-unbearable tension, while Kyre's shocked mind wondered if he had imagined what he'd thought he saw in the instant before the brazier was extinguished. Then a new light began to glow from the pallet where the child lay: a cold, green-white glow, phosphorescent and sickly. It gained strength until Gamora's body was haloed by it, and when Kyre looked down at the pallet he felt his stomach lurch violently.

Gamora's eyes had indeed opened. She was staring into the room, and on her face was a smile never seen before on the face of any child ever born. Behind her, Simorh's expression was frozen into a look of paralysed horror; as DiMag started forward she held up her hands, palms out, warning him to stay back.

The little girl began to sit up. She moved as though controlled by invisible hands, her back rigid, arms by her sides, and there was something repulsive about the apparent lack of effort it took her to rise. She sat bolt upright, and her head turned slowly, jerkily, first to one side, then to the other. Her gaze swept the room and the four appalled witnesses, then her mouth opened, and a voice that made Kyre swallow back bile issued from her throat.

Calthar's voice.

'I believe I almost pity you, Simorh who calls herself sorceress!' The familiar mockery lent an uglier edge to the words. DiMag stared at his daughter, transfixed, and Simorh could only utter a faint, gagging sound. It was echoed by Calthar's laughter.

'You can't lift the enchantment, foolish child. The little one sleeps, and only I can wake her – should I choose. But you have angered me. You have angered my Mothers. It would be fit punishment, I think, were I to reach out my hand and sever the fragile cord of your daughter's life!'

'No!' Simorh's cry was anguished with impotent fury, and Kyre felt his pulse throb with a rage that matched

hers. He spoke without thinking, unable to prevent the words from spilling out.

'I should have stayed to see you dead, and consigned you back to the putrefaction from which you came! May the Eye help me, I should have dismembered your corrupting body and scattered the pieces to the tide for sea-worms to devour!'

'*Ah* . . . ' The dreadful voice issuing from Gamora's lips took on a quality like poisoned honey. '*So Haven's little dog is among you, is he? My salutations, Sun-Cur. You did well to escape me, but you should have realised that the Mothers take good care of their own.*'

'Damn you!' Simorh shrieked, 'Release my daughter!'

Gamora's head turned, the small body twisting about until she faced her mother. Simorh started to shake violently, but forced herself not to look away. '*It seems we have reached the heart of this matter,*' Calthar said sweetly. '*You want your child restored to you. And I, in my turn, want something from you.*'

There was a sharp silence. Then Simorh took a deep breath, and whispered: 'What . . . ?'

Calthar laughed. The low chuckle from the little girl's throat was horrible. '*This, Simorh who calls herself sorceress, I tell you now, and I tell you once. If you want your child to live, then the girl Talliann must be brought to the ruin on the shingle strand, on the night of the Great Conjunction. There you will give her into my keeping – and only then will I lift the bewitchment.*'

Kyre spat an involuntary protest and, forgetting in his fury that Calthar wasn't physically present in the room, started towards the pallet with murder in his eyes. DiMag moved quickly to intercept him, grabbing hold of his arm and hissing urgently in his ear, '*No!* Hear her out!'

'*Prince DiMag?*' Gamora's head swivelled again and her unseeing eyes glared at the prince. '*It seems I am in the most exalted of company. How interesting to*

*encounter you again, after ... what must it be? Nine
years?'*

DiMag's expression tightened, but he kept his voice
even. 'Don't waste your breath mocking me. You say
that you will break the spell you have cast on my
daughter if Talliann is returned to you on Dead Night.
Do you seriously expect us to believe that if such a
bargain is made, you'll keep your word?'

Gamora uttered a long, fluttering sigh, and Calthar's
voice said, *'Prince, you flatter yourself. I have no interest
in you, or your witch-wife, or your child, or the
troublesome mongrel you keep on your leash. Your
options are simple. Do as I have told you, and I will
release the little girl. Fail, and as the Hag's light strikes
your gates, your daughter will die and my Mothers will
destroy Haven.*

*'You have heard my terms, Prince DiMag, and I have
no more to say to you. You have five more nights to
ponder your decision. And then I will be waiting.'*

As Calthar spoke the last word, the cold halo around
Gamora's small frame flickered and dimmed. The
child's eyes rolled and, for an instant only, something
resembling terrified intelligence flickered behind their
blindness. Then the halo vanished, and the child fell
soundlessly back on to the pallet.

'Gamora!' Simorh almost stumbled over in her frantic
effort to reach the little girl's side. She grasped her
shoulders, hugging her, shaking her. 'Gamora!'

DiMag pulled her back, gently but implacably.
'Simorh, it's no use!' He drew her against him, and
buried his face in her hair. 'You won't wake her – you
can't fight this!'

She was quiet for a few moments, her shaking
gradually subsiding. Then, her voice under an iron-hard
but painfully thin shell of self-control, she said,

'Light. I want light. The lamps, the curtains ...
quickly!'

Kyre stumbled across the room to where he could just

make out the faint outline of a heavily-curtained window. He dragged the curtain back, but it made little difference; only the faintest hint of dawn glimmered through the mist outside. But it was enough to show him a lamp bracket, and flint and tinder on a table beneath. Fumbling, he lit the lantern and a yellow glow banished the worst of the shadows. Talliann hastened to light a second lamp, and as it flared he felt the thick, claustrophobic atmosphere receding a little. They all looked at each other, no one knowing what to say. Eventually, it was Talliann who broke the silence.

'She tried to touch me ... ' Her voice was barely audible. 'I felt her, like a – like a dead hand inside my mind. But she couldn't reach me.'

'No ... ' Simorh said. She glanced quickly at Kyre, frowned. 'You're safe from her here. As Kyre said you would be. But Gamora ... ' She bit her lip, hard.

DiMag turned towards the window. 'Five nights.' His tone was grim; then he shook his head and pinched the bridge of his nose tiredly between thumb and forefinger. 'I must summon the council. We daren't lose another moment – I have to tell them what's happened.'

He started towards the door without waiting for anyone to reply, and Kyre caught his arm. 'Prince DiMag, you don't believe that Calthar meant what she said? That she'd keep her part of any bargain?'

'Of course I don't believe it!' DiMag fired back angrily.

'The council may not agree with you.'

'That's a risk I'll have to take. I can't face this alone, Kyre. None of us can.' The furious light died from his eyes then and his shoulders slumped. He disengaged his arm from Kyre's grip and patted the other man's shoulder. 'You'd best come to the court hall. You'll want to hear what the council has to say.'

'Prince DiMag ... '

DiMag and Kyre looked in surprise at Talliann. The black-haired girl's eyes were wide and frightened, but

there was a determined set to her jaw. She met the
prince's gaze and said,

'I'll go back.'

'*No*, Talliann!' Kyre was aghast.

'*Yes*,' she argued stubbornly, and looked unhappily
around the room. 'I can't stay here. It isn't right; I – I'm
endangering you all. And the little girl . . . '

'Talliann, you can't!' Kyre protested. 'If I were to –'

DiMag held up a hand, forestalling what Kyre had
been about to say. He addressed Talliann, and his voice
was gentle.

'Lady, there's nothing to be gained from sending you
back to the citadel. Believe me, if I thought my daughter
would profit from giving you back into Calthar's hands,
I'd drag you to the temple on Dead Night myself – Kyre
might put your wellbeing first: I don't.' He smiled thinly.
'But Kyre's right. Calthar won't keep her word – but
while we have you, she won't dare do Gamora any
further harm for fear of losing her bargaining power. So
you must remain with us, and we must find a way to
thwart her.' He glanced at Simorh for confirmation, and
the sorceress nodded curtly.

'Yes. You must stay, Talliann. You're our hostage to
Gamora's survival.'

'It's a miserable stalemate,' DiMag said, to no one in
particular. 'And we have so little time.'

Simorh crossed the room to join him. As she stood
beside him DiMag thought that she was about to reach
out and touch him, link her arm with his, and though
the contact would have been unfamiliar he found
himself longing for the comfort it might bring. But
instead she withdrew her hand, and only gave him a
quick, sad smile through the tawny curtain of her hair.

'You'd best send for the councillors,' she said quietly.
'Take Kyre with you – Talliann can stay with me for a
while. I want to ensure Gamora is watched and guarded.
We'll join you as soon as we can.'

DiMag nodded. 'There are a few councillors who

won't take kindly to being hauled from their beds before daybreak. They'd best get accustomed to it – I doubt if any of us will sleep soundly again until this is over.' He turned, gazed at her for a moment, then kissed her, lightly and briefly, on the brow.

Simorh stood very still as DiMag and Kyre left the room. The kiss had been unexpected, and it both gladdened and hurt. Such a small, apparently meaningless gesture; and it had cost DiMag little. But it was a beginning.

Morning was advancing but the sun was invisible behind a dense layer of cloud when the meeting in the court hall came to its chaotic and unhappy end. As the councillors filed out with his words of dismissal still ringing in their ears, DiMag sat rigid on his great chair, listening to the sounds drifting to the hall from the palace's main courtyard. Distant, stentorian voices, the clash of metal, the concerted tattoo of a myriad boots stamping on flagstones . . . Haven's army drilled intensively under the commands of its sergeants and masters-at-arms, and DiMag wondered wearily what point there was to it all. Whatever Dead Night held in store, it wasn't the readiness or otherwise of the fighting men that would decide the outcome of the battle.

Nor, he thought bitterly, would it be the wisdom of the court council that would come to Haven's aid now. He had expected some scepticism in the face of the story he had told them; he had expected opposition to the decisions he had made: what he hadn't anticipated was the intensity of that opposition. And he realised now that he might have made a very grave mistake.

It was, of course, Vaoran who had led the main faction against him; though the swordsmaster had cleverly managed to give the appearance of merely being swept along by the prevailing tide of opinion, DiMag had seen the triumph in his eyes when the arguments began. The prince had told the council the full truth – he had revealed the identities of Kyre and Talliann, had described Simorh's attempt to break the bewitchment of Gamora and the consequence that had followed; he had apprised them of Calthar's ultimatum. They had listened in silence, they had conferred together while the prince watched uneasily and Kyre sat cross-legged on the dais beside him – and then the condemnation had started.

The council were not willing to believe that the Sun-Hound had returned from the dead. With respect, as Councillor Grai, whom DiMag had never trusted, unctuously prefaced his speech, if such a miracle were possible it would be enshrined in the city's historical manuscripts. But their most erudite historians, over many generations, had found no trace of such a concept.

'Councillor,' DiMag retorted sharply, 'you are as aware as I am that our records are flawed. The old tongue has declined; we can't be sure of the accuracy of our translations. Besides, we have the Sun-Hound's lost amulet. I don't think even you can deny the reality of that!'

'Indeed, my lord.' Grai bowed in thin acknowledgement of the point. 'No one here disputes that the quartz is what it purports to be: that at least is documented. But if it has been in the possession of the sea-demons, who's to say that they might not use it for their own ends?' He glanced over his shoulder at the councillors behind him, and more than a few nodded assent. 'We have no proof that this Sun-Hound is anything more than a cipher who has been corrupted to their use!'

'Or was in league with them from the beginning,' someone said in a deliberately carrying aside.

DiMag turned a basalt gaze on the speaker, who stood just two paces from Vaoran. 'You presume to doubt the integrity of my wife?' he demanded ferociously.

The man reddened. 'No, my lord: I merely – '

Vaoran interrupted smoothly. It was the first time he

had spoken directly to DiMag, and that, the prince thought, was a dangerous sign. 'My colleague intended no slight to the Princess Simorh's efforts to aid our city by creating a cipher to be its champion, sir,' he said. 'But he fears – as many of us fear – that the princess might also have been an unwitting victim of the sea-devils' duplicity.'

The innuendo was clear. DiMag sat back. 'Then you believe I have been duped?' There was a challenging undercurrent in his voice.

Vaoran inclined his head. 'I'm not in a position to judge, my lord. But if this man is Kyre – the *real* Kyre – I might have anticipated some more positive evidence to back his claim.'

Kyre's eyes narrowed. 'I'm not in the business of performing miracles, swordsmaster. I never was, as you'd know if you read your own history.'

'Nonetheless, Prince DiMag, I'm sure you must appreciate the council's reluctance to accept his story without sound proof. We have only Haven's interests at heart, and – if I may speak bluntly – we've seen enough of what the sea-demons can do to take nothing on trust now.'

Grai stepped forward again before DiMag could respond. 'My lord prince, as your senior adviser my considered opinion is this: we accept and acknowledge that our astronomers were mistaken in their calculations, and that the Dead Night conjunction will occur five nights from now. To that end, Swordsmaster Vaoran has already issued orders to our army to intensify their efforts to make ready in what little time we have left.'

Vaoran gazed modestly at the floor and smiled faintly. Though he begrudged it, DiMag had at least to give him credit for his prompt reaction.

'As to the other matters you have placed before us, I cannot accept the assertion, nor even the likelihood, that the Sun-Hound has truly returned to us.' He licked his lips. 'Indeed, under less urgent circumstances I'd urge the council to look on such an assertion as blasphemy.'

DiMag sighed, but said nothing.

'And the third matter – the ultimatum delivered by the sorceress Calthar.' Grai shook his head. 'My lord, the choice is clear. We can't trust the sea-demons, but neither can we afford to lose the smallest chance to help our little princess. On Dead Night, the girl must be returned whence she came. And her return must be part of our own strategy to best the sorceress.'

Kyre jerked forward as though he meant to start to his feet, but DiMag gripped his arm, fingers digging painfully into his bicep.

'Strategy?' the prince said dangerously. 'What strategy?'

Grai looked at Vaoran, who cleared his throat.

'As yet I can't be more specific, my lord. There hasn't been the time for concrete proposals to be suggested, but that can soon be rectified. If our scholars and historians join forces with our military tacticians, we can find a means by which the sorceress can be overpowered, and – '

Kyre could keep silent no longer. '*Overpowered*?' he interrupted explosively, and this time DiMag's restraining hand wasn't enough to stop him from leaping to his feet. 'Are you *insane*?' He fought back the impulse to wade in among the councillors and smash Vaoran's complacency with his fist, and with a great effort brought his fury under control. 'If you have ever come face to face with Calthar, swordsmaster, you'd know that what you're suggesting is *suicidal*!'

Vaoran smiled thinly. 'We're speaking now of a full military detachment, my friend; perhaps an ambush, perhaps something more subtle. That bitch from the sea is only mortal – '

'She is *not* mortal!' Seething, Kyre wondered if the councillors had listened to a word of the story DiMag

had recounted to them. 'Not in any sense that you or
I understand the word! By all the laws of nature she
should have been dead half a century ago, yet she lives,
and she has the appearance of youth! How long do you
think your military strategies will last against the kind
of power which can grant her *that*?'

Vaoran inclined his head and made a gesture that
suggested the helplessness of a man faced with blind
unreason. When he spoke, it was to DiMag.

'My lord, I fully appreciate the – ah – Sun-Hound's
agitation. However, I submit that his arguments are
unhappily coloured by his personal concerns – and I
believe that my views accord with those of the majority
in this hall?'

The interrogative brought murmurs of assent; too
many, DiMag realised, to give the lie to Vaoran's
presumption. He waved to Kyre to sit down again,
shaking his head in a swift warning gesture as the other
man seemed about to speak again, and cleared his
throat.

'Swordsmaster Vaoran – Councillor Grai –
gentlemen. You have heard the facts of this matter from
me, and I in turn have listened to your arguments.' His
eyes were as hard and cold as unpolished brass. 'I was
unaware, before Councillor Grai gave us all the benefit
of his considered opinion, that the question of Kyre's
identity was at issue. I have all the evidence I need to
convince me, as does the Princess Simorh. I have also
decided that there will be no attempt to treat with
Calthar, duplicitously or otherwise. Talliann will not be
used as part of any scheme to outwit her.'

'My lord!' Grai protested. 'If the ultimatum is ignored
–'

'If the ultimatum is ignored, it won't make our
situation any worse. No, Grai: I won't be argued with.
Talliann is and will remain under my protection.'

Vaoran glared at him. 'Prince DiMag, I must add my
protest to Grai's! I would remind you – '

'*No!*' DiMag was rapidly losing his temper. 'I would remind *you*, Vaoran, that the Council is my servant and not my master! Talliann stays in Haven – and if she is what I believe her to be, then by the Eye you'll thank me for that decision before this is over!'

Vaoran's face was granite and the prince saw rebellion in his eyes. DiMag's command of the situation was teetering on the edge of a deadly precipice: his decision had added a good deal of fuel to the fires of those who were subtly trying to prove him unfit to rule. If Vaoran chose this moment to challenge his leadership, he could well have enough of the council behind him to sway a large majority in his favour.

Vaoran said, with great care, 'My lord, duty compels me to urge you to think again.' The words had a clear double meaning.

'Your duty,' DiMag retorted, 'is to ensure that our armed forces are properly drilled and trained, and in that capacity to keep me informed of progress. I'd suggest, Vaoran, that you look to that, rather than to matters on which you are *not* qualified to advise your prince.' He smiled, but the smile was coldly hostile. 'Do I make myself clear?'

There was a long pause. Then Vaoran, face flushing with anger, said: '*Quite* clear, my lord.'

'Good. Then I wish you good morning.' DiMag's gaze raked the entire assembly. 'All of you.'

And now the great doors had closed behind the last of the councillors, leaving DiMag and Kyre alone, but for a handful of silent stewards, in the court hall.

Kyre got slowly to his feet and stood looking at the prince, who ignored him. 'My lord – '

DiMag's head turned. His face was rigid with tension. 'Don't call me that,' he said. 'Coming from you, it sounds ironic to say the least.'

'It shouldn't,' Kyre replied. 'You are the ruler here.'

'Am I?' DiMag countered bitterly. 'I'm beginning to wonder.' Then as Kyre was about to say something more he waved an impatient hand. 'I don't want to discuss that, or anything else, at the moment. Let it be, Kyre; keep what you were going to say for another time.' He stood up stiffly, then paused as the small door behind the dais opened.

Simorh entered. She looked weary but there was a resolute set to her face: seeing that the hall was all but empty, she stopped, surprised, and looked queryingly at the prince. 'Is the meeting over?'

'It's over.' DiMag stepped awkwardly down from the dais. 'You missed all the fun, Simorh.'

'What was the outcome?'

He stared resentfully at her, but the resentment was for the world at large. 'Precisely what I should have anticipated,' he said, and headed for the door. Simorh made as though to follow, but the anger in his face, the rebuff in his eyes, stopped her. She watched until the door had closed behind him, and the curtain had fallen back into place, then turned slowly and looked at Kyre.

'It went badly.' It was a statement, not a question, and Kyre nodded.

'Very.' Briefly, he told her of the councillors' views and the near-confrontation that had prefaced DiMag's angry dismissal. She listened in silence, then, when he had finished, sighed.

'I expected something like this.' She shivered, hugged herself, then added with a trace of defiance in her voice, 'DiMag won't be persuaded to change his mind.'

'There's no reason why he should.'

Simorh looked up at him. 'You and I might be alone in that view.'

There was still a faint edge of resentment in every word she addressed to him. She mistrusted him – now that she knew what he was, she too wondered whether he might have ambitions to rule in her husband's stead.

She said abruptly, 'I thought better of bringing Talliann with me. She's sleeping now, in my tower. The poor child's close to exhaustion.'

'And . . . Gamora?'

'Guarded, and as safe as any power I possess can make her.' She looked towards him again, but didn't quite seem able to meet his eyes directly. 'I haven't . . . thanked you for what you did. Without you, Gamora would have been lost to us forever.' A pause. 'I don't want you to think that I'm not aware of the debt I owe you.'

'You owe me nothing, princess,' Kyre said gently, suddenly pitying her. '*I* owe *you* my life – or had you forgotten that?'

She grimaced. 'Perhaps I had.'

'Or perhaps you wanted to?'

She frowned. 'I don't understand you.' But her expression was wary.

On an impulse Kyre moved towards her and laid his hands on her shoulders. She flinched away, then froze, staring at him with the frown fixed on her face.

'Simorh, I tried just now to explain to DiMag, but he didn't want to hear me out. But I *must* say this – I have to make you understand.'

'Understand what?' She was still reluctant to look at him.

'That I don't present any threat to the prince, or to you. I might have ruled here once, but that was long, long ago; I don't have ambitions to rule again.' He smiled. 'Even if I had, so much has changed in Haven since my time that I wouldn't know where to begin.'

A sharp colour had come to her face. 'I didn't think – '

'Yes, you did. And I don't blame you. But believe me, Simorh, I don't want to oust DiMag from his rightful place!'

She gave a curt, bitter laugh, shrugging his hands away, and turned her back. 'If that's true, then you must be one of the few men in the palace who hasn't harboured such thoughts!'

'Maybe. In which case I want to help you ensure that

none of those men fulfil their secret ambitions.'

'I wish you could.'

'I think I can. I, and Talliann. If only we can find the lost amulet.'

She looked back at him then and there was such agonising despair in her eyes that his heart went out to her. He said: 'Simorh, I can only ask you to trust me. Even in the midst of this crisis I know there are knives poised at DiMag's back. Will you try to believe that mine isn't one of the hands holding them?'

She thought about that for a long time, then finally nodded.

'I understand you, Kyre,' she said. 'And I think I believe you.' Now the barrier was down and she looked fully at him, her eyes candid. 'I *want* to believe you.'

'Isn't that a beginning?'

'A beginning . . . yes.' An odd smile played about her mouth. 'It's a beginning.'

Vaoran was gratified to find that fifteen men of the seventeen to whom he'd sent his cryptic message were ready and able to answer the summons. Uncluttered though his room was, such a number made it crowded, and the majority were forced to choose between perching on the narrow window-ledge or standing.

Vaoran dispensed with the social niceties; no wine was offered, no idle small-talk preceded the matter at hand. The swordsmaster spoke bluntly and to the point, and the fifteen were equally pragmatic in their responses. Their view – as he had hoped but not dared to assume – was unanimous.

'So it's decided.' Grai, who had elected himself spokesman for the visitors, nodded with satisfaction. 'We will make our move on the day of Dead Night itself.' He blinked sidelong at Vaoran. 'My only reservation concerns the advisability of leaving it so late.'

'I take your point,' Vaoran said, 'but to act earlier might be to take an even greater risk. We need to ensure that anyone who might oppose us will be too preoccupied with the imminent conflict to cause any trouble. Our strategy – our own strategy – for facing the sea-demons needn't suffer in the meantime. We may not have overt control of the army, but we have all the influence we need in practice. The vast majority of our soldiers aren't, of course, privy to court matters; they simply obey orders, and it doesn't occur to them to question where those orders originate. We need only ensure that all concerned are well drilled in precisely what they must do, and precisely when they must do it.'

Grai smiled, satisfied. 'Then I have no further reservations. And I congratulate you, Vaoran, on such a skilled and thorough plan.'

There were murmurs of agreement to which Vaoran inclined his head in acknowledgement. 'Thank you, my friends. And before we go our separate ways, I'd remind you once more that our first priority must always be the safety of the Princess Simorh and the little Princess Gamora. If DiMag has his way, that poor child will never open her eyes on this world again.'

A short, burly army captain cleared his throat. 'The sea-demon girl won't present any problem in that regard, sir. But I'm a little concerned about the – ' he hesitated, not sure how to refer to Kyre in Vaoran's presence, then finished, 'the one who calls himself the Sun-Hound.'

'Mmm.' Vaoran stroked his chin. 'You're right to mention it, captain. I've been thinking about that, and I suspect it might be wiser to modify our original intention. Rather than take him prisoner as we intended, I think it would be more prudent to kill him.'

He looked around the room to gauge the general reaction to his remark. No one spoke for a minute or so, then Grai coughed delicately.

'If I may add my voice to Vaoran's, I agree. That one could be trouble – safer to despatch him altogether, rather than run the risk.'

Any who might have had doubts found them submerged in the majority view. Vaoran nodded, and rose
to his feet.

'Very well, gentlemen. We have only to await the
moment. I thank you for coming, and I wish you all the
best of fortune. Let's hope that this marks a new
beginning for the city we all love!'

They left, as they had arrived, in twos and threes to
avoid arousing comment. Grai was among the last to go,
and as Vaoran escorted him to the door the plump
councillor turned and smiled.

'Prince Vaoran,' he said, and looked the other man
up and down. 'It suits you well, my friend. And it's my
belief that yours will be the best dynasty Haven has had
in a very long while!'

Chapter 17

Haven prepared itself for Dead Night, and with each day that dawned Kyre's forebodings grew.

He had to acknowledge that DiMag's forces were doing all they could to meet the threat from the sea, but he knew in his heart that it wasn't enough. On the rare occasions when sheer exhaustion forced him to snatch an hour or two of sleep, images of Calthar as he had last seen her stalked his dreams – Calthar, and her monstrous, rotting predecessors, the unbroken chain of Mothers that had passed down the centuries from that first traitress and founder of the city in the sea.

Malhareq: the quintessence of spirtual corruption; a rogue scion of her race – but as well as sorcerous power she had possessed charisma, and that charisma had been enough to earn her a willing following ready to challenge the Sun-Hound's rule and elevate her in his stead. With Brigrandon's help, Kyre had pieced together much of what had taken place after the attempted uprising that led to his demise. Malhareq had failed in her ultimate ambition to rule Haven: far from ensuring her victory, the death of their lord had aroused such fury in the warriors who opposed her that she had been forced to flee with her followers. She had taken refuge in the deeps of the sea – in those days, Kyre remembered, the people of Haven had been at home in both elements – and in her new domain she had founded a dynasty that had now grown strong enough to destroy the people from which it sprang so many centuries ago.

The two races could be one again, if only the cancerous legacy of the Mothers could be defied and their sway broken. But all Haven's army, and all Simorh's sorcery, couldn't hope to prevail against the power Calthar would wield on Dead Night. If there was any hope left for the city, it lay in the discovery of the lost amulet that was twin to Kyre's own.

Sometimes, as he sat in Brigrandon's rooms among the mind-numbing heaps of manuscripts, scrolls and documents that the scholar had unearthed from the palace archives, Kyre came close to despair. Though Brigrandon had pressed every man and woman capable of understanding the old tongue into his service, their chances of finding the manuscript that would lead them to the talisman – if, indeed, such a manuscript existed at all – were remote, and worsening with each hour that passed. Their efforts were further hampered by the fact that their ability to translate the ancient language accurately was flawed at best: Kyre himself was the only man alive who could read the oldest of the documents with any fluency. And though he had learned much of Haven's history since his death, he had found not the smallest reference to what he so desperately sought.

If only Talliann could have remembered ...

Simorh had tried to unlock the memories frozen in Talliann's mind, but she had failed. And the black-haired girl's inability to recall her past life brought Kyre another and more personal pain. She had been his lover, his consort, his wife; the moon around which his sun revolved. But although those memories were alive and vital in his mind, to her they meant nothing. She had lost the past, and he couldn't touch her, couldn't reach her – and couldn't explain to her what they had once been to each other. If he had tried to take up the threads of their old life, Talliann couldn't have understood his reasons, and he would run the risk of alienating her. And when he looked at her, and saw the blankness in her dark eyes, the emotion he felt was worse than bereavement.

For that reason alone he had forced himself to keep his distance from Talliann. If she wondered at his reluctance to spend time with her she never voiced it: Simorh had had a room prepared for her in her own tower, and the girl spent most of each day either there or closeted with the sorceress. She had found an unexpected champion in Simorh; a bond had developed between the two, and Kyre sometimes wondered if Simorh saw in Talliann's estrangement from him an echo of her own estrangement from DiMag.

As for DiMag himself, the prince seemed to have become possessed by a ravening energy that drove him day and night. He never slept – the daylight hours saw him roving the palace, arguing with councillors, watching the drilling of the soldiers, conferring with those few advisers he still felt he could trust; while at night he kept vigil with Gamora or joined the weary-eyed scholars in Brigrandon's rooms to pore fruitlessly for hour upon hour over the ancient documents. The desperation he felt was eating to the core of his being, his health was deteriorating fast; but nothing would persuade him to allow himself a moment's ease.

And with each hour that trickled by, each manuscript that yielded nothing and was set aside, Dead Night drew nearer: until at last the sun set in a blaze that shot ominous, angry shadows through the rising bank of fog on the last night before the conflict.

Kyre felt as though his legs were about to give way under him as he climbed the stairs to his own room in the Sunrise Tower. He had been banished from his labours by Brigrandon when he fell asleep for the third time over the pile of parchments before him: the scholar, himself red-eyed with weariness, had ordered him to sleep until morning; his place would be taken by another and the search would continue. Kyre was too dazed to argue. He simply nodded, and walked slowly, joints stiff, from the room.

His own chamber hadn't been occupied since his

return from the sea-citadel and was damp and bitterly cold, but he was past caring. He shut the door behind him, stumbled to the bed, and didn't have the strength to do more than pull a blanket roughly over himself before he was asleep.

As soon as he opened his eyes in the darkness, he realised that he hadn't woken naturally. Something had disturbed his sleep; and as his eyes grew a little better accustomed to the dim, unnatural light refracted through the window by the fog outside, he realised that he wasn't alone in the room.

A fearful reflex made him sit up and reach out for a weapon that wasn't there, but before he could co-herently challenge the human-shaped shadow lurking by the door it moved, groping towards his bed.

'Kyre . . . ?' Her voice was soft and frightened, and recognition stunned him. He had time to speak her name, wonderingly, before Talliann had reached him and flung her arms around him, her body quivering. He held her tightly, unable to speak, kissing the crown of her black hair. She was crying – he could feel the wetness of her tears on his shoulder – and at last she whispered. 'I can't sleep. Not tonight, not – knowing what tomorrow will bring.' Her whole frame shuddered. 'Kyre, I'm so afraid!'

He turned her face up towards his and kissed her again, first her brow, then her cheek, then, very lightly and tentatively, her lips. Fresh tears welled in her eyes.

'Don't send me away, Kyre. Please don't. I don't think I could bear being alone . . . '

Kyre pulled back the blanket and she climbed into the bed beside him. There was barely room for them both, but neither cared; Talliann nestled as close as she could to Kyre and he held her, protectively as he used to do, her head cradled in the crook of his arm. Her body felt as familiar to him as his own and her touch awoke yet more memories, insignificant in that they recalled only fleeting moments of their lives, yet precious to him nonetheless.

They didn't speak again. They simply lay in the moonshot darkness, easing their fear by sharing it in silence and stillness, only thankful not to be alone. And after a while, they slept.

In the chilly grey light of dawn, the city was unnervingly silent. From her window Simorh had seen the sky turn briefly roseate with the sunrise before a blanket of cloud moved in to cut off the brilliance. She had refused to look for an omen in the weather, good or bad, feeling that she could no longer trust her instincts. But her heart felt like a solid ball of lead beneath her ribs.

Thean came in softly, bearing a covered tray which she set down on a table near the sorceress's bed.

'Bread and a herb beverage, lady, as you asked,' she said.

Simorh turned her head and managed a bleak smile. 'Thank you, Thean. I won't need you again for a while yet. You should try to sleep a little longer.'

The girl nodded and left as quietly as she had come. Simorh stared at the tray for a few moments – bread was all she would allow herself to eat today, but she didn't even want that – then she left the window and walked down the stairs and through the anteroom to her inner sanctum, where she stood for a long time gazing at the motionless figure on the couch.

The curtains had been drawn in the room, and the only illumination came from four small lamps set at the cardinal points around the couch. Gamora lay under a light blanket with her feet together and arms folded over her breast: her face was a peaceful mask and she might have been naturally sleeping.

Or dead. Though the room's trappings were a vital precaution to protect the child, the tableau reminded Simorh of the day twelve years ago when the body of DiMag's father had lain in state to receive the last

farewells of a grieving family before he went to his
funeral pyre. *Omens*, she thought again, and to reassure
herself she moved to the couch and touched Gamora's
forehead with light fingers. Her warmth banished the
worst of Simorh's fears but gave her little comfort, and
she turned and left the room – to find DiMag waiting
for her.

'Thean said you were awake.' DiMag looked hag-
ridden, then glanced towards the door of the inner
room. 'No change?'

'Nothing.' She shook her head and blinked back tears,
angry with herself for giving way to weakness at this late
hour. 'You should try to sleep yourself, DiMag.'

He shrugged. 'I would if I could. But it doesn't matter
now, does it? When tomorrow dawns I'll either be
resting easy in my bed, or sleeping for eternity.' He tried
to smile, but the attempt at levity hadn't worked for
either of them. Sighing, he turned towards the window.
'Kyre at least has rested. Brigrandon ordered him to bed
last night when he all but collapsed over his
manuscripts.' This time he did smile. 'I sent a servant
to check on him a little while ago. He's still asleep – and
Talliann's with him.'

'Talliann? She went to him?'

'So it would seem. Perhaps after all she's beginning
to regain her memory without the aid of the amulet.'

Simorh felt a pang of bitter envy stab through her, and
quelled it. 'I wish that could be true,' she said, then
added: 'The manuscripts – I suppose there's still no
clue?'

'Nothing.' DiMag shook his head and scuffed at a
threadbare patch in the carpet with the toe of one boot.
'We must, I think, face up to the prospect of meeting
our enemies without the help we'd hoped for.' He
blinked, then his expression hardened and his voice
became brisk. 'With that in mind, I've ordered the full
council to meet three hours before sunset, in the court

hall. There are bound to be last-minute details to clarify. I thought you'd better know, in case you want to attend.' His eyes were frank. 'I'd appreciate it if you did.'

'Of course I'll attend.' If she could do nothing more than lend her voice in support to his, Simorh thought, it would at least be something.

The prince nodded. 'Then I'd best get down to the courtyard. Our foot-soldiery are about to be put through their paces one last time; for whatever little good it may do, I should give them the benefit of my moral support.' He hesitated, then moved towards her and, to her surprise, took hold of her hand. 'I'm sorry, Simorh,' he said, and there was terrible weariness and terrible sadness in his voice. 'I wish things could have been different ... ' And he raised her hand to his lips and kissed her fingers.

'Don't, DiMag!' She turned her head away in distress, and abruptly he released her.

'I know,' he said. 'It's too late. I'm sorry ... ' And he turned and limped out of the room.

Haven was as ready as it could ever hope to be. The army had completed its final drill; in the city itself, every able-bodied man and not a few women prepared weapons that ranged from well-honed swords and daggers to fish-gutting knives, staves and horsewhips. DiMag had issued no order to press the citizens into service, but, knowing what was at stake, they would fight without the need for compulsion, lending their numbers to the ranks of trained soldiers.

The sun passed meridian, and the first thin trails of mist formed again in the lower-lying streets. As councillors began to file into the court hall for their final meeting, Kyre and Brigrandon sat in the scholar's room with the now nighmarishly familiar heaps of documents before them. Brigrandon had slept for a while in the pre-dawn hours while his team worked on, and when Kyre returned he had despatched the others to their beds; now they were alone with the manuscripts and their diminishing hopes.

Talliann, too, was sleeping. When Kyre woke he had found her gone, and when he went in search of her Falla had told him that she was with Simorh, helping the sorceress to make her preparations. When the sun set, Kyre thought, he would go to her . . .

In the court hall, the gathering was all but complete. Liveried stewards opened the double doors for DiMag and Simorh as they approached together, Simorh's hand resting in a formal posture on DiMag's arm. She wore her black robe rather than more customary court attire as a deliberate reminder to the council that she was a sorceress as well as a princess; seeing her, DiMag had acknowledged the gesture with a small smile and his eyes had been momentarily warm. They walked side by side towards the great chair, watched by the silent ranks of advisers. Together they mounted the dais, and DiMag took his seat.

'Gentlemen,' he said, 'As you are all aware, this is our last meeting before Dead Night – and there's little point in pretending that it might not be the last meeting that will ever be convened in the court of Haven. I thank you for taking time from your urgent duties, and I assure you that I won't keep you longer than necessary. I intend simply to apprise you of the position as it now stands, and to reiterate the strategy that will be put into operation at sunset. I – ' And he stopped, frowning, as a group of councillors moved aside suddenly and Vaoran stepped out of the ranks to stand before the dais.

The swordsmaster looked up at the throne, and there was a smile on his face. He laid a hand on the hilt of his sheathed sword, and said in a cool voice that carried easily through the hall,

'I think not, my lord.'

Thean and Falla tried to stop the six men who forced their way into the tower ten minutes after Simorh had left, but against such a strength they could do nothing. Two of the intruders – one sporting livid parallel scratches on his face where Thean's nails had raked him as they struggled – pinned the girls' arms behind their backs and held them, while another went into Simorh's inner sanctum and the remaining three took the stairs to the rooms above. Moments later the girls heard shouting, scuffles, a woman's scream of protest, and the three reappeared with Talliann struggling like a wildcat in their grasp. She was biting, kicking, flailing wildly; only when one of the men bunched his fist and hit her on the jaw did she subside.

They dragged her towards the door, and the sixth of their number emerged from the sanctum with Gamora in his arms.

A short, burly army captain entered the barracks flanked by two of his most trusted sergeants. His men, who had gathered in the mess hall, were baffled by his unexpected summons – but the captain soon allayed their puzzlement. A minor change in strategy, nothing more; and it took only minutes to clarify. The soldiers were content.

The small detachment of armed men who gathered in the palace's entrance hall had been carefully and precisely instructed in their task. The man they wanted would be with the scholar Brigrandon, and their orders were clear. The old man wasn't to be harmed beyond the demands of restraint, but his companion was another matter. Their sergeant had told them to do what must be done as quickly and as cleanly as possible, then bring the corpse back to the barracks.

The men waited until their numbers were complete, then they formed up and moved off towards the terrace.

DiMag stared white-faced at Vaoran and said, his voice shaking with rage:

'I don't think I believe what I'm hearing! You *dare* to stand before me and speak such treachery – '

'I dare because I must, Prince DiMag!' Vaoran raised his voice to cut across the prince's fury. 'You have left Haven with no other choice, for you have proved yourself unfit to rule – therefore your rule must end!'

DiMag got to his feet. 'Guards!' He gestured to the uniformed men ranged in a line behind the dais. 'Arrest Swordsmaster Vaoran! The charge is treason!'

The guards didn't move, only continued to stare blank-faced ahead of them. Vaoran smiled.

'The guardsmen are aware of their duty to Haven, Prince DiMag. Their loyalty is to our city before all else.'

Realising the full extent of the betrayal, DiMag snatched at the hilt of his sword. He had half drawn it from its scabbard when Vaoran spoke again.

'The guardsmen also have orders to kill anyone who makes an attempt on the life of an appointed councillor,' he said, and his smile widened sardonically. 'As a matter of self-defence, such an order is quite justified.' He nodded to the guards, and as one they drew their swords and held them at a threatening angle towards the throne.

DiMag felt Simorh's hand take his in a vicelike clasp, but he couldn't respond. Shock made his pulse pound as though his whole body were being assaulted by hammers, and his only coherent thought was: *I should have known ... may the Eye help me, I should have known!*

'Traitor ... ' His voice grated and he could barely get the word out. '*Traitor!*'

Grai cleared his throat and stepped forward to stand at Vaoran's side. The prince turned a searing, accusing gaze on him, but Grai ignored it. 'This is not treachery, Prince DiMag, but the just and necessary decision of the properly appointed members of the court council of Haven,' he said. 'And as spokesman for that council, it is my duty to inform you that the decision to remove you from office has been ratified by a sufficient majority to make any question of treason irrelevant.' Beside him, Vaoran glanced round at his colleagues, his eyes speculative as his gaze rested on certain individuals whose support he couldn't yet count on. That, he thought, would change in good time.

DiMag continued to stare at Grai for a few moments longer, then slowly sat down as the last vestiges of his strength suddenly drained away.

'Grai,' he said desperately, 'Do you have any idea of what this insanity means? In three hours the sun will set, and we'll face the deadliest threat we've ever known. To choose this moment to pursue your self-seeking ambitions, when Haven is on the brink of disaster – ' He shook his head helplessly. 'You're mad; *all* of you!'

'Plans for fighting the sea-demons will suffer no setback,' Vaoran countered. 'But not your plans, Prince DiMag – ours.'

DiMag sucked in breath with a hissing sound. 'You've been scheming for this moment since the first – '

'For long enough to ensure that we give our city its best chance – its only chance – of survival!' Vaoran snapped. 'We've suffered under the burden of your whims and obsessions for too long, prince! You can rant, you can rage – but there's not a thing you can do to stop us!' He shook off Grai's attempt to lay a restraining hand on his arm. 'We have had enough, *my lord*.' He gestured to the guard behind DiMag's chair. 'Disarm the prince, and detain him.'

DiMag hadn't the time to do more than rise and turn before strong hands pinioned his arms and pulled him from the dais. His sword was dragged from its scabbard and he found himself surrounded by armed men. He couldn't react in any way. Shock had taken him in a rigid grip, and he felt as if he was dreaming.

Vaoran looked up at Simorh, who still stood on the

dais. She seemed as stunned as DiMag, and the swordsmaster gave her a smile that was intended to be encouraging.

'Lady – may I assist you down?'

She snatched her hand away as he reached towards her. 'Swordsmaster Vaoran,' her voice was pitched low. 'What you have done here today, your perfidy, is – is' She grimaced, striving to control herself. 'You are *scum*!'

Vaoran's face clouded. 'Lady, it pains me to hear such condemnation from you, and I hope that when this crisis is over I can convince you of my sincerity. We have no quarrel with you – indeed, your wellbeing is of paramount importance to all loyal citizens, as is that of the Princess Gamora.'

She looked at him with withering contempt. 'You are a liar, Swordsmaster Vaoran.'

'Madam, I am not.' He placed one foot on the dais, chagrined by the way she immediately stepped back, then suddenly drew his sword and held it up before his face in a formal salute.

'Princess Simorh, it will now be my privilege to take the throne of Haven as its new ruler. In that capacity, I pledge to you the honour which is your right.' He completed the salute, returned the sword to its scabbard, and though his smile was for her alone he was unable to resist glancing surreptitiously at DiMag. 'And though I make no presumptions, madam, it's my fervent hope that you will one day consent to take up again your role of consort.'

Simorh stared at him in utter disbelief, and DiMag made a violent movement to free himself from his guards which was instantly restrained. He didn't speak, and Simorh struggled to find words that would adequately express her loathing for the burly man who stood before her. She longed to raise one hand and blast Vaoran where he stood, but she had no such power: her sorcery wasn't of the order of Calthar's. But Vaoran must have seen something of that longing in her eyes, for he stepped back, and signalled to the rest of the guardsmen.

'Please escort the Princess Simorh to her tower,' he said, and bowed to the sorceress. 'With your permission, lady, I'll wait on you as soon as my business here is concluded. I've prepared a strategy that I hope will restore the Princess Gamora back to us and it's only right that you should know the details.'

White-lipped, Simorh said curtly, 'Very well. You have my permission.' She was aware of DiMag's hot gaze on her, but didn't dare look at him lest she gave herself away. Intuition was telling her to make no attempt to argue with Vaoran, but instead to appear to comply with his wishes. If she could keep some measure of her freedom, she might yet find a way of working against the usurper. She only prayed that DiMag didn't believe she would betray him.

DiMag watched as she was led from the hall. His face was a mask, and if Vaoran had hoped to see distress or fear in his eyes he was disappointed. When Simorh and her escort had gone, he stepped up on to the dais and looked first at the throne and then at the man he had deposed.

'Take the ex-prince to his rooms, and see that he's well guarded,' he said. DiMag went without demur, and Vaoran turned to face the council.

'Gentlemen.' He lowered himself slowly on to the great chair, settled himself on the uncomfortable seat. 'To business . . . '

Brigrandon said in a tightly controlled voice: 'Kyre . . .'

Kyre looked up, blinking as his eyes tried to re-focus from the crabbed script he had been reading, and when he saw Brigrandon's face his heart missed a beat painfully. He stood up. 'You haven't – '

'I don't know. A lot of it's badly faded, and I can't translate some of the words. But I think you'd better come and look.'

The scholar pulled the lamp on his table closer as Kyre bent to peer over his shoulder at the document. It was, Kyre saw from the first few words on the page, an account of the construction of a temple to honour Haven's dead hero, and the thought that it was the same building which now stood in ruins on the shingle bar gave him a peculiar *frisson*.

'Here,' Brigrandon said, stabbing with one dusty finger. 'That sentence; something about an enshrining. What, exactly, does it say?'

Kyre's eyes followed the line he indicated. For a moment he couldn't let himself believe it ... but it was there. *It was there!*

'Brigrandon,' he said, his voice soft with awe, 'this is it ... this is what we've been searching for. *Talliann's amulet is in the old temple!*'

And at the dedication of the crypt, beneath the central flagstone was placed the talisman of our Sun-Hound's beloved consort – a symbol here which, Kyre remembered, had always been used to depict Talliann's name – who gave herself to the embrace of death in grief at her lord's passing. This amulet will stand sentinel between Haven and her enemies, until such time as it may be reunited with its lost twin and shall bring back to us all that we have lost ...

'Oh, Kyre ... ' Brigrandon said in an old, old voice. 'And we'd almost given up hope ... '

'DiMag must be told – and Simorh.' Kyre started towards the door, but before he reached it it was flung open from outside. On the threshold stood Nirn, Brigrandon's young servant. His face was flushed and he was breathless; he stumbled into the room and slammed the door at his back.

'Master, there's a detachment of soldiers on their way here – '

'Soldiers?' Brigrandon was nonplussed, and Nirn nodded, gulping down lungfuls of air.

'They're coming for the Sun-Hound – to arrest him.

Master, the palace has been taken over, the prince
deposed, and – '

'*What?*' Brigrandon was on his feet. '*Deposed?* Nirn,
are you out of your mind?'

'No, Brigrandon; wait.' Kyre waved the old man to
silence and addressed the breathless servant. 'Nirn, are
you sure of this?'

'Yes, sir. It happened a bare twenty minutes ago;
there was a meeting in the court hall, the royal guard
had been corrupted, and Swordsmaster Vaoran – '

'Vaoran ... ' Suddenly disbelief changed to understanding in Brigrandon's eyes. 'Of course: *Vaoran*. But
I didn't think he'd be so stupid as to choose a moment
like this!'

'On the contrary; he couldn't have chosen better,'
Kyre said grimly. 'Nirn, what else do you know?'

'Very little, sir; only that it all seems to have been
accomplished without trouble. There's talk of prisoners,
but not many.'

Prisoners ... *Talliann!* Kyre thought in alarm. He
moved towards the door. 'Brigrandon, I must go!'

'No, sir!' Nirn cried. 'The soldiers are coming for you
– if you go out on the terrace you won't be able to avoid
them!'

'The lad's right,' Brigrandon said tersely. 'And with
Vaoran in power, you can be sure they don't mean to
carry you into the palace with a laurel crown on your
head.' He looked round the room, and his gaze lit on
a window. 'Can you get through that?'

Kyre eyed it. 'I think so.'

'Then go. Out there is a disused herb garden; it isn't
overlooked, and it's overgrown enough to offer plenty
of hiding places. I'll send the soldiers on a wild goose
chase and find out as much as I can at the same time.
Stay put until I come for you personally.'

'Brigrandon, there isn't time to waste hiding! If I
could get to the old temple – '

'You'll never get out of the palace, let alone the city.

Don't argue, Kyre – if they find you here, we three won't be able to fend them off!'

He had no choice . . . Kyre stepped up on a table and, as Brigrandon thumped the window open with a clenched fist, squeezed himself through. The scholar slammed the window behind him, and as he did so, the sound of tramping boots approached along the terrace.

'Sit down,' the scholar said hastily to Nirn. 'Sit where Kyre was, spread those documents around and pretend to be asleep. Did anyone see you coming here?'

'No, master.'

'Good.' Brigrandon hesitated, then snatched up a half-full ale jug and refilled the cup by his own chair, taking care to spill a fair amount. 'They'll find us both sleeping, and me more than a little drunk. When they wake us, we've been here since this morning going through the manuscripts. Kyre was here, but he left just after noon. You don't know where he's gone; I'll offer several confusing suggestions. Got that?'

'Yes, sir.' Nirn slid into his place. When the soldiers hammered on the door, both men had their heads pillowed on their arms, eyes shut, and Brigrandon was snoring gently.

'So,' Simorh said carefully, 'you believe that you will succeed in leading the sea-demons' sorceress into a trap.'

Vaoran inclined his head in acknowledgement. 'It's the best chance we can give to the little princess. And believe me when I say that every man involved will fight to save her.'

'Oh, yes; I believe you.' She rose and went to the window; at her movement the guard by the door tensed, but Vaoran waved him back. Simorh was no threat: he'd ensured that all her sorcerous accoutrements were removed to a place where she couldn't reach them, and beyond that no other precautions were needed. Indeed, he'd made better progress with her than he'd thought possible, for the simple reason that he knew and had played on her one weakness: Gamora. He was aware of the value in presenting himself as the child's champion; and if his plan succeeded – as he believed it would – then he would earn Simorh's lifelong gratitude, and in time that could develop into far more.

'The girl will be taken to the strand at sunset, as I originally exhorted the pr – the ex-prince to do,' he told her. As he spoke he watched her face to see how she would react to the change in DiMag's title; but her expression gave away nothing. 'The trap will be set, and – providing only that Calthar keeps the rendezvous – there's no reason why she shouldn't take the bait.'

Simorh nodded. 'And the – and Kyre?'

His mouth pursed. 'I'm reluctant to say it, lady, but he could be a danger to our plans and therefore to the little princess. There's no doubt in my mind that he has attempted to dupe us with his claim to be the true Sun-Hound, and I suspect that he may even be in league with our enemies in some way.' He studied her for a moment, then decided to take the risk of being frank. 'I dared not take any chances, madam, and by now Kyre will be dead.'

With a tremendous effort Simorh managed to maintain her expression, though inside she felt horribly sick. *Dead* ... With DiMag locked and guarded in his room, Gamora taken to a 'place of safety' and Talliann imprisoned and awaiting the moment when she would be taken to the strand, Kyre had been her last hope. Now, there was nothing.

She gazed out of the window. The cloud was beginning to break up, and long shafts of light lay low and mellow across the city. Two hours or less until the sun set ...

A step sounded behind her and a hand came to rest lightly on her shoulder. She forced herself not to shudder at Vaoran's touch, but her stomach muscles tensed involuntarily.

'Don't despair, lady.' The swordsmaster's voice was kind. 'Haven will triumph. I'm sure of it.'

She couldn't bring herself to answer him: if she had tried, she would have lost all self control and spat in his face. The hand withdrew from her shoulder and she heard his heavy tread as he and the guard made their way out, leaving her alone with the hatred burning like a volcano inside her.

Chapter 18

Brigrandon prided himself that he knew the lesser byways of Haven's palace better than almost any man alive. But he'd never dreamed that his knowledge would be put to such an urgent and alarming use.

Walking along the terrace to the main entrance, he knew he was in full view of anyone who might be watching and so took good care to weave and stagger a few times to keep up appearances. By now, he calculated, the soldiers would have searched the Sunrise Tower and found it empty, and they'd be spreading out through the palace, looking for their quarry and cursing Brigandon for his drunken incoherence. Kyre would be safe enough from their efforts: the old scholar doubted if the soldiers even knew of the herb-garden's existence.

He turned in at the main door and loitered in the hall for a few moments, as though he'd forgotten where it was he meant to go. Two servants scurried by, but ignored him; Haven's new master had no interest in an ageing sot of a scholar and, provided he didn't arouse anyone's suspicions, Brigandon would be left alone.

The servants disappeared, and for a moment there was quiet – then a slight figure moved out of the shadows of the stairwell and beckoned. Brigandon checked quickly over his shoulder and hurried to meet her.

'Falla – you had Nirn's message? What news?' He kept his voice to a whisper.

The dark-haired girl hugged her shawl around herself. 'The princess is unguarded, Master Brigandon; she's free to move about the palace. I told her you needed to see her urgently and she said she would meet you in your rooms. She's on her way there now.'

He patted her shoulder gratefully. '*Thank* you, Falla! Is there any word of the prince?'

She shook her head. 'No. The princess tried to see him, but he's too heavily guarded. All we know is that he's still alive.'

'Very well. You'd best go back.'

'If I can do anything more – '

'I'll send word.' Brigrandon patted her shoulder again and hastened away.

As he opened the door of his room, Simorh rose from where she had been crouching before the fireplace.

'Brigrandon – ' She got to her feet, and only force of habit stopped her from running forward to embrace him. 'Falla gave me your message – is it true? Is Kyre still alive?'

The tutor smiled reassuringly at her. 'Unless Vaoran is more concerned with gardening than I think he is, madam, yes.' And as she frowned uncomprehendingly he crossed the room and thumped open the window. 'Kyre!' His voice was soft but carried on the still air. 'It's Brigrandon – you can come back now!'

A tangle of bushes in the overgrown herb-garden rustled, and Kyre emerged. He ran to the window, keeping low, and Brigrandon helped him over the sill.

'Princess . . . ' Kyre froze, surprise and relief on his face as he saw Simorh. He recovered himself, brushed dry leaves from his hair and clothing. 'I'd thought – when we heard the news – '

'Oh, it's true, all right,' Brigrandon told him. 'Vaoran is now effectively ruler of Haven, and controls both the council and the army. The prince is a prisoner; but we know at least that he's still alive.'

'Vaoran has other plans for me,' Simorh interjected bitterly, her tone leaving them in no doubt of what she meant. 'So far, that has enabled me to keep my freedom.' She shuddered.

'What of Talliann?' Kyre asked urgently.

She met his eyes. 'They've taken her, Kyre. Vaoran took good care to explain his plan to me, because he thinks his concern for Gamora will inveigle him into my favour. He means to keep the rendezvous with Calthar.'

Kyre swore, then looked at Brigrandon. 'What's the hour?'

Brigrandon knew what he was thinking, and glanced towards the window. 'Less than an hour until sunset.'

'Will the tide have cleared the strand yet?'

The scholar made a rapid mental calculation, then nodded. 'By the time you can reach the temple, yes.'

Simorh looked quickly from one to the other. 'What is this? I don't understand.'

'Princess,' Kyre said, 'when we heard that Vaoran's men were hunting for me, Brigrandon and I had that very moment discovered the whereabouts of Talliann's lost amulet. It's in the ruined temple, under the central flagstone of the crypt floor.'

Her face was immobile with astonishment for a moment – then hoped flared in her eyes. 'Oh, by the Eye ... Kyre, are you sure?'

'There's no possible doubt.'

'Then we must retrieve it, and return it to Talliann! If the two stones can be linked – '

'Lady, there isn't time,' Brigrandon interrupted. 'If Vaoran means to take Talliann to the strand at sunset, he'll be moving out in less than an hour, and the army will be on his heels.'

He was right. 'There's only one chance,' Kyre said. 'Vaoran's party must be intercepted, and stopped!'

'And where would you find enough trustworthy men to stand against them, let alone in such a short time?' Brigrandon demanded. 'No, it wouldn't work. It – '

'Wait!' Simorh held up a hand. She was staring at something propped in one corner of the room. The sea-warrior's spear that Kyre had snatched in the citadel

– he had left it with Brigrandon, almost forgotten its existence.

'They say you wield that like a master,' Simorh said, her look wry. 'Is it true?'

'Yes ... '

'Then take it, and you and I will go to the temple. Now, before Vaoran and his men set out.'

'Lady, we can't hope to prevail against them!'

'It needn't come to that. If the amulet is in our hands before they arrive, there'll be no need for fighting.' Her eyes were ablaze now. 'There's a spell – I learned it as part of my training, though without the two amulets it can't be used. If I can remember it, and I believe I can, Vaoran will present no threat to us!' She smiled at him, vulpine. 'I may not be a warrior, but I have other skills which are as valuable. All I need is for you to guard me while the work is done.'

Kyre hesitated – then returned her smile and with it a good measure of respect. There was still a chance for them all ...

'Lady,' he said, and kissed her hand, 'We may triumph over Calthar yet!'

Their leave-taking of Brigrandon was hurried but intense. Kyre and the old scholar clasped arms, neither able to voice the thought that this might be the last time they would ever meet. Then Simorh hugged Brigrandon, and kissed his cheek soundly.

'We'll return,' she said, resolution and emotion making her voice harsh. 'And when the Hag rises, we'll be ready to meet her!'

Brigrandon nodded, and Kyre realised the old man was biting back tears. 'I'll try to get word to the prince, madam. I'll tell him what you've done ... '

She hugged him again and whispered, 'Thank you, Brigrandon – thank you for your loyalty!'

And then Kyre and Simorh were outside in the raw, crimson glare of the lowering sun.

The city was a place of ghosts. Empty streets, silent houses, the few windows not yet shuttered staring into the evening light like blood-filled eyes. Mist crept around their ankles, sometimes to their knees, intensifying the quiet. Somewhere in the distance a young child was crying ... the people had done all they could, and now they waited.

As they hastened through the still town Kyre glanced occasionally at the woman beside him. He had begun by hating Simorh; now he had learned to respect her, pity her, and, in a strange, brotherly way, love her. She was a true champion of the city and the husband and child she sought to save, and she deserved better fortune than life had so far dealt her. He thought of DiMag, imprisoned and under threat of his life; Gamora, little better than dead with Calthar's enchantment still upon her ... reflexively his hand went to the amulet which now hung on its repaired chain about his neck. He had failed Haven once, though Haven might argue it, and his failure had brought them all to this. If any power in the world could prevent it, he wouldn't fail again.

The wind was rising. As they emerged from the sandstone arch it came blustering to meet them, ripping their hair back from their faces, punching and buffeting them, and raising whirling clouds of dry sand that stung their skin like whiplashes. Vast shadows reached out from the cliffs towards the sea, and the sea itself where the sun still touched it was gory, waves beginning to tumble and agitate as the wind strengthened.

Simorh ducked her head aside and said, raising her voice to be heard, 'This may be to our advantage! The wind will wipe out our footprints – otherwise, we'd have had to keep to the cliff edge and waste precious time!'

He nodded, and took her arm as she stepped out from the arch's comparative shelter. Leaning into the gale, they ploughed through soft sand towards the shingle bar, both painfully aware that Vaoran's party might emerge from the gateway and see them before they could reach cover. The bar loomed ahead; reaching it, they paused and looked back.

The bay was deserted. But the sun was now no more than a sliver of furious brilliance above the headland: in minutes it would be swallowed.

'There'll be no fog tonight!' Simorh shouted, trying to counter the terror that was threatening to dig its claws deep into her. 'We mustn't delay – come on!'

They ran, as far as running was possible, along the shingle bar towards the monstrous silhouette of the ruin ahead. Once Simorh fell, swore, but was on her feet again before Kyre could stop to help her. They hastened on, and he tried not to look at the brooding sea to his right or listen to its booming, angry voice. Then shingle and shale gave way to rubble and the twisted shapes of fallen masonry, and they came to a gasping, breathless halt amid the towering pillars of the temple.

For a few moments they stood still, gratefully dragging air into their burning lungs. Kyre was about to speak to the sorceress – but as he opened his mouth, a cold wing of shadow seemed to brush by him. He looked seawards. And the sun's last crimson glow was gone, turning the ocean to a churning, endless grey.

He gripped Simorh's arm. '*Sunset!*'

She looked, and bit down hard on her lower lip. 'Quickly,' she hissed.

They found the narrow embrasure that was all that remained of the crypt's original entrance, and squeezed through. The stairs beyond were pitch dark – neither of them had thought to bring a lantern – and they felt their way carefully, step by uneven step, down the short flight to the chamber below. Here, phosphorescent algae and sea-lichen gave off a faint, eldritch glow, and Simorh stepped cautiously across a litter of stones and small rocks to the middle of the floor. Judging where she thought the central flagstone must be she crouched down and Kyre joined her. As they cleared away the debris that covered the floor – weed, broken shells, a thin covering of sand – the sorceress said:

'When the temple was built it stood on a bank fifty feet above the high tide line. Until nine years ago, the sea had never entered this chamber.' She paused in her work and looked up. 'It makes me wonder what our fate might be this time.'

'Only pray, then; that we'll be in time.' Kyre brushed at a layer of sand – and abruptly stopped as his fingers encountered something that didn't yield to his attempt to move it aside. Quickly he crouched lower, peering in the gloom, and Simorh said tensely, 'What is it?'

'I don't know ... a pattern I think, slightly raised...'

She all but shouldered him aside in her eagerness, putting her face close to the floor. 'I think ... oh, *damn* this darkness; I should have had the sense to bring a lamp!' Her fingers traced the outline Kyre had found, then she sat back on her heels. In the dimness her face was alight with excitement.

'*Yes!*' She clenched her fists triumphantly. 'This is the one – I remember it; there's a relief of the Eye in the very centre. Hurry – we must clear the debris from the slab!'

Feverishly they cleared the litter, and in less than a minute the outline of a single massive flagstone was revealed.

'How can we lift it?' Kyre asked.

The sorceress scrambled to her feet and backed away from the stone. 'Take your spear, and insert the blade into the crack between it and its neighbour.'

He didn't argue, though the idea seemed ludicrous: the spear-blade would snap long before the slab could be levered up. But a new light had crept into Simorh's eyes, and as he did as she bade him he realised that she intended to use other means.

'There – hold it there!' Her voice had taken on a harsh timbre, and she closed her eyes, drawing in a deep breath. He saw her lips move though she made

no sound; then her body tensed and an aura – faint,
but clearly discernible – flickered into life about her.
The salty air seemed to shiver and he felt a sensation
like the close, tingling awareness of an electric storm
raise the hairs on his arms and shiver through his scalp.
The spear in his hand bucked; momentarily the floor
lurched under his feet –

And the stone slab came up. It moved as though an
immensely powerful fist had punched it from below,
springing upright, teetering for a moment on its end,
before it crashed with a heavy thump on to its
neighbour, and cracked across.

Simorh's eyes met Kyre's over the hollow space that
had been exposed, and he grinned, suddenly feeling
light-headed with their triumph.

'I never was a sorcerer,' he said. 'That was always
Talliann's skill, not mine.'

The light faded from Simorh's eyes. 'Talliann ... '
she said; and glanced towards the stairs. 'They must
be on their way, if not already at the rendezvous.'

The thought sobered him abruptly and he dropped
to his knees beside the dank, musty hole. It wasn't
deep, and at first it seemed that there was nothing
there but sodden sand and the broken foundations of
the temple. Then he saw the faint, metallic glimmer ...

Centuries had neither worn the quartz pendant nor
tarnished the chain from which it hung. In size and
form it was the perfect twin to the one that hung about
Kyre's neck, but he could just make out that the quartz
of Talliann's amulet was a deep orange-red, and
embedded within it was not the Eye of Day but an
image of the eye of night – a silver-flecked pearl.

Kyre's fist clenched around the amulet as old
memories flooded into his mind. Now that both stones
were in his possession he recalled some of the
properties they had had when used in harmony; the
power that Talliann, with her seeking mind and her

magical skills, had been able to wield. Suddenly, on an impulse, he held the pendant out to Simorh.

'Wear it,' he told her. 'For Talliann's sake. You stand in the place she once occupied – you can use her power!'

Her eyes widened and she made no attempt to take the quartz from him. 'I can't, Kyre. It wouldn't be right.'

'It *is* right! Until it can be restored to her – wear it, Simorh. Please.'

She hesitated a moment longer, then reached out to take the jewel, looping the chain over her head so that the quartz lay between her breasts. Kyre saw surprise register briefly in her eyes as she sensed the stone's power; then she reached out and took his hand.

'We can't delay any longer,' she said, and there was a warmth in her voice that he'd never heard before; the warmth of sharing even the direst danger with a known and trusted friend. 'Whatever awaits us out there, we must go and meet it.'

Emerging first through the slit of rock that formed the crypt exit, Kyre saw something that made him freeze and hold out a hand to halt Simorh.

'What is it?' Her whisper echoed eerily in the confined dark, and he put a finger to his lips, flattening himself against the rock wall and pointing to the visible patch of nightscape beyond the entrance.

Etched in the last dim glow from the sky, a man was standing alert and attentive among the shattered pillars. His back was towards them, but Kyre saw the glint of an unsheathed sword, and recognised the uniform of a Haven warrior.

He put his mouth close to Simorh's ear. 'They're waiting for Calthar. They've set an ambush.'

'*Fools!*'

'I can't see Vaoran . . . he must be on the shingle bar.' Kyre frowned. 'We've no chance of helping Talliann while we're trapped here. But that guard – '

'Wait . . . ' Simorh touched his arm, gesturing towards
the embrasure. He looked, and saw that the warrior had
dropped to a crouch, leaning tensely forward. As they
watched, the man began to inch his way awkwardly
towards the cover of a broken wall. He reached it,
settled, and Simorh touched Kyre's arm again.

'We daren't wait for a better opportunity – we have
to be able to see what's happening!' she whispered.
'Ease out, and turn to the right; there's a fallen pillar
there that will shelter us well enough. And watch the
rubble under your feet.'

He nodded, and they moved forward. The soldier's
back was still towards them; the man didn't move as they
emerged from the rock slit and made for the shelter of
the pillar. Deeper shadow swallowed them, and Kyre
heard Simorh let out a pent breath. He turned his head
to get his bearings – and his heart lurched.

'*Simorh!*' His urgent hiss was barely audible over the
sounds of the sea and the rising wind, but she heard him,
and swung round as he pointed out to sea.

Something moved among the tumbling chaos of the
waves, a dark shape against the sea's uneasy
phosphorescence. As they watched, the shape drew
nearer – and a figure, lithe-limbed, crowned with a
nimbus of wild hair, rose from the shallows. For a
moment she stood motionless, her outline etched by a
cold, silvery glimmer from somewhere out over the sea;
then she shook a stream of water from her hair and
stalked towards the shingle bar.

Simorh looked at Kyre. '*Calthar?*'

He nodded, his face grim. 'Calthar.' With a gesture
warning her to silence, he eased himself out from the
shelter of the pillar and crossed quickly to the lee of a
jagged wall.

And from this vantage point he could see all he
needed to see.

Vaoran stood just off the shingle bar, some twenty

yards from the ruin. Behind him, two men held Talliann,
who stood erect and immobile, facing the sea. The wind
whipped her hair back, and her face in the night's eerie
glow was a sickly white. She looked just as she had done
when he first saw her on the strand, and Kyre had to
fight back a compulsive urge to break from his cover and
attack Vaoran and the two guards single-handed.

A hand closed on his forearm as he still struggled with
himself, and he started, then looked down into Simorh's
eyes.

'No, Kyre,' she said, her voice hard. 'Don't do it –
don't think it. There's a better way.' She smiled, a
ghastly grimace in the dimness. 'The spell I told you of:
it may turn the tide in our favour, and with the amulet's
help I think I can make it work. Wait, watch, and take
your chance when it comes.'

Calthar had emerged from the sea. She stepped on
to the shingle and stood gazing at Vaoran's small party.
Though the hump of the bar set her at a height above
them, Vaoran, on firm sand, had the better advantage.
Talliann turned her head abruptly away as the sorceress
stared at her.

'A strange welcome.' Calthar's husky voice carried
clearly even above the moaning sea and the gusting
wind. 'No Prince DiMag or his little wife to greet me?
No ranks of soldiery to form a guard of honour?' Her
voice was mocking, and her gaze raked the ruin with
undisguised contempt. 'Or are your men too shy to show
themselves?'

Vaoran ignored the taunt, and shouted back, 'It has
been decided to grant your request, Calthar. The girl
Talliann, in exchange for our little Princess Gamora's
release from bewitchment. A straightforward bargain.'

Kyre glimpsed movement at the edge of his vision.
'*Down!*' he hissed, and drove the heel of his hand
between Simorh's shoulder-blades, sending her sprawling as he fell almost on top of her. From the far side of
the broken wall another warrior emerged, crouched

low, edging round the ruin towards the strand. They
held their breath; the warrior slowed, stopped, froze . . .

'A straighforward bargain,' Calthar repeated, smiling
in a way that Kyre recognised all too well. 'So be it.' She
held out one hand, an imperious gesture. 'I have no
further interest in Haven's brat. You may release the
girl. She won't try to flee.'

As she spoke she was staring at Talliann again and,
drawn by a compulsion she couldn't fight, Talliann
raised her head and looked directly into Calthar's eyes.
Vaoran stepped aside and the two guards led the girl
forward. One pace, two, three – they were now walking
up the gentle slope of the shingle bar, and Calthar took
a lazy pace towards them. Kyre's stomach muscles
tensed agonisingly; the motionless warrior a few feet
from their hiding place began to move stealthily forward
again –

The amulet at Simorh's breast was suddenly lit from
within by a vivid glow like a tiny flame. The sorceress's
hands moved convulsively, covering the quartz; but still
the light shone through the lattice of her fingers, its
intensity growing. Her face was lit by it, her eyes were
tightly closed and her lips moved rapidly, silently, as she
mouthed the words of a conjuration. Kyre moved
quickly to shield her and the amulet from sight: as he
did so Calthar raised both arms, holding them out
towards Talliann as though to enfold her in an obscene
embrace. The two guards released their hold on the girl
and pushed her so that, involuntarily, she stumbled the
last few paces towards Calthar before falling at her feet.
She lay huddled on the shingle like a mesmerised
animal, and did not move.

Calthar stared down at the two men who had guarded
Talliann, then turned her face towards Vaoran. Her
mouth widened in a smile that was almost pitying.

'Go back to Haven, little man,' she said. 'Go back,
and watch over your city in the hour of its death.' She
snapped her fingers, once, and Talliann, like a puppet

whose strings had abruptly jerked it to life, rose. 'Your little princess will wake, for I would have her see the final destruction of her heritage! Her life, like all your lives, will be short enough.' The smile became a terrible grin. 'You are a gullible fool, my friend. A very gullible fool.' And, the tatters of her robe sweeping around her, she turned – and stopped.

Vaoran said evenly: 'You speak a little too soon, Calthar.'

Haven's warriors stood between Calthar and the sea. Each had drawn his sword, and they formed an apparently impassable barrier. For a few moments no one moved as the sorceress gazed at the men, and Kyre almost felt pity for Vaoran. The swordsmaster still believed that he could best this monster. He had so much to learn ...

'Ah, little man,' Calthar said. '*Such* a little man. Such a simple trap. Do you know no better than that?'

She turned – and met the point of Vaoran's sword as he lunged at her. The blade rammed into her heart; she stopped, rigid, and for an instant a look of surprised irony showed on her face. Then it metamorphosised into a sly and ugly smile. Slowly, deliberately, she gripped the hilt of the sword protruding from her body, and with a swift, economical movement wrenched it free.

There was no blood on the blade. No blood spilling from what should have been a fatal wound. Calthar's smile widened, and as Vaoran stared in dumb shock, eyes almost bursting from their sockets, she took a single pace towards him.

Kyre had a premonition of what was to happen. Vaoran was transfixed, his body immobilised by the impossibility that his mind couldn't assimilate. Calthar tossed the sword carelessly into the air. It hung unsupported, drawing the swordsmaster's hypnotised gaze – and the sorceress clenched her fist in a swift, violent gesture.

The sword twisted in mid-air, turned and hovered quivering for a single moment, before it came sweeping down in a murderous, arcing slash. At the last instant before the sword struck, intelligence and appalled understanding returned to Vaoran's eyes; but it was too late. The blade sheared through his neck, the impact not even slowing its deadly sweep, and the swordsmaster's decapitated body crashed to the sand.

Calthar turned her face up to the sky, her laugher echoing from the cliffs –

And at Kyre's side, Simorh shrieked a single word. Kyre felt a terrific jolt hit him as a blast of raw power ripped from the amulet at her throat and almost threw him to the ground. An instant later the sky was torn apart by a howling, thunderous crimson flash that lit the scene with stunning brilliance. Calthar whirled round, the soldiers fell back, yelling in fear –

'*Now!*' Simorh screamed. Kyre didn't stop to think what he was doing; he *couldn't* stop, couldn't control the surge of furious and desperate energy that erupted within him. He broke from cover and leaped up the slope of the shingle bank towards Calthar and Talliann. The sorceress spun to face him, snarling like an animal; he swung the spear, bringing the blade shearing towards her, saw her jerk back as it skimmed by an inch from her skull. She recovered her balance instantly, sprang at him as the sky split open again – he had no time to do anything other than snatch at Talliann's arm, pulling her out of Calthar's reach, before the sorceress's hands clamped on the spear haft.

Talliann fell heavily, rolling from the bank on to the sand, but Kyre could do nothing to help her. For a moment that seemed to freeze them in another dimension he and Calthar were locked motionless, face to face, only the spear a flimsy and precarious barrier between them. In the grim light he saw Calthar smile, and the deranged eyes of Malhareq, alive even in death, glared out from her twisted face. Hatred gave him strength; he wrenched, kicked out, and his heel slammed against Calthar's breastbone, sending her spinning backwards.

'*Simorh!!*' Kyre's frantic yell resounded over the howl of wind, sea and sky. He plunged down the bank, almost losing his footing, and saw Simorh's pale figure emerge, running, from her hiding place.

'The amulet!' He grabbed Talliann, who was trying to climb to her feet but seemed too dazed to co-ordinate her limbs, and lifted her up as Simorh reached them. The princess was trying to pull the pendant from around her neck, but the chain had caught in her hair: she struggled with it, cursing – and suddenly Talliann gave a small, moaning cry of fear, and pointed back towards the shingle bar.

Calthar stood on the crown of the bank, framed by a ghastly, phosphorescent halo. For a moment Kyre thought that the Mothers were again manifesting their unholy, vampiric existence through her living flesh – but no; the cold glow was spreading along the bar, shimmering on the wet shingle, etching the temple ruins into stark relief. And the churning, rolling wavetops beyond the bar were shot through with silver light.

The Dead Night moon was rising.

Calthar spread her arms wide, and her wild laughter rang to the sky, challenging the wind as it rose to a yelling gale. Raw power radiated from her; as though summoned by her voice, the first furious edge of the Hag's livid silver face lifted above the sea on the distant horizon, and a single shaft of light speared across the bay to strike full on the gate of Haven. Calthar howled like a wolf, and her triumphant cry ricocheted from the cliffs.

'*You are too late!*'

'*No!*' Simorh's answering protest was a shriek of defiance. She tore the amulet free, ripping out a hank of her own hair with it, and lunged towards Talliann. The chain slipped over the dark girl's neck: Talliann

gasped as the quartz touched her skin, and Kyre saw the
deep colours within it flare briefly into a brilliance that
challenged the rising Hag –

'*Kyre!!*' It was a wail, a cry of agony and joy and
despair, as Talliann's memories smashed out of their
prison and into her conscious mind. Her body jerked
violently as though some titanic force had struck her full
on; Kyre caught her as she reeled, and they staggered
chaotically back together. Simorh was buffeted aside,
stumbled – then every muscle in her body locked rigid
as, beyond Calthar's wild figure, the light of the moon
went out.

Far out in the bay, a black wall of water was lifting
itself from the surface of the sea, blotting the Hag's
deadly brilliance from view. The vast wave gathered
strength, gathered speed, and Simorh's mind was hurled
nine years into the past, to the hideous night when the
tide had flowed twice without ebbing.

No sorcery she knew, nor any power that Kyre and
Talliann might command, could combat this. Calthar
was summoning the full, awesome power of the Mothers
– and the huge tidal wave racing chaotically towards
Haven was their herald!

Simorh tore at Kyre's sleeve, wrenching him round
with more strength than she'd believed she possessed.
She sucked salt air into her lungs, and screamed to him
at the top of her voice, striving to combat the howling
of the elements and the distant, shattering roar of the
oncoming wave.

'*RUN!!*'

Kyre and Talliann both looked seaward, saw Calthar
now in silhouette, saw what was eclipsing the Hag's
light. Horrified understanding dawned on their faces;
they turned and, with Simorh beside them, raced for the
sanctuary of the portal. Behind them Calthar's laughter
rang madly on the back of the gale, but her mockery
meant nothing – to stay on the beach and face what
hurtled towards them would be insanity; their only hope

of survival lay in flight.

Kyre thought suddenly of Vaoran's ambush party and the fate that would await them if they didn't reach safety, and he slowed, turning to look back. Far behind, three or four figures pelted across the sand; of the rest there was no sign.

'Kyre, don't stop!' Simorh yelled. 'It's too late to help them – run for your own life!'

She was right: to delay now would be to kill them all. The warriors must take their chance. With a last, despairing look at the frantically running men, Kyre turned again and raced on.

The lights of Haven's gateway shone ahead, but they still seemed impossibly distant – and behind them, the sound of the oncoming wave was swelling towards a crescendo. The sand beneath their feet vibrated, the cliffs shouted back the wave's roar in deafening echoes. *They wouldn't reach the arch in time* – then suddenly they were on drier, looser sand, whirlwinds of it stinging their bodies and whipping them to greater effort. The green witchlights danced crazily, closer, closer; the arch opened up before them. And as they hurled themselves through the sandstone gateway, a massive, thundering concussion of sound smashed into their ears as the tidal wave exploded against the cliffs.

Chapter 19

Titanic columns of spray reared hundreds of feet into the night sky, and the roaring sea funnelled into the bay. Kyre was behind Talliann and Simorh, trying to shield them as they ran, flagging now, through the lower streets of the town, when what felt like a gigantic fist slammed into his back and lifted him off his feet. Water struck like a solid wall and he fell, the two women flailing beneath him; he swallowed a mouthful of sea and rolled, gagging and choking. The edge of the wave swirled around them, but its strength was expended, and as suddenly as it had come the water drained away, leaving them sprawled, drenched, on the paved road.

They staggered to their feet, clutching each other for support as water streamed from their clothes and hair. Kyre was the first to recover from the shock, and as he looked back he felt as though his stomach had turned over within him.

The arch and the wall that protected Haven from the sea were gone. The furious energy of the tidal wave had smashed the sandstone to rubble, and though the massive undertow had already dragged water back from the gate, there was nothing now to save half the town from being overwhelmed by a second onslaught. Out in the bay, where minutes before there had been smooth sand, the sea roiled and churned like a gigantic, boiling cauldron, its surface turned to a maelstrom of tossing silver as the Hag, a huge hemisphere now on the horizon as she continued to rise, glared malevolently over the scene.

And far away, carried on the shrieking wind, he heard a sound that made him feel that his veins were filled with ice. A wailing, howling sound, as though a thousand voices joined together in a monstrous nightmare of a song. *Or a battle cry.*

He had heard that dreadful howling once before, and when he looked at Talliann and Simorh he knew that they, too, recognised it. Coming towards them over the sea, challenging the courage and resolve of every living soul in Haven, it was the war-song of the citadel army.

They were out on the sea, and they were mustering their forces. At the moment when the malignant moon cleared the horizon, the Dead Night battle would begin. And that wailing song would be the signal for Haven's warriors to march out from the city to meet their nemesis.

He had to reach DiMag! Haven's only hope lay in the power invested in the amulets; but he couldn't use them, *dared* not use them, until the prince was restored to his rightful place. The quartz gems would smash open a gateway between the present and the long-dead past – time and space would collide, and their collision could hurl the world into chaos. Only through DiMag and Simorh, the true inheritors of the throne of Haven, could he and Talliann hope to control the forces that would be unleashed.

He looked wildly at Talliann, saw that she shared his unspoken knowledge, and yelled above the turmoil of gale and sea and the eerie swell of the far-off voices. '*Simorh!*' He snatched at the sorceress's arm. 'Get to your tower, *quickly*! Talliann will go with you – we need your strength, and we need your skill! *Go!*'

He caught Talliann in his arms, kissed her briefly, fiercely, then turned and started away at a run up the street.

'*Kyre!*' Simorh yelled against the gale. 'Kyre, where are you going?'

'To DiMag!' And he was gone.

Talliann pulled ferociously at Simorh's wrist. 'Hurry!' she cried. 'There's so little time left!'

Simorh didn't understand; couldn't even begin to understand – but the frantic urgency in Talliann's voice sheared like a knife through her confusion. Her fingers tangled with the black-haired girl's, and hand in hand they raced away through the streets in Kyre's wake.

Kyre burst through the wicket-gate into the palace gardens with the faraway wailing of the sea-warriors ringing in his ears above the racket of the wind. He stumbled on to the path that cut through the dying shrubbery, gagging at the decayed flowers' stench – then from the direction of the palace he heard something that brought him to a flailing halt.

It came from the barracks courtyard – the sound of hundreds of tramping feet, the stentorian shouts of sergeants: and then, like a physical blow on the air, the rhythmic, relentless war-chant of Haven's warriors.

They were moving out. And DiMag, who should be leading them, was still a prisoner ... Kyre inhaled a deep lungful of the sickly-sweet air and ran on towards the palace, taking the terrace steps four at a time and sprinting for the main door.

Only two lamps glowed dimly in the entrance hall, casting foreboding shadows and lending an eerie un-reality to the scenes embroidered on the worn tapestries. Kyre started for the stairs – and as he ducked into the stairwell arch, he cannoned into Brigrandon.

'Kyre!' The old scholar's face was pale. 'I feared you must be dead – thank the Eye for your safe return! But where's the Princess Simorh?'

'Gone to her tower, with Talliann.' Kyre leaned against the wall to catch his breath. 'We found the lost amulet, and Vaoran's dead – '

'*Dead?*'

'Calthar killed him. Brigrandon, there's no time to

explain – I must reach DiMag: the army's moving out
and he has to lead them!'

'He's still guarded,' Brigrandon said. 'I tried to see
him just now, but – '

'Damn the guards!' Fury rose in Kyre: he quelled it
with difficulty and grasped the old man's shoulders.
'Stay in the palace and do what you can, Brigrandon.
The battle's about to begin, and those who shelter here
will need all the strength and comfort you can give
them.'

Brigrandon's eyes narrowed angrily. 'I'm joining the
city's defenders.'

'No. When this is over, Haven will need you as a live
scholar, not a dead warrior!' He set one foot on the first
stair. 'May the Eye watch over you, Brigrandon!'

Brigrandon stared at the shadows of the stairwell as
the sound of Kyre's running footsteps diminished up the
steps.

There were two armed soldiers outside DiMag's door.
They were little more than children, Kyre realised;
clearly Vaoran hadn't been willing to spare more
seasoned men at such a time of crisis. He ran towards
them and they raised their swords menacingly.

Kyre stopped. 'Get out of my way.'

Whether or not they recognised him he didn't know;
but he sensed fear underlying their uncertainty. 'No one
is permitted to see the ex-prince,' one said, his unsteady
voice belying the challenge. 'Not without Prince
Vaoran's express permission – '

'Swordsmaster Vaoran is dead!' Kyre snapped, and
had the sour gratification of seeing their eyes widen in
shock. 'He was murdered by the sea-sorceress not half
an hour ago – and that means that *Prince* DiMag is still
your ruler!'

These two weren't traitors, he realised: they had
become embroiled in this whole ugly affair through no
fault or will of their own, simply because they were

soldiers constrained to obey their commander or suffer for it.

More kindly, he said, 'Haven's forces are leaving the barracks now. You'd best join them, quickly.'

They glanced at each other: then, hastily, their spokesman bowed to him. 'Yes ... sir.' He licked his lips. 'Thank you ...'

Kyre paused only a moment to watch them go, then unlocked DiMag's door.

The prince was standing by the window. At the sound of the latch he whirled – and his face went rigid with astonishment.

'*Kyre!*' He stumbled forward. 'They told me you were dead!'

Kyre smiled grimly. 'They were premature. Vaoran took my place.'

'Vaoran?' DiMag swung back towards the window. 'But the Hag has risen – the army are moving out to meet our enemies! *Who leads them*?'

'Only their captains. And I doubt if half the men even know what happened in the court hall.'

The prince paused. 'You mean ... ?' He saw confirmation in Kyre's eyes and didn't finish the question. Instead he limped to a cupboard, opened it, and began to rummage hastily through its contents. Moments later he pulled out a heavy, padded black jerkin made of supple leather, black trousers, a wide belt, a pair of boots.

'Tell me what happened,' he said as he began to dress.

Briefly, Kyre recounted Brigrandon's discovery of the amulet's whereabouts, his hasty flight to the ruined temple with Simorh, Vaoran's attempt to dupe Calthar which had resulted in the swordsmaster's death, and the tidal wave – invisible from DiMag's window – that had roared in to the bay as they fled back to Haven. When he finished, DiMag looked up, his face drawn with worry.

'Gamora,' he said tensely. 'What happened to her?'

'I don't know; I've had no chance yet to check. But I think Calthar might be perverse enough to have meant what she said. She wants to savour her triumph in any way she can.'

DiMag nodded dourly. 'Yes. I can believe that of her.' He sucked air sharply between his teeth. 'I can't afford the delay of finding out. All I can do is hope ... ' He reached into the cupboard again and, with some difficulty, pulled out a massive scabbard from which protruded the ornate hilt of a broadsword. It must, Kyre thought, have been twice as heavy as the blade the prince habitually carried.

'This belonged to my father,' DiMag said with a wry grin. 'Vaoran took my own blade, but he didn't know of this one's existence.' He hefted it, raising his eyebrows at its prodigious length and weight. 'My father was a taller man than I am.'

'Can you wield it?' Kyre asked.

He laughed bitterly. 'There's strength in my arms, if not in my legs. While I can still sit a horse, I can handle this well enough to cause some havoc among our enemies' ranks.' He looked up. 'You'll ride with me, Kyre?'

'Yes.'

DiMag cinched the belt at his waist. 'Then let's be on our way.'

Simorh raced breathlessly up the last stairs to her tower door, thankful to find it unguarded. Behind her came Talliann, glancing back over her shoulder to ensure they weren't being followed. They hastened into the anteroom and Simorh ran to the window, from where she had a clear view over the city. Though the chanting and tramping of the departing warriors could be heard on the wind, they weren't as yet in view. *So little time*, she thought, her mind in chaos, and turned to Talliann.

'I don't know what I must do!' Panic welled up in

her; she felt so bereft, so impotent. 'Talliann, help me – tell me what you need of me!'

'I need your mind, and your will,' Talliann said. A great change had come over the black-haired girl; all trace of the bewildered and hapless innocent were gone with the return of her memories, revealing the formidable strength of the soul beneath. Her aura was almost tangible, and Simorh realised with a shock just how great a sorceress she had been when she had ruled at Kyre's side.

'Kyre rides out with DiMag,' Talliann continued. 'When they reach the bay, my mind and his will become one, and we'll awaken the amulets and call their power into the world from our own time. But it's dangerous, Simorh – by summoning that force we break down the barriers between past and present: they can't rightly exist together, and they'll clash. We *must* keep control of that force if we're to prevent time from running amok, and only you and DiMag can help us. We need you to hold us to *your* time, to this night, by any means you can. And it won't be easy.'

Simorh looked into her stern yet sad black eyes, and understood. Time running amok ... the thought was awesome. But a price must be paid for calling such power out of the distant past – and it was Haven's only hope.

She said, forcing strength and conviction into her voice, 'We won't fail you.'

DiMag and Kyre burst out of a side alley into the main thoroughfare just as the first ranks of Haven's warriors reached the junction. They had taken a short cut to intercept the army, urging their horses at dangerous speed through a maze of narrow lanes, and as they hauled the animals to a snorting, rearing stop, the two captains at the head of the first mounted column yelled in consternation for their men to halt. A horn sounded, echoing; there was confused shouting as horses bumped one another; a standard-bearer was almost unseated – then the captains were staring, opened-mouthed in astonishment, at their prince.

In the moonshot darkness DiMag looked dangerous. His black war-garb made his body a shadow among shadows, and his tense, pale face, framed by the fair hair streaming in the gale, was ghastly and almost unhuman. His eyes were alight with the anger that had lurked pent and twisted within him for nine years – but at last that anger had an outlet to cleanse it of its taint. He stood up in his stirrups, ignoring the pain that shot through his leg, and smiled grimly as the ripple of shock at his unexpected appearance ran back through the ranks like a breaking wave. He looked at the two captains. One, the younger and stockier, had been Vaoran's right-hand man; the other – Revannic, the prince recalled – had taken up arms as a foot-soldier under DiMag's father, and was a militiaman above all else. The prince's gaze rested a little longer on the older captain, then he shouted, the wind carrying his words across the heads of the throng.

'Swordsmaster Vaoran is dead, and his attempt to overthrow me has failed! I come to lead you to triumph over our *real* enemy, and I bring the Sun-Hound with me!'

From somewhere behind the horsemen, among the lines of foot-soldiers, a ragged cheer went up. Vaoran had had many followers among the higher echelons, but he had never been popular in the ranks. DiMag smiled again, less grimly this time, and looked once more at the two captains.

'Gentlemen,' he said, and his voice was eerily counterpointed by the scream of the gale and the more distant roar of the sea, 'you have a simple choice. Accept me as your rightful leader, and Kyre as our champion – or kill us both here and now.'

From far away they could all hear the chanting of the sea-warriors, rising towards a crescendo now as they prepared to move in on the tide. The younger captain shifted uneasily in his saddle and made as if to speak, but the elder held up a warning hand. The look in his eyes, as he glanced at his fellow commander, froze any words the other might have uttered. The stocky man hesitated – then he cast his own gaze down and conceded with a curt nod of acquiescence.

Captain Revannic drew his sword and in a practised, economic gesture, saluted the prince.

'My lord,' he said crisply, and there was relief in his eyes. 'We hadn't thought to see you lead us tonight.' He glanced at the prince's maimed leg, his meaning clear; then he smiled. 'Your father Prince MeGran would have been proud of such courage.' And with no further pause he signalled to the herald who rode beside him.

A long, wailing horn-blast wound the length of the street, followed by three short, staccato notes. DiMag returned both Revannic's salute and his smile, then turned his horse about and spurred it forward. Kyre swung his own mount around as the horn sounded again, imperative now; the standards of Haven rose, snapping on the wind with a sound like cracking whips – and the army surged towards the city wall.

The mass of men gathered momentum, spurred on by the racket of the elements and by the ever more urgent howling of their enemies far out on the sea. The shattered wall loomed before them, the sandstone arch and its eternal witchlights smashed and indistinguishable among the rubble: they were gaining speed –

'*KYRE!*'

At the same moment that Talliann's disembodied voice resounded in his head, Kyre felt the quartz around his neck pulse with a violent flash of awakened energy. He yelled aloud without realising it as his consciousness locked with hers, and with a peripheral part of his mind saw DiMag look round in surprise as he urged his horse on. What he saw Kyre couldn't even begin to guess, but the amulet at his throat burned suddenly hot, and a cold light sparked from it that lit the prince's face and his vulpine smile as he understood.

Talliann was chanting a litany in Kyre's mind, and he joined his voice with hers. Somewhere deep in his soul he felt a lurching sensation, and his inner vision focused on a gate, a dark, titanic gate, that stood between this world and the ancient past over which they had once reigned together. He saw Talliann's face within the gate, powerful and knowledgeable as she had been then, her black eyes almost closed in trance and only the twin brilliant slivers of her pupils shining through the blackness. He felt another surge of searing heat as the fire-red glow of her amulet merged with the glacial brilliance of his, and he saw her mouth open, as his opened, to scream the final, the ultimate word of the rite that would shatter the gate and bring the ancient forces roaring through.

And as the word rang out, the Hag cleared the horizon like something from a primeval nightmare, hurling her silver-green spear across the surface of the tossing sea to strike the leading ranks of Haven's army full on. With a suddenness that sent a shock through Kyre's bones, the sea-warriors' eerie chanting stopped – then DiMag's voice called above the wind's howl:

'They're coming! Haven – Haven, and our triumph!!'

The horn shrieked a challenge, a wild, primitive incitement, and a yell of furious defiance rose from massed throats. Kyre's horse bucked under him, smelling battle and terror on the battering gale, and like a living wave the warriors of Haven streamed through the shattered city gate.

And as the wave of humanity smashed into the bay, Kyre's voice and mind and soul joined with Talliann's in a cry that rang like supernatural thunder on the night.

'NOW!!'

Beyond the shining sand where the tidal wave had drawn back, the incoming sea erupted like a volcano. And riding the maelstrom, carried on the back of the silver spear of light that the grim moon flung across the ocean, came a howling host, distorted by the pounding surf into an army of unhuman phantoms, monsters made of spray and foam, leaping and diving shorewards and shrieking demonically.

DiMag howled a war-cry, and Kyre heard his own voice screaming in cacophonic harmony. They were galloping now, their mounts crazed and racing while the warriors of Haven streamed and yelled behind them. As they crossed the smooth acreage of sand where half of Kyre's city and DiMag's city had been buried nine years before, the ground beneath them rumbled and shifted, as though something that slumbered deep under the bay had awoken and was clawing its way towards the surface –

In Simorh's tower, Talliann shrieked. Simorh clutched her, tried to hold her, but the dark girl's arms flailed with a mad, unhuman strength and she was flung aside, against the wall. She scrambled to her feet as the room rocked wildly, then threw herself towards Talliann, grasped her, held her, screamed at her –

Kyre saw the first of them explode from under the sand as the horses thundered over their graves. They had the hideous semblance of living statues, their flesh shrunken, petrified, bones and muscles standing out like cords under skin stretched taught over their frames. *But they lived!* The dead of Haven, men, women, children, rising through the sand that had been their tomb and joining their howling voices to those of the charging warriors. Their eyes were livid sparks of hellfire in sand-encrusted skulls, their ossified limbs jerked and bent in motions their dead brains had long forgotten. They carried swords, staves, axes, knives, clubs – anything that would serve as a weapon – and they hurled themselves into the ranks of the army, the living and the dead racing together to meet the sea.

*Talliann screamed again while Simorh struggled to pin
her arms to the floor, and out on the bay Kyre screamed
with her –*

They were galloping at breakneck speed towards the
surging surf and the creatures who rode howling
towards them. Closer, closer to the line of the tide –
and ahead, where the sea crashed on the shingle bar,
water boiled suddenly into a foaming explosion and
something blacker than night, blacker than the ocean
depths, erupted from the waves. It was a shell – a
gigantic shell, towering into the night, blotting out the
moon – and in the shell, riding in it like passengers in
a nightmare chariot, stood Calthar and her Mothers.
The sea-sorceress had performed the ultimate rite, and
her appalling predecessors had risen from death as
Haven's own had risen, decayed, grinning corpses,
their mortal remains reanimated to join with their
spiritual daughter in the last conflict. And presiding
over them all, most evil of them all, most deadly of
them all, Kyre saw the rotted, triumphant face of
Malhareq, his own betrayer.

He thought he cried out, but he could never know.
The sea was roaring to meet them – then he felt a
massive shock wave strike him full on, and time and
space imploded around him as the enemy army came
surging out of the tide.

DiMag heard his own voice yelling insanely as the
leading ranks of Haven's horsemen clashed with the first
line of the sea-warriors. His blade was a murderous
steel-silver blur in the chaotic darkness; alien faces
sprang out of the night and he hewed at them, felt the
sword bite home, saw blood flying like dark sea-spray.
His horse reared and shrieked in warning, and he arched
his body to block the shearing glitter of a spear,
disarmed its wielder with a powerful twist of his arm,
hacked at a pale shoulder and saw the wounded

sea-warrior go down into a melee of trampling hooves.
To his left he glimpsed the fiery flicker of Kyre's hair
and the flash of the spear in his hands; then suddenly
he was beset by three more howling warriors coming at
him from the right. The sword sheared down and the
first enemy flailed back with an ugly, dying shriek, but
the second lunged in behind his comrade and the prince
felt blood flow over his leg as the spear gashed his
horse's flank. The animal bucked crazily under him,
panicking; struggling to control it he had no chance to
defend himself as the third warrior attacked. For a
terrible instant DiMag saw the spear-blade hurtling out
of the dark towards his torso and he knew in that second
that he couldn't evade it – then another horseman
appeared from nowhere; a massive blade, swung two-
handed, cut the spear in half and, as its owner turned
in shock, sliced again with a sharp, whining whistle, to
sever the warrior before he could jump clear.

The horseman grinned ferally at DiMag from a
blood-streaked face – and the prince recognised the
hawk nose, dark beard and lean body of his own father,
MeGran, in the instant before horse and rider winked
out into nothingness.

MeGran, who had been dead twelve years! Shock
slammed DiMag back in his saddle as his horse wheeled
and plunged once more into the battle, and suddenly his
mind and his body and the raging world around him
were out of control as the tides of past and present
collided into a maelstrom. DiMag rode a black horse
that bore a great scar along its neck where it had been
cut down in the battle of nine years ago to die shrieking
and kicking on the sand, and at his side fought MeGran,
while a lithe young woman with short dark curls and a
warrior's garb and Gamora's face sounded the horn that
rallied the Haven army, living and dead, to fresh
onslaughts. And there were children among the
carnage, children with his own fair hair and hazel eyes
who yelled and shouted and wielded swords and spears.

And Brigrandon was young again and fighting with the rest, and on the prince's right flank Vaoran yelled a warning and spurred his horse to intercept a silver-faced warrior launching himself at DiMag, and between them they slew the attacker and three more who came behind him, and their eyes met and they laughed together, while DiMag thought of his baby daughter sleeping in the palace and of the wife he loved and whose sorcery was aiding him.

And everywhere he looked was Kyre. Kyre riding through a press of enemy warriors, his spear twisting and turning and spinning in his hands; Kyre on foot at the edge of the sea, his horse dead beside him, in hand-to-hand combat with three silver-haired warriors; Kyre leading a charge of foot-soldiers, the royal standard of Haven streaming above his head. He saw Calthar, a sinuous and vicious-faced child; he saw sea-warriors he'd slain nine years before, he saw dead men and living men and men not yet born, and over the deafening clamour of the battle came again and again the frantic, insistent winding of the horn. Out on the shingle bar the temple was changing and changing and changing, one moment a ruin, the next new-built and whole, the next gone without trace. Only the moon was constant, glaring down on the carnage with her mad eye – the moon, and the monstrous black shell that rose above the waves while the impossible, hideous parodies of humanity that rode within it laughed and screamed and urged their followers to further madness.

'*I CAN'T CONTROL IT!!*' The words thundered in DiMag's head and he realised that they didn't come from within himself, but from Kyre. Somehow their minds had fused, and the prince felt the Sun-Hound's desperation ricochet through his bones. The warp of time was running amok as two ages and the chaotic centuries between came together and battled to tear each other's fabric apart.

'*WE SHOULDN'T EXIST TOGETHER! HELP*

ME, DIMAG – HELP ME, OR YOUR WORLD WILL BE LOST!!'

DiMag's horse reared, whinnying, and through a forest of writhing, clashing forms he saw Kyre again. He was at the tide's edge, mounted still, and he was trying to fight his way through to the prince. Goaded by a violent intuition, DiMag spurred his horse towards the tideline, only to find the path blocked by some twenty embattled men. He swerved, saw a gap, kicked his mount's flanks – and he was flung backwards as a sea-warrior sprang from the dark, spear whirling low and deadly to slash the horse's legs from under it. The animal shrieked in terrified agony and DiMag pitched out of the saddle, hitting the wet sand with bone-cracking force and rolling clear as the animal's body crashed down an inch from his head. Pain shot through the prince's crippled leg as he got to his feet, but five more Haven men were closing on his attacker and he was able to get clear – to find himself at the edge of the crashing, tumbling sea.

'*DiMag!*' This time Kyre's voice wasn't in his head: DiMag looked wildly round and saw the Sun-Hound, also dismounted, racing towards him. They were on the fringe of the battle now, clear of the tumult – but as the prince limped into the shallows to meet Kyre, a warrior appeared seemingly from nowhere, stumbling across his path. He was unarmed and blood ran down one shoulder: the prince caught a glimpse of black-streaked silver hair, and snarled, raising his sword –

'*No*, DiMag!' Kyre flung himself between the two men as he recognised the distinctive hair, the disfiguring facial mark. The sea-warrior faced him, shoulders heaving as he fought for breath. Wounded and disarmed, he'd broken free from the melee only to find himself confronted now with almost certain death. He stared at Kyre with glazed eyes – then recognition dawned.

'Sun-Hound ... ' Akrivir coughed, and spat.

Impulsively, Kyre held out a sword he'd taken from a dead Haven warrior. 'Take it, Akrivir. Save yourself, if you can!'

The young man's hand closed round the hilt, and he flashed Kyre a look of intense gratitude. 'Kill her, Kyre,' he said. 'It's the only way to save us all!' And before the astounded DiMag could stop him he was gone, running back into the chaotic dark.

The prince grasped Kyre's arm, shouting above the din. *'What d'you think you're doing? That was –'*

'There's no time to explain!' Kyre yelled back. 'DiMag, I can't hold the power! It's running out of control – I've got to lock my mind with yours, we must fight as one!'

The prince shook his head, utterly confused but knowing he had to trust Kyre. 'I don't know how!'

A riderless horse careered out of the chaos straight towards them; they sprang aside and it galloped by into the surf, its hooves hurling up a fountain of spray and soaking them.

'The amulet!' Kyre shouted. 'You've got to take the amulet! It'll hold your mind to this world, this time – I can control the power through you!'

He snatched at the chain around his neck, pulling it free, and thrust it over DiMag's head. The prince's consciousness jolted as the quartz touched his skin: for an instant he thought the entire bay was lifting, humping towards the black sky like a vast, uncoiling serpent, and he flailed out as he seemed to pitch backwards, over, tumbling into limitless dark.

'Hold on to the present, DiMag!' Kyre shouted. *'Don't let go!'*

His voice was eclipsed suddenly by a shriek of unhuman delight and triumph that snatched DiMag back into the world. A wave broke against the prince's thighs; as he swayed with its onslaught his eyes snapped open and he saw a vast black silhouette looming towards him. *The giant shell –*

'Kyre!' DiMag yelled in horror as the shell disgorged a plethora of flowing, serpentine shapes. Under the moonlight they resolved into hideously animated corpses, skeletons with tatters of skin clinging to their fleshless bones, worm-eaten monsters with empty eyes and brittle, colourless hair flying like scum about their skulls – the Mothers, the dead, reanimated Mothers, spilling from their carriage and surging towards the prince. Ten of them, fifteen, twenty, impossible horrors that opened their rotted mouths and screamed mayhem above the gale. And at their head – DiMag staggered back, clapping a hand over his mouth in a desperate effort to stop himself from vomiting – at their head was a skeleton with eyes like twin coals in the crumbling skull. Oldest of them all, founder and inspiration of them all, she was – she was –

She was changing, flesh growing on the bones, sinew and muscle overlaid by shining, green-tinged skin, while a wild corona of hair whipped about a face whose eyes and smile the prince knew all too well. And as she changed it seemed that the rest of the hell-inspired horde flowed towards her and around her and into her, until she stood alone, tall and erect and evil, the tattered robe clinging obscenely to her sinuous body, her eyes glittering white slits and the gigantic spear, twice the length of that borne by any of her followers, balanced effortlessly in her hand.

The years rolled back and the battle raging around him seemed to recede into a vast distance as DiMag, lonely and suddenly cold as ice, faced Calthar for the second time in his life – and for what he knew must also be the last.

In the tower, Talliann cried out as the echo of Kyre's frantic call to DiMag resounded in her mind. The room still rocked madly like a ship in a tempest, and she and Simorh staggered back from the window as lightning-shot darkness engulfed them. In their inner vision they could

*see the battle and the terrible clashing and warping of
time, and Talliann felt Kyre's terror as the chaos of the
amulets' power roiled uncontrollably about him. She
saw him reach DiMag, felt the sudden surge of his
intention –*

'*Simorh!*' Talliann clutched at the sorceress in the
swirling blackness that churned ever more wildly as time
ran crazed. 'Simorh, the amulet! You must take the
amulet – *you must be strong!*' Even as she called out she
was pulling the chain from around her throat, and
Simorh, understanding the peril, ran to help her.

Then suddenly Simorh was Talliann and Talliann was
Simorh, and the fair-haired sorceress flung back her
head and raised her arms heavenward as power surged
through her veins. All around her she felt it vibrating,
calling, holding her to the world: she drew on her
strength, fists clenching as she focused all the will she
could muster to the aid of DiMag and Kyre. Through
the channel opened by Talliann's mind she felt other
presences: names from history, faces from her own past
and from an indefinable future. Her own mother,
MeGran's sister, fair and serene, a sorceress in her own
right. The dead consorts of princes past, who had
worked their own magic down the long centuries to the
aid of Haven. Gamora grown to beauty and to power.
Thean and Falla, old and skilled in arcane ways. Her
nurse, at rest these twenty years. And Talliann, black-
haired Talliann, the greatest of all Haven's sorceresses,
who stood beside her and held her like a sister and
merged her mind with Simorh's as the great wheel of
power spun faster, faster, faster –

Calthar laughed. She moved towards DiMag through
the waves, and DiMag stood his ground. In her face,
glaring out through the sockets of her eyes, the awful
madness of the Mothers shone like white-hot fire, and
in his mind's eye DiMag saw again the countenances of
the appalling creatures that had merged their bones and

their souls and their power with her.

*He couldn't fight that power! Something so old, so
corrupt – he was nothing more than a mortal man; he
couldn't hope to triumph over such evil!*

She came on, slowly, like a predator savouring a
paralysed and helpless victim. DiMag tasted bile in his
throat, and hefted his sword, though he knew, *knew*,
that he was lost.

Calthar smiled – and suddenly she was Calthar no
longer. Her form changed, shifted – great ropes of
wine-dark hair swung about her shoulders and cascaded
down her back, and her face was younger, her pale body
clad in a long, slit-skirted robe, belted at her narrow
waist, and over her shoulder was slung the crimson sash
of a Haven councillor –

And where DiMag had stood, Kyre's green eyes and
flame-red hair flared in the darkness as he faced the
woman who centuries upon centuries ago had betrayed
her city and her people and her prince, and by whose
hand the glory that had once been Haven had been
sundered.

Then suddenly there was no battle. It was as though
every other living soul had flared out of existence,
leaving only the dark bay, the sand and the sea, and the
old, pocked moon riding the sky above. There was just
the entity that was both Kyre and DiMag, a lone figure
facing the creature into which Calthar and Malhareq had
merged. The gale was gone; and the stillness was acute.

The woman with the wine-dark hair raised her spear
as though in mocking salute, and Calthar smiled. Kyre's
voice broke the silence.

'Ah, Malhareq.' DiMag heard the words in his
tumbling mind, and in sharing Kyre's thoughts he at last
understood the truth of the legacy that the Sun-Hound
had left behind. 'Will you kill me, this time?'

Her voice was warm, rich. 'I will, prince. The Hag's
hand is on me, and she will not fail.'

'The Hag is no enemy of mine. Your people were

Haven's people once: before you fled to found the city
under the sea. It could be so again.'

Malhareq laughed softly. 'It will not be so again,
Kyre. Not while my daughter Calthar lives.'

'And if Calthar should die?'

'There will be others.' That smile again, alluring,
beautiful, deadly. 'Your day is long gone, prince.'

'As is yours, sorceress.'

'Ah, no. Through the Mothers, I live on.' Her outline
flickered, wavered; maggots moved under her translucent skin and the part of her adversary that was DiMag
recoiled in revulsion. He felt Kyre's mind touch his,
drawing him back: the fear faded and he knew what he
must do.

*She was the heart of it, the core of it, this monstrous
creature who lived on still through the Mothers. Once
there had been but one people – the people of Haven. And
then had come this power-hungry predator . . .*

*Without Malhareq, there need be no war. Without her
malignant influence crossing the centuries to feed still on
the minds and wills of her descendants, Haven and the
sea-citadel could live at peace together. She was a
vampire, she and her daughter-in-spirit, Calthar.
Through Calthar's living flesh, dead Malhareq fed on
power and lust, and her thirst would only be slaked when
the last of Haven's citizens lay dead among its shattered
rubble.*

*It must not be. Time must be defied, and the sway of
the power that Malhareq had handed down through the
long and grim line of the Mothers must be broken in the
only way possible – at its source. Malhareq must die. And
he – Kyre, DiMag; he no longer knew who he was, and
it hardly seemed to matter – was the only one who could
slay her.*

He raised a weapon that was both sword and spear,
and in his mind, from a great distance, he heard Talliann
and Simorh cry out as the power of the amulets swamped
him. The spell that had held them in limbo shattered,

and the world of the shrieking gale and the screaming, battling warriors erupted volcanically back into being as DiMag and Calthar, Kyre and Malhareq, lunged forward and met in a clashing cacophony of steel.

Chapter 20

Hands clamped on Simorh's wrists, and Talliann's voice shrieked in her ear.

'Now, Simorh! Call on the power – now!!'

Simorh's mind seemed to spear upwards into the night, until she gazed down from a vast height on the tumult of the battle. Men struggled like a single writhing black entity on the beach, the tide of bodies surging this way and that as the armies fought. And where white surf churned at the edge of the sea there were other men, horses milling about them, knee-deep in the water and engaged in desperate single combat. Simorh looked for DiMag, but couldn't find him; at her neck the amulet pulsed hotter, hotter –

'There!' Talliann screamed, and a stunning force turned Simorh's disembodied mind about. 'On the shingle bar!'

DiMag! But his hair was red, and he wielded a spear instead of a sword as he swung and hacked at a shimmering, leaping creature who seemed to be composed of flesh and foam and light and decay all at once . . .

'Call on the stone!' Talliann cried, and in the tower room her hands gripped Simorh's shoulders and shook her with a violence that made her teeth snap together. *'Now!* Call on it – *that monstrosity must die!'*

Simorh's mind swept back nine years and she saw again DiMag being dragged into their bedchamber on a makeshift stretcher, his face grey with shock and pain, blood from Calthar's festering, sorcerous wound soaking his clothes, while she, struck dumb by the ravages of her own failed sorcery, could only stare and stare at him, too weak even to cry. Calthar had destroyed their lives that night . . . and with the thought came a wild uprising of hatred and vengeful fury that took hold of her like a whirlwind. Her hands clawed around the quartz and the quartz burned her as she dragged from it, from her mind, from Talliann's mind, the last vestiges of the power she needed, and found the strength to hurl it on flying black wings at the battling figures on the shingle bar before the world spun madly about her and she collapsed.

Kyre saw the spear coming down at him in the instant before a fireball of brilliant scarlet light exploded above his head. It lit Malhareq's upturned, snarling face, froze her lithe figure like a stone statue in its glare, and in that one moment he realised what Simorh and Talliann had done. He yelled a name – DiMag's, his own, he didn't know – and heard an answering scream from the amulet as his consciousness ripped free from the entity that was himself and the prince, and merged with the blazing wheel of light. Blue and red spun together, he felt Talliann in his head, in his soul, her power blending with his as Malhareq's face twisted in dawning horror –

And DiMag, his mind spinning as the link with Kyre was torn apart, saw Calthar bearing down on him. Simorh's last power-bolt fired his mind with the strength of vengeance, and he swung the great sword as a woodsman might swing an axe. He saw the blade bite deep, heard Calthar's howling laughter as it embedded itself in her flesh. *She didn't bleed* – and in an instant the prince's mind went spinning back nine years. He saw her snarling face as he had seen it on that night; saw the spear glittering, felt again the agony as it slashed his leg open, baring muscle and bone and searing his flesh with its sorcerous poison.

He couldn't kill her! He had failed then; he would fail now –

And something seemed to take hold of his free arm. With an involuntary jerk his hand came up and he felt the cold quartz of Kyre's amulet beneath his fingers. *And suddenly he knew what had to be done!*

Calthar was twisting her serpentine body in an obscene, contemptuous gesture, to rid herself of the sword. DiMag snapped the amulet's chain, gripped the quartz tightly – then lunged again and drove the pendant at her heart.

Her scream was something he'd remember in his nightmares for as long as he lived. It wasn't human, nor even animal: as she doubled over, jerking in a fit, the scream rose above the gale, above the din of battle, higher and higher as rage and frustration and disbelief and terror and a hatred beyond comprehension was ripped from Calthar's throat along with her life and the hideous, unnatural life of the Mothers on whose black legacy she had fed for so long. Her hands became claws that tore at her own hair, her legs kicked, out of her control: the scream went on and on, while behind Calthar's eyes Malhareq writhed in horror and agony, and the long line of Malhareq's unholy progeny squirmed and shrivelled and shared Calthar's death as they had shared her living.

The sorceress rolled over, and for one moment stared madly at DiMag in a last blaze of impotent loathing. The prince felt pain shoot through his leg and his head together; he reeled, then the world swelled, receded, roared in his ears, and he keeled unconscious to the ground as the spark of life fled from Calthar's eyes.

The darkness in the tower room seemed to swell to a suffocating density – then with a vast, silent concussion it was gone. Simorh raised her head but couldn't focus her eyes; she'd cracked her skull on a table leg and any sudden movement made her feel sick and dizzy. But there was light . . . the faint glimmer of a single lamp, and moonlight shining in at the window . . .

Trying to remember what had happened, she crawled slowly and painfully across the floor, clutching the window sill for support as she dragged herself upright. Her legs were weak and the sickness still roiled in her stomach: but the power, the shattering force, the madness were all gone, and the room was quiet.

Quiet . . . She shook her head, winced at the pain – and remembered.

'Talliann?' Her voice was hollow against the silence, and no one answered her. She was alone in the room. But Talliann had been with her. Together, they had called on the power of –

Something fell from her right hand, which she didn't even know she'd been clenching. A shower of tiny, glittering fragments, scattering on the floor like glass shards and winking redly up at her. Simorh gasped and dropped to a crouch, her hands scrabbling. And there, under her fingers among the broken scraps of orange-red quartz, was a single, silver-flecked pearl . . .

'Talliann . . . ' The sorceress jammed a fist against her mouth, biting back a flood of emotion. Talliann was gone – and her amulet, her legacy, lay shattered on the floor at Simorh's feet.

But where could she –

The door eased open a crack, stopped, opened a fraction more, stopped again. Simorh's heart pounded and she whispered, 'Who's there?'

'Mother . . . ?' The door opened wide at last and Gamora stood on the threshold, her small face drawn with fear and her eyes huge under the tousled curls. 'Oh, Mother!' She flung herself across the room to Simorh, hugging her with all her strength. 'I was so frightened! I woke up in a room with drawn curtains and candles, and there was no one else there, and I couldn't find anyone, and I've had such horrible *dreams!*'

Simorh dropped to her knees on the worn carpet,

clutching the child to her. *She was alive, she was safe,
the enchantment was broken* – 'Gamora, Gamora!' She
couldn't say anything more; grief and joy combined to
make her incoherent. Tears streamed down her cheeks
and Gamora was crying too: they stayed, hugging each
other without speaking, sharing feelings that neither
understood, in the silence of the dimly lit room.

It was Revannic, the captain DiMag had confronted as
the army rode out, who finally found the prince
sprawled among the rubble of the ruined temple, and
in his carrying, parade-ground voice he shouted into the
confusion of milling horses and bewildered troops
whose sergeants were trying to muster them into some
semblance of order. Two men detached themselves
from the nearest of several small parties engaged in the
grim task of separating the wounded from the dead on
both sides, and came running to the strand.

'The Eye preserve me!' One of them stared down at
DiMag in amazement. 'We'd thought the prince must
be dead, sir! We've already combed most of the bay,
and – '

'Then let's be thankful you were wrong.' Revannic
ran his hands over the prince's legs and along his back.
'I'm no surgeon, but I don't think he's broken any
bones. And there's no blood.'

DiMag stirred. Hastily the men moved to help him
as his eyes opened dazedly, and he struggled into a
sitting position on the wet shale.

'Revannic ... what – '

'The battle's over, my lord. Haven's safe.'

'But the moon's still up ... ' He could see her
pockmarked face lurking near the cliffs, throwing
grotesque black shadows over the sand and the turning
tide.

'I know, and I can't claim to understand it, sir.'
Revannic took off his jerkin and cast it round DiMag's
shoulders as the prince began to shiver. 'My detachment

were in the thick of it when we heard this sudden noise:
like a scream, a wailing. It must have been some kind
of retreat signal, because they just turned, the sea-
demons I mean, and started fighting their way back to
the shoreline.' He paused, licked his lips. 'When it
became obvious what they were about, I – forgive me,
my lord, I called our men off and let them flee.' He
frowned. 'We thought you dead and someone had to
make a decision; and we'd already lost so many . . . '

DiMag nodded. 'You did right. Thank you.' He knew
now what Revannic had heard, and why the enemy
warriors had withdrawn. It all made sense . . . but –

'Kyre!' he said suddenly. 'The Sun-Hound – is he
alive?'

Revannic's face, which had cleared at his approbation, clouded again. 'He hasn't been found yet, sir,
among the dead or among the survivors.'

'You're *sure*?'

'Certain as I can be; though there are still several
parties yet to report back to me.'

He had to be here . . . DiMag tried to get up, and
grimaced as his maimed leg refused to support him.
Revannic steadied him until he could settle the hilt of
his sword under his arm to use as a makeshift crutch,
then the prince looked speculatively round at the gaunt
shadows of the temple. He couldn't even remember
reaching the place, and his recollection of what had
happened was hazy at best. All he knew was that he and
Kyre had fought side by side . . .

'Search the ruin,' he said grimly, praying that they
wouldn't find what he feared they would. 'If Kyre's
alive, he must be injured. I want him found!'

The two warriors saluted and hastened away, and the
prince looked at Revannic. 'Are there many dead?' he
asked quietly.

Revannic hunched his shoulders against the chilly,
invasive breeze that had replaced the gale. 'It could have
been worse.' He paused, staring down at the uneven

ground, then said in a peculiar voice: 'My lord ... '

'What is it?' Though DiMag thought he already knew.

The captain bit his lower lip. 'My lord, I – I don't know how to put it: you'll think I'm mad. But ... ' He met DiMag's gaze, but only briefly before looking away again. 'At the height of the battle, sir, I thought I saw ... Prince MeGran. Your father. And others. I couldn't be sure about them, but I thought I recognised friends who died in the last conflict: it was just that I knew your father the old prince so well ... ' His throat muscles worked as he swallowed. '*Am* I mad, my lord?'

'No,' DiMag said gently. 'You're not mad, Revannic. I, too, fought alongside dead friends. And Prince MeGran saved my life.' He smiled bleakly, sadly. 'If you knew my father well, I knew him better. I don't think either of us was mistaken.'

Revannic hugged himself, and shivered. 'I don't understand, sir ... '

'Neither do I; not fully. But something happened here tonight that ... ' DiMag's voice tailed off as he realised he had been about to say *that will change the course of all our lives*, and that it would have sounded pitifully banal. Instead he shifted awkwardly round until he was facing the muttering sea.

'When the aftermath is over, there'll be changes, Revannic. And maybe then I'll be able to explain it to myself and to you.'

A voice rose hoarsely from the deep shadows among the ruins, and both men looked up. One of the soldiers was signalling frantically and DiMag made what speed he could towards the man, cursing his lameness and wishing that Revannic would go on ahead. As they finally came up to where the two warriors waited, one pointed to something that lay beside a shattered pillar, and DiMag swallowed back sickness as he steeled himself to look.

It wasn't Kyre. It was the body of a woman with an ugly, bloodless gash in her stomach. She was curled, limbs locked rigid, in a crude foetal posture, and her skin shone with the faint but growing phosphorescence of decay. Her eyes were empty, and her full lips were drawn back in a snarl that was frozen forever on her face; and for a moment only DiMag saw wine-dark hair like a rich cloud around her shoulders. He blinked, startled – and the hair and the evilly beautiful face changed to the silver nimbus and the cruel countenance of Calthar.

The prince looked sidelong at Revannic just in time to catch the other man's eye. Revannic, he realised, had seen the change, the fleeting echo of Malhareq in Calthar's corpse; now, staring down at her again, DiMag saw that she was already ageing and withering. It was final confirmation that the sorcery which had allowed her to live years beyond her rightful time was broken.

'So that was it . . . ' Revannic spoke softly, with the reverence, DiMag thought, of a soldier's grudging respect for a hated but defeated enemy. 'They must have known. And when she died, it broke their power. That was why they went back to the sea . . . '

'She was our only real enemy,' DiMag said quietly.

Revannic frowned, not comprehending. 'My lord?'

'Never mind . . . there'll be time enough to explain.' Something glittered among the shreds of Calthar's rotting robe, and DiMag dropped to a clumsy crouch to look more closely. Glass . . . or quartz . . . tiny, brilliant blue shards, as though a jewel had shattered and fallen among the decayed fabric. And draped across the sorceress's motionless breast, a thin, silver chain.

Suddenly DiMag knew why Kyre hadn't been found, and he got to his feet, staring out to sea as the pain of sorrowing regret twisted within him.

There had been so much he wanted to say. Haven owed all it had to Kyre and Talliann; and DiMag in particular had the Sun-Hound to thank for his life. He and Talliann had brought hope where before there had been only despair; there was a chance now that the city might live again, and the prince wished with all his heart that he could have seen and spoken to the Sun-Hound one last time. Thanks were desperately inadequate; but he wished he could have expressed them nonetheless.

But it was too late now. Time had opened its black gates for him once: it wouldn't do so again. And though he was gone, Kyre had left Haven a legacy beyond price.

He turned to Revannic once more, and asked quietly, 'Are there prisoners?'

'Some fifty or more wounded.'

The prince nodded. 'Have them taken to the city, and see to it that they're tended and treated well.'

Revannic was a wise soldier, and the prince's earlier remark had given him a small insight into the nature of Calthar's influence upon her followers. There was more behind DiMag's command than was yet clear, and Revannic believed it boded well.

'As you say, my lord.' He bowed; a quick, economical inclination of his head. 'And . . . that?' He indicated the thing that had been Calthar.

DiMag looked for the last time on his enemy, then turned away. 'Let the sea have her,' he said. 'She means nothing now.'

They had returned in small bands, swimming into the sea-cave and somehow finding the strength to pull themselves on to the rock ledge and make their way through the maze of tunnels to a place where they could rest. Many were wounded; more still were dazed, shocked by the impossible event which had stunned them all. None spoke a word, and the forebodings of the men who had taken no part in the battle but who now watched the returning warriors from the shadows grew.

Akrivir was among the last to return. One arm was stiff where blood had caked into a scab at the shoulder-joint, and there was a long, fierce gash above his hairline which was still bleeding sluggishly.

Hodek saw him emerge from the water, and hastened forward from the knot of anxious senior councillors. To Akrivir the old man looked like some scrawny and wind-tossed scavenger bird, and he felt the dully familiar hatred rising in him again. But this time, there was a difference . . .

'Where is she?' Hodek's voice was shrill with petulant frustration. 'Where? Answer me!'

Akrivir stared at his father, and his face was like stone. 'Where is who?'

Unease flickered in Hodek's expression; he'd never seen Akrivir behave in such a way, and it worried him. *But no matter – when she came back, she'd deal with the whelp easily enough* . . .

'Calthar!' he snapped back. 'Why does she delay? And what's the meaning of – '

Akrivir interrupted him in a voice so cold that Hodek's unease flowered suddenly into real fear. He said: 'Calthar is dead.'

'Wh . . . wh . . . ' The pale eyes before him bulged in a mixture of disbelief and helpless horror. 'No . . . ' Hodek croaked. 'You're lying, you're – '

'Calthar is dead,' Akrivir repeated, and the ghost of an icy smile cracked the stony indifference on his face as he realised the full extent of his sire's terror, and what Calthar's demise would mean to the old man in particular. 'Calthar, and her Mothers. Gone, father. *Gone*.' He raised the sword Kyre had given him; the movement was calculatedly slow, and Hodek hardly seemed to notice it. Suddenly Akrivir felt as though the sea was flowing through his veins and washing away a taint so old and so deep-rooted that he'd barely been aware of its existence. He felt clean – and freer than he'd ever done in his life.

Hodek's mouth was working in ugly spasms, but he couldn't utter a word; shock had robbed him of speech, and spittle foamed on his lips, dribbling down his chin.

Akrivir's fist tightened on the sword hilt.

'There'll be no more of it, father,' he said, almost kindly now that the moment had come. 'You're the last of the corruption.' And with a swift, economic movement he thrust the point of the sword into Hodek's heart.

He turned away, with the blank and terrified stares of his father's fellow-councillors fixed on him. Akrivir looked at the bloodied sword for a few moments, then released his hold on it and let it fall to the ground.

The warriors who had struggled back through the sea with him were gathered at the tunnel mouth. He couldn't read clearly what was in their eyes, but they didn't fear him. And they had no reason to do so. One of them had taken a bad sword-cut to the leg and had lost a good deal of blood; a companion had tied a crude tourniquet round his thigh, but the man urgently needed attention. Akrivir approached him, nodded to a second warrior, and between them they put their shoulders under the wounded man's arms, supporting him. Ignoring the cowering councillors, the small group turned and moved away into the tunnel.

From where they stood, they could see the dark figures moving on the bay, the quiet exodus that began back to the city as the tide turned and the sea began to cover the strand once more. In Haven's streets and squares, and in the palace whose three towers rose loftily above the town, lights began to glow, scattered at first but increasing in number like tiny, distant beacons; and Kyre's thoughts went back over the centuries to Haven as it had once been; not the sad remnants of a city on the brink of disaster, but thriving, its walls and its thoroughfares spreading cheerfully and triumphantly out over the bay. Those days couldn't be recalled. The clash of time engendered by the amulets had broken down the barriers, but briefly: now the sand lay smooth over the buried streets, the dead had returned to their graves and would not rise again. The gates of time had closed on the past, and that was as it should be.

But with the closing of the gates, there was no place now in this world for Kyre and Talliann. They had returned to the city they had once ruled and loved, and they had fulfilled the promise of the ancient legacy they had left behind. Now, their names must pass again into memory and history. At the moment when Prince DiMag had slain Calthar – and with her the soul of Malhareq – the amulets had given up the last of their power and, their work done, had shattered. As they had left the world, so, Kyre knew, a part of himself and his consort had also departed. They stood now between dimensions, gazing into DiMag and Simorh's world as though looking at a window through which they could no longer pass.

But Haven no longer needed them. Kyre had glimpsed the sea-citadel captives being led or carried back towards the town, and knew that their fate would be very different from that of comrades who had gone before them. With Malhareq's black spell finally broken, there would be wise and far-seeing minds on both sides who would meet and talk and understand the follies of the past. Not blind and self-aggrandising fools like Vaoran or Hodek; but others with enough courage to admit to their own wrongs and forgive those of others, and bring about a lasting peace. One day, perhaps, the Hag would be a friend to Haven again, and the sea-dwellers would no longer fear the sun.

Talliann's small hands touched his arms and he turned to her. The pillars of the old temple cast strange and fleeting shadows over her face; but her black eyes shone serenely and he knew she had seen and understood his thoughts.

'They will prosper, Kyre,' she said softly. 'This is their world; and they will make it thrive again.' Her gaze left his face and focused at a distance, taking in the dark strand and the shimmer of moonlight on the slowly-moving sea. 'There's nothing more for us here.'

He stroked her face. 'Does that sadden you?'

'No.' She smiled up at him. 'DiMag and Simorh are what Haven needs now, and I have no ambitions to take their place. I want only peace, with you. We were parted for so long – '

'Never again,' he said.

'No,' she agreed softly. 'Never again.'

'There are other places,' he told her. 'Not worlds as we've known them, but places where time has no meaning. Where neither the past nor the future need exist.' His fingers hesitated on her brow, then he bent forward to kiss her, a light touch. 'We could find peace.'

'Peace after strife, and after centuries of nothing . . .' She looked at the sea again. 'Yes. I would like that.'

He smiled, a slow, quiet smile. 'Haven no longer needs us. We can be free, Talliann.'

'Free . . . ' Her arms slipped through his; her skin was chilled by the night wind. There was no more to say, and no farewells to make to the city or the sea or the old temple. They looked just once towards Haven, but neither spoke. Then they turned, two figures as faint as phantoms or dreams against the towering ruin, and moved slowly towards the shimmering, endless ocean. A mote of light danced briefly on the sea's surface then flickered out; and only the restless, ever-moving surf remained to disturb the night.

Epilogue: Haven

Dawn had broken quietly through veils of pale, shimmering mist that crept in from the sea to soften harsh edges and cast a milky luminescence over the city. As the morning wore on the mist slowly cleared, and Haven basked in the mellow and faintly melancholy warmth of a perfect autumn day.

In the market squares a few traders set up their stalls, though they knew that more talking than trading would be done at their booths today. Children ran shrieking through the streets, playing games incomprehensible to their elders; now and again a woman's voice would call out from a window, admonishing them to quiet lest they wake the exhausted menfolk who slept in the aftermath of the battle. Other people, in twos and threes, stood on the heaps of broken rubble where the city wall had been, watching the full tide surging in the bay and thinking their own thoughts.

In the palace the barracks were quiet. Most men slept, though one or two wakeful sergeants sat drinking mugs of ale and tried not to think of the numbers of empty pallets in the sleeping quarters. And in the lofty palace rooms with their faded tapestries, lamps were extinguished as the sun shone through tall windows, and servants prepared the court hall for the meeting that Prince DiMag had ordered to be convened that afternoon.

DiMag hadn't slept. He had allowed himself only the luxury of bathing and changing his war-regalia for a loose woollen shirt and trousers, the comfort of which

contrasted sharply with the dull ache suffusing through
his bones, the stiffness of his sword-arm and the
frequent stabbing pains that assailed his maimed leg. He
had wondered, briefly, if with Calthar dead that old,
sorcerous wound might now begin to heal: ingrained
cynicism made him doubt it, but he was no longer sure
whether it mattered. Crippled or whole, to his army and
his people he had become a hero. Word had travelled
like fire in dry kindling, and the story of his slaying of
Calthar was already widely known; though Haven's
accolade discomfited DiMag, he could neither stem it
nor escape it. And, in ways he was reluctant to admit
even to himself, he was glad of his people's approbation,
for it gave him the chance he needed to put right so much
that had been wrong these past nine years. There would
be no more talk of deposing him. And though by rights
the heroic mantle should have been placed upon Kyre's
shoulders, DiMag believed that the Sun-Hound would
have understood and been glad for him.

Before he completed his preparations to attend the
court hall, the prince made one visit; and it was the most
important of all. He stood in Gamora's room, looking
down at his daughter's peaceful face as she slept with
one thumb in her mouth. Simorh stood beside him, her
arm linked with his in a posture that was neither casual
nor quite formal. Her expression was pensive and a little
wistful; though her face still reflected great strain he
thought that the lines were beginning to soften, showing
reawakened hints of the beauty she had possessed
before the bitter times had darkened both their lives.

There need be no more bitterness ... DiMag pressed
her arm gently against his and she looked up quickly,
something close to a smile flickering across her face.

He said: 'We should leave her to sleep. If I know
Gamora, she'll come running to find us the moment she
wakes.'

Simorh made as if to laugh but quelled it, suspecting
that it might have turned too easily to tears. 'If she

comes to the court hall, they'll cheer her even more
loudly than they cheer her father,' she replied quietly,
and smiled. 'She deserves it. She's had little enough joy
in her life.' They moved towards the door, and she
added, 'But she'll miss Kyre. I wish I could have seen
him and Talliann one last time before they left us. We
owe them so much.'

'I believe they must know it.' They would have much
to say to each other about Kyre and Talliann, but not
yet: memories were too close, and private contemplation must come first. But it wasn't too early for some
of the lessons they had learned to take form. Twelve
years ago, Prince MeGran's dying wish had been that
his son should rule Haven justly, strongly and wisely:
a duty that, DiMag believed, he had sorely neglected.
That would change now, along with so much else. He
had lost his fears and his suspicions, and in their place
was hope.

In the corridor outside Gamora's room, a senior
steward was waiting. He bowed as they emerged, and
there was an odd expression on his face that the prince
couldn't interpret.

'My lord – lady. Please forgive my intrusion, but there
is an emissary in the palace, asking that his presence be
made known to you.'

DiMag frowned, surprised. 'An emissary? From
where?'

'He says his name is Akrivir, my lord, and that for
want of a better title he has styled himself Protector of
the Citadel. A temporary measure, he says, sir, until
such time as true order can be restored.' The steward
paused. 'He was careful to stress the word *true*, sir, as
though it has some special significance.'

Akrivir . . . the name was familiar, and then DiMag
recalled a face in the madness of the battle, a wounded
warrior to whom Kyre had given a sword. And he
remembered, too, that Kyre had told him about
Akrivir . . .

'Yes,' he said thoughtfully. 'Perhaps it has ... Tell me, does he come alone?'

'Quite alone, my lord, and unarmed.'

DiMag looked questioningly at Simorh. 'It could be a beginning ... ' she said, and she couldn't disguise the eagerness in her voice. They exchanged a look of shared understanding.

DiMag turned to the steward again. 'Have our welcome guest conducted to the court hall,' he said, 'and tell him that the princess and I will join him immediately.'

The man bowed and hastened away, and DiMag held out his arm to his wife.

'Are you ready to greet the Protector of the Citadel?' he asked, and his eyes were warm.

She smiled a brilliant smile that recalled the Simorh of a decade ago, and laid her hand over his. 'I am, my lord.'